FATES DIVIDED

Copyright © Jules Barnard 2015

USA TODAY BESTSELLING AUTHOR

J. BARNARD

JBARNARDAUTHOR.COM

N
Old Kingdom
Tales River
Sunland
Dark Kingdom
New Kingdom
TiRNaN

CHAPTER

ONE

Elena's hands shook as she burst through the front door and scanned the apartment for her roommate. "Reese!"

No answer.

Reese must still be on campus.

Elena raced into the kitchen and slammed open cupboard doors until she found what she was looking for. She grabbed a metal pot, filled it with water, and placed it on the tile counter across from the fridge—clear away from any potential heat source, like the stove.

It was ridiculous to stare at a pot of water, but to run a true test she needed to repeat what she'd done in class forty-five minutes ago.

A few seconds passed, and then she felt it. The tingling beneath her skin erupted like before, which wasn't reassuring, though she supposed it was good for experimental purposes. She thought about how water molecules reacted when heated, just as she'd thought about the solution's properties in class. By instinct—the way she'd done with the class chemicals—she ran her hand over the pot.

The water boiled. With nothing to warm it.

Elena flinched as steam billowed up. *Not again. What the hell?* She eased back until she bumped into the fridge, her pulse racing. What was happening?

After a second, she grabbed the handle and tossed the pot into the stainless steel sink before it scorched the tile. Or did something else it wasn't supposed to do.

Leaning forward, she carefully held the back of her hand over the place where the pot had been and sensed the warmth there. She curled her palms around the edge of the counter and gripped hard.

"It's okay." She sucked in a deep breath and let it out slowly. "Everything is going to be *okay*."

She'd gone straight home to collect her thoughts after her solution had boiled over in class without heat, but she couldn't run an experiment in her kitchen. Something wonky must have gone on with the chemicals in class. Maybe a leftover residue had been stuck to the bottom of the beaker. That didn't explain the water boiling just now, but there *had* to be a logical reason.

Hurrying into her bedroom, Elena grabbed her laptop. She needed to return to ground zero where the liquid anomalies had begun—in a campus lab. There she could access the right equipment for measuring and calculating every step, every nuance, to determine what was making the liquids boil.

Reese took that moment to storm into Elena's bedroom, and Elena jumped, startled.

Oblivious, Reese plopped onto the bed. "Guess what?"

Elena returned her attention to the laptop, her shoulders still tense. "Where'd you come from?" She scrolled through the online campus map for an open lab.

But it was no use. All of the labs were closed, except

during class hours. She sank her head onto the desk. How the hell was she going to experiment if she couldn't get inside a lab? Her next class was a week from now, and what if the chemicals did something weird again? She'd managed to hide it from her classmates today. The chances of that a second time were slim.

"I just got home," Reese said, "but listen to this." The bed squeaked as though Reese had shifted closer. "You're going to have to cook me meals for the rest of the school year after what I scored for us."

Reese's words cut through the fog of Elena's distress. She glanced over incredulously. "How is me cooking for you everyday any different from what I do now?"

Reese's expression was pure innocence. "You know I'm not domestic."

"And I am?"

The off-campus dorm they lived in offered meal plans on campus, but that required a two-block trek she and Reese rarely managed without strong motivation.

"At least your aunt taught you how to cook," Reese said. "My mom paid people to do that stuff. How was I supposed to learn?"

Reese had grown up a rich kid in Los Angeles with chefs and cleaning people—Elena wasn't exactly sure about the extent of their domestic help. Despite the obvious differences in their backgrounds, Elena got lucky in the roommate lottery. Reese had become one of her closest friends in the two months since they'd started their freshman year at Dawson University.

"Fine, you made your point." Elena might joke about Reese not lifting a finger in the kitchen, but she secretly didn't mind cooking. Much like creating solutions in her chemistry labs, fussing around with food and experimenting with spices calmed her. Only today's lab hadn't calmed her. It had turned her into a frazzled mess. "I'm kind of busy, Reese. What's up?"

Reese stared at her shiny, cobalt-painted nails. "Oh, nothing. Just that you might want to toss in laundry duty along with meal prep after what I've arranged."

"Don't get your hopes up." Elena quit the online map and rifled through her backpack for the piece of paper she'd scribbled her professor's email address on. She hated going to one of the professors, but who else could get her inside a chemistry lab? "I'm in a rush, Reese. Tell me what it is already."

Her roommate rose quickly from the bed, excitement pouring off her as she paced the room. "Let's just say if everything works out, we won't have any problem getting into bars."

"Bars? You're thinking about..." Elena shook her head. "It doesn't matter. I have no interest in going to bars. And anyway, we're underage. There's no way the bouncers would let us in."

"They will if we have IDs that say we're twenty-one. You said you didn't like partying at the fraternity houses. This solves the problem."

Elena closed her eyes. She loved Reese, she really did, but sometimes they might as well be from different planets for how alike they were. "I'm not even going to ask how you managed to get us fake IDs."

Reese winked and walked toward the door.

"Wait," Elena called out. "Before you go, can you help me with something? I need a lab. One that's open after classes. I...screwed up an experiment today. I have to work it out before the exam or my grade will take a beating." Which was partially true. Elena was on scholarship; grades mattered. But mostly she needed to make sure she wasn't losing her ever-lovin' mind.

Liquids boiling without heat? Not possible. Yet it had happened. Twice.

Reese had crafty ways of getting what she needed on campus—case in point, the fake IDs—and it often involved something not altogether legal. But Elena was past caring about stuff like that. This was an emergency.

Reese rested her hand on the doorknob. "Try our neighbor. He's a chem geek like you, only way better looking than the students you hang out with."

Elena rolled her eyes. She and her chemistry friends might be geeks, but Reese was one of the biggest geeks—just in a pretty, less socially awkward package. She was a double major in political science and philosophy. Elena had learned the first week of school to never debate with Reese unless she wanted her ass handed to her.

"He seems connected in the department," Reese continued. "He could be a good resource."

"How do you even know these things?"

She blinked innocently. "Did you not hear my reference to his hotness? Need I say more?"

Elena closed her eyes and gave her head a shake. "No. No, you don't."

Even if the only reason her roommate knew about this guy was because she'd scouted out all the attractive coeds by major and place of residence, this was a good lead. The best Elena had that didn't involve speaking to a professor. She preferred begging their neighbor to help her find a lab over hiding the truth from someone who could get her kicked out of the chemistry department.

What person made liquids boil by waving their hands?

No one, that's who. Which was why she needed to find the scientific cause.

Elena slid on her leather bomber. The jacket had been her late father's, and now she wore it, along with the amethyst necklace her mother had left behind. Her parents had been gone a long time, but holding on to their things made her feel less alone. If ever there was a time she needed a piece of them near, it was now.

"Don't come home too late," Reese said. "You just turned eighteen; we have cake to devour. I queued up *She's All That* on Netflix. And if I can convince you to go, there's a party on A Street. We need to celebrate."

Elena had almost forgotten it was her birthday. She'd woken not feeling well, and the day had deteriorated from there.

Reese didn't say the party was at a fraternity, but most of the parties she went to were. If Elena had wanted to hang out in a place that smelled like men's gym socks and stale beer, she could have invited her cousin Mateo to stay for a few days. No offense to the fraternity party, but a calm night with trashy food and a nineties movie worked.

She grabbed her backpack and followed her roommate out. "Cake and a movie sounds perfect. I'll see you a little later."

With any luck, her neighbor could help her gain access to a lab and she'd find a reasonable explanation for why crap was boiling. She prayed it was that simple.

But life had never been simple.

Elena rapped twice at the house next door. Her street was a mix of off-campus dorms, like the one she and Reese lived in, and regular student housing.

After a moment, the door opened, and the sharp scent of pot smoke billowed out. A boy with a long knobbed nose, whose head came to her shoulders, stood on the other side.

He leaned against the doorjamb and raked his gaze down her body.

Elena groaned internally. Most bizarre thing ever. At five foot ten, she never failed to attract guys she towered over. But she'd stopped trying to figure out the opposite sex ages ago. Her boyfriends were her beaker and the periodic table—two things in life that never failed her.

Well, until they had. That's why she was standing on her stoner neighbor's doorstep. Her beaker boyfriend had just dropped her on her ass.

"Which one of you is a chem major?" *Wow, smooth. Simmer down already and show some social skills.* She cleared her throat and tried again. "Sorry, I'm Elena, your neighbor. I heard one of you studies chemistry. I could use some advice."

Okay, not advice, per se, but no need to get into the dirty details until she was talking to the right person.

The guy in front of her banged a fist against an interior wall. "Derek!" he yelled, and sauntered to the left.

Elena tentatively stepped inside. Another stoner sat on a couch in the living room, zoned out and with a psychedelic-swirled bong in his hand.

Excellent. So far, neither of these guys looked like they could hold a pencil, let alone measure the pH of an acid.

Footsteps thundered down the stairs and a third person emerged, causing Elena's stomach to hitch. This guy must be Derek. And yes, she got why Reese had noticed *him*. Elena was antisocial, not dead.

Reese was right. Derek wasn't like the other students in her department. His clothes were normal, if a bit baggy, and his golden-brown hair was a rumpled mess, as if he'd risen from his bed and hadn't even bothered to run his fingers through it. But with a square jawline, heavy brow, and sensual lips, he was rather intimidating in the holy-hotness department. And tall.

Because Elena was the height of an average man, taller men turned her head. If she was paying attention.

Derek took in her face, his eyes widening. For a moment, it seemed as though he recognized her, which was odd, because he didn't look familiar. He peered down on her from a good half a foot, but she would have noticed him even if he didn't have the height to make her insides gooey. Derek lived in the house next door—an entire lawn away. And that might explain why she'd never seen him before. Elena was observant in class, not so much with her fellow students.

"You're a chemistry major?" she asked.

He blinked but otherwise made no response.

Okayyy. She took that to mean yes.

She glanced at the two characters on the couch, their eyes rimmed with red, glassy, and half-lidded. They weren't paying attention, but she wanted privacy. "Can we talk somewhere?"

Derek led her to a dingy kitchen and turned a mismatched chair around. He slumped into it, facing her, and draped one long arm across the dining table. His hand was as big as her foot, and she wore size eights. He wasn't overtly muscled like the athletes at Dawson, but his broad back and shoulders stood out beneath the oversized T-shirt he wore. In some ways he was like a puppy—all limbs and paws—but he carried himself well for such a tall guy.

And why was she focusing on the way this guy looked? She had important things to worry about.

She sat in the seat beside him and smoothed back her wavy hair before reciting the speech she'd prepared on her way over. "My name's Elena. I live in the complex next door. I'm a chemistry major too." In a moment of inspiration, she flashed the Rosales smile her cousin Mateo claimed opened doors.

Derek's hand flexed, but his face remained unmoved.

Gahh. Why did she think she could charm this guy? She'd never had Mateo's ability with people.

She sat up and came straight to the point. "I was wondering if you know of any campus labs available for private use."

"Private use?" They were the first words Derek had uttered, and they delivered the same punch to her gut as his entrance in the hallway.

Elena shifted in her seat. The low, warm tone of his voice or the fact that she was asking for something highly unethical—probably both—sent prickles across her shoulders.

His gaze narrowed, and he took more than a cursory glance at her face this time, his look delving, as if he could see inside her head to the secrets she hid.

"My class labs aren't open after hours," she hurried on, "but tonight I have to practice." She nervously rubbed her thigh with the heel of her hand, freezing when his eyes caught the motion.

"Practice." His tone mocked.

Okay, he was right not to believe her, but still. "Yes. Practice."

This wasn't going well. Arrogant men drove her nuts, and there was something inherently superior about Derek's demeanor. Her frustration rose, and he hadn't even said yes or no yet. She mentally counted to five...

The liquids shouldn't have boiled. There had to be a reason, and she'd figure it out with or without this guy's help.

Should she leave?

Elena shoved a dark curl from her face and huffed out a breath. Derek's assessing stare rose from her eyes to the curl—and lingered.

Was he passing some sort of judgment based on her looks? And okay, maybe she'd just done the same to him. Elena was lighter due to her mother's coloring, or so she'd been told—she'd never known her mom. But even with half of her mother's genes, she looked Mexican with her big, wavy hair, according to the white people in her hometown. Could Derek tell what she was? Did he have something against it?

Discrimination back home was subtle—little things like shop owners being less welcoming to her and her aunt compared to how they greeted white customers. Elena had learned to ignore it, but in this instance, the judgement rankled.

"Forget it." She stood and reached for her backpack. She might be jumping to conclusions about the prejudice thing, but it was obvious Derek wasn't going to help her.

"Stop." Though he'd spoken softly, his voice commanded.

Normally a tone like that would have ticked her off, but for some reason Elena eased back into the seat.

"I know of a place," he said carefully. "My mentor's...out of town. You can use his lab."

Seriously? She'd hoped for this, but she hadn't actually believed an undergrad would have access to a private lab.

Before she could second-guess his motives or consider all the reasons why this was a bad idea, she said, "Thank you."

Derek tapped his finger on the table, his dark blue eyes studying her again.

Her heartbeat spiked, and she broke eye contact. She wasn't used to attractive guys staring at her, unless they were five foot four and fantasized about dating an Amazon. "So can I go there now? Do I need a key?"

Derek stood, pulled out a cell phone from his pocket, and glanced at the screen. "Give me five minutes. I'll walk you over."

He's going too?

She jumped up and jerked on her backpack, accidentally knocking into Derek's arm. With her chest.

Not the first time her boobs had collided with an unsuspecting object, just the most embarrassing.

Elena froze then carefully eased back an inch, only to find that the air between them had changed the way it did before a lightning storm—positive and negative molecules separating, creating the urgency to rush back together. She glared at the empty space between them, as if it, like the liquid anomalies, had betrayed her.

Slowly, she scanned up Derek's broad chest and shoulders, beyond the firm jaw, tangling momentarily with his full lips, and landing on his eyes. He was staring down, his beautiful gaze almost threatening, as though he sensed the crackling and blamed it on *her*.

And maybe it was her fault. She didn't know what came from her and what didn't. Or why strange things kept happening today.

"You don't have to go with me," she said. "I can find it. There's no need to put you out."

Of course he'd *want* to go. It was his lab. But she didn't need a witness. Bad enough her classmates had been around for the incident this afternoon. She'd cleaned it up quickly without anyone noticing, but privacy, a safe place to figure things out—that was what she needed.

Derek's jaw hardened. "Either I go with you or you can forget about the lab."

She didn't like his tone, but how many people had access to a private lab? It was a strange coincidence her neighbor happened to, but Elena wasn't going to question her good fortune.

Maybe she should have.

CHAPTER

TWO

Derek's heavy tread on the pebbled path fell silent as he turned up a campus sidewalk and loped up concrete steps to a two-story beige building with steel overhangs. Elena had seen the building before, but she'd never been inside. From what she understood, it housed upper-division professors' offices.

She followed Derek up the steps, and he held the door for her. As soon as she entered the building, he passed her in two long strides and jogged up a flight of stairs.

The air on the second level smelled of formaldehyde and cleaning products, leaving a bitter taste on her tongue. Some of the doors were labeled with professors' names, while others were numbered laboratories. Derek stopped at the last lab on the right, and Elena's grip on the padded straps of her backpack tightened.

Her hands had been trembling all day. This morning she'd assumed she drank too much caffeine, but her last double latte had been hours ago, and still the shaking continued.

Derek opened the door to the lab and flipped on light switches.

Elena's breath caught. For a moment, she forgot everything—her trembling hands, the liquid crisis...

She stepped inside and spun slowly around. Aside from an odd section of antique devices and bottles—*was that a vintage Bunsen burner?*—every piece of cool chem equipment she'd ever dreamed of using stood in front of her. Some were so high-tech even her class labs didn't carry them.

Derek's gaze narrowed on her face, and his lips compressed.

So maybe she'd been grinning from ear to ear. Who wouldn't be in the mecca of all labs?

Refocusing, she set her backpack on one of two work islands. "Any special rules you want me to follow?" If she couldn't figure out a solution to her problem with access to this equipment, she never would.

"Yeah. Don't use anything you've never used before. And don't blow anything up."

Haha, funny—if it wasn't actually a risk. But he didn't know that. "I'm not an amateur."

His sculpted eyebrow rose. "Aren't you? Isn't that why you wanted to *practice*?"

He wouldn't believe her if she told him about class and the water at home. She had no one to confide in. Reese had become her closest friend since starting Dawson, but their friendship was new. Elena wasn't ready to share this with her, let alone a guy she hardly knew.

She ignored the question and let out a slow breath. *Act normal.* "Who else uses this place besides you and your mentor?"

"No one."

"You have it all to yourself?" She peered around. The lab was large enough to support several scientists. "How'd you get so lucky?"

Derek unloaded books from his backpack onto a desk in the corner. "I published in a major medical journal in high school."

Elena chuckled, then noticed his serious expression.

Holy crap. Only kid wonders published in scientific journals. The rest of the authors were seasoned experts. "So you're, what, some kind of genius?"

"I'm not a genius. My memory is—" He stacked the last book on his desk. "Advanced," he finally said.

"What do you mean *advanced*? Are we talking photographic?"

He shrugged. "Something like that. I took extra classes during high school at the nearby university. My dad's a cardiologist. With his help, I researched proteomics and immunization. Professor St. Just, who's now my mentor, heard about my project and asked me to work with him at Dawson."

Most high school students weren't far enough along in school to take college courses. Even so, the chemistry class Elena had taken at the junior college near her podunk farm town was nothing compared to what this guy had done. His accomplishments made her look average.

"If that's the case, why did you choose Dawson? Why not attend Harvard or Johns Hopkins?" Not that she was putting down Dawson. It was a top university. But there were *top* schools and then there were *elite* schools.

He shrugged, tucking his backpack beneath the desk. "Marlon—Professor St. Just—offered something those programs couldn't."

"A sports car?"

His gaze slid to her. "Funny." No hint of mirth crossed his handsome face. "He offered exclusive anytime access to his lab."

"I would've taken the car," she said, though it wasn't true. She would have taken the lab as well because it was kick-ass. But for some reason, she needed to ruffle this guy's steely exterior.

Derek's mouth twitched. "Don't make me regret bringing you here."

Grumpy with no sense of humor. But beggars couldn't be choosers and all that. She needed his lab. For her sanity, if nothing else. Still... "Why did you bring me?"

He shrugged and paced to a locker. He pulled out a lab coat and other protective equipment. "You seemed desperate."

She hadn't said anything to that effect, which meant he'd read her without words. And that was unsettling.

She didn't want this guy reading her and discovering the truth.

Stupid, Derek thought. Why *had* he brought Elena? Because she'd seemed desperate? Partly true. He wasn't sure about the complete answer, didn't want to think that deeply. All he knew was that the minute they stepped into Marlon's lab, he wanted to take it back. Tell her she shouldn't be there, that he couldn't help her. He couldn't risk ruining what he'd built with Marlon, and he'd had his reasoning rock-solid in the kitchen, totally prepared to say no. Then she'd smiled.

Blinded by a pretty girl.

Derek wasn't normal under any circumstances—why

he'd gone and done the most stereotypical guy thing and given in to a pretty girl's smile, he hadn't a clue. It was annoying as hell.

Elena didn't explain outright why she wanted the lab, but she wore her fiery emotions like a neon sign. He could tell she wasn't giving him the whole truth. He couldn't decide whether getting involved had been smart or stupid, but he was leaning toward stupid.

Derek couldn't risk distractions from his work. Not if he wanted control over his life.

He pulled out his notebook, attempting to relax. So far, Elena had done things correctly. Worn the proper safety equipment, laid out her tools in the order in which she'd use them, and retrieved chemicals he deemed safe for a rudimentary chemist. She was pretty methodical about the whole thing, which surprised him. Maybe he hadn't watched his neighbor closely enough. She knew her way around a lab better than he'd expected.

Tapping his finger, he stared at her hands. He couldn't be sure from this distance, but he thought they might be trembling. If they were, that wasn't a good sign. Measuring chemicals requires a steady hand for precision. Still, she seemed competent enough, and more important, the chemicals she had before her were harmless.

Long, dark lashes shadowed the smooth skin on her cheeks as she focused on the flask over the burner... This was totally distracting. He needed to stop staring.

Elena didn't realize it, but he knew who she was, had noticed her months ago. Not that he had any intention of telling her that.

He attempted to study his notebook, but his attention, if not his gaze, was still on his neighbor. From his periphery, he saw her glance up and turn her back to him. He peered over. Was she waving her hands?

The flask in front of her rattled, and Elena lurched back. The solution hissed and spurted, shooting everywhere—including onto her—right before the container holding it crashed onto the floor, piercing the room with the sound of shattering glass.

Derek's heart stopped, then pumped double-time as he careened across the room, knocking over a stool.

Elena pressed her hands to her face, her eyes wide. The strange liquid glowed fluorescent across her lightly tanned skin, dripping down her chin.

He yanked off her lab coat and pushed her toward the emergency shower.

She followed him blindly for a moment, then pulled back, wiping the solution off her face with her sleeve. "I'm fine. I just used too much heat. I'll clean up the mess right away."

He stared in disbelief. "What are you talking about? That stuff's all over you. We're taking decontamination measures." He wasn't sure how she'd managed an explosion with the materials in front of her, but he wasn't taking chances.

"It's not necessary. I wasn't using anything dangerous." She tried to walk past him, and swayed as though she was lightheaded.

Derek caught her by the shoulders. He studied her face and the skin of her neck. Whatever that fluorescent crap was, it had scorched her flesh a light shade of pink. "You're taking a cold shower."

"No. I don't need it." Her tone came out adamant, but her body shook.

Chemical accidents were nothing to mess with. She

could be in shock, and he didn't trust her to make sound decisions right now. She attempted to duck around him again, but he reached under her knees and swept her into his arms. She weighed nothing. But with his unusual strength, everything weighed nothing.

Elena glanced around, her eyes widening. "What are you doing? Put me down!"

He set her beneath the shower and turned on the nozzle before she could wiggle her way out. Water drenched her hair and clothes in seconds. She sucked in a startled breath.

If Elena couldn't think clearly right now, he needed to. "Take them off." He gestured to the long-sleeved shirt and jeans she wore.

Water poured down her face, her eyelids fluttering beneath the onslaught. *"No way.* You're being ridiculous. I told you, the chemicals were harmless."

He sighed in frustration. "The chemicals you started with were harmless, not the fluorescent stuff that ended up all over you. I don't even know what that shit was. This is for your safety; we don't have time for modesty. Take them off."

Her body trembled and her teeth chattered—the water pouring over her was cold. Her eyes darted to the side as though she were considering what he'd said. "I was wearing a lab coat. No—nothing got on my clothes. Only a little on my skin where the coat didn't cover. I could have flushed my face beneath the faucet."

She had a point. "At least remove your shirt. That solution was dripping down your neck."

Elena huffed out a sigh of annoyance, then reached down and whipped off her top.

It landed with a splat on the shower floor. Or at least,

he thought it did. He wasn't looking at the piece of fabric on the ground.

This was bad. Worse than he could have imagined.

Her skin was fine. No scorch marks below her neck, just like she'd said, but he could see everything down to her toned stomach.

Beautiful didn't begin to describe Elena. She was...more.

Derek's mouth went dry. He tried not to look at her curves beneath the pale lace bra that had become transparent with water, but—yeah, that was impossible.

She shivered as she rinsed her face and hair, her technique choppy and not nearly thorough enough. "Happy?"

"No." He kept his eyes above her neck and shoved up the sleeves of his shirt. "Hold still."

He traced her cheekbones with the tips of his fingers, making circular motions over her face, careful to reach the places she'd missed. He rubbed her stubborn chin and down her long, delicate neck, moving the necklace she wore aside to reach her skin. Working his way farther south, his hands stilled above the slopes of her breasts.

Sweat beaded on his temples, the room suddenly burning hot despite the cold water that was still running. Derek dabbed his forehead with the sleeve on his upper arm and looked at her face. Big mistake.

Liquid hazel depths stared back, the pupils dilated to half the iris.

Elena slapped his hands away. "We're good. You got it all."

He stepped back and thrust wet fists into the front pockets of his jeans. He had to get a grip. She had caused a damned explosion in Marlon's lab. He needed to distance himself from her, not feel things for her.

She turned off the water and swayed as she bent down for her shirt.

Derek's jaw clenched. He went to steady her again, but she stepped around him and wrung out the fabric. "I'm fine, just cold."

She didn't look fine. The scorch marks had gone away—surprisingly fast, actually—but she looked pale and ready to pass out.

He peeled off the long-sleeved shirt he'd worn over his tee and handed it to her.

"Thanks." She slipped it on, and the material draped her like a dress.

Wrapping her arms around her waist, she turned and walked toward her work area, her legs moving stiffly in the damp jeans.

"What are you doing?"

"Cleaning up," she said without looking back.

"Do *not* take another step. Matter of fact, grab your things and walk out the door. You're done."

Elena's back tensed. She looked over her shoulder, blinking several times. "It was an accident. It won't happen again."

"You're right, it won't," he bit out. "I need this lab. I should never have brought you here."

Elena couldn't have caused an explosion with the materials she'd been using, and yet somehow she had. She was trouble, and she wasn't coming anywhere near his lab again. He had enough to worry about with his mentor missing. "Leave. Now."

A flare of fire turned her hazel eyes deep emerald. She stormed to the locker, grabbed her things, and slammed the door shut. When it didn't catch, she slammed it again.

Why was she so pissed? He was the one with the contamination zone to clean up. "Wait outside. I'll walk you home when I'm finished."

Elena grabbed her folder from the island, water trickling off her jeans in a wet trail as she swept out the door without slowing.

Of course she wouldn't wait.

He assessed the mess and rubbed his forehead. If Marlon suddenly showed up and walked in on this, he'd be pissed, but Derek couldn't let Elena walk home by herself in the dark. He'd become paranoid since his eighteenth birthday. He didn't take chances.

He strode out of the room and spotted her at the end of the hallway. She shot him an icy glare he interpreted as *Stay the hell away*.

Change of plans. He'd follow her to make sure she got home safely, but she wouldn't know he was there.

No one saw him once he Blended.

THREE

Elena stared at the PowerPoint slide on the large screen in the physics auditorium. What the hell was going on? She didn't need her reading glasses today—a first for her. But it wasn't just her eyes. The percussion of hundreds of fingers flying over keyboards as students took notes sounded like a million tiny mice scampering across a wooden floor, each key pounding into her skull.

This morning, she'd hoped things would be back to normal, that yesterday would be some weird dream she'd wake from. But the liquids *were* real, her hands still shook, and now her senses were in hyper mode.

She hunched in her seat and winced. After gaining access to the most amazing chem lab she'd ever seen last night, she was no closer to explaining how she made the liquids boil. She didn't dare experiment at home after the mess she'd created in front of Derek. Which had been followed by one of the most embarrassing shower scenes ever.

Elena had been so shocked by the explosion she'd lost

all sense of safety. Derek was right to throw her in the shower. Harmless chemicals or not, they hadn't reacted as expected. But when he helped her remove the solution, she wasn't thinking about the danger of the chemicals on her body. She was too busy being stunned by the effect his *touch* had on her.

Her attraction to him should have been the last thing on her mind, but her breath had quickened and her heart raced in her chest. She was sure he could tell what he was doing to her.

It was no surprise Derek told her to leave. He'd been a bit of a jerk about it, but she couldn't blame him for getting her out of there. Overnight, she'd gone from a budding chemist at the top of her class to a menace with lab equipment. Everything she knew about science was dissolving. If she could accidentally boil her solution, what else could she accidentally boil?

Jesus—people were roughly sixty percent water. What if she boiled the liquids inside herself? *Or inside someone else?*

She had to figure this out before something terrible happened.

Elena breathed deeply, attempting to calm down, but it wasn't working. Because as soon as she returned her attention to the professor, her heightened senses zeroed in on a door behind the podium that was the same color as the wall.

A door she'd never seen before.

Maybe it had been there all along. She could just be searching for things because she'd become an overanxious crazy person these last twenty-four hours.

The door swung open.

Dammit. And if that wasn't enough to convince her the door was strange, another classroom lay beyond. A classroom that shouldn't exist because it was physically impos-sible. Her physics auditorium filled the entire first floor of the building.

Elena stared into the other room. Everything in there appeared larger: the people, the ornate desks spread farther apart than the stadium seating of her auditorium. It was like looking through a magnifying glass. What the hell?

She wrapped her arms around her chest and clenched her elbows. Right now, sprawling farms and the single stoplight of her California hometown sounded nice.

A tall blond guy in dark, fitted clothes sitting near the door in the strange classroom turned and looked right at her, a slow, knowing smile spreading across his face.

Her back tensed. Why was he looking at her like that?

Before she could consider it further, he rose and strolled out of sight, giving her a clear view of the rest of the students. A few of them had light brown hair, but most were blondes or redheads with smooth, pale skin. All of them were unnaturally attractive like the first guy, who could have been a Viking warrior with his height and broad shoulders.

Dawson University was known for its diversity. This Norse group looked out of place.

Elena glared at her physics professor, but the woman didn't seem aware of the room behind her.

She nudged the girl next to her, who was texting. "Do you see that?"

The girl's gaze went straight to the professor, as though the other room wasn't important—or not there. Her long, side-swept bangs dropped over one eye. "See what?"

Elena opened her mouth to say something, then shook her head. "Nothing, I—did they paint the wall a different color? Wasn't it maroon?"

Her neighbor edged to the far side of her seat. The girl's body was angled away, but the screen of her phone was visible. She texted, *Freak next to me in Phys 4.*

Great. A quick scan confirmed the rest of the auditorium wasn't looking at the strangers in the other room either. Their attentions were focused on the PowerPoint images overhead, even though the room stuck out like Elena's wavy hair on a humid day.

Rubbing her temples, she faced forward—and her heart launched into her throat.

The strangers beyond the wall had gathered into a semicircle. And they were all watching her.

The physics professor clicked off her laser pointer and crossed the podium, showing zero signs that she noticed the people inches away. She flipped on the auditorium's bright lights. Lecture over.

Students emptied desks—Elena's neighbor like a fire had been lit beneath her butt. The crowd blocked Elena's view of the podium and wall for several minutes.

By the time the last person moved out of the way, the door to the other classroom had closed, all evidence of the strangers gone.

Elena shoved her laptop into her backpack and swung the bag over her shoulder. She strode to the front of the classroom. The professor was busy talking to students and didn't seem to notice her. She hesitated for only a moment before reaching for the indentation of the hidden door.

The surface was smooth, no grooves, but she could still see the edges. How was that possible?

She peered from various angles and continued to feel around the wall, pressing in different places. That was when she saw the faint outline of a doorknob the same color as the wall halfway down.

Elena reached for the knob. And her fingers slipped straight through as if it were air, her knuckles bumping the wall instead.

She stepped back, shaking her head. The door had opened. It was real. She'd prove it.

She ran out of the auditorium toward the end of the building where the other classroom should be.

And came to a dead end.

No doors. No creases in the wall. Nothing to indicate anything lay beyond.

Elena kicked the surface hard with the tip of her sneaker, the impact reverberating up her leg. The wall was solid.

Why was this happening? She sank to the ground and pressed her fingers to her eyelids. She tried to concentrate on what she knew—to piece it together and make sense of it all.

Logically, the room couldn't exist. She'd walked past the Physics Hall every day for the last two months. No buildings backed the structure, not even a temp, but the door and the classroom—the students—she'd *seen* them.

Last night, she'd humiliated herself in front of Derek, could have injured both of them. Nothing should have happened with the chemicals she'd been using, but it had. And now her hearing was elevated and she was seeing things she couldn't explain?

She needed to see a doctor, because something was seriously wrong.

Nothing in life had come easily. Her mother had left her and her father on Elena's first birthday, and then the universe took away her father a few short years later. Those were things she couldn't control and had never understood. But school made sense—science and chemistry, molecules and the predictable ways they reacted. She trusted it to be there for her.

Now her foothold in life was failing her too.

Her head pounding, Elena lumbered to her feet and started to run, her backpack slapping her spine, threatening to unbalance her.

She rounded a corner, desperate for an exit—and slammed into a large body. Air burst from her lungs, stars flittering across her vision. And then the giant wall of a human she'd bounced into grabbed her and picked her up.

"I wondered where you had gone." The unfamiliar, melodic voice rumbled through the chest her face was plastered against.

Elena couldn't breathe and her arms were pinned. The man began to move, carrying her away.

She angled her mouth past the thick fabric of his shirt and sucked in air. "Let me go. Help!" she yelled, but his grip tightened and the slight view she had revealed the hallways were empty.

Her struggles grew frantic and she kicked her legs to free herself. The man shifted her body to the side, and that was when she saw his face.

The Viking with the wry smile.

She hadn't imagined him...and now he was abducting her?

Elena's blood whooshed through her veins, the throbbing increasing the headache her heightened senses had triggered.

Before she could figure out how to get away, the Viking opened a door and unceremoniously dropped her on her feet.

She spun around, ready to dart in the opposite direction, and froze. Ornate desks, intricate plasterwork—it was the classroom that shouldn't exist.

Three adults sat behind a wide table like magistrates. A woman with silver, wavy hair and piercing blue eyes nodded to the Viking. "Thank you, Keen." She regarded Elena. "Good morning."

Elena glanced behind her to find her kidnapper blocking the exit. "What's this about? Where am I?"

The woman's smile was cold. "In due time. For now, all that matters is that we know about you, Elena Rosales."

Elena had never seen these people in her life. "What do you mean, you know me?"

A man and another woman sat there too. The man had a spray of gray at his temples and the other woman had short red hair, but all three of them had smooth, creamy skin. They wore fitted, dark clothing, like the Viking who'd grabbed her, and were slender and unusually tall, even while seated.

It was the first time Elena had ever felt like the short person in the room.

"We know who your mother is, why you were recruited by Dawson, and what you've done."

Elena had received a full-ride scholarship. It was more than she'd ever hoped for... Had that been intentional? "Wait—" She shook her head. "How do you know my mother? I don't even know my mother."

The woman smiled that cold smile again. "No, you wouldn't."

That's all she was going to say? No explanation?

"You've been using your magic." This time the comment came from the man. His features were Nordic, like those of her captor, but sharper, more chiseled, with a longer nose and high cheekbones.

Elena's brain blew a fuse at his words. A long pause followed while she wrapped her head around it. "My *magic?*" The prickles along her skin returned full force. "I'm sorry—" She gestured to him.

"Leo."

"—Leo. If you're referring to the lab—ah, labs—that was an accident. Won't happen again." *She hoped.*

Leo exchanged a look with the two women at his side.

"Oh, but we want it to happen again," the silver-haired woman said. "In fact, we count on it."

The red-haired lady with delicate features remained perfectly silent.

Elena fought a shiver. The liquid disasters, these people with their strange doors and knowledge about her missing mother—there was something very, very wrong with this situation. Still, given the size of Keen behind her and how easily he'd deposited her here, she chose her next words cautiously. "I don't know what happened in the labs."

"Don't you?" the older woman asked. "I think you know exactly what you did, Elena Rosales."

The solutions had exploded, but there was something —something she'd ignored yesterday because it was insanity. Before the explosions, the shaking and tingling in her fingers had magnified...as if an energy simmered beneath her skin.

This was nuts.

The woman nodded. "I see from your expression that you agree."

Elena's control slipped, panic tightening her chest. "Who are you?" she choked out, glancing around the room more thoroughly.

A large map with odd land formations hung behind them, and there was state-of-the-art computer equipment below wavy-paned diamond glass windows. The contrast of old and new reminded her of Derek's lab and the antique equipment next to modern devices.

"You've already been introduced to Leo," the silver-haired woman said. "I am Portia, and this is Deirdre." She gestured to the silent redhead. Portia pursed her lips as though she'd tasted something sour. "They said you were bright for a human, but you are proving particularly dense."

"For a *human*?"

Portia waved her hand to Keen and the others at the table. "We are Fae. And you are Halven—half Fae from your mother's side."

CHAPTER

FOUR

Elena held back a maniacal laugh. These people had lost their minds. "What do you mean you're Fae? Like a fairy? Where are your wings? You're not going to tell me vampires exist too, are you?" The last question was facetious, but she glanced around instinctively, searching for fanged creatures ready to pounce. It had been that kind of day.

Portia sighed and met Leo's gaze. "Vampires are a part of human make-believe. Again, your intelligence concerns us."

Maybe it wasn't the best moment to allow the insult to bother her, but it did. She might not be a genius like Derek, but when she wasn't boiling liquids with her hands, she was a damn good student.

Given the events of yesterday and today, Elena wasn't in the mood for this—whatever *this* was. "What do you want from me?" she asked bitterly.

"Your assistance, of course," Portia said. "To answer your earlier question about who we are, we must go back to an earlier time when angels still ventured into the human

32

realm. There are those who refer to us as Nephilim, but Nephilim are a separate race. They were created by angels rejected from heaven who mated with humans. A mistake much like you, Elena, though you are at least descended from Fae, whose existence was ordained by God." Her chin tilted up pompously. "God created us, and with our powers, we are the closest relation to angels."

Elena glared at her. "So Fae and Nephilim are both the result of angels mating with humans." Portia was attempting to draw a distinction, but Elena was pissed and confused, and she wasn't above annoying them to get the answers she needed.

Portia's eyes blazed and she leaned forward. Leo placed a hand on her arm, urging her to settle back in her seat. He studied Elena calmly. "Nephilim were created by disobedient angels mating with humans, while Fae were created by angels ordained by God to create a new race with powers and immortality. It is the difference between good and evil."

His words were myth and legend, but a part of her couldn't entirely discredit them. She'd witnessed things science couldn't explain. And these people touched on something else she'd never understood—the puzzle of her mother.

No one knew why her mother had left on Elena's first birthday. She'd been told her mother had simply disappeared—literally during the party. She was never heard from again.

Did Portia and Leo know what happened to her mother?

Portia grinned rigidly. "You are descended from the beloved Fae created by God. Is it any wonder you have come into your powers? On your eighteenth birthday, you reached your majority, a time when Halven present with abilities, if they possess them."

She *had* turned eighteen yesterday. "If this is true, why am I only now learning of it? If I'm part Fae, I'm one of God's beloved," she said half-mockingly, because dammit, these people waited until unexplainable things occurred before telling her she wasn't human?

Portia and Leo visibly stiffened, but Deirdre looked on with an expression of sadness. Something Elena had said apparently hit home.

"No." Portia leveled her with a look of disdain. "Halven are far from beloved. I suppose Halven may be perceived as a bit of disobedience on the part of a few willful Fae. But Halven are an abomination, much like the Nephilim."

Elena gritted her teeth. She was sick of the insults. "Then why am I standing here? I've got school and friends and better things to do than be kidnapped and verbally abused by you."

"There is nothing more important than the battle Fae face," Portia spat. "Abomination or not, you were sired from a powerful bloodline and possess an ability we need." She looked away, as if exasperated.

Leo's hand once again came down on Portia's arm. She glanced at his expression and let out a sharp breath. Plastering on a tight smile, she turned to Elena. "Are you up to the challenge we have to present to you?"

The light tone of her voice after that anger could be nothing short of fake. Portia sucked at diplomacy. And a challenge? Hadn't they dumped enough on her? "I doubt it," Elena mumbled, her mind buzzing from the emotionally charged moment.

Portia's eyes narrowed. "Your mother and the rest of the Fae are in grave danger, and you stand here—"

Elena's head lifted. "My mother? Where is she?"

"For now, she is safe, but she will not be for long. Unless you help us."

Elena stared in disbelief. "How do you expect me to help you?"

"You may be a half-blood, but you are still Fae. Have you not noticed additional strength, healing, or sensory input, along with your abilities?"

Elena swallowed. She had noticed some of those things.

"Fae have never been susceptible to disease in all the millennia of our existence. But someone managed to create a virus that kills our kind. It will kill your mother as well."

"My mother left me," Elena said, without thinking. Of course, she didn't want people hurt, including her mother, but this was insane.

"Elena," Portia said in a voice filled with warning. "Consider your options very carefully. We may be injured as a race, but we are not weak. If what we believe about your particular ability is true, it makes you valuable to us. We are asking for your help. We will not ask again."

There was an eerie finality to her words. Elena looked to the others at the table. Leo's expression was stoic, but Deirdre glanced away as though she was uncomfortable.

"What do you want from me?"

"We want you to build your powers and create a cure for the disease sweeping our land."

FIVE

Elena couldn't deny the things she'd done and witnessed the last two days. Or that the Fae's story provided an explanation for her mother's absence, if not a highly unusual one. But how did they expect her to cure them of a deadly Fae disease?

The atmosphere in the strange classroom had been charged from the moment Elena was thrust inside. With so much going on, she couldn't dissect what the Fae had told her in a rational manner. Their question about her helping them had been more of an order than a request.

"I'd like to go home before I answer," she said.

Portia shot her another tight smile. "You have one hour."

How would she figure anything out in an hour?

Elena turned unsteadily. A little time was better than no time. She needed to process everything that had happened —needed the comfort of her apartment and Reese to figure out what was real and what wasn't.

She walked toward the door that led to the physics auditorium, her limbs heavy. Keen allowed her to pass, but she sensed him behind her while she exited the building.

Elena glanced back. "You don't need to follow me."

He stared straight ahead. "I am your guard while you work on the antidote. Until the disease is contained, I will ensure your safety."

She stopped in mid-stride. "I haven't agreed to help." Nor did she think she could help, even if she was considering it. Abilities or not, how the heck did they expect an undergrad to create an antidote to a virus? "And Portia didn't say anything about me being in danger."

Keen shrugged. "Whoever created the virus targeted our people. If you try to help us, they'll want you dead."

That was the craziest thing she'd heard so far. In the span of two days, she'd transformed from a bookworm to a magic wielder in mortal danger?

"This is madness, you know," she said, and continued walking.

"For you, perhaps." Keen's long stride equaled two of hers. "For us, battle is a part of our existence."

"Well, I'm not sure I want to know my 'other culture' if that's the case."

"We do not choose our family, Elena."

His face remained expressionless. She suspected there was a story there, but since she had bigger issues to worry about, she left it alone.

Keen insisted on driving her home, though she lived only a short distance from campus. Elena probably should have refused, but her abductor had lost his dangerous edge once he'd started talking about not being able to choose family and how he was ordered to protect her.

She idly ran a finger along the leather seat of his sleek black sedan. It somehow appeared sporty, but she supposed real sports cars didn't come in jumbo size for seven-foot Fae. Between their turn-of-the-century classroom and modern cars, these people were old-school thrown into modern times. "You and Portia said a person created the virus. What did you mean by that? People don't create viruses, unless they're of the computer variety."

Keen looked for oncoming traffic and turned a corner. "Human viruses do not affect us. This is no ordinary affliction. Someone created a disease designed to destroy our healing capability."

"Right. Your healing capability." Whatever that meant.

He glanced over, taking in the skeptical expression she didn't bother to hide. "You are fresh into your abilities. You may not have experienced it yet." A small knife flashed in his hand.

"What the hell?" Elena pressed her shoulder to the door. Why had she thought for one second that she was safe with this guy?

He ran the blade over his steering arm where the sleeve of his shirt didn't cover his wrist. Blood dripped onto his black pants. He continued driving with the bloodied wrist and flicked on the blinker to turn another corner.

Okay, so he wasn't going to kill her, but…"What are you doing?" Elena glanced out the window. They were only a couple of blocks from her apartment, nowhere near the urgent care. "We have to go to the hospital. You need stitches for that."

"Not necessary." Keen reached across her and popped the glove compartment. Pens and a tire gauge clattered around as he unearthed a stack of napkins. He used them to wipe the blood off his arm. "We heal."

His flesh was smooth and unblemished where the blade had slashed.

Oh hell. What had she gotten herself into?

They were immortal, Portia had said. With the exception of this virus that was killing them, they were immune to disease. And apparently that meant they healed from injuries in seconds.

Elena sank in her seat. "Let's say, for argument's sake, that what you're telling me is true," she said shakily. "And I'm in danger from—from certain people. How do I protect myself?"

"What I say is always true, as you will find of all Fae. As to the other, I will protect you." A languid smile spread across his face, one hand splaying down his body, as if to show off the package that was Keen.

The gesture was so arrogant and male she snorted—before she realized what she was doing. Keen wasn't a man. Not in the sense she knew.

"Do not worry," he said. "If all goes as planned, a cure will soon be devised and no one will know of your involvement."

His words didn't reassure.

Keen pulled to a stop in front of Elena's complex, and she yanked the car door open, desperate to get away from the madness. "Thanks for the ride."

She hurried up the cement path, but before she could reach the door, Keen came out of nowhere. He swept past, lightly bumping into her, but his body was massive and his little nudge sent her stumbling off the path and onto the lawn between her building and her neighbor's house.

She straightened and caught a blur across the yard in front of Derek's door. Or was that her vision doing weird things again? Keen grabbed the keys dangling from her fingers while she was distracted.

"Hey." Elena scrambled onto the pavement. "What are you doing?"

He unlocked the front door of the building, then the door to her apartment on the first floor. He stepped inside.

How had Keen known which apartment was hers?

Because they'd been following her; how else would they know the things they did? Awesome.

Elena skittered after him as he opened bedrooms and peered inside closets. "Stop!"

At least Reese wasn't home. Explaining why there was a seven-foot Fae barging into her room would have been a challenge.

"Get out of my apartment, Keen. I agreed to you taking me home, not *making yourself at home.*"

Ignoring her, he walked down the hall and into her bedroom.

She rushed after him and peered around the doorjamb. He stood in the center of her room and regarded it for a moment before fluidly ducking his head beneath her bed. Seemingly satisfied with what he saw—or didn't see—he rose and strode to the closet.

She'd met Portia and the others less than an hour ago. There shouldn't be danger lurking around. Should there? "Is this really necessary?"

Keen reached inside the closet, and his arm reappeared with a lacy blue bra dangling from his cigar-sized finger. He grinned.

"*What the*—let go of that!" She stalked across the room and tore the unmentionable from him. "You're taking this too far. This wasn't a part of the bargain."

Keen's eyes lost their glint. "You don't know what you bargained for."

"Bargain?" The question came from behind them.

Elena swiveled to find Derek standing in the doorway, his gaze piercing Keen.

She threw the bra behind her. What was he doing here?

Keen's chest rose and fell on a sigh. "I'll be outside when you wish to leave. For all our sakes, make your decision quickly. Things will go better that way."

"What does that mean?" she asked.

But of course Keen didn't answer. He moved toward the door, only Derek was blocking the exit. A second passed as the two stared each other down.

For the love of God... "Let him pass, Derek." Just what she needed, a pissing war.

Derek didn't take his eyes off Keen, but he stepped aside and Keen walked out.

"He'll be here when you wish to leave?" Derek's tone was casual, but his jaw clenched as he glared at the doorway. "Charming guy. Sounds like a jail warden."

Elena sank onto her bed and flopped back. She closed her eyes. "Why are you here?"

"Uh-uh, tell me what's going on." His footsteps grew closer, and the heat of his large body brushed her side. "First, you almost blow up my lab, and now this...*person* is in your house talking about bargains? I have a right to know what's happening."

She blinked her eyes open. "Why? What does Keen have to do with you?"

"Maybe nothing. But if he's why you needed the lab last night, I want to know. Some of your compound got on my hands, and now I'm seeing things."

Okay, so he lied.

Derek wasn't seeing things. He was worried about her, that was all. Last night in the lab, Elena had been unsteady on her feet after the explosion. He'd followed her home to make sure she returned safely, but he couldn't shake the feeling she was keeping something from him. And considering what he'd hidden the last couple of years, he knew a little about secrets.

Elena sat up. "This is so not what I need right now." She wagged her head, then her eyes narrowed. "How did you get in, anyway? The front door to the building is always locked, and I never told you which apartment I live in."

"I walked in as someone was leaving. And the front door to your apartment was cracked open. I heard voices and recognized yours." Derek omitted that he'd already known which apartment was hers. Had known for months. He kept track of all his neighbors.

The blond girl Elena lived with burst into the bedroom, holding up two cards. "Check out our kick-ass fake…" Her voice trailed off, and she eyed Derek. "Hey." She smiled and turned to Elena. "Did another guy just leave?"

Elena waved toward him absently. "Reese, this is Derek, one of our druggie neighbors. Derek, this is my roommate."

Druggie neighbor? Good. Let her think he was like his roommates. He'd chosen them because they were too busy getting high to notice anything odd.

Elena glanced at the cards in her roommate's hand. "What's up, Reese?"

Reese smiled and rushed over to sit beside Elena on the bed. She handed her one of the cards. "It only took three weeks of heavy flirting with the computer nerd in advanced calculus, but I got them." She bounced up and down.

Elena held the card up to the light. "This ID looks real."

"Of course it does. The guy has connections." She

nudged Elena in the shoulder. "What d'ya say, *Phyllis Downs*?"

Derek coughed into his palm, stifling a laugh, and Elena glared.

She pressed her fingers to her temple and sighed. "That's the worst name ever, Reese. It sounds like a porn star." Her shoulders were slumped, her body filled with tension.

Her reaction to the fake IDs was heavier than he thought the situation warranted.

Reese's mouth parted. "Whatever. My name's Mona Pratt. They were the computer nerd's suggestion. He was doing me a favor. I didn't complain." She nudged Elena again. "*Come on*, Phyllis, let's get our drink on. Big Billy's has twenty-five-cent beers until five. If we leave now, we can make it in time." She stood and looked at Derek. "You should join us."

Elena hadn't smiled once during the exchange with Reese. Something was up, and Derek suspected it had to do with the giant blond ninja who'd left. What had the guy done to her?

"I'm changing," Reese chirped, and whirled from the room. "Be ready in a few minutes, Elena. This will make up for last night's lame birthday celebration."

Derek's brow quirked. "Birthday?"

"Yesterday. I turned eighteen," Elena said absently.

A prickle of unease jogged down Derek's spine. His eighteenth birthday had been memorable, and not for good reasons.

But that couldn't be what was wrong with Elena. As far as Derek knew, no one experienced the kind of birthday surprise he had.

Elena stared emotionlessly at the license in her hand as

though she wasn't even seeing it. A grayish tinge replaced the tan and rose in her cheeks.

"You okay?" he asked.

Her gaze drifted to him, filled with an emotion that looked an awful lot like panic.

Shit. He walked over and crouched, his shoulders level with hers. Her body shook, her breath coming out in spits and spurts. She wasn't crying, was she? "What's wrong?"

Her throat bobbed in a swallow, but she didn't respond.

Derek sat on the bed beside her. "Was it the ninja? He didn't do anything before I got here, did he?" Anger filled him. He knew he didn't like that guy. If he'd hurt her...

"The ninja...? You mean Keen. No, he didn't do anything. Not the way you're thinking." She buried her face in her hands.

What was that supposed to mean? The guy had either hurt her or he hadn't, and it sounded like he had.

Derek stood, unsure whether to hunt the guy down, remain with Elena, or stay out of it entirely. He didn't need this shit.

Elena fisted a handful of his T-shirt in her small palm. "Don't go."

Her stormy hazel eyes were his undoing.

Elena came across as independent and strong, though some of that armor had cracked last night. To see her this upset meant whatever was bothering her was big.

Derek could be a cold SOB, but he couldn't turn his back on a weeping woman. He was from the Midwest, his mother a born-and-bred Southerner.

That was the only reason he sat back down and pulled her into his arms. It had nothing to do with the spasm in his chest at the sight of her crying.

After a moment, Elena reached for a tissue on the side

table, one arm still clamped around his waist. A strand of dark, wavy hair brushed his chin, leaving a wake of fruity, Elena-scented air behind.

His head automatically dipped closer.

She dabbed her eyes, then pressed the heel of her palm to her forehead. "All this—this trying to fit in and have fun —it's impossible. My world will never be the same after today."

Elena breathed in, registering for the first time the body lock she had on her neighbor.

What was wrong with her? Now she was clinging to people she barely knew?

She peeked at Derek from beneath her hand, and dropped her arm from his waist. She held her middle and scooted to the edge of the bed.

Derek's mouth twisted in a frown. "What did you learn today that has you upset?"

How could she tell her brilliant neighbor the truth? Who would believe her? She barely believed it, and Derek already thought her a nuisance after the explosion in his lab. Now he blamed her for his health problems—which she might very well be responsible for. Wonderful.

She shook her head. "Nothing. I—it's nothing."

"Do you want me to ask your roommate to come back? Would you rather she comfort you?"

God, she couldn't tell Reese something like this. "No. I should go."

Elena rose and crossed the room. She pulled her phone

and wallet from her backpack and jammed them in a small purse.

"Wait." Derek stood. "You're upset. You shouldn't drive."

"I'm not driving. I'm walking."

"I'll walk you wherever you need to go."

Why? Was he trying to keep tabs on her? Still worried about the solution and what it had done to him? Well, he could get in line, because she had bigger issues to deal with.

"Thanks, but I need to be by myself. Tell Reese I"—she stared at the license that had slipped off the bed to the ground—"I'll talk to her later. I can't do this right now." She darted out the door.

Being different wasn't new. Elena's physical appearance deviated enough that the Mexicans in her community thought her white, while everyone else in the world considered her Latina. But now she couldn't claim either, if what Keen and his people said was true. She was part "other species" and part Mexican, a messed-up mix if ever there was one.

Until today, she thought she'd finally found a place where she belonged in Dawson University. A place where cultural ambiguity didn't matter and an obsession with science was encouraged.

She was wrong. She didn't belong here either, but maybe if she helped the Fae she'd regain something she'd lost. Her mother. Because if her mom was still alive, she had questions. Like why her mother had abandoned Elena seventeen years ago.

Oblivious to students and everything else, Elena made it halfway across campus before registering the vibration of her cell phone in her purse. She reached for it and peered at the picture of her cousin on the screen.

"Mateo, I can't talk right now."

"Too bad. I'm checking in to make sure you're not out partying. Or maybe you're too hungover after your birthday? Are you hungover? You better not be hungover. Don't make me come down there and shove your nose in a book. Never had to at home, but I will if you're getting into trouble." His voice grew deeper with each sentence.

Really? This? *Now?* Could his timing be any worse? "I'm not out partying." Mateo didn't need to know she'd gone to one last week after Reese managed to drag her to a fraternity house.

"Good, 'cause you need the grades if you're getting into medical school."

"No shit, Mateo. Back off, will you?" Her family was obsessed with her becoming a doctor, and sometimes the pressure got to her.

A dark figure brushed against Elena's arm, and her heart lurched. She swiveled her head to the side and realized it was only Keen. "*Craaap.* You're supposed to keep me safe, not give me a heart attack. Were you behind me the entire time?"

Keen nodded and stared straight ahead. "They're waiting for you."

"Who is *that?*" Mateo nearly shouted into the phone. "It sounded like a guy. And why do you need someone to keep you safe?"

"I misspoke. I'm fine, Mateo. Someone just took me by surprise. Look, I have to go. I'll call you later, okay?" She hung up before he could say any more.

Elena raised her head to the darkening sky, blinking back tears. She didn't know what she was doing—not really. But she couldn't return to her apartment and pretend that everything was okay. She'd been vulnerable back there with Derek, but she hadn't lied when she said nothing would ever be the same after today. How could it be?

"I want to find my mom... and do what I can to help the Fae."

Keen glanced at her with a mixture of concern and weariness. He nodded. "This way." He veered toward the buildings at the heart of campus. "We'll reach them through the classroom. You'll always be able to enter, as long you are with me."

They made it to the darkened physics building and Keen pulled out a set of keys.

Who gave Fae keys to the buildings? Exactly how much influence did they have at this school?

He unlocked the outer door and waved her inside. They stepped through two more doors before entering the hidden Fae room through the stage of the physics auditorium.

Just as Keen had said, the Fae were waiting. But this time Elena was greeted by elevated voices. Portia's to be exact. She seemed to be in some kind of argument with the redheaded Fae, Deirdre. Elena didn't catch the whole of it, but enough to know it had been about her.

Leo looked up at their entrance and appeared relieved. Portia cut off her heated conversation with Deirdre and proceeded to look on with a calculating intensity that had Elena's skin rising in gooseflesh.

"I am sorry, Elena," Deirdre said, speaking to her for the first time. "This must all come as a shock to you. There's nothing we can say that will make it better." Her tone was soft and gentle, but Portia flashed an annoyed glance her way.

"We are pleased you returned of your own accord," Portia said. "That makes it easier."

Of her own accord? Would they have forced her?

Portia stood and walked around the wide table. "We mustn't waste more time. You will need all of it to master your abilities."

She turned to the odd map on the wall Elena had noticed the first time she entered this room. "The disease is killing our people within a human week. It is unheard of in our realm. We do not get diseases." Portia punctuated the last sentence, as if humans were inferior for their contagions. "Those of us in this realm are safe, but the others..." She gestured to the map. "Soon only a few will remain in our land. We will do whatever is necessary to stop the virus. Even work with a Halven."

Ouch. Portia had hinted at it earlier with the *abomination* comment, but it was still a shock to witness prejudice between species, not just skin colors.

"I'm sorry your people are suffering, but how can I save them? I'm a first-year college student, not an immunologist."

Portia yanked on the wrist of her immaculately pressed sleeve. "With your bloodline, you've inherited a rare gift. You will tap into your ability to manipulate matter and create an antidote to the virus. You've already commanded your elemental ability with disconcerting ease."

Portia said this like it was a bad thing. Considering they needed her, that made no sense. And hello? *Elemental ability?* "Technically speaking, I've only blown things up."

"Yes." She peered over at Leo, who didn't meet her gaze. "That is distressing. Perhaps with training you'll be able to master your powers," Portia said indifferently.

Portia didn't seem like much of a believer, and Elena couldn't blame her.

She rubbed her temples, her fingers shaking. "How much time do I have?"

"As I've already stated, we have but one human week to create a cure before the rest of the realm is infected."

"A human week? That differs from a Fae week?"

Portia's mouth compressed as if she were irritated, but Elena wasn't trying to annoy the woman this time. She was serious. Time mattered. Particularly when she had no idea how to control this elemental ability they said she possessed.

"Of course, if your mother is not careful, she could be exposed sooner," Portia added.

Another threat? "Look, I'm not even sure I believe my mother is still alive, or who you say she is. Stop trying to bully me. It won't work."

"Not even if the lives of your precious Mateo, Aunt Leti, or grandfather are at risk?"

Elena swallowed. Hard. Portia had listed Elena's entire remaining family—everyone she cared about, save Reese. She didn't know what they could do, but the magic door, the little healing trick Keen had pulled off—she wouldn't risk finding out.

"Help us," Leo said, "and we will do our best to keep your mother and family safe."

Was he telling the truth? Elena stared at their stoic faces, then at the map on the wall that looked genuine, and absolutely foreign. Even if they weren't telling the truth, she wasn't willing to take a chance on the alternative.

And if her mother was out there somewhere, Elena might be able to find her.

"Fine, yes, whatever you need. I'll help."

Deirdre blanched. Portia's mouth curved up at the edges.

A sense of doom filled Elena's chest. She thought she understood what they had asked of her, but now she wasn't so certain.

Portia focused on something off to Elena's right, her eyes rolling up in annoyance. "You may show yourself."

A faint ripple flickered in Elena's periphery. She jerked to the side as the pixelated image of a large man slowly formed a few feet away.

What the hell...

Derek?

He grabbed her arm while she gaped. "What have you done?" he said.

SEVEN

Derek—her hot, possibly pothead neighbor—could make himself invisible? Of course he could, because that went right along with magic doors and self-healing Fae.

Elena sank to the floor, her head bent between her knees, breathing slowly so she wouldn't hyperventilate.

Derek stepped up next to her, his leg a steady presence against her side. "What the hell is going on? Who are you people?"

Elena blinked and rolled her head against the firm surface of his thigh, looking up. He could make himself invisible, but he didn't know Portia and the rest of them? If he wasn't Fae, what was he?

"I asked you not to follow me," she said.

A look of chagrin crossed his face for a split second before he stared back at the Fae. He laid a strong hand on her shoulder, his face furious. "I overheard one too many threats directed at her."

Regardless of Derek's overbearing streak, he seemed to

be on her side. Sensing the tension building, she pulled herself together and stood.

Portia slowly returned to her seat. "Derek O'Brien, how fortuitous of you to join us. I see from whom you inherited your temper."

If Portia knew Derek's parents, and he wasn't a Fae, was he a Halven like Elena?

Portia tapped the side of her chin. "It is an interesting pairing, but you may be of use. You live next door to Elena. We do not anticipate a problem, as long as she draws no attention. But an extra guard would not hurt. With your ability to disappear, you have an advantage over other protectors. And your grasp of the sciences is an asset—your knowledge of immunology particularly useful." She nodded. "Yes, this could work out nicely."

Derek stabbed Elena with a glare.

What? She wasn't responsible for this. And anyway, he'd kept secrets too, considering his invisibility trick.

Portia cut off their silent exchange with a wave of her hand. "Enough. Elena must begin her training. You will go with Leo to one of our laboratories."

Portia stood, along with the other two Fae, and opened a door on the back wall. Keen's presence pressed at her and Derek from behind, and they followed the Fae out.

Elena paused just outside the door, her breath catching. The corridor beyond the classroom resembled the hallways of the palaces Elena had researched for her art history paper. Fine plasterwork, hardwood parquet floors, intricately painted ceilings. How did this place exist at Dawson without anyone knowing about it?

They continued down the hallway until Portia and Deirdre split off to enter a separate corridor.

Portia stopped and turned to them. "Follow Leo. And Derek, should you decide to abandon Elena, you will find your secret is no longer a secret. I wonder what your father would think of his brilliant son if he discovered the truth? Do conventional parents stand beside a child who is truly different? They accepted your school preference, but will they accept who, or what, you are?"

With that parting shot, Portia walked away.

Derek's breathing grew loud and unsteady, tension radiating off his body.

Up ahead, Leo went through a door in the middle of the hallway.

Elena wrapped a palm around Derek's balled fist and urged him forward, but he shook her off.

He lowered his mouth to her ear. "What is all this? Has it got something to do with your experiment last night? How do these people know who I am?"

Elena glanced at Keen, following a discreet distance behind them, and nodded. "How long have you been able to turn invisible? Did"—she winced—"did my solution do that to you?"

Derek blew out a breath and shook his head. "No. I lied about it making me see things. I wanted to find out what you were up to." His humility didn't last long. With his next breath, he glared down at her and said, "Now, tell me the rest of it."

His tone grated, but she reeled in the urge to snap back at him. No matter how angry he sounded, Derek had stood up for her to the Fae, and he'd paid a heavy price. "I woke feeling off yesterday, my hands shaking. I didn't think much of it until I made the solution boil in chem lab—without heat."

"Go on," he said cautiously.

"The same thing happened at home with water. I went to you yesterday because I was searching for someplace safe to experiment and figure out what was going on." Her face heated. "You know how well my experiment went."

He shook his head incredulously.

"I'm sorry about what happened in your lab. I thought that if I could just test out a few things, I'd figure out why the liquids were boiling."

"Seriously?"

She threw up her hands. "What? It's not like I knew any of this was possible. Not until these people confronted me today."

"I get that part, but why are you making deals with them?"

"They're dying. I can't just walk away if I can help."

"Yes, you can. I followed you and the giant into the room. Those people threatened you. If you were smart, you'd stay away from them."

"My mother is a Fae. If I don't help, they'll make sure she's exposed. Granted, I don't know my mother—she left me when I was young—but she's still my mom and I don't like the idea of anything happening to her. More important, they threatened the family I *do* know, which you heard if you were sneaking around. They're serious, Derek. I can't risk it."

She grabbed his arm and made him face her. "What they said makes weird sense—about my mother. They told me I inherited abilities from her and that I'm a Halven."

"*Halven*. Portia called you that." He turned to Keen. "Is that what I am? This Halven thing?"

Keen nodded.

Derek tilted his head to the ceiling, his face strained, eyes blinking.

"You didn't know?" she asked quietly.

He looked down and shook his head.

"I'm sorry. If you've had your ability for a while, you must have wondered."

"You think?" His tone was sarcastic.

She tried to come up with something to say that would make him feel better. She'd only lived with not knowing what she was for a day, and that was long enough. She couldn't imagine waiting years.

"I know it's hard to take in. I don't fully understand it myself, but we have to try and move forward—because we have a very big problem on our hands. The Fae want me to use my magic to cure them of some Frankensteined virus, and you just agreed to help."

Her words must have gotten through, because Derek started walking again, then he suddenly stopped. "Wait— did you just call what you did last night *magic*?"

"I don't call it that, the Fae do. Why? What do you call your invisibility thing?"

He gave a closed-mouth grin. "Useful."

Elena couldn't breathe, let alone respond when he smiled at her like that.

She forced her gaze from his sensual lips, back to his arrogant eyes. "So useful, you're afraid to tell your family?"

His grin faded. "Fine. What do we need to do?"

"Help them come up with an antivirus to the disease."

"Oh, that's all?"

"Supposedly they think I can. I don't know much about the virus. Honestly, I'm getting the impression they don't either. It couldn't have been a Fae who created it. Not when it puts all of their lives at risk. Portia and Keen didn't say so, but it's possible a human made the disease."

Derek's face paled. "I wonder..." He didn't finish his thought.

"You wonder what?" she asked.

He shook his head, but his eyes darted away. "Nothing. We better catch up to Leo."

CHAPTER

EIGHT

Derek glanced back at the large Fae they called Keen, and let out a frustrated breath. Right now, the blond giant was the least of his worries.

It was an understatement to say that discovering what he was after two years of fear and confusion was a relief. Ironically, the idea of a link to Fae loosened a string of nerves taut inside him. The Fae's existence meant he wasn't as big a freak as he'd thought he was.

What bothered Derek wasn't his link to Fae—it was his potential connection to the virus they spoke about.

Unlike Elena, when Derek had turned eighteen two years ago and had gone through "the change," it was beneath his parents' roof, a few short weeks before he was to leave for college. Derek's father wanted him to study cardiology and partner in research back home, and Derek had been on board, until the day he changed.

Professor Marlon St. Just came calling around that time, promising an interesting research project, and a private, well-equipped space in which to work while Derek finished his degree. Derek saw it as a way to add distance between him and his parents—and everyone else. Because if anyone ever discovered what he could do, they'd never understand, especially his adoptive parents.

Portia was right. His parents were conservative. He didn't have faith they'd accept him if they found out the truth. He'd already lost one set of parents the day he was born; he didn't want to lose the people who'd raised him.

Derek had agreed to attend Dawson and work with Marlon, changing his college plans at the last minute. In light of current events, however, and the fact that his mentor had disappeared without a word, he wondered... Was Marlon's super-flu virus connected to the Fae virus? Had his mentor known Derek was a Halven?

He glanced at Elena next to him. As much as Marlon's virus concerned him, he had other pressing issues to deal with. These people thought Elena could cure them. Were they paying attention? Obviously, the Fae hadn't seen her use her "magic." Unless there was something he was missing, there was no way Elena would achieve anything close to a cure if her efforts in his lab last night were any indication. She wasn't even close to mastering her ability.

Derek opened the door to the lab Leo had entered, and walked in behind Elena. An old-fashioned room, like the other rooms inside this place, had been converted into a fully functional laboratory.

Leo was waiting for them in front of a counter, his arms crossed. "What do you know of your magic?" he asked Elena without preamble.

"I can make liquids boil. I've practiced with water."

"Elemental manipulation, yes, but what of your experience with transmutation—changing one substance with specific properties into something else entirely? Something that does not exist?"

Derek caught Elena's sheepish glance, and stifled a groan. She'd better not be considering the experiment she'd performed in his lab last night. That had been a disaster. He didn't think she knew what she'd done, and he certainly didn't. He shook his head, and she frowned.

"Not much," she finally answered.

"Strengthen your magic and perform transmutation and you will have the power to create a healing serum for anything, including the Fae virus. The speed at which the disease spreads means we have but one week to create a cure before our entire realm becomes symptomatic. Nothing less than magic will stop it in time."

"A whole week?" Derek said, and shook his head. Were they nuts? No way would she be able to do it in that short a time. Most likely never. "Why haven't other magic users found a cure? I'm assuming all of you are capable of transmutation."

Leo turned his back and began aligning glassware on the counter. "Fae powers vary. Most may be traced through lineage. Half of our people possess mental powers, such as spirit reading, persuasion, and telepathy. Others possess control over the elements." He stopped what he was doing and looked up. "You, Derek, manipulate your body atomically to make yourself invisible. Though it appears an elemental ability, like Elena's, in that you commune with the atomic structure of, say, water, your magic is actually mental. You cannot change what isn't connected to your body as an elemental magic user can, and that is the ability we need."

"I get it. I'm not as talented as the rest of you, but why

Elena? She's a Halven. Why not recruit your gifted Fae brethren with her ability?"

"Most Fae possess mastery over one of nature's elements, such as air or fire. So far, Elena can manipulate liquids with ease, but she comes from a line of those capable of manipulating multiple elements. A rare gift few possess. We believe that with training, Elena will master several skills."

This conversation was about Elena, but considering she'd turned into a pale statue at some point during the discussion, Derek continued to grill Leo for answers on her behalf. Someone had to find out what was really going on.

He decided to say the words Leo appeared to have difficulty admitting. "And that makes her special."

"Yes." Leo's gaze flickered toward the door. "Though not all would agree."

"If her Fae family possesses these powers, why not go to them for help?"

Leo's eyes cut away. "The creator of the virus made certain the first exposed were those capable of curing it. A clever tactic," he muttered. "Those in her family with the ability are gone. Consumed by the disease."

Derek glanced at Elena, who seemed to sway at Leo's words. He pressed his hand to her lower back. She may not have known the people who died, but she was related to them. Leo's news would be difficult for anyone to hear.

Elena's breathing seemed to even out and she straightened her back. She glanced at him, a fire burning in her hazel eyes, and turned to Leo. "I'm ready to get started."

ELENA HAD BEEN FREAKING out while Leo explained her powers and how rare they were. Then he spoke of her Fae relatives who'd died because of their powers—murdered so that they couldn't stop the disease. Well, the murderer hadn't counted on Elena being around and she was ready to help.

"What do I need to do?" she asked Leo.

Elena would find a cure the way she'd done everything else in her life—by busting her ass until she achieved the right result. Now that she knew who she was and what she was capable of, she wasn't walking in blind. That had to count for something, right?

"Only with transmutation can you formulate a healing elixir never created before," Leo said.

No stress. Elena squeezed her eyes shut and let out a deep breath. "How am I supposed to do that if I don't know what I'm doing with liquids?"

"You will practice in stages. We will begin with the ability that comes easiest—elemental manipulation of a liquid. From there, you will work toward more complex manipulations. Once you succeed, you'll move on to transmutation, changing one substance into something entirely new."

Leo moved aside and gestured for her to approach the beakers. "The first vessel contains water. Change the water into ice, but pay attention to the sensations running through your body. All Fae tap into their powers differently. Determining how your body responds when using magic will help you grow it."

Elena stepped forward, sensing Derek's hard gaze. She wouldn't be surprised if he was nervous—when it came to this magic business, he'd had a front-row seat of her screwing it up.

Elena lifted her shaking hands, and a rush of heat seeped into her fingertips. Invisible sparks of energy jumped beneath her skin. She'd felt the tingling before, but hadn't known it was her magic.

"Ice," she whispered, and relaxed her shoulders, releasing the energy as though exhaling on a deep sigh.

The liquid in the beaker instantly solidified and cracked, bursting the glass. Shards shot into the air and Elena threw her hands up to block her face—in the same instant Leo's arm flashed out and held the glass and ice suspended.

She looked at Derek and saw a wide-eyed expression on his face that matched her own.

Okay, then. Leo's power was telekinesis.

They might not be able to perform transmutation, but Elena should never allow herself to forget that Fae were powerful.

Leo slowly lowered the shards to the counter. "That was too quick, Elena. Part of your training will be to learn control. Remember, water expands as it freezes. You must measure out the release of your magic. Perform the exercise again, but this time, allow the water to expand within the beaker until it fits inside the vessel as a solid block."

For several hours into the early morning, Elena manipulated the elements, learning to control her power. She managed to manipulate water, fire, and air. Leo was pleased that his prediction about her abilities had turned out to be true. She *could* command more than one element. And the power that yielded was mind-boggling.

Exhausted and overwhelmed, it would take her a month to wrap her head around what she could do with her ability. But she didn't have a month. She had a week to master these powers and save the Fae, and she was nowhere near where she needed to be in order to transmute *something* into *something entirely new.*

Her head pounded and the muscles in her body—even internal ones, like her diaphragm—burned with fatigue. Her movements became jerky and unsure.

Derek grabbed her arm, steadying her. "Enough, Leo. She needs rest."

Leo took in her appearance, which must have looked pretty sad, considering the surprised furrow in his brow. She could barely lift her arms, and the room wavered like an ocean.

"Very well," he said, but she sensed his disappointment. He turned his back and began clearing the beakers and other glassware they'd used. "You will rest here."

What? she thought, at the same time Derek said, "No. She'll go home. I'll take her." He led her toward the door.

Elena's head spun. She didn't appreciate his bossy tactics, but in this case, she wholeheartedly agreed with him. She didn't care where she put her body down, but she'd prefer that it be in her own home.

"It is not safe for Elena at her apartment," Leo said from behind. She would have faced him, if she'd had the energy. At the moment, standing like a zombie and allowing Derek to handle it seemed perfectly reasonable. "She will stay where she can be protected."

"*I'll* protect her," came Derek's response beside her. "She needs sleep. Look at her."

Elena finally peered up to find a frown on Derek's face. A look of similar distaste rested on Leo's. This kind of scrutiny could eat at a girl's self-esteem. Did she really look that bad?

"She'll sleep better in her home," Derek said.

"He's right," she managed to get out. "I'd like to go home."

She wanted to help the Fae. That didn't mean she felt comfortable around them.

"You'll need peak strength in order to develop your ability in the time we have left." Leo's voice was low, as though he was speaking to himself as much as to her. "You're an asset I do not wish to lose." He gave a brief nod. "Very well, you may take her home, Derek. We could surround her with guards, but that would draw attention. Our kind stand out amongst humans. I'll send hidden soldiers, and of course Keen will stay with her."

Elena nodded woodenly, willing to agree to anything as long as it got her a pillow.

Leo studied her a moment longer. "One more thing. I insist you both learn fighting skills—Derek more so than you, Elena. Your focus must be on your powers, but you should learn basic battle maneuvers while you're working with us in case you run into danger. It will do us no good if you get killed because you put up no fight in a confrontation." His mouth twisted in annoyance. "It is a disgrace that this world does not teach its youth the fundamentals of battle. Keen will arrange the training."

In what world were fighting skills fundamental? "I have two bodyguards, and you just added a few incognito ones to hide in the bushes. Why would I need to learn to fight?"

"No guard can shadow your every move. Whoever created the virus is deadly. There is no doubt the mastermind would come after you if they discovered your involvement. If at any point we find they suspect you, you will have no choice but to remain in Emain. No exceptions."

"Emain?" she asked.

"The Fae realm embedded in the Dawson campus. That is where we are."

Leo turned to his tasks, effectively dismissing them. Derek nudged her forward with his hand on the small of her back, which she appreciated. It helped keep her upright.

"Don't worry," Derek said low near her ear. "We'll do the fight training together. It'll be fine."

Would it? She didn't feel fine. She felt frightened and utterly drained.

Keen followed them to her apartment. Elena managed to walk the entire way on her own, though she wobbled a few times and was pretty sure her eyelids were at half-mast; her vision had constricted to a narrow strip.

Once inside the apartment, Keen took up residence on the couch, and Derek walked her to her room.

Elena fell facedown on her bed and everything—the world, her fears—faded.

Elena blinked her eyes open—to Reese leaning over her in a fuzzy pink bathrobe. "*Gahh*. What are you doing?"

Reese yawned, her golden hair plastered to one side of her head, sleep lines marking her cheek. "You were talking in your sleep. Woke me from an awesome dream. What's going on? And why is our hot neighbor sleeping on your floor?" She wagged her eyebrows suggestively.

Elena sat up, her arm quivering from exhaustion under her own weight. She peered past Reese to where Derek sprawled like the dead in the corner of her room. He took up a good portion of it too, with his long limbs.

She didn't remember anything after landing on her mattress last night, but she'd assumed Derek would walk the few feet across the yard back to his house.

"We worked late on a project," she said.

If Elena was lucky, Reese wouldn't stumble into the living room where Keen slept on the couch. *His* presence would be harder to explain.

"Is that why you ditched me yesterday? I thought we

were going out. You could have told me you had something to do."

Crap, she'd totally run out on Reese. She'd asked Derek to explain things, and considering he'd followed her into Emain, he'd clearly failed in his task, though it really wasn't his job. Reese was Elena's friend. She should have said something.

How could she keep her agreement to help the Fae from her roommate? Reese was her closest friend at Dawson, maybe her best friend. She was bound to wonder what was up with all the late nights. Then there was school. School was her world, but getting through another lab would be impossible with her powers wreaking havoc.

Elena didn't want to lie to Reese, but the Fae's existence wasn't something you told someone if you didn't need to. She'd barely wrapped her head around it. She didn't expect Reese to understand. "I should have said something. I'm sorry. I appreciate you getting the driver's licenses, though I don't know how comfortable I am using mine."

Reese twisted her hair in a knot at the nape of her neck. "We'll work on that. For now, finish your project with Mr. Hottie Neighbor. And while you're at it, get him to come out with us."

Elena dropped her voice. "Really? You don't think he's kind of...irritable?"

Reese smoothed an errant curl on the top of Elena's head that apparently had been sticking straight up. She shrugged. "I thought he was nice, and he's been coming around a lot, so he's interested. He'll go out with us if you ask him. I don't know why you had him sleep on the floor instead of in your bed." She waggled her eyebrows again, and Elena shoved her shoulder.

"Keep your voice down," Elena whispered. If only Reese

knew why Derek was glued to her side. It wasn't because he wanted to be. He'd made that clear when he'd kicked her out of his lab. Though Reese was right about one thing, Derek had followed her today... *No.* He wasn't interested. He was just being nosy. He should have minded his own business, then he wouldn't have gotten caught up in everything. "I can't explain it, but he's not interested. Trust me on this one."

Reese didn't look convinced, but before she could argue —with Derek only a few feet away—Elena asked, "What time is it?" She batted Reese's fluffy bathrobe out of her face and glanced at the clock. "*Six fifteen?* I'm late."

Elena swung her legs off the bed and staggered to her closet to grab a pair of jeans.

"Late?" Reese stared at her in groggy disbelief. "What is this project that has you working inhuman hours?" She held up a hand. "On second thought, tell me later. I'm going back to bed."

She shuffled to the door. "See you in a few hours when I wake up with the rest of the student body."

ELENA, Derek, and Keen made it to the lifeless physics building an hour late, yet still too early for the doors to be unlocked. Thanks to Keen's all-access keys, they entered without a problem.

"Leo mentioned something about Emain and a different realm," Elena said as they crossed the auditorium toward the secret door. "How does that work? How do Fae classrooms exist if we can't see them from the outside?"

Keen paused behind the lectern. "Emain is a part of our realm, but not a part."

Derek looked at her with a *What the hell is he talking about* expression.

Her thoughts exactly. "Make some sense, please. We don't understand Fae-speak."

Keen gestured to the door and the knob Elena's palm had slipped through like air yesterday. "The rooms beyond here are in a place we call Emain. Emain is owned by Tirnan, the Fae realm, but separated geographically, the way Alaska is separated from the rest of America. That is why Fae residing within are safe from the disease. Emain shares a timeline with the human realm, making transfer between Earth and Emain simple. This doorway is a portal to Emain. Humans don't know it exists because they haven't been granted access."

"Okay, that only makes a little bit of sense. Why Dawson University? Why not plop your portal to Emain someplace remote?"

Keen's mouth quirked. "You don't believe your university—situated amongst agricultural fields—remote?"

"I'm talking *really* remote. Like the Gobi Desert or the Himalayan mountain range."

"A natural energy field plumes below the campus, spreading wide from coast to highland. The energy field allows us to maintain portals with minimal magic. Humans are interested in energy conservation; the concept shouldn't be foreign to you. As for the setting, we built a university because it provides an ideal monitoring station."

A shiver slid across her ribs like invisible fingers. Fae had *built* Dawson? No wonder they had access to the buildings.

"What are you monitoring?"

He leaned forward as if divulging a secret, a lock of pale hair falling across his cheek. "The Halven."

Derek inched closer—close enough to touch without touching.

Keen straightened and shrugged one shoulder. "As Portia said, millennia ago, angels mated with humans and created Fae." He turned the knob to the Fae classroom without opening it. "Fae only mate with Fae. At times, they've lain with humans and created a diluted, lesser being, the Halven. It doesn't happen often. Fae do not generally desire humans. But when it happens, we must watch the offspring for signs of abilities."

Doesn't happen often? Must happen enough that they'd built the university.

Derek snorted. "Sounds like some serious denial you've got going on there, buddy."

Keen shot him a look and opened the door.

Before Elena could walk through, Derek pulled her aside and spoke low in her ear. "Mating with humans? Tirnan and the Fae realm?" He shook his head. "We stick together inside Fae-U, got it?"

Elena wet her chapped lips. The things Keen had said, Derek's deep voice in her ear and the protective way he'd been acting toward her—all equally distracting. "What about when I need to use the bathroom?" she whispered. Clearly the stupidest thing that could have come out of her mouth, but she was flustered.

He shifted his jaw. "I'm not up for your jokes today. Your floor was hard as hell last night."

"Hey, no one asked you to stay the night."

He bent closer. *So* not helping the pounding in her chest. "I'm not leaving you alone with that guy."

"He's big, but harmless. A little flirty, maybe."

"Exactly." Derek stalked through the door Keen held open.

Elena's shoulders slumped, her breathing, which had pitched in funny ways with Derek bearing down on her, calming slightly. Why was he acting like this? Reese had said he might be interested, and she'd brushed her roommate off. Was Reese right?

"You'll begin the day with me," Keen said as they made their way into the corridors of Emain. "Best that you train with me now while you have the energy." His smile was sinister.

Combat training. *Ugh.* And he looked like he was going to take great joy in pushing her to her limits. She'd rather memorize the molecular structures of the lanthanide elements. Who was she kidding? That would be fun. Combat training, not so much.

A few minutes later, Elena emerged from a bathroom down the hall from the gym where Keen planned to torture them with fight training, wearing the same clothing Portia and Deirdre had on yesterday—thick black tunics and fitted black pants. Keen had insisted they wear the clothes, which she sort of understood. The smooth fabric had a stretchy quality, making the tunic and tight pants surprisingly comfortable. The boots were made of an all-in-one stretchy material that hugged her legs from her knees to her toes, rendering every footstep silent.

Elena was still marveling at her soundless boots while tugging at the hem of her top to cover her rear, when she nearly ran into Derek. "Sorry—" she started to say, then lost her train of thought.

Derek in Fae gear... Had she actually thought him on the slender side?

Muscles—there were muscles. Not bulging, but thick and heavily padded along his arms and broad chest. The stretchy fabric clung to intriguing angles, his torso narrowing to a black belt that looked to be made of some sort of rubber instead of leather. Black fitted cargo pants stretched over more muscles, tapering at the bottom and disappearing inside dark combat boots.

Elena tried not to stare, but her eyes wouldn't cooperate. Her gaze trailed up from his fit chest to his handsome face. His deep blue irises and golden brown hair glowed against the dark material, making his presence that much more powerful.

Keen might be beautiful, in that perfect Fae sort of way, but Derek was something else entirely. Oh, he was hot enough to make her mind stutter, but there was also this magnetism—he pulled her.

Seemed to always be pushing and pulling her.

Her heart bounced around in her chest, and she told it to simmer the hell down.

Then she watched in horror as Derek's gaze dipped to her own chest. His face tensed.

Elena squirmed, remembering the image in the bathroom mirror. Of course he'd noticed. That was what warm-blooded men did. Not that he hadn't already gotten an eyeful of her boobs in the emergency shower of his lab. As if that weren't enough, the low slit at the neckline of her tunic made the view easy. She'd had to adjust the clasp on her mother's necklace so it wouldn't show above the fabric.

Elena appreciated the Fae clothing hugging Derek's body, but her own? She'd never shown this much cleavage in her life.

If Fae were going to recruit curvy Latina Halven, they needed to make wardrobe adjustments.

"Let's go," she said, her face warm. She swept past him toward the gymnasium, and Derek tracked her without a word. She didn't see or hear him behind her to know he was there, but she *felt* him.

They entered the Emain gym, and suddenly Elena forgot all about her wardrobe issues. The gymnasium looked like your average workout room, with padded mats, exercise equipment, knotted ropes dangling from the ceiling—*Keen better not expect her to climb those*—along with a wall of weapons.

Weapons. Holy crap.

Knives, swords, long, narrow objects, razor-sharp star thingies, and all manner of scary-as-heck killing devices were secured in an array along one wall.

Weapons were the last things she should be handling. The shaking she'd acquired along with her Fae abilities hadn't gone away.

Leo, the magic taskmaster, had rolled his eyes several times as she fumbled the glassware during lessons yesterday. Apparently, shaking was a side effect of new magic users and went away in time—not that Leo was the least bit understanding.

Keen followed her gaze. "Don't worry. We won't work with the armory. Today."

Sweet Jesus. They actually meant for her to train with that stuff? Elena turned to Derek, eyes wide, but he didn't seem to notice her distress. He was too busy ogling the wall of killing instruments.

He took a casual sip from his water bottle. "Why not?" he asked Keen.

Elena silently groaned. "Maybe I should sit this part out. You guys seem to have a handle on things."

"No sitting," Keen said. "Once you have a solid grasp of hand-to-hand combat and basic martial arts—a particularly useful fighting tactic your world created and we've perfected—I'll show you a few knife maneuvers. Derek will focus on the main weapons training, but knives are easy to conceal, and Halven are particularly susceptible to guns. If there's time, I'll show you how to fire one."

Considering how much work she had ahead of her with Leo, she was confident most of her time would be accounted for, and that made her feel better. "Why the focus on weapons that kill Halven?"

Keen swung one of the dangling ropes out of the way and into the rafters, thank God. At least she wouldn't be expected to climb it. But Keen's long pause following her question made her suspicious.

"We've found unusual patterns among Halven. Clusters," he finally said. "We suspect they're responsible for the virus."

Wow. A Halven created the virus? And Fae were asking a Halven to cure it? That had to be some kind of conflict of interest.

"Halven have known of our existence over the years. Some resent us for not treating them as equals." Keen scoffed. "As if that were possible."

Fae arrogance was beyond annoying. If they were so great, they wouldn't be relying on a *Halven* to protect them from other *Halven*. "Aren't you worried we'll join them?" she said. "They'd probably treat us better than you do."

Elena had only known what she was for a couple of days, but already she felt a kinship to her half-breed brothers and sisters and their place between worlds. Not that she was in any way planning to join up with the murderer who created the virus.

"Your loved ones' lives guarantee you will not." Darkness edged Keen's tone.

She'd heard threats from Portia and Leo, but never from Keen. He'd always seemed to be on her side in some weird way. "Are you threatening me now too?"

His expression softened—as much as it was possible. "Think of it as a reminder. False moves on your part will not be tolerated by my people. Additionally, if the Halven discover you work for us, they will not trust you, no matter what you are. Do not underestimate them. They used extreme cunning to weaken our people."

Derek crushed the empty plastic water bottle in his hand. "Smarter than you thought, were they? Maybe you shouldn't underestimate any of us."

Keen circled Derek. "Bioterrorism is underhanded and weak. Be careful to whom you compare yourself."

With that final thought, Keen proceeded to exhibit his superiority by kicking their asses in combat training.

Elena only trained for an hour, while Derek was stuck with Keen for several more, but her muscles still felt like Jell-O after throwing punches and breaking holds. She was a runner, but that didn't seem to be keeping her in shape.

She bundled up the empty wrapper from the extremely bland sandwich Keen had procured for her, and tossed it in a trashcan. "I need to change and meet Leo in the lab."

"Do not change your clothing." Keen shoved used sweat rags to the side of the mat with his foot for whatever minions cleaned up around here. "You are required to wear Fae gear henceforth until you complete your mission."

"You can't expect me wear this around Dawson," she said. "I'll look like a freak—uh, not that you look like a freak. You know what I mean."

Keen crossed his arms over his wide chest. "While you reside within Fae lands, you will wear Fae clothes." He scanned her figure, the corners of his mouth curling up as his gaze passed over her cleavage. "The fabric will keep your body warm and protected from the chemicals you'll be using. It has magical properties."

But it can't cover boobs.

TEN

Another row of glassware lined the counter when Elena joined Leo in the lab.

"These are elements arranged according to the human periodic table," Leo explained. "You will manipulate each element into its various states: liquid, gas, solid. Your final test will be to manipulate two of the elements into a third, new substance."

Elena stared at the glassware. She'd accomplished more than she thought she would yesterday, but... "You really think this is possible?"

"If your gift is as powerful as I believe, yes."

And Leo was right.

She managed to manipulate every element into its individual states without completely draining herself, though she was tired. The first part of the exercise also revealed her weakness, or magical mental block, according to Leo.

The greater the atomic weight, the more she struggled to manipulate the element. Leo had her reform elements with light atomic weights first. In other words, taking the process of manipulation in baby steps.

Derek joined them after his fight training, right as Leo brought out two tanks for phase two of the exercise. The first tank contained hydrogen, and the second, oxygen, according to the labels. "What's this for?" he asked.

Leo methodically filled airtight vials with each gas and set a third vial nearby. "Elena will use her power to combine hydrogen and oxygen and form water inside the third, empty vial. We will examine the results to ensure that she did not simply manipulate a single element into its liquid state."

Elena approached the counter and raised her hands. Her palms vibrated with the power building beneath. She envisioned running her fingers over the atomic pattern of each element, sensing the contours and nature as if turning over a wooden puzzle and figuring out how each piece fit inside another.

She stood there with her hands raised for several minutes, maybe as long as a quarter hour. The intensity of her concentration and the power spreading inside her made her weak all over. When she thought she'd read the atoms correctly, she voiced a command for the elements to combine into water, and released the energy.

A burning sensation spread from her shoulders down through her fingertips, culminating in an invisible spark that jerked her hands back like the kick from a gun.

She gripped her stinging palms above her heart and stumbled back shakily, staring at the liquid inside the once empty vial.

Leo reached for the vial and held it to the light. He angled the glass and tipped the liquid. "Good."

Elena's head went dizzy and her legs buckled, knees slamming to the floor. She caught herself by one stinging palm before pitching face-first onto the ground. Mind numb, she sensed Derek lifting her and setting her on a chair. She clung to his shoulder, her head still spinning.

"Are you all right?" His voice was gruff, his body crouching in front of her protectively. He ran his hand across her forehead and down her throat, pausing above her pulse.

She focused on his worried eyes, attempted to put words together, but it was as if her tongue was surrounded by peanut butter.

Across the room, Leo seemed to be testing the liquid for pH. He smiled.

She must have done it—combined the two elements.

Derek ran his fingers forcefully through his hair. "What are we doing here? They don't care what happens to you. Dr. Evil only cares about achieving his goal, not what it costs you. Come on." He wrapped his arm around her back and under her arms, easing her up. "It's getting late, and he won't notice if we leave. Not at first, anyway. He's too excited about the progress you made."

She nodded.

Once she was standing, Derek bent to pick her up.

"No. I can walk," she croaked, and cleared her throat, relieved to form words again. She fought a new wave of dizziness as they made their way to the door.

"Tomorrow. Same hour." Leo's words drifted darkly from behind. "Do not be late this time."

Of course Leo noticed them leaving.

No matter how crappy her body felt or how worried she was about what Leo would ask of her tomorrow, she couldn't pretend she wasn't excited about what she'd accomplished.

In just two days, she'd more than doubled her powers.

With a week of training, what else would she be able to do? The possibilities seemed endless.

Elena changed her clothes inside the Emain bathroom, but with each exhausted step home, a flicker of doubt crept into her consciousness. "Derek, what do you think happens to Halven who know about Fae? Do you think they'll let us walk away once it's over?"

He glanced at Keen, who was a safe distance behind them. "I don't know. I haven't figured out the endgame." After a few seconds he added, "When I think back, the reason Marlon recruited me may have had less to do with my high school transcripts and more to do with my genes. I just haven't determined how he would have benefited from it. Up until he disappeared—"

Elena stopped and stared. "Your mentor disappeared?"

Keen had paused as well, presumably to give them privacy, though she suspected he heard more than she wanted him to.

Derek placed his hand on her arm and urged her forward. "Not here. Let's get you home. I'll stay the night and tell you what I know about Marlon."

She looked at him out of the corner of her eye. "You don't need to stay the night. You live next door."

He shook his head. "I'm staying. I don't trust...anyone."

When they reached Elena's apartment, Derek secured them inside her bedroom with a towel tucked beneath the door. He paced the room, tapping his finger vigorously against his leg, his jaw working as though he were warring with something inside.

"Marlon had me run tests on a flu virus," he finally said, glancing over hesitantly.

She sat on her bed, exhausted, but focused. "What kinds of tests?"

"Basic tests, nothing unusual, but the findings showed the virus mutated at an astronomical rate." More pacing before he added, "Marlon claimed the virus was a regular flu strain, simply more adept at survival than others. We were studying its hardiness, using the properties to research a vaccine to immunize against all flu strains. It was supposed to be cutting-edge science meant to change the world for good. But—" His voice cut off and he peered at Elena, a growing panic simmering there. "What if that's not what it was? What if *Marlon* created the Fae virus and had me help him because of my background in immunology and because I'm a Halven?"

He sat on the bed beside her, his mouth close to her ear as if he feared Keen might hear even through the towel he'd tucked under the door. She understood the precaution. Her hearing had improved since she'd reached her majority; what must Keen's senses be like if he was full Fae? But Derek's close proximity was extremely distracting.

Elena's head might be muddled from exhaustion, but she still had enough sense to smell his clean scent, feel the warmth of his body beside her, and remember the sexy image of him in his Fae clothes.

She inched back, but Derek only moved closer, obviously not understanding what his nearness did to her. "Marlon is the only professor on campus working on something like this—at a university run by Fae. And he hand-picked me—a Halven—to be his assistant. It's a pretty big coincidence, don't you think?"

She did, but she didn't want to jump to conclusions just yet.

"The last time I saw Marlon, I'd just completed another series of tests. There was nothing special about them, except that we discovered how rapidly the virus gained in its ability to spread from cell to cell. Marlon was happy with the findings and his behavior turned erratic. He stayed in his lab all night. Missed important appointments with students and colleagues. 'This virus will right the wrongs, Derek,' he told me. He was eccentric and kind of kooky, so I didn't think much of it at the time. I figured he needed the most aggressive flu virus he could find to create the vaccine. But what if that wasn't it?" Derek's head dropped back and he stared at the ceiling. When he looked back at her, his hands were balled into tight fists on his thighs. "What if Marlon is the madman, and I helped him kill all those Fae?"

Elena grabbed one of his hands between both of hers. "Even if that's true, you didn't know. It's not your fault. And with the advances we made today in my training, we'll find a cure before it's too late."

He shook his head. "No. I put you in this position. If I hadn't helped Marlon—hadn't wanted to get away from my dad so badly… I could have gone to another school—the one my father had encouraged me to go to—and this would never have happened."

He was rattling on and she didn't understand every-thing, but she understood his intent. He blamed himself.

"That's not true. Marlon would have found another research assistant. Any number of people could have run those tests. Your absence wouldn't have stopped him from developing the virus—if it was, in fact, Marlon who created it."

He turned to her, the tension in his eyes diminishing some as he took in her face. His gaze dropped to her mouth, and her cheeks warmed. He reached over and tucked a curly lock of hair behind her ear.

The gesture would have been exciting—this touch that had nothing to do with practicality and everything to do with touching for the sake of touching. Except that the hair he'd tucked away slipped its confines and bounced back onto her cheek.

Without breaking eye contact, Elena twisted her lips and blew it to the side.

The hair landed across her eye.

Derek's mouth curved into a smile that made her stomach flutter. "Your hair is crazy."

"Hey, I can't help it." She pressed her hands to the sides of her head, attempting to smooth the waves.

He frowned. "Don't. I like it the way it is."

He reached out and ran his fingers down a long strand, turning it over and studying it. His gaze moved from her hair to her face, and the look in his eyes made her heart bounce around in her chest.

He wound the strand of hair around his finger and gently drew her closer. His gaze dropped to her mouth again and—

A loud knock sounded on the bedroom door.

Elena jerked back at the same time Derek sighed and mumbled something uncomplimentary about Keen.

"May I come in?" Keen said from the other side.

How did Derek know it was him?

"Just a minute," she called, her voice higher than normal.

She walked over, kicked the towel out of the way, and opened the door.

Keen looked her up and down, then glanced at Derek sitting rigidly on the bed. Keen smirked.

Derek scowled and clasped his hands between his legs.

"You're expected at dawn," Keen said. "We will put in more combat training in the morning, and you will need rest for the next phase of lab work. You should get sleep for the exhaustion and"—he waved his hand uncertainly toward her body—"make necessary healing preparations... for any soreness."

It took her a moment to figure out what he was referring to. "Do you mean pain medication?"

"Ah, yes. That is it."

Elena rolled her eyes. Fae and their lack of medicine was a serious nuisance. Had they had any hands-on knowledge of disease, they might not be in this situation.

Keen returned to the living room, and Derek pulled off his shoes.

"You really don't need to stay," she said, watching him. "I'll be fine."

"I'm staying." He walked over to where he'd slept the night before.

She sighed and left the room to retrieve a pillow and blanket for him. But if she was being honest, she didn't mind him here. It was a comfort after the day she'd had.

Elena handed Derek the linens and changed in the bathroom, where she brushed her teeth. When she returned, Derek was lying on the floor a few feet from her bed—closer than he'd been the night before. How was she supposed to sleep with him so close? Comfort or not, he still made her pulse race.

She crawled under the covers and watched him toss and turn on the hard floor for a few minutes. She felt safe with him, even if he sent her senses into stimulation overload.

Had he really been about to kiss her before Keen barged in?

Her face heated just from thinking about the look in his eyes. The boy had beautiful, penetrating eyes she swore saw down to her soul.

They each had a stake in this business with the Fae now, but there was a part of the situation they never spoke of—that positive and negative charge between them that was a fraction away from snapping them together.

How in the world was this going to work without one or both of them getting hurt? The Fae wanted her help, and Derek's project might have been the catalyst that had forced them to come to Elena in the first place.

Her eyelids grew heavy with the enormity of it. Because no matter what she'd told him earlier to reassure him everything would be okay, she was frightened for the both of them.

CHAPTER

ELEVEN

Elena shook Derek's shoulder. "Wake up. We have to go."

He didn't move or make a sound. The guy slept like a champ.

Elena nudged him harder and was rewarded with an irritable grunt. Derek rolled onto his side, his back to her.

"Suit yourself. I'm taking a shower and leaving for Emain in fifteen minutes."

Ten minutes later, Elena returned to her room to find Derek gone. She assumed he'd left to swing by his house, but she hadn't heard him walk out the front door. Then again, he could turn himself invisible and walk through walls.

And—wow—this was her life now.

She shook her head and rushed into the kitchen to make bacon and egg burritos—enough for the three of them if Derek returned in time.

Keen stationed himself on the couch like a Fae prince, as she rushed around the kitchen. "Don't worry, Keen. I've got it," she said, heavy on the sarcasm.

Keen stretched out his legs, tapping his watch as if to say, *Hurry it up*.

Damned Fae. He could help with the dishes, or something.

Derek walked in the door right as she wrapped the last burrito in tinfoil. His hair was a wet mess per usual, but his clothes were fresh and seemed less baggy.

He picked up her backpack. "Get a move on, Elena, we gotta go."

"Oh, for the love of—you were still asleep fifteen minutes ago! And I'm feeding you, so don't give me any lip."

He peeked over the kitchen peninsula. "What'd ya make?"

"Breakfast burrito."

"Just one?"

Mateo amazed her with the volume of food he consumed, and he was half the size of Keen and Derek. She hadn't taken any chances. "Three. For each of you."

A boyish, unbelievably hot grin spread across Derek's face, nearly making her drop the pan in her hand.

Keen scooped up his burritos and opened the door. "We must go."

Elena gently set the pan down. She ducked her head, glancing slyly at Keen as she came around the peninsula. "Sure, just let me grab a book. I have a test today."

For so long Elena's priorities had been clear: family, school, self. Now they were a jumbled mess, with Fae mixed in. She'd put off thinking about exactly how far behind working with the Fae had made her in school, because what she was doing for them was important. Possibly the most important thing she'd do in her life. But she couldn't ignore the exam she had today. She'd already missed numerous class hours and one small test, but her

O-Chem midterm was critical to her overall grade. A black mark on her transcripts could ruin her chance at medical school.

Elena had realized long ago that she loved chemistry far more than biology. But her family wanted her to become a doctor. They'd come from nothing and built everything they had. She couldn't let them down, and she figured she'd turn the MD into a career as a medical chemist anyway, so it wouldn't be a loss.

Keen pressed his shoulder against the doorframe and crossed his long legs at the ankle. He wore Fae combat boots, but he had changed into dark jeans and a dark, long-sleeved T-shirt. Trying to blend with the student population? "Leo will not be pleased. You haven't the time for classes right now."

Elena pulled stiff fingers through the wavy hair at her temples. Saving Fae lives was important, as was keeping her family safe. On the other hand, if she failed in school, it would crush her family. They didn't know their lives were at risk.

Keen seemed to sense her hesitation. "Elena, school, your grades—they do not matter. More is at stake than you realize."

Derek stopped chewing his burrito and stared at the Fae.

What more could be at stake than her family's lives and the survival of a species? "What if I stay late and make up the two hours I miss? I can work however long Leo needs me to."

"We were in Emain until after midnight last night," Derek said, irritably.

She looked at him. "You're not helping."

Keen straightened. "This is all very stimulating, the

married couple banter. But I'd like to point out that you are no longer late. You are *very* late."

Elena performed more tests with Leo, then Derek and Keen joined her for the second phase of experiments, like yesterday.

Keen quietly took up residence on a stool by the door, and Derek went to the back of the room to work on—whatever it was he worked on during her elemental manipulation sessions. He always seemed to show up once Elena couldn't hold up her head any longer, as though he had one ear to her training no matter what he was doing.

Leo had a new battery of chemicals and glassware waiting for her for the afternoon session, and he was drumming his fingers on the counter. Which was bizarre. Did Fae have nervous tics? "This school exam you wish to take should be the least of your worries."

Elena shot Keen a dirty look. She'd wanted to smooth things over with Leo herself.

Keen shrugged with an innocent smile and crossed his arms over his chest. Traitorous bodyguard.

School had been *everything*—before she discovered the truth about her mother. Keeping her family safe and helping the Fae were her top priorities now, but if she could do both? Take her midterm *and* help with the virus?

"I'm trying to stay in school and make something of myself," she said to Leo.

Leo cocked his head. "And are you not, Elena Rosales—making something of yourself?"

What did he mean by that?

"I understand the stakes you face, and believe me, I'm

doing my best to help, but the only thing I have besides my family is school."

"I've given you a new education."

"I liked the old one! None of this is a comfort." She stared around the lab, taking in the walls of Emain. "None of this is predictable. I don't know where I fit anymore."

Derek stood and walked over to her side.

She expected Leo to order her back to work after her outburst, but instead, he stepped forward and placed his hands on her shoulders. "You cling to what you feel you can depend on, but you are missing the opportunity before you. By building your powers, you have a new life with which to explore. A life kept secret from you until now."

She'd been so focused on tasks—saving her family, doing what the Fae asked—she'd lost the big picture. Her life *had* changed and she was still trying to travel down the same road she'd laid out for herself.

Leo turned away. "We don't have time for your classes. That should be obvious." He glanced back, but his expression wasn't hard—it may even have been a shade sympathetic. "You will remain here. It is best."

And for the first time since all this began, she wondered if he was right. She'd clung so hard to what was familiar she hadn't embraced something that might be her true purpose in life—not school and becoming a doctor to make her family proud, but her powers and the life of a Halven chemist.

Hours later, Elena stared quizzically at the four-inch blue crystal she'd created. "It looks like blue glass. Is it real?"

"As real as any manmade diamond," Leo said. "Under

extreme pressure and heat, humans can create diamonds that are optically, chemically, and physically identical to mined diamonds. Though it is expensive without magic."

And she'd done it with nothing but carbon, a little boron to create the blue hue, an atomic diagram, and some hand waving.

As long as she knew what to turn the elements into—from personal experience with the end result or an atomic diagram from a book—she could create anything. Scary and fantastic at the same time. Her ability with the elements was like performing chemistry on steroids, and how could she not love that just a little bit?

The experiments had gone more smoothly this afternoon. She'd managed to make multiple elemental manipulations without draining herself, which was a huge step. Now, the only problem was to create something without firsthand knowledge of the end result.

A cure for cancer? Didn't exist. A cure for the Fae virus? Didn't exist either. So where did that leave her? Pretty much nowhere at the moment, with the exception of a rather impressive raw diamond and all sorts of interesting possibilities, none of which would help her cure Fae.

She needed to figure out how to modify known into unknown. "How have people achieved transmutation in the past?" she asked Leo.

He didn't answer at first. He turned his back and put away chemicals. "Only one Fae in recent history possessed the ability to transmute elements," he said over his shoulder. "He was the first to succumb to the virus. We believe they targeted him to prevent development of a healing elixir."

"What about his family? Maybe one of them has the ability and they don't know it?"

"We are well aware of the abilities of his descendants. I am an expert on the lineage of Fae nobility, and particularly his line. That is why I chose you."

God, he was annoying. How about a direct answer? "Just so I'm clear, you said abilities are passed genetically?"

A pause. "Yes."

"If this other guy was the only Fae with the ability to transmute and he was a part of the nobility, then… I'm related to a friggin' Fae nobleman?"

Leo stopped his busywork, his pale eyes grave as he finally looked at her. "Yes."

Her jaw dropped and she snapped it shut. "What about my mother? If I have the ability, she must—"

"Powers run in ancestral lines. That does not mean everyone acquires the same abilities. In this, Fae genetics work similarly to those of humans. In your world, a grandfather with dimples may see the feature in his granddaughter, but not his son. Similarly, your mother cannot manipulate elements the way you can. But this talk detracts from our goal. All you need to know is that your powers differ from those of others."

Leo never wanted to talk about her mother. Why?

Elena paced a few steps. "What about pooling resources? You can't work with Fae from Tirnan without risking exposure, but shouldn't Fae in Emain with like abilities work together?"

"We are utilizing those with applicable abilities, but power manifests differently. Tapping into that power differs as well, so they would not be able to help one another with the magic. And"—another long pause—"your powers are unique."

Derek had kept quiet, surrounded by his books after the initial argument over her missing the O-Chem exam. He paid attention when she did something interesting—or stupid, depending on your perspective, like when she'd accidentally melted a dropper—and when Leo provided nuggets of information on Fae, such as now.

Right now, Leo had Derek's attention. He walked over and joined her again.

"Why are my powers unusual? Is that the reason my mother left me?"

Leo didn't answer, and Derek put his hand on her arm. "She deserves to know about her mother. Tell her the truth, Leo."

Leo's eyes narrowed. "Fae do not lie." He turned to Elena. "Your mother gave you up, Elena, as penance for her disloyalty to our people. We followed your progress. It was inevitable you would come into powers."

Elena swallowed, her throat dry, body shaking in anger. "Where is she? What did you do to her?"

Leo's head tilted up. "Nothing she didn't deserve."

Elena held back the burning behind her eyes. She'd been orphaned after her father's death. If it hadn't been for Fae and their punishments for the crime of bearing a half-human child, Elena could have had a mother all these years.

Derek pulled her close and she pressed her face to his chest, breathing in his familiar scent. She took a shuddering breath and tilted her head to Leo. "What did you mean when you said it was inevitable I'd come into powers? If all Halven have abilities, why haven't you asked others for help?"

"Not all Halven inherit powers. You and Derek are...special."

She shook her head. "That makes no sense. How can we have powers and not others?"

No response.

He wouldn't lie to her face, but that didn't mean he'd tell her everything. "I want to see my mother."

"No. Reuniting with your mother was never an option. The agreement was to save your mother's life and the lives of your family. That is all."

He hadn't said she could see her mother. It was Elena's hope, not a promise from the Fae. "You can't keep her from me!"

Leo raised his brow. "We can. We have. You would do well to perform your job and not press your luck, as the human saying goes. Unless you wish to risk your mother's life?"

Elena sucked in a sharp breath. Leo was hot and cold, showing signs of compassion one moment and threatening her in the next. She was exhausted, and with Leo keeping her mother from her, she wanted to scream. To run from this place. But the threats they'd issued hung over her head. She wouldn't risk the people she cared about, even the one she'd never known.

They might not *help* her see her mother, but that didn't mean they wouldn't *lead* her to her.

In only a few days, Elena had come closer to her mother than she'd ever been in her life. She wouldn't give up hope now.

TWELVE

Leo removed his lab coat and stepped to the center of the room. "I've asked Beatrice to introduce you to the Tertullian Codex. It is a seventeen-hundred-year-old text said to possess the key to transmutation, among other things. Now that you've mastered elemental manipulation, it is time to move on to the next level."

"Why can't you show me the book?" Elena didn't trust these people, but at least she knew Leo.

"The Codex is written in a dead language. Beatrice has the ability to place a glamour over the text. You will see the words translated in your language, but the writing is convoluted like poetry, and subject to interpretation. Only the reader may decipher the meaning."

The Tertullian Codex didn't sound like the perfect solution, but it was a *book*. Books she understood.

He looked toward the door, and a slender girl about Elena's age and only a couple of inches taller—all Fae were taller; this one just seemed slightly shorter than the rest—entered the room. "Here is Beatrice now."

Beatrice wore the same fitted clothes as the other Fae,

her strawberry-blond hair swept rigidly from her face in a ponytail.

"Go with her. The Codex is integral to devising the anti-dote. Some spend months studying it. Perhaps you will be lucky and have a sense for its meaning the first time you read it."

The look on his face said he wasn't convinced. She would have to make the best of the time she had.

Elena nodded and followed Beatrice out the door, along with Derek. The girl's shoulders were stiff as she led them down the mazelike corridors of Emain, the walls blood red above mahogany paneling. The inside of Emain looked like a Victorian building that had mated with the Pentagon, with numerous wide hallways and modern fluorescent lights buzzing and clicking above her.

Their guide wasn't giving off a friendly vibe, but it seemed strange to work with her and not know anything about her. "Are you one of the Fae researching a cure?" Elena asked.

Beatrice's mouth tightened. "Do what you're told and don't ask unnecessary questions."

Ouch—definitely not friendly.

Derek stopped Elena, glaring at Beatrice's back as she continued down the hall. "I don't want to leave you with this chick, but I've got to take care of something. Will you be okay for a bit?" He leaned down, warm, peppermint-scented breath brushing her ear, sending a shiver down her spine. "While you're looking at that crusty old book, I'm going to my lab to check things out."

She peered up to find his sapphire eyes intent. "I'll be fine, but are you sure it's safe for you to go back? What if Marlon returns?"

"I have skills." He winked. "No one will know I'm there."

She considered bringing up the We Stick Together Inside Fae-U policy, but a library was about as sedate as it got. No point in making him stay for that.

"I'll be fine," she said, but he seemed to hesitate.

After a moment, he must have decided it was safe, because he squeezed her arm. "I'll meet you back here at five. Be careful."

Fae would be stupid to hurt her when she was helping them. But if Derek's mentor was involved in creating the disease and suspected Derek had betrayed him, *Derek* could be in danger. "You be careful."

His gaze dropped to her mouth and a splash of heat spread through her belly, reminding her of the near kiss last night. "I will."

At first, it annoyed the heck out of her that Derek had followed her to the Fae classroom and insinuated himself into her drama. But now...now she valued having him near.

Elena didn't trust these people. Why she trusted her neighbor she couldn't explain. But she did. It was the way he watched her, the look in his eyes when he worried over her safety. And the fact that he wasn't anything like the cold pretty boy he first projected.

Beatrice hadn't slowed, and Elena worried she might lose her in the labyrinth of hallways. "I better go," she said.

Derek nodded, and she gave him a quick smile before hurrying after the girl.

Elena turned the last corner where she'd seen Beatrice go, and came to a skidding halt. Beatrice was there, but so was Keen. And they were in some sort of heated discussion.

Beatrice reached up and slid her hand behind Keen's neck, drawing him closer. She brushed her mouth along his cheek and the corner of his lips. Not a kiss—more of a caress—then she whispered something in his ear that Elena couldn't hear from this distance.

Keen straightened and blinked several times. He walked away, never once looking at Elena.

Wasn't he supposed to be guarding her?

Keen rarely made a sound while shadowing her and Derek, and sometimes she'd forget he was there, but he always was. She hadn't realized he hadn't been behind her until now.

They suspected a Halven had created the virus, not a Fae. Keen must think it safe for her inside Emain. In that case, she needed to have a little chat with her bodyguard. If he was going to pick and choose his lax moments, he could quit following her to the bathroom.

Beatrice glanced directly at Elena, as if she'd known she was there all along. She opened a door and stepped inside, the door closing silently behind her.

Wonderful. Why had Leo paired her with this person? Beatrice didn't have any love for Halven. Or maybe she just didn't like Elena.

The hallway went eerily silent, not even the buzzing and clicking of the overhead lights sounding. Elena jogged down the intricate parquet floor to the door Beatrice had entered.

Taking a couple of steps inside the darkened room, she called out, "Beatrice?"

Elena felt along the wall for a switch just as the heavy door slammed shut behind her, turning the room pitch black.

Her head went dizzy without a speck of light. She crouched and placed a hand to the floor, grounding herself.

"Beatrice, turn on the lights, or I'm leaving," she said in a firm voice.

A feminine giggle sounded from above, like laughter on the wind. Or was it inside her head?

Oh, hell no.

Screw this. Elena shifted to her hands and knees and crawled toward the sliver of light a couple of feet away that streamed beneath the door. She slid her palms up the hard wooden surface to reach the knob.

And found nothing.

She traced every inch of the door. No knob, no hinges—she couldn't even fit her fingers beneath the gap at the bottom. Not that it would have mattered. The door didn't rattle or budge as she pushed and kicked its surface. It was as though it had been sealed closed. The rasp of her breath was the only sound inside the cool, empty space.

Elena concentrated on the rise and fall of her chest to keep from going into full panic mode. No reason to be afraid, she told herself. It was just a dark room.

A dark empty room with no door. Inside Emain. And Beatrice had vanished.

THIRTEEN

The moment Derek stepped outside the physics building, a sense of panic filled him. His heart sprinted and he searched the windows of the brown building, as if he could see through to the Fae realm. Which was ridiculous. He might be able to *merge* with walls, but he couldn't *see* through them.

He pulled his shoulders back and took a deep breath. Leaving Elena alone with the Fae was better than the alternative of taking her with him to Marlon's lab. If Marlon was responsible for the Fae virus and he discovered Elena's involvement, who knew what his mentor would do? A man capable of mass genocide was capable of murdering one innocent girl.

Derek needed the truth about Marlon without putting Elena in harm's way. Leaving her with the Fae was a necessary risk. Keen was an ass, but the combat training he'd inflicted on them proved him a capable ass. He'd take care of Elena while Derek was away. *He'd better.*

Derek walked on. Just a couple of hours to check out Marlon's lab, then he'd be back with her. Not *with her* with her, but to protect her. Course, that wasn't what he'd done last night. He'd almost lost his head and *kissed* her. And for a stupid moment he'd thought she wanted him to.

Elena had always been a distraction, and it had nothing to do with her elemental abilities. He'd only learned about her powers when he followed her into Emain. But he *had* known who she was before she approached his doorstep.

Derek had scoped out his neighborhood regularly while Blended. It was possible he paid special attention to his beautiful, dark-haired neighbor.

Whatever. Getting involved with her was a bad idea. He couldn't protect her while she worked on a cure if he was distracted by the idea of kissing her.

He trudged across campus to the building that housed Marlon's lab, determined to keep his head in the game. Entering the building, he climbed the stairs to the second floor, which was deserted, as usual. Few people frequented this part of campus, composed of private labs and offices for esteemed faculty.

Derek didn't bother with the key to the lab like a normal person. He tucked his backpack into an alcove and let frustration and anger over everything he'd witnessed these last few days build inside him.

Adrenaline crashed through his ribs, down his arms, his heartbeat thudding in his ears. The adrenaline and rapid tempo of his pulse pushed the transition along faster. He could stop the process by clearing his mind and relaxing, but he let the visceral response to his anger course through him, speeding his ability to Blend.

Bit by bit, down to the molecule, his body changed until it merged with the surrounding air, the structure of his body visible like a shadow when he looked down.

No matter how many times he'd gone out in public—

first at night, later during the day—no one saw him once he had Blended.

Derek entered the laboratory by stepping through the door, registering the light zap of contact with a solid surface. Keeping the lights off, he studied the surroundings to make sure no one was there. Satisfied the room was empty, he made himself solid and flipped on the light switches, going back out to grab his bulky backpack and bring it inside.

He knew every inch of Marlon's lab, save the jars Marlon kept in the corner. Marlon hadn't gotten around to explaining what they were for before he'd disappeared a few weeks ago. After visiting Emain and seeing similar bottles in the Fae lab, Derek now wondered about their contents.

His first priority, however, was to search the locked cabinet next to Marlon's desk. A cabinet Marlon kept off-limits, and that Derek suspected held secrets.

Only problem? Derek didn't have the key.

He could bust through the cabinet and take a look at what was inside, but that wasn't discreet. Marlon would know someone had gone through his things. He didn't know how powerful his mentor was, but he didn't want to risk discovery.

With all the elemental training Leo had put Elena through, which was having a surprisingly positive effect on her abilities, Derek wondered about his own powers. Instead of breaking the cabinet door, he thought he'd try something else—honing his own abilities.

He could get through the cabinet while Blended, but he wouldn't be able to take anything out without going solid, grabbing the object, then Blending it. And part of him would still be halfway outside the cabinet because he was so large. Which meant he had to Blend part of himself while making part of himself solid. Something he'd never tried before.

He spent several minutes attempting to remain solid while turning his arm invisible. It was about as much fun as patting his head and rubbing his stomach in a circle at the same time, but he finally got it to work. He'd managed to bisect himself so that a part of his body was invisible while the rest remained whole.

Going entirely Blended, Derek slid his arm and head through the cabinet and made his hand solid. He began feeling around, since he couldn't see anything in the dark.

Most of what he felt were file folders and paper, but soon he came across an item the size of his thumb that was cool to the touch and rectangular in shape. He could Blend items close to his person, like his clothes or the keys in his pocket, so he fit the object inside his palm and Blended it along with his hand, drawing both out.

A thumb drive.

With the lab and hallways deserted, and seemingly safe from anyone barging in, Derek fired up his laptop and plugged in the drive.

His hand shook as he scrolled through the files, opening them one at a time. The drive appeared to be some sort of backup for Marlon. Which made sense. Marlon probably didn't want this information floating around on a cloud somewhere, because, based on the documents Derek read, what Marlon was doing was dangerous, illegal, and highly unethical.

Not to mention paranormal.

In some ways, Marlon hadn't lied. He had studied a flu strain for decades. His life's work. It was his purpose for studying the virus that came into question.

Typically, a single influenza virus dominates during the flu season and doctors provide an immunization for common strains. The problem that occurs is that some people get sick even if they've been vaccinated because they catch a different, less active strain of the virus.

The virus Marlon created, which contained elements of every flu strain in existence, was meant to curb the flu vaccine problem. In theory, by providing a vaccination with this supervirus, a person's body could fight every influenza strain.

Marlon had fed his objective to Derek and the funding agencies for years. But the documents on the hard drive proved that this was not what Marlon had intended at all.

Before he disappeared, Marlon had merged a mysterious ingredient labeled *F-18* with the supervirus Derek had worked on. F-18 reacted to Fae tissue Marlon had acquired from somewhere, circumventing Fae healing and causing cells to die within minutes. Marlon didn't call the tissue *Fae tissue*. He'd labeled it *Tirnan*, the name of the Fae realm.

Derek slammed his fist onto the desk. He'd been so careful. Changed his life to avoid suspicion by his family, by other students—everyone. And here he was in the heart of a catastrophe, and partially responsible. Elena had said it wasn't his fault, but he'd trusted Marlon. Had *helped* Marlon.

F-18 was the ingredient that changed the virus and made it dangerous to Fae. Derek had to find F-18. But Elena should be done with the library soon and he didn't want her in Emain by herself any longer than necessary. He'd return to Marlon's lab once he got Elena home safely.

He downloaded the information he'd found on the drive onto his computer as a precaution—he'd already memorized most of it—and returned the drive to the cabinet.

Leaving the building, he hurried back to the physics auditorium, and found Keen in front of the portal door to Emain, zoning out.

What the hell?

The panic Derek had pushed aside when he left the building to go to Marlon's lab came crashing back. "Where is she?" he yelled at the Fae.

That got Keen's attention. He glanced around, as if just now realizing where he was.

Without a word, Keen tore through the portal door to Emain, winding quickly through the hallways, while Derek hauled ass beside him.

They passed a few other Fae—some of the first Derek had seen besides the ones he and Elena had been introduced to—and it made Derek realize how dangerous this place could be. These men were giants. All of them as tall and muscular as Keen.

"You're supposed to be guarding her! Why would you leave her alone in this place?" Derek growled as they sped through the corridors.

"Silence, human, I know where she is." Keen slowed to a stop in the middle of one of the hallways near a door. A small smile appeared on his face. "She's attempting to create a crowbar from paper clips."

Derek glared. "What are you talking about? *Find* her."

Keen stepped forward and swung open the door.

Derek stepped inside the darkened room. He reached along the wall for the light switch and flicked it on.

Elena was huddled on the floor, a wad of paper clips in her hands, inches from her face, her eyes closed in concentration.

She squinted up, blinking as if she'd been sitting in the dark for a long time. "Derek?" A wash of relief crossed her face. She stood and lunged at him, wrapping her arms around his neck. She pressed her face to his throat, brushing her lips and nose over his skin, sending a spark of heat to his lower back. "You came." Her voice was faint, fractured.

The fear he'd felt when he thought something had happened to her, the way she smelled, her soft lips on his skin—he wanted to press her closer and never let her go.

He grabbed her arms and eased her away. "What happened?"

"I called out. No one came. Didn't have my cell phone..." Her broken voice suggested she'd been yelling for a good long while. "Derek." Her gaze tangled with his. "Beatrice trapped me in here."

FOURTEEN

Derek swung open the door to the lab, the wood slamming into the plaster wall. Elena flinched at the sound, her nerves still jumpy after the library. "Your prodigy abandoned Elena," he said to Leo. "Left her stuck inside that dusty library with no way out."

Elena entered the lab behind him, along with Keen.

Leo quickly looked up from where he stood over a microscope.

After being locked away for several hours, Elena hadn't wanted to confront Leo. She'd wanted to get the hell out of Emain and never see this place or these people again. Why would they ask for her help, then lock her away? They weren't making sense, and she had a bad feeling about it.

Then Keen had started acting strange as they'd hurried to Leo's lab, as if he was worried, she'd daresay panicked, which wasn't like him at all. That man never got ruffled. Something truly bad had happened. Worse than her being locked in the library for hours. Keen's distress convinced her to talk to Leo.

Leo looked at Elena. "Explain."

"I followed Beatrice to the library to read the book, like you requested. But when I entered, no one was there. The door locked behind me, and when I felt along the door and walls, there was no doorknob or light switches. I called out, but it was as if a sound barrier had been erected. No one heard me. I was stuck in there for hours before Derek and Keen found me."

Elena didn't know what was going on, but it was almost as if someone didn't want her to read the Codex. As if they wanted her to fail.

Leo's gaze darted to Keen. "Why weren't you with her?"

Keen's expression hardened. "I don't know."

"I see," Leo said slowly, his gaze never leaving Keen's face, as if he was reading it.

"Well, I sure as hell don't," Derek said. "Someone want to explain to me what is going on around here?"

"No," Leo and Keen said in unison. Keen spun on his heel and walked out of the room.

Derek threw up his hands. "Of course not. You force Elena to risk her life making a cure that puts a bull's-eye on her back for the psycho who created the virus, but you won't tell her what's going on?"

Elena had never seen Derek so angry, and that was saying something, because she'd nearly destroyed his lab when she first met him.

"Forget it." Derek put his hand on her lower back and urged her toward the door.

"Where do you think you're going?" Leo demanded.

"She's not staying here tonight. It's not safe."

Elena didn't want to stay in Emain, and a few minutes ago, she would have readily marched out. But Derek's indignation on her behalf had doused her anger. What would Leo do if she didn't cooperate? Would he and Portia make good on the promise to harm her family? What would happen to the diseased Fae?

Elena looked back and caught Leo staring after them from the doorway of the lab, his expression dire.

She grabbed Derek's wrist. "We can't leave..." Her voice trailed off at the fierce glance he shot her. He was clearly not in a negotiating mood.

She allowed him to guide her down the hall a few more feet, then she stopped. She pulled him to the side, out of the way of a militant blond guard passing them. Derek stared after the guard with a snarl.

"Believe me, Derek, I'm just as upset as you are by what happened this afternoon." She shut her eyes, blocking out the memory of being trapped inside the library. She was safe and other things mattered now. "But if something happens to my family, I'll never forgive myself." She looked away and took a deep breath. "I lost my father, and I've never known my mom. If I back out of my agreement with the Fae, will they hurt the people I have left? What would happen to *you*? They're serious, Derek; I see it on their faces. They will harm those we love to get what they want."

He shook his head as if he didn't want to hear her. He leaned his forearm against the wall above her shoulder, dropping his gaze to hers. "All I know is, you're not staying here after what that bitch did to you."

He was trying to intimidate her into leaving because he was worried—but it was awareness that swept through her when he looked at her like that.

Of his body heat...the masculine size of him inches away.

Elena swallowed and rested her head against the wall, breaking eye contact. "I don't think Beatrice planned to hurt me. We were alone; she could have easily done so if she'd wanted to. But you're right. I won't get any sleep if I stay here. If they want my help, I'll need rest."

"Elena?" A feminine voice sounded from down the hall.

Elena ducked beneath Derek's arm to see who it was, and to clear her head. She couldn't think when he looked at her that way.

Deirdre approached. "May I speak to you? Alone?"

"Hell no," Derek said from behind.

He was being pushy, but he had a good point. "If you don't mind, I'd rather talk here. It's been a rough day. We can walk a little ways if you like, though."

Deirdre's forehead furrowed, but she nodded.

Elena followed the redheaded Fae down the hall several feet until Deirdre turned and tucked her short hair behind her ears. She clasped her hands at her waist. "I am afraid for you."

Out of all the Fae she'd encountered, Deirdre was the most compassionate, but still, her words surprised Elena. "I didn't appreciate Beatrice's prank, but it's over and I wasn't physically harmed. The guy who made the virus *could* be a danger to me. So far, I don't think he knows I exist."

"Beatrice? A prank?" Deirdre shook her head. "I don't know this game you say Beatrice played. And I am not only referring to the creator of the virus. Elena"—Deirdre grabbed her hand, her slender fingers surprisingly callused —"you don't know who you are, and that is a danger to you."

Elena had no idea what Deirdre was talking about. "I'm the daughter of a farmer. And I guess my mother is Fae. What else is there to know?"

"Not only Fae—your mother is a princess."

The crackling of those stupid overhead fluorescents suddenly became audible, magnifying to deafening levels.

Elena dropped Deirdre's hand. *"What?"* Leo had said she possessed powers because she was descended from noble Fae, but she'd assumed the relationship was a distant one.

Deirdre guided Elena farther down the hall, talking as she went. "Tirnan, the place we come from, is divided into three kingdoms: Old Kingdom, New Kingdom, and Sunland." She pulled Elena toward an alcove and Derek started to follow.

Elena raised her hand to stay him, and he frowned, crossing his arms and glowering. "What does that have to do with me?"

"Your maternal grandfather rules New Kingdom. He is very powerful. Many believe he will someday control all of Tirnan."

Elena wagged her head. "That can't be right." But even as the words left her mouth, Elena caught herself.

Hadn't the Fae told her all along that she was different? Her powers were unusual, even for a Halven.

"There is no mistake, Elena."

Derek was a full dozen feet from the alcove, leaning against the wall, but even at that distance she sensed the coiled energy he gave off. He was ready to protect her at any moment if she needed him.

"Is my mother with the king? Is that where she's been all this time?"

"She left you because she had no choice. If she had stayed in the Earth realm, they would have returned both of you to Tirnan, and you would never have known this world, or your father. More importantly, your mother feared for your life. Halven are not accepted among our people."

It was pretty obvious Fae held prejudices toward

Halven. It explained why her mother had left her behind, though it was difficult to swallow.

Deirdre rested her hands lightly on Elena's shoulders. "Show extreme caution. Trust no one." She glanced at Derek. "Perhaps the boy, but the others—I don't know their motives. I'm beginning to wonder..." Deirdre's voice trailed off as if she were about to say something but changed her mind. "Help them find a cure. Promise nothing else."

Of course she wouldn't promise more. As soon as this was all over in a few days—hopefully, after being reunited with her mother—Elena would have nothing to do with these people. "Why are you telling me this?"

Deirdre had always come across as compassionate, but this seemed like sneaking around.

She dropped her hands to her sides, her expression wistful. "You must survive."

Elena held her breath for a heartbeat. "Did my mother send you?" It was the only thing that would explain Deirdre's behavior.

"No," she said sadly, and glanced down. "One last thing. Never forget, Fae cannot lie. We tell the truth, but we manipulate the truth. Be careful what you agree to."

"You're Fae. How do I know I can trust you?" Elena thought she could trust Deirdre, but she'd also thought herself relatively safe in Emain—until she'd met Beatrice.

"You don't. Think about what I've told you." She turned and walked quickly away.

"How do I protect myself if I can't trust anyone?" Elena called, but Deirdre glanced past Elena and Derek, surveying the area, before disappearing down another corridor.

Stupid Emain labyrinth, Elena thought, right as Keen burst through a door a few feet away.

"Jesus," Elena gasped, slapping her hand to her chest. "Quit sneaking up on me like that."

"We're leaving," Derek told him.

"Yes, that is best. Let us go." Keen's expression was grim.

"*Now* you're my protector?" She stared in disbelief at the Fae.

His gaze flickered to her before he strode to the door that led to the classroom out of Emain. "You are fine. That is all that matters."

No, it wasn't all that mattered, according to Deirdre, and Elena had no reason to doubt her, since Fae didn't lie. Elena wasn't just an asset to them because of her powers— she was important because of the family she came from.

Keen had said she didn't know how high the stakes were, and now she realized why he'd said it. She was a part of a royal family, and she'd bet that put her in more danger.

Excellent.

FIFTEEN

The walk back to Elena's apartment was silent. Derek didn't know what Elena was thinking, but a riot of anger and frustration rolled around in his head. How was he supposed to protect her from these people? Leo kept secrets, Beatrice was up to no good, and Derek had no idea whose side Deirdre was on.

Since the day Derek had turned eighteen, he hadn't known whom he could trust, and it was getting worse. Marlon had betrayed him, and now he was involved with the bastard Fae and the bullshit they hung over his and Elena's heads. He'd assumed Keen had Elena's best interests in mind, but even Keen had failed her today, the jackass. And if Derek was being honest with himself, he'd failed her too.

That was what really ate at him.

They walked into Elena's apartment and she set her backpack by the door, letting out a deep sigh that ended on a light shiver, as though she was finally relaxing. After the day she'd had in Emain, she had every right to be stressed out.

"Are you hungry?" she asked. "I know it's late, but I should eat something. I guarantee my roommate hasn't had anything. Reese doesn't eat the dorm food. She could order out, but she's gotten used to me cooking."

Elena directed her next question to Keen, who stood near the couch. "How about you? Are you hungry? Or do you eat other things like, say, innocent babies or young maidens?"

A lazy smile spread across Keen's face. "Are you offering your virtue?"

Son of a bitch. Derek inhaled, holding the air inside his lungs until it burned. Better that than wrapping his fingers around the Fae's neck. "I'll stay, Elena. Food sounds good."

No way would he leave Elena alone with that unreliable bastard, and hell yes, he wanted food. He wasn't capable of passing up a meal. It would have to be rancid and growing fur before he turned it away. He hadn't eaten in about an hour, and already his energy waned. Derek carried a stash of snacks inside his backpack so he could eat every hour on the hour, because his appetite was huge.

After his eighteenth birthday two years ago, Derek's metabolism had shot through the roof. He'd grown eight inches in height since then. He had to buy clothes so often, the mall employees were beginning to recognize him. He'd gotten in the habit of buying things a couple of sizes too large to avoid a mall rat reputation and save time. Derek's adoptive parents associated the growth with late blooming, but they were wrong. The increased appetite and height coincided with his ability to Blend.

Topping six foot six, Derek wondered when the growth spurt would end. Every guy wants to be huge, but there comes a point when it's too much, especially for someone interested in a scientific career. Handling dropper pipettes gets tricky with hands the size of Frisbees. Not that he'd mind a few more inches. It would put him in a better position to protect Elena from Fae. The men he'd come into contact with inside Emain, including Keen, had nearly a foot on him.

Elena set pans on the stove and pulled ingredients out of the refrigerator. She cut carrots and other vegetables, her hands moving expertly and quickly.

"You need any help?"

She shook her head and waved him off. "Might as well relax while you can. We'll be back in Emain before we know it." Her pretty mouth twisted to the side, a light crease forming between her eyebrows.

"You're not relaxing," he pointed out.

"Actually, I am. I like to cook." She smiled, masking some of the worry on her face, but he'd seen it.

Of course she was worried. Today had sucked. And with the information he'd discovered about Marlon, something told him it would only get worse.

Keen slouched on the couch and Derek joined him. Maybe he'd figure something out about the Fae based on his channel-surfing preferences—or maybe Keen would let slip what he hadn't told them this afternoon about Beatrice.

Keen stared at the remote like he'd never seen one before.

"You drive a car, but you don't know how to operate a remote?" Derek said.

Keen handed Derek the controller, and Derek turned on the television, flipping through the channels rapid-fire. Out of the corner of his eye he caught Keen hold up a hand.

"What is that?" Keen pointed to the screen.

Where did this guy come from? "A television, dude."

Keen's gaze slid to Derek. "Not the device, human. The people. Who are they?"

Derek glanced at the TV. "Lacy Lamoor. It's an episode of *My Train Wreck Life*. Reality television?"

Keen stared at the images, entranced. They had cars and electron microscopes, but no cable? Fae were weird.

Derek gave up the idea of watching something decent, like sports, or solving the secrets of Fae, and stood to use the bathroom. Keen's arm flashed out, palm up.

The only thing Derek held was the remote, so he handed it to him. Keen set the controller on the armrest.

Keen hated humans but he liked reality television —*about humans*. Derek shook his head and walked down the hall.

When he returned from the bathroom, two things hit him. One, the smell coming from the kitchen made his stomach rumble like he'd starved it for a year. And two, Keen's attention had shifted from overdramatized reality television to Reese, Elena's roommate, walking through the front door.

"I'm home!" Reese called out cheerily, head bent as she juggled a truckload of shopping bags dangling from her arms. "Oh my God, I'm starved," she said to Elena. "Went to Kira's after shopping and a bunch of guys showed up. Did you know she tutors? That chick makes bank. Practically writes their papers for them. I didn't even know..." Her voice trailed off as she took in the two men in her living room.

Keen stood and tracked Reese as she crossed to Elena, setting her bags by the kitchen peninsula.

Reese raised an eyebrow. "Guests? Girl, what have you not been telling me?"

Keen hadn't stopped staring at Reese. With a predatory

look, if Derek had to peg it. One that took a leisurely sweep of Reese's figure while watching her every move.

This could not be good.

Thank God Keen never stared at Elena that way. He might flirt with her, which was bad enough, but the way he was staring at Reese was...possessive.

Elena tossed ingredients into a pot on the stove. "Reese, this is Keen. He's working with Derek and me on that project I told you about." She glanced nervously at her roommate. "And, uhh, Keen spent the night last night. Sorry, I should have asked if it was okay. It was a last-minute thing."

Reese gave Elena a you'd-better-tell-me-all-about-it-later look.

Elena nodded subtly. "The guys are staying for dinner."

"Nice name," Reese said to Keen. She twisted back to Elena before Keen could reply, hand outstretched for a bite of food.

Must not have noticed the drool dripping off Keen's chin, or his forward-leaning attack pose, like he was one step from clubbing Reese and dragging her to his lair.

Elena didn't miss the look, though. She stared at Keen, eyes silently pleading for him to chill, if Derek read it right. She handed Reese a carrot stick and smiled stiffly.

Keen finally snapped out of predator mode and sank onto the couch.

What was wrong with the guy today?

Derek sat next to him. "You can pick your chin up off the ground now."

Keen made a disgruntled sound, his attention supposedly on *My Train Wreck Life*, though Derek would swear it was on the two girls chattering in the kitchen.

Thirty minutes later, the only thoughts passing through

Derek's mind were: *Marry her. Now. Food so good. Have to marry this girl so I can eat like this all the time.* The strange rice meatball stewed soup thing she'd made was the best damn food he'd had since his mom's cooking.

Mexican food in the Midwest? Sucked. But this?

This was heaven.

Eating at Elena's and hanging out was the most normal thing he'd done in the last few days. Damn, for the last year or more. He'd kept his distance from everyone, not just his family and roommates. He knew there had to be a reason his neighbor had intrigued him from the start. She liked to cook and he liked to eat. They were a perfect match.

Belly filling with delicious food, he almost forgot the shitstorm they'd found themselves in. Almost.

Elena's cell phone rang partway through Derek's third helping. "Sorry." She smiled shyly, and pushed out her chair. "I gotta take this."

Keen spooned out his fourth bowl, a competitive smirk on his face, as Elena walked away.

Derek shoveled down his next bite, then picked up his bowl and drank the broth. No way was this guy outmatching him when it came to eating. Derek could best a food champion.

He was sloshing down bowl number four when Elena's voice rose, part of her conversation floating over.

"*Mateo,* a friend snuck up on me, that's all. I'm sorry I haven't called back." There was a pause, then he heard her say, "I know..." before her voice trailed off and he couldn't catch the rest of it.

Elena ended the call shortly afterward anyway, staring at the phone in her hand. Her fingers braced her forehead and the strain around her mouth returned.

The food in Derek's stomach turned into a brick.

He was about to ask if everything was okay, when she plastered a smile on her face. "How's the meal?"

"Quite nice," Keen said. "I enjoyed the spices you applied. It gave the food a zest I'm not accustomed to."

Derek clenched his teeth. The food was freaking fantastic. "It was great, Elena. Thanks for cooking."

She walked back to her seat and idly stirred her soup without eating. "Good—well, there's more. I'm used to cooking for a lot of people. My aunt taught me after..." An uncomfortable silence filled the room.

Reese straightened. "After you moved in with her."

"Yeah," Elena said, and took a shaky breath, as if the weight of the world rested on her shoulders. And in some ways, it did.

He hated the weight she carried. Wanted to unburden her.

"It's getting late, guys. If you don't mind, I'm gonna crash." She peered uncertainly at Keen.

"I will rest on your couch for the evening," Keen said.

Reese glanced between them. "He's staying? Again?"

Derek stared at the Fae. "This is overkill, man. I'm next door. I can be here in thirty seconds if need be." Elena was in far more danger in Emain with people like Beatrice around than inside her home. And for some reason, the idea of Keen hovering around Elena rankled, rational or not.

Keen placed his spoon on the table, his eyes hard. "I stay with the girl. No exceptions."

"Elena?" Reese pulled a lock of thick golden hair over her mouth in a nervous gesture. "What's going on?"

Derek's anger built, energy making his blood pump faster. His body wanted to Blend, but he didn't flip that switch. He sat solid and furious, glaring at Keen, but the guy's expression didn't budge. "Fine. I'll stay, too."

"What?" Elena and Reese said at the same time.

"I'm not leaving you alone with this guy," he said to Elena, without taking his gaze off Keen.

"It's fine, Derek." She lowered her voice, but everyone could hear. "He's not going to hurt us."

Derek exhaled slowly, his fists clenching and unclenching above his thighs. What was his problem? He didn't do the jealous thing. He needed to get out. Back to his house and the sham existence he'd created with his roommates. Even his damn research was a sham now.

"Thanks for the food." He pushed back his chair with too much force, straightening it before it toppled. Then he grabbed his backpack and stalked out the door.

SIXTEEN

Elena wrestled her arms through the sleeves of her nightshirt, her head popping out the top just as Reese entered her room.

Reese hooked her thumb over her shoulder. "Why is that guy Keen sleeping on our couch? Not that I'm complaining, 'cause—" She fanned a hand in front of her face and leaned against the door. "Do you think the resident advisor cares if he stays?"

They might live off campus, but the building was all freshmen and housed an RA. "I doubt it. The walk of shame is practically a daily occurrence."

"True. But that's not what's going on, right? I mean, if you like Keen..." She looked down. "That's fine. I just—I didn't get the sense you guys had something going on."

"You think—no, Reese." Elena shook her head vehemently. "Nothing like that is going on. He's here to... to protect me," she said carefully.

Reese stared for a moment, then methodically moved to the bed and sat in the center, crossing her legs. "Why would you need protection?" Her tone was serious, and Elena wondered how much she could tell her roommate. She couldn't keep everything from Reese. Not with Keen shadowing her every step and staying the night.

"I know something's going on," Reese said. "You've not been yourself. I mean, you're always a hermit bookworm, but I don't know. There's more, isn't there?"

Listening for the television, which appeared to be at full volume, Elena decided it was safe to talk without being overheard by the superior Fae hearing in the living room.

She moved to the head of the bed and tucked her feet beneath the sheets. "If I tell you, you can't freak out."

Reese yawned and balanced her chin on her hand, elbow propped on her knee. "My dad writes for Hollywood—you think I'm not used to drama? I can handle whatever life crisis you're going through."

"Oh, really?" Elena laughed humorlessly. "In that case, Keen's a Fae."

Reese stared, as if waiting for more.

"A Fae, Reese. Do you know what that is?"

Reese furrowed her brow. "Fine, I'll play along. A Fae? Like a pretty little fairy with wings?" She giggled, and Elena was tempted to as well. Keen with delicate wings was a funny mental image.

"Not quite." Elena's mouth twisted wryly. "Supposedly, Keen isn't the small, winged variety. He looks normal, and so do the others I've met. They're exceedingly tall, slender, and—attractive. You've seen him. You know what I'm talking about."

Reese nodded automatically, then her face sobered. "Wait—what? Elena, he's playing you. That's like the oldest pickup line in the player handbook. You think a guy hasn't told me he's a superhero before? How could you fall for that?"

"It wasn't a pickup line, and he's not playing me. His people have powers. They told me I have powers too."

Reese raised her eyebrows pityingly.

"Fine, you need proof?" Elena shoved aside the papers on her nightstand and centered the glass of water she kept there. Focusing on the liquid, she read the molecules and commanded them to re-form, her hand passing over the glass.

The water bubbled.

Reese jerked back. "What the...?" She pointed. "You—what did you do?" She unlocked her legs and scooted off the bed, walking backward toward the door.

Elena might not understand her ability, but it was freaktastic—*freak* being the operative part.

"Simmer down, Reese. You didn't believe me, so I'm giving you proof. You just got done telling me you wouldn't wig out. What happened to your hardened Hollywood experience?"

Reese waved her hands around wildly. "That was before you went all hocus-pocus on me. I thought you were going to tell me your family was part of a Mexican drug cartel, not *this*." She glared at the glass. "How did you do that?"

"Remember how I told you I never knew my mother?" Reese nodded. "Well, she's a Fae. That's why she left me and my father all those years ago."

Reese's jaw dropped and she stared without blinking.

"Tell me about it," Elena said.

Reese looked around. "Shit, Elena. What the hell? That guy on the couch, can he do this too?"

"No." Elena shook her head, then reconsidered. "At least, I don't think he can. I don't know what Keen's abilities are. They assigned him to protect me."

"They?"

"The other Fae. On Dawson campus. They live inside an alternate realm in the physics building."

Reese walked forward and sank onto the bed. "You realize you sound psychotic, right?"

"Oh, I'm well aware. Why do you think I didn't tell you sooner?"

"If I didn't just see you hocus-pocus that glass of water, I'd be checking you into a mental health institution."

"*Thanks.*"

"You're welcome." Her mouth twisted. "Let's say that I believe you about realms and whatnot. Why is Keen protecting you? Is it about your mom?"

Elena spent the next thirty minutes telling Reese what she knew about the virus and why Fae had come to her for help. She also explained who her maternal grandfather was, and how she could be in danger—from the man who created the virus, from her grandfather's enemies—kind of terrifying when she laid it all out like that.

"You're a *princess*?"

"My mother is, I'm not. And Reese, you utter a word of this to anyone and I will take my hocus-pocus hands and incinerate your designer wardrobe."

She cocked her head. "Did you just stereotype me? I come from a wealthy family, so all I care about are clothes?"

"Why are you being touchy? I'm the one with—"

Reese waved her hand in an all-encompassing manner, then more pointedly at the glass. "What do you expect? The world's gone psycho!"

Some of that drama Reese had grown up with in Hollywood must have rubbed off.

"Relax. Everything's going to be fine," Elena said. She *hoped* it would be fine. "But I do have a favor to ask."

Her cousin's call this evening had hammered home

what deep shit she was in. Mateo was the voice of her family, and they were counting on her not to fail. No one in her family had made it to college. Shoot, most of them hadn't finished high school. Elena couldn't blow her chances at Dawson, no matter what Leo had said.

"Can you take notes for me tomorrow?"

"Um, yeah-h-h," Reese said cautiously. "I can help, but I can't promise I'll understand a word of your nerdy science lecture."

"That's okay. Thank you." Elena reached across the bed and squeezed her roommate so hard she squeaked.

"Ouch, Elena. Did you gain muscles along with those powers?"

"I don't think so, but I have been working out. Can you tell?" She flexed.

"Nope. Same wiry arm."

Elena twisted her head to stare at her biceps. Damn, all that training with Keen for nothing.

"I could help in other ways too." Reese glanced at the bedroom door. "He's watching reality television," she whispered. "Maybe I'll join him." She waggled her eyebrows. "See what I can discover."

Oh, good God. Elena pressed her fingers to her temples. "I just finished telling you he's a Fae. As in, *another species.* Do you really think it's a good idea to be alone with him? Keen seems harmless, but it's not like I know him that well."

"But he's H-to-the-O-to-the-T. Besides, in addition to giving me free shopping rein, my parents booked me in extracurricular activities." She ticked off her fingers. "I'm a decent gymnast, I play the piano, and I have a black belt in Tae Kwon Do. I can drop a man twice my size."

"I'd like to take this opportunity to point out that the Viking is three times your size."

Reese snorted. "Viking? Is that what you call him?"

"Sometimes. He has all those Nordic features. Stick to the point."

"First of all, you worry too much. Second, I doubt he's three times my size. Two and a half, at most. And anyway, it won't come to a fight."

Elena looked to the ceiling and sighed. "Somehow, that doesn't reassure me." She scooted further under the sheets and stifled a yawn. "But I'm too tired to argue. It's been a rough day, and I have to wake in a few hours. Just be careful..." She thought about it for a moment. "And scream if you need me. Derek will probably come running too."

"Yeah—what was the deal with him tonight?"

Elena frowned. "I don't know. I think he's upset he got dragged into my problems. He sort of stumbled upon me with the Fae. That's why he's involved in all this." Elena left out the part about Derek's ability. It wasn't her secret to share.

She pointed at Reese. "That's why it's important you not get too involved. I couldn't see how to keep you out of it entirely with us living together, but I don't want you to become a target, Reese. I don't trust them, so don't provoke Keen."

Reese pressed a hand to her chest. "Me provoke? Never. I'll simply work my own little magic." She waggled her fingers.

Several things worried Elena about that statement, but Reese had a way with men. Considering the way Keen had stared at her earlier, even Fae weren't immune.

SEVENTEEN

The next morning, Elena walked out to find Keen relaxing on the couch, his legs spread in a wide guy sprawl. In contrast, Derek sat next to him, tension and annoyance radiating off his body. His hair was damp from a recent shower and ruffled like a rat's nest. He avoided her eyes when she walked into the kitchen.

She didn't understand why he'd gotten so upset at Keen last night. Keen was just doing his job. He might have slipped up yesterday, and she wasn't happy about that. She still didn't understand how Beatrice had convinced Keen to leave. But even though Keen had screwed up, Elena didn't think it warranted Derek's animosity when the Fae had said he'd stay the night.

If Derek's frustration was about getting caught up in this mess, she couldn't blame him there. But no one had told him to follow her onto campus that day. He was as much to blame for being ensnared by Fae as she was for unknowingly leading him into danger.

"Do you want to take a shower?" she asked Keen.

"Towels are in the hall closet. Just make sure you lock the bathroom in case Reese forgets you're here."

Keen stood and smirked at Derek before walking away. Derek peered hard at the Fae's back, then rocked his head from side to side, as if releasing tension.

What was with these guys?

Keen wasn't making it easy. She'd have to have a little talk with him later.

Elena went into the kitchen to make breakfast and calm her nerves. After yesterday, who knew what Emain would bring today?

Maybe she could pull Derek aside later and ask him if he discovered anything at Marlon's lab. He'd left last night before she got the chance. She didn't think Keen could hear with the shower on, but that conversation would need to be top secret, and she didn't want to risk it.

Elena handed Derek three egg sandwiches and he mumbled his thanks, then ate a third of the first one in a single bite. The tension in his face didn't go away, though.

She rinsed out the sink and peered at the hard lines of his expression from beneath her lashes. "You don't have to do this, you know—help me."

His mouth twisted in a cynical smile. "They didn't give me a choice, Elena. They threatened my family too, just in a different way."

She braced her hands on the counter. "You could go home. Take a few months off. My family's *lives* are on the line. There's no reason to put your life at risk just to spare yourself a difficult conversation with your parents."

"It's more than that." He swallowed and looked at her intensely. "I can't walk away."

For a moment, she couldn't breathe. Suddenly this didn't seem as though it was about getting caught in something he never wanted to be a part of. It seemed as though it was about her. And him.

Them.

He hoisted his backpack on his shoulder. "They told me to protect you, and that's what I'm going to do."

"Okay. But if that's the case, you need to get along with Keen." She nodded toward the hallway. "He screwed up yesterday, but he's here to help too."

Derek grunted and popped the rest of the sandwich in his mouth.

Keen emerged from the hall, his hair wet like Derek's, but combed and slicked behind his ears. Keen didn't have an overnight bag, which begged the question of whose comb he'd used.

Probably best not to think about that.

"Ready to go?" she asked.

Keen nodded, and Derek opened the door, letting Keen pass first. He seemed to have lightened up somewhat, which was a good thing, because they all needed to work together.

But she hadn't forgotten what else she'd read in his eyes —longing and maybe more. And that was dangerous, because she felt it too.

There was no room in her world for longing like that.

Derek sat in the corner of the Allon Library, flipping through a book on plant alchemy, the tang of leather and aged furniture filling his nose. Hundreds of books, spanning modern science to a fourteenth-century edition of *The Travels of Marco Polo,* covered every wall surface inside the octagonal room. The oldest texts, written in some archaic language, had been printed on clay tablets and sat within glass cases. They had to be worth a fortune.

"Come on." Elena threw up her hands, leaning forward as she stared at the Tertullian Codex—a crusty old book they kept under lock and key. "'Blood of thy nobleman, in thy land trust. What is ancient breeds growth. Cross thy barrier and strengthen thy bond.' What is this, poetry? I can't interpret this crap. I'm a science geek." She propped her elbow on the pedestal that held the book, sinking her chin on her hand.

She was talking to herself again, frustrated with the book Leo said held all the answers.

"What do you *think* it means?" he asked. "Leo said it's up to the reader to determine the meaning of the Codex."

Beatrice wasn't involved in their trip to the Allon Library today. Portia had escorted them and cast the glamour over the Codex so Elena could read it. She had excused Beatrice's actions yesterday by claiming a miscommunication.

A miscommunication? Derek called bullshit. But the Fae weren't talking about what really happened. Or why someone had intentionally frightened Elena and delayed any progress she might have made in building her powers.

The more he thought about his discovery in Marlon's lab regarding the virus, the more he wanted to keep it to himself. Oh, he'd use the information to help Elena find a cure—he'd already started schooling her on viruses, particularly flu viruses. But he wasn't telling the Fae what he knew about Marlon. He didn't trust them not to use it against him.

Elena's pretty mouth twisted. "Deirdre said Tirnan is divided into three kingdoms. She said something about my mom being a Fae princess—which I'm having a hard time believing, but if it's true, it would make me a part of their nobility. When the Codex says, 'Blood of thy nobleman, in thy land trust,' I think it's saying Fae nobility will find what they need to improve their powers in the land—in Tirnan."

Derek pushed aside his book and folded his hands, his knuckles locked in a death grip.

He didn't want Elena inside Emain, let alone Tirnan, the Fae's home base. Maybe she hadn't read far enough. "What else does it say?"

"More about something ancient, but it doesn't say what it is." She shook her head. "A lot of what I'm reading is confusing, but there's one thing my instincts keep screaming. Our world is old, but Fae are really old. I don't think the lines about something ancient are referring to anything on Earth. I think I need to go to Tirnan."

CHAPTER

EIGHTEEN

Elena worked with Leo on transmutation all afternoon. No matter what she tried, she couldn't advance from elemental manipulations to transmutation—and she couldn't stop thinking about the words in the Codex.

Blood of thy nobleman, in thy land trust.

What is ancient breeds growth.

Cross thy barrier and strengthen thy bond.

Interpretation of the book was about instinct, and to her the passage meant the land would help with her powers. The land in Tirnan.

While she worked, she told Leo about the Codex, but not what she thought it was saying, because that was a dangerous interpretation. Traveling to Tirnan would put her life at extreme risk. But as she inserted her key in the door to her apartment just before midnight, she felt certain her instincts were right—that she had to travel to her mother's homeland.

The notion wasn't all bad. There was a chance she'd

meet the woman who'd left her and her father all those years ago.

To meet her mother after all this time... What would that be like? Would her mom be happy to see her?

Keen and Derek trailed behind her as she jerked her key out of the lock and pushed the door open—to find Reese sitting on the couch watching television. With Mateo.

All thoughts of Tirnan and her mother vanished at the sight of her cousin in her living room. "Mateo, what are you doing here?"

He rested his arm over the backrest behind Reese's shoulders. "I have a *pinche* cousin who doesn't return phone calls. Dragged my ass up here to check on you."

He was using his authoritative voice, which was annoying as hell, because he was only a couple of years older. Mateo went overboard in looking out for her while she was away at school.

He grinned at Reese. "Your roommate has been sweet enough to keep me company."

A low hiss sounded from behind. Keen walked around Elena into the room, waves of aggression rolling off him as he stared at her cousin.

Derek stepped between Keen and Mateo, thank God, because some kind of Fae shitstorm was brewing. What was wrong with Keen? Her cousin wasn't a danger.

Elena looked at Reese, who had a bit of a smug expression on her face. Reese inched closer to Mateo.

Reese wasn't interested in her cousin. What was she doing?

Keen growled.

Wait—was Reese baiting her Fae bodyguard? Keen had seemed oddly interested in Reese last night, and Elena had never gotten the scoop on what happened after her roommate had gone out to watch television with him. Elena had been too busy passing out, then waking up at the crack of dawn, to question her.

"Reese." Elena grabbed her roommate's hand and pulled her up. "Can I talk to you?"

Reese trotted behind her. "Uh, yes? Back in a minute, Mateo."

Mateo patted the couch. "Got your spot saved right here."

Elena dragged Reese into her bedroom and shut the door. "Is there something going on between you and Keen? What happened after I went to bed last night?"

Reese crossed her arms over her chest. "Nothing. We watched television."

"Then why is Keen acting like a jealous lover?"

Reese's chin notched back in shock. "Jealous? No, that guy is an *ass* who couldn't see a good thing if it slapped him in his hot Viking face."

Elena might be going through some sort of magical adolescence, but she'd swear everyone around her was hormonal. "Soooo, there's nothing going on?"

"No. He's just a big Fae ass, is all."

Okayyy. "'Cause you're not making a lot of sense. And you've called Keen an ass twice now."

"Thinks he's so superior," she muttered, and threw up her hands. "Like he's the last man on earth and all women want him."

"Um, he's Fae, Reese. Not a man."

"Whatever. He's an arrogant, self-righteous—"

Elena held up a finger. "Wait a minute. Do you *like* him?" The notion was kind of out there, given that guys chased Reese, not the other way around. But when Mateo liked a girl—really liked her—he acted all contrary… kind of the way Reese was behaving.

Reese squinted. *"Are you kidding me?"*

Hmm, she hadn't said no. "Reese, how do you feel about helping me with something? Again."

Okay, so she'd been asking for a lot of favors from her roommate lately. But really, with Fae nipping at her heels and murderous virus-creating Halven out there, she kinda needed the support. Elena would make up for it in food prep for the rest of the year. Not a bad deal for Reese.

This plan was on the fly, but Elena's best idea was to go to Tirnan to gain the power she needed to create a cure. Not the most prudent solution. The Fae weren't telling her everything. If she knew more, would she be able to come up with a cure without traveling to Tirnan, a land where an entire race of beings hated her? The few disgruntled Fae in Emain, even Beatrice, were preferable to the hatred of an entire population.

"Keen's keeping secrets," Elena said. "Derek and I can't figure out what's going on, and we need more information if we're going to find a cure. Leo seemed less confident today when I made no progress. It scared me. The things the Fae implied if I didn't help them—it's not good. If I don't figure something out soon, this could all go down very badly."

Reese sat on the bed. "What do you need me to do?"

"Well, you sort of came up with the idea on your own. I'd like you to flirt with Keen and get him on our side. Maybe he'll confess to something."

Reese shook her head. "No way."

"You don't have to *do* anything. Just work your 'magic charm,' or whatever you called it last night."

A strange look crossed Reese's face. "It won't work,

Elena. I tried talking to him. It was like speaking to a brick wall. Your Fae bodyguard told me to put more clothes on."

"Why? What were you wearing?"

She shrugged. "Pajama shorts and a tank top. Perfectly decent."

Reese held her own in the curves department. Her pajama shorts barely covered her rear. Her tank tops—well, let's just say they were formfitting, and she often skipped wearing a bra around the house. She wasn't the least bit modest.

Elena could just imagine the things that would go through a guy's mind if he saw Reese in her pajamas. No matter what Keen said about humans, Elena saw how he watched her roommate. In some ways, he was all male, Fae or not. Approval of what she wore had nothing to do with it.

Reese was *temptation*.

Mentally, Elena rubbed her hands together. *Think yourself impervious to the charms of humans, Keen? We shall see...* "Humor me, Reese. Go out there and ask Mateo for a foot massage or something. I promise to grab Mateo before Keen kills him."

Reese snorted. "Keen couldn't care less. I'm going to embarrass myself." She picked at her nails. She'd managed to peel off half the paint at some point during the day.

This from the girl whose nails were always perfectly manicured? Something was definitely up.

Elena covered Reese's fingers. Maybe this was a mistake. "You sure you don't like him?"

Reese's gaze flickered briefly. "Of course not. Let's get back to the issue at hand. Are you whoring me out?"

"What? No. This is Mateo. Foot massages come customary from a man-whore like him. You're my roommate. He won't try anything. He has *some* sense of boundaries. I just want to make Keen jealous and see if he'll cough up information on what the Fae are planning."

"That ass is not jealous. And even if he was, why would he give me information?"

"Because he'd be wooing you, and he'd say anything to get close to you."

Reese shook her head, her eyes narrowed. "This is some serious masterminding. Where did you scheme it up?"

"*Telenovelas.* Mateo's addicted." Elena flashed a bright smile. "Why, am I doing good?"

"Not really... Mateo watches soap operas?"

"*Hellooo*—everybody does."

"Uh, no. They don't."

"Will you please try? You don't actually have to touch Keen, just flatter him, or whatever it is you do to reel in guys."

"I'm not a fishing pole. I'm a blonde with brains. I tend to attract men." Reese frowned. "Although that guy's not normal. I'm telling you, he doesn't like me."

Reese was wrong. Keen liked her, Elena would swear to it. She smiled. "We'll see."

Moments later, Reese plopped onto the couch next to Mateo. That was all it took for Mateo to pick up where he'd left off. "Hey, beautiful." He flashed his signature Rosales smile, and even Reese blushed.

Elena sat at the kitchen peninsula next to Derek and pretended she wasn't watching the action on the couch. Derek leaned over. "What are you doing?"

"Shush. I have a plan," she whispered.

He glanced at the others. "Yeah, well, I don't like it."

"You haven't heard it." She peered back to see what was happening behind her.

Mateo pushed a strand of golden hair off Reese's shoulder. Keen turned away and punched the remote with his large finger, flipping through the television channels. He edged his knee toward the center of the couch cushion, taking up more space than necessary.

"Whatever it is, it might end in bloodshed," Derek murmured.

Mateo glanced at Keen, a look of annoyance on his face. "Guess we need to squeeze in," he said to Reese. "Why don't you put your legs over mine?"

Reese smiled flirtatiously. "Why, are you going to give me a foot massage?"

You are brilliant, Reese.

"Because I could use it after running across campus to take notes for Elena."

No, don't tell him that!

Mateo frowned, but he scooted closer and grabbed the foot Reese draped over his lap. "Why did you take notes for her?" He glanced at Elena, and she ducked her head, pretending to show Derek an assignment from her backpack.

Reese closed her eyes. "That feels soooo good, Mateo," she said, deflecting his question.

Mateo leaned into the massage. "Such pretty toes."

Wow, she really owed Reese. *Was* she pimping out her best friend?

No matter what Reese had said in the bedroom, it seemed like a part of her show earlier had been to piss off Keen. This was just more of the same. Besides, Mateo was a good guy and not bad to look at, from what she'd been told.

Reese's head lolled to the side, a smile on her face. She didn't look unhappy. Maybe Mateo had skills... *Eeew. Get thought out of head.*

"Enough!" Keen shouted.

Elena jerked in her seat, and Derek leapt off his stool.

"Your cousin cannot stay here tonight." Keen stared daggers at Mateo.

Mateo scrunched his nose as though he smelled something foul. "Who do you think you are? Elena, who is this jerk? You shouldn't have guys like him hanging around."

"He's my study partner, Mateo. Can I talk to you, please?" She pointed toward the hallway. "My room. Now."

Mateo flipped up his hand. "What did I do?" He rolled his eyes at the look she leveled at him, and sauntered toward her room.

"Don't you need to go next door?" she asked Derek before she followed her cousin back. Elena jerked her head at Keen and Reese on the couch, ignoring each other.

"Oh—right," Derek said, finally catching on. "I have to grab...that book we'll need."

Derek walked out, and Elena went back to her room, where Mateo was waiting. She closed the door behind her.

Mateo was standing in the center of the room. "What's this all about, Elena? And what's with these guys hanging around? You're supposed to be studying."

She threw up her hands. "You can't just show up and tell me what to do. What's wrong with you?"

He pointed toward the living room. "I'm protecting you from guys like that. We shouldn't leave your roommate with the basketball player." He looked at the door, as though considering. "She's so small and he's...not."

Elena swatted the air. "They're fine. We're all fine. Maybe you should think about returning home?"

He scanned her face. "Why do you want me to leave so badly?"

"Because I'm busy," she practically shouted.

He shifted his jaw, his gaze narrowing on her face. "I think I'll stay the night for the heck of it. I want to make sure everything's okay."

"Are you listening? Everything's fine. And you can't stay."

"Of course I can. You got any food around here?" He rubbed his belly, and walked toward the door.

She grabbed his arm and ran around in front of him. "*No.* I mean, yes, I have food, but there's no room, Mateo. Keen needs a place to sleep for a few days. He's on the couch."

Mateo lifted his lip in an irritated snarl. "Has your brainiac program cracked a gasket inside that head of yours? You can't let that guy stay the night. Tell him to find someplace else. You know what, forget it." He had his manly voice going now. "I'll do it."

He moved to step around her and Elena yanked him back. "No, you won't. He's my... friend. He stays as long as I say he does. The resident advisor lives next door. There's nothing to worry about. Keen's harmless." *To me,* she silently added.

She was pretty sure Keen had had nothing to do with the locked Allon Library yesterday. He seemed equally upset in his reserved, show-no-emotion sort of way. Reese, on the other hand? Elena wasn't sure what Keen wanted with Reese, but he definitely wanted something. Though she didn't think he would hurt her.

"I don't like it, ER—"

Elena clenched her fists and sucked in a strained breath. "I hate that freaking nickname."

It had been funny when she was ten and had told her family she wanted to become a doctor. Now the nickname just annoyed the hell out of her.

"He's a creep. I don't want him in your house."

"You don't like him because he's bigger than you."

Mateo's chest puffed out.

"I told Keen he can stay, and he stays."

"Then so do I. I'll crash on your floor like I did last time."

"I don't want your stinky feet in my room."

He brushed her off and walked around her. "Don't be such a priss. My feet smell like daisies."

She put her fingers to her forehead and closed her eyes, resisting the urge to hit him. "Fine, sleep here. I'll sleep with Reese. But you should think about cutting your stay short. I appreciate you coming." She let out a deep sigh. "I really do. I know you're just looking out for me, but it's bad timing."

The corner of his mouth pulled back in annoyance. "I can see that."

Of course Mateo would show up the one time she had men in her house. "Do me a favor and hang out in my room until I return."

"I'm not staying in your room—"

"Here." She reached for a stack of women's magazines Reese had brought in the other day. "Read these. Maybe you'll learn something."

"Learn something? My techniques are masterful," he said, though he was already flipping through *Cosmo*. Without looking up, he walked to her bed and sank back, one arm behind his head, legs crossed at the ankle.

Thank God Mateo was easily distracted.

She reached for the door. "I'll be back in a little while."

Mateo didn't answer, already engrossed in the latest ways to "please your man."

After quietly closing the door behind her, Elena crept down the hall and peeked around the corner.

"—for the last time, I don't need to cover my legs." Reese's tone sounded angry and her face was flushed as she glared at Keen. "Where are you from, anyway, the Baltics? This is California."

Keen waved his hand in the general direction of Reese's formfitting T-shirt. "I merely suggested you use the clothes you clearly possess and properly cover yourself."

A breeze tickled the side of Elena's face. "Anything going on?" a deep, masculine voice whispered in her ear.

Elena gasped and flattened a hand to the wall. "Mother effing—"

Derek covered her mouth, wrapped his arm around her middle, and carried her into Reese's bedroom.

"*Jesus Christ*, Derek," she said, after he'd closed the door. "Warn me before you do that. What is it with you and Keen sneaking up on me?"

"You'd better get used to it if we're going to be hanging out."

"Do I have a choice?"

"You want my help, or not?"

Her shoulders sank. "Want."

This drama masterminding was harder than it looked. Based on what she'd just witnessed of Reese and Keen, Derek was right. This was a bad idea.

"You think you can do your invisibility thing and see what they're up to? So far, it doesn't look promising. All they're doing is fighting. We might need to abort mission."

Derek didn't answer. He simply disappeared pixel by pixel, as if he were a computer screen.

"Where are you?" she whispered, but he was gone. No

sound, nothing, except a slight shimmer that disappeared by the door.

Several minutes later, Derek reemerged and sat on Reese's bed, his back to the footboard. "They've found common ground. They're watching reality TV, and Reese made popcorn. Could take a while for her to get anything out of him, though; he's stiff as a board. Not his... Never mind."

Derek flicked a piece of fuzz off the bed. The light blush that crept up his cheeks was sort of sweet.

"The good thing is," he added, "whenever Reese isn't paying attention, Keen follows her every move. It's only a matter of time."

"You really think this could work?" she asked.

He shrugged in the universal guy gesture for *yeah, probably*.

"Wow. How long does this sort of thing take?"

"You're a chick. How long does it take to manipulate a guy?"

She raised her brow. "Bitter, are we?"

"Not at all. You women are trained early to maneuver men to your will. Common knowledge."

"Well, I've never manipulated a man—annoying cousins not included." Elena tucked a lock of hair behind her ear. "And since I don't have a lot of experience with this sort of thing, how long does it take to break through a guy's defenses?"

"Sometimes it never happens. Depends on the girl."

There was something about the way he said it that had Elena wondering if Derek was referring to her—*them*.

She became very aware of several things all at once: they were alone, on a bed, and he was looking at her in a way that did funny things to her stomach.

Tonight wasn't the first time they'd been in a bedroom together. They'd even slept in the same room before. But this was the first time Elena hadn't been so utterly drained that all she could think about was her head making contact with her pillow.

Right now, every part of her was alert and taking in her attractive neighbor who'd made it his mission to look out for her, for reasons she hadn't yet determined. There was the obvious reason, because Portia had threatened him if he didn't. But there was another reason he'd been hinting at, yet hadn't outright said.

This sort of boy analysis was above Elena's pay grade. She didn't understand men, not really. She'd barely grazed second base with a guy. She sure as heck wasn't going to figure out Derek tonight.

She cleared her throat. "So you don't think she'll get him to talk?"

"Oh—she'll get him to talk. That guy's been drooling over your roommate since the first moment he saw her. I'm just saying, not all guys cave. It depends on how they feel about the person. In this case, we're safe. As soon as that jackass gives up the pretense he's not interested, he'll be putty in her hands."

He stretched out his legs and crossed his arms over his chest. "Don't worry, she'll wear him down. And I agree, if he likes your roommate, he might be more willing to help. It'd be good to have Keen on our side."

CHAPTER

NINETEEN

Derek took in Elena's features as she rested her head against the upholstered headboard of Reese's queen-sized bed, her soft, wavy hair fanning around her face. If her mother was Fae, no wonder she was so pretty. Physical flaws didn't seem to be a part of the Fae gene pool. Though even if Derek didn't know what Elena looked like and had only heard her talk or banter with him, he would have been drawn to her.

Elena was smart, which he'd always appreciated in a girl, but she was also funny and feisty—not characteristics he often found in women. Then again, most girls were intimidated by him, which he'd never quite understood.

Elena had never been intimidated by him, not even when they first met and she'd appeared anxious to find a lab.

"Okay, well, it looks like we have time until Reese breaks down Keen's man barriers," she said. "My schoolbooks are in the other room, so studying is out. I don't want to disturb the lovebirds. We could get some sleep...or we could talk?"

"Talk," Derek said dryly. That sounded about as much fun as waiting for Keen to make a move.

She rolled her eyes. "Don't be such a guy. Tell me about your family. That's a safe subject."

For some people it might be, but not for Derek. "What do you want to know?" he asked reluctantly.

"Where are you from?"

"Columbus, Ohio."

"What's your family like?"

"My mom's a housewife. I already told you about my dad—cardiovascular surgeon. No siblings."

She blinked in irritation. "Very factual and to the point. Thank you. Now give me something good. Do you have a girlfriend? What's your biggest fear? What do you want to do with your life?"

He studied her for a moment. "Why do chicks always want to know that stuff?" A faint blush pinkened her cheeks. Yeah, he'd caught the girlfriend reference.

"Because it's interesting. Don't be such a wuss. Just answer the questions you're comfortable with."

"No girlfriend, my parents discovering my ability, and... I'm not sure. About the future. I wanted to take after my dad and go into cardiovascular health, but it's not safe for me to be around my parents anymore."

Her brow furrowed. "You can't be worried about both of your parents finding out what you are. One of them is Fae. Chances are, they both know about alternate realms."

"I was adopted. My real parents gave me up. Considering how enamored Fae are of Halven, I'm not surprised."

Her expression turned serious. "I'm sorry... I shouldn't have brought it up."

"Don't be. I've never had a problem with my adoptive

parents." That didn't sound right. His parents stressed him out, but he loved them. "They're good to me."

The space between her brows pinched. She wasn't buying it, and neither did he. "It sounds like your adoptive parents care about you. Why don't you trust them with who you are?"

Derek thumbed the footboard. "They come from perfect families and have lived perfect lives."

Elena sighed loudly and her hazel eyes flared a deep green. "Screw what Portia said about acceptance and being different. She was trying to scare you. If your parents love you, they'll support you."

"How would you know?" he said gently. "Your family didn't give you up. They adore you. You're their shining star."

"Yeah, no pressure there."

There was the feisty. Girls never talked to him like this. And why Elena's never giving him an inch drew him, he couldn't explain. "I know you mean well, but you know nothing about what I've gone through the past two years—"

"Well, I think I know a little." She smiled her pretty smile, the one that made his heart trip. "I'm in the same situation, remember?"

"And have you told your family who you really are?"

"Well, no, but that's different. I haven't seen my family since I discovered my ability. There hasn't been time for a family sit-down. You know, saving Fae and all."

He jerked his head toward the door. "Your cousin's in the other room. Why don't you talk to him? At the rate Reese is getting things done, we have the time."

Elena sat straighter. "Reese doesn't need to do any of this. She's making a sacrifice for us."

"First of all, nice way to change the subject. Second, yeah right, your roommate is making a sacrifice." He snorted.

Elena's jaw dropped. "What's that supposed to mean?"

"Nothing. Just that she enjoys dating around. Not that there's anything wrong with that."

"Reese has never even had a boyfriend."

"Maybe not a boyfriend, but..."

Her face contorted in anger. "You don't know what Reese has or hasn't done."

He was being an ass, but he was well aware of all the guys who visited Reese. He'd seen them come and go plenty of times. Of course, Elena didn't know that, and maybe it was time he confessed.

"I do know, Elena. I've kept tabs on the people in our neighborhood."

She blinked several times. "How... *You.*" She reached across the bed and poked him in the chest. Hard. It didn't hurt, but he found himself inching into the footboard anyway. "I saw the shimmer earlier when you left the room. I've seen it before, when Keen brought me home for the first time. Have you been spying on us?"

Shit. She can see me while I'm Blended?

Elena couldn't believe what she was hearing. How long had Derek been watching them?

"You're nothing but a peeping Tom!"

"That's an exaggeration," he said. "I've been inside the dorm when you and Reese were talking outside your apartment, but I don't enter people's homes. Well, I did once, but it was because I needed to make sure some guy wasn't up to something. He seemed suspicious."

She opened her mouth to respond, but he cut her off.

"What did you mean when you said you could see me? No one sees me when I'm Blended."

She shrugged one shoulder impatiently. Who cared? The fact was, he'd kept his sneaking around from her. "The air wavers like refraction—a sidewalk on a hot day, that sort of thing. Let's get back to the point. Why were you spying on us?"

"Scouting. I don't spy."

She folded her arms over her chest. Did he really think she was buying that?

Derek ran his fingers through his messy hair and sighed. "When I first Blended, a lot of things ran through my mind, but mostly I became paranoid. I worried someone had done this to me. I started looking over my shoulder and keeping tabs on the people around me. I've checked out all our neighbors, not just you and your roommate."

"If you don't routinely go inside people's homes and you're such a paragon of morality, how do you know what Reese does with guys?"

"I don't, but I assume when she brings guys home—"

"Well, don't assume. You don't know Reese the way I do. She's not like that."

His expression fell and he let out a resigned sigh. "You're right. I don't know her. I wouldn't want to be judged."

Derek sat forward and reached for her wrist, forcing her to loosen her arms folded across her chest. "I shouldn't have said that, Elena. I'm sorry. Reese seems like a great girl. I made a snap judgment before I knew her, and it was wrong."

He tucked a loose strand of hair behind her ear, and this time the curly lock stayed put, but all she could think about was how close he'd been to kissing her the last time he'd touched her hair.

She looked up and drew in a breath, her frustration and anger melting as his gaze moved from her hair to her mouth. Her cheeks warmed and her heart pounded.

He slowly leaned forward and touched his lips to hers. A kiss of apology—and so much more. His mouth lingered, the sensual caress sending a light shiver down her spine.

Derek had always been attractive, but he'd become a part of her in some fundamental way she didn't understand because she'd never felt this connection before. Maybe it existed because they were both Halven, but she didn't think so. That lightning storm of tension had been there from the start, long before they knew what they were.

He lifted his mouth, but only a fraction, his gaze trained on her lips. Then he angled his head and deepened the kiss. A tightening sensation swept through her middle. She threaded her fingers through his soft, messy hair and kissed him back.

Derek lifted her on his lap as if she weighed nothing, her legs dropping on either side of his waist. He pulled her close until no space existed between them.

After a moment, Elena broke the kiss to catch her breath. They were at eye level and she could see the sapphire flecks of his beautiful irises, the outer rim a midnight blue.

"Are you still mad?" His voice came out gruff.

She shook her head and pressed her mouth back to his. The feel of him beneath her—surrounding her—had all the muscles in her belly contracting, the sensation migrating down her thighs. He kissed her while she ran her hands up his muscled neck to the angle of his jaw, her fingers smoothing over the light scruff there. Derek pressed her lower back until her body rocked flush with his. He did this over and over, his tongue moving in a similar rhythm inside her mouth. And that was when her breath started to come out in short, sputtered bursts between kisses. The friction—the closeness—sent her heart racing.

Elena had made out with boys in high school, before she'd hermitted herself away in order to earn entrance into college. But never had she felt *this*. Raw, consuming, she wanted—*wow*—more.

In the distant recesses of her mind, she took note of a door closing. A moment later, a knock sounded at Reese's bedroom door.

Elena broke away from Derek, nearly falling off the bed in her effort to climb off his lap. His gaze was half-lidded and more intense than she'd ever seen it, and he was looking at her as if he was ready to ignore the knock and pull her back on his lap.

For a second, she considered it.

"Yes?" she said, without looking away from the magnet in front of her.

"I'm not going to wait in your room all night, Elena."

Holy crap, Mateo. How could she have forgotten her cousin in the other room?

Leave it to Mateo to interrupt the hottest kiss of her life. He officially had the worst timing ever.

Elena scooted off the bed and ran her fingers through her hair, taking a deep breath to cool the heat in her face. Did she look like she'd just had the sense kissed out of her? Her gaze moved to Derek, but she had to look away. Seeing his half-lidded expression only sent warmth back through her body. She smoothed her top, though it wasn't ruffled, and opened the door.

Mateo's eyes darted around the room, narrowing on her face. He glared at Derek.

"We're studying," she said, like she'd been caught. Which she had, but still, she was an adult. Kissing and all the rest of it was allowed.

According to half of her high school student body, Elena was way behind in sex education. Not that she felt the need to keep up with the rest of them. But with Derek, she was beginning to appreciate what all the hype was about.

Mateo's mouth twisted, as if he didn't believe her. Okay, so there were no books out and she could feel her face was still flushed.

"I've been looking at *Cosmo* for over an hour. I can't believe girls actually read that garbage. I'm grabbing food from the kitchen and going to bed." A pause. "You should too. *Alone.*" He frowned in Derek's direction.

Elena glanced heavenward. "Give it a break, Mateo."

He notched his shoulder toward Derek. "Where's he sleeping?"

"He—"

"Here," Derek said, and she looked at him. "I'm not leaving, Elena."

She didn't want him to leave. She wanted to keep kissing him, but that wasn't what Derek was referring to. He was worried about her.

She rubbed her forehead. "Okay—I guess you can sleep in the living room with Keen."

"No," Derek said. "That's not a good idea." He looked pointedly at the wall, as if trying to communicate something silently.

Was he worried about interrupting Keen and Reese?

"Let's get food, and see what's going on," she offered. "Maybe Reese knows something by now."

As the words left Elena's mouth, they heard shouting. Mateo's head swiveled toward the living room, and Elena and Derek joined him in the hallway.

"—how can you be such a misogynistic pig?" came Reese's elevated voice.

Mateo stepped forward as if to go in there, and Elena pulled him back. "Wait."

Derek moved beside her. His arm brushed her shoulder, sending sparks across her skin. She sucked in a breath. How was she supposed to concentrate after those kisses?

"Derek," she said. "Are you sure this is going to work? It doesn't sound like they like each other, let alone want to know each other better."

Mateo stared at her in disbelief. "What are you doing trying to set your sweet roommate up with that creep?"

"Be quiet, Mateo," she whispered at his loud voice. "And it's none of your business."

"You're right," Derek said to her, and let out a strangled sigh. "It shouldn't be taking this long."

She stared down the hall. "I think I made a mistake forcing them together."

"Come on." He nudged her. "Let's see what's up."

They walked into the living room and Derek headed for the kitchen.

Keen and Reese didn't seem to notice them at all. Reese was on the couch, leaning away from Keen with her arms crossed, her face set in a scowl, and Keen hovered over her, one long basketball arm, as Mateo had put it, on the back of the couch. His mouth was close to her ear as he spoke in low tones Elena couldn't hear.

Considering Reese's expression, whatever Keen was saying was pissing her off.

Reese scooted farther away and shook her finger at him, the majority of her hushed tirade making its way into the kitchen. "You are not more intelligent... I'll have you know..."

"We have to do something," Elena whispered, as she sat at the counter across from Derek, whose head was halfway in the fridge.

He glanced over at Reese and Keen. "Nah, it's going to be okay. It's on."

"*What?* Are you nuts? They're about to come to blows."

Mateo was watching Keen and Reese too, his brows raised in interest.

He was no help. Mateo loved *telenovelas,* and this was like a live version.

Derek closed the refrigerator door and rifled through the cupboards. He pulled down a cereal box. "Honey flavored"—he popped a little O in his mouth—"and still fresh."

At the sound of food, Mateo grabbed bowls from the cupboard. "Don't eat 'em all, man. I need nourishment if I'm gonna maintain my guns." He flexed and kissed his biceps.

Elena gaped at the two of them like they'd lost their minds. How could they think of food with Reese and Keen fighting?

"What?" Mateo said, at the look on her face. "Don't worry, ER. I'll pick up more groceries tomorrow."

Elena ground her teeth, her eyes crossing briefly. "Mateo, what did I tell you about that nickname?"

Derek smirked and poured cereal to the rims of the

bowls, followed by milk that toppled little Os on the counter.

A screech of frustration came from behind. Derek gave a cursory glance behind her and Elena spun on her stool to see what was happening.

"Yup, so on," he said.

She turned back to find him shoveling a heaping spoonful of cereal in his mouth.

"They're going to kill each other," she whispered. "This was the worst idea I've ever had."

Mateo grinned. "Ten bucks says we find them spooning on the couch in the morning."

Derek shook his head. "Don't make that bet, Elena. Guys can be cavemen when they like a girl, and Keen's exhibiting all the signs. Trust me on this."

She stared at the two guys across from her, pouring food down their throats as though they'd been starved. "I will never understand men. All I see are two people hating on each other." She shook her head. "Mateo's wrong. I'll take his bet, because I know Reese."

Without looking up from their food, Mateo and Derek high-fived each other loudly enough to elicit a moment of silence from the couple on the couch.

TWENTY

Apparently, Mateo decided he wasn't that tired after all, or he simply didn't trust Derek alone with Elena. And Derek didn't blame the guy. The way Derek was beginning to feel about Elena, he didn't trust himself around her either.

Mateo's interrupting them earlier was one of the few things that could have splashed cold water on him. Derek would have stopped if she'd wanted him to, but she didn't seem any more eager to end what they'd started than he was.

He'd always been attracted to his pretty neighbor, but now that he knew her, his attraction had grown tenfold.

After spending an hour trapped in Reese's bedroom, trying to keep his mind off inappropriate thoughts about Elena while her cousin surfed his phone two feet away, Derek decided to slip out and check on the cranky lovebirds.

He waited until he was in the hallway to Blend. No need to give Elena's cousin a heart attack.

Entering the living room, he found Reese standing behind the couch with Keen leaning over her, his body tense. Keen said something quietly and Reese's eyes widened. She wasn't tall, and looked even smaller in front of Keen. That didn't stop her from bending her knees and driving a perfectly formed punch to his stomach.

Derek jerked forward, prepared to stop the fight Elena had called, then halted.

Because Keen, in some ninja Fae move, had caught Reese's fist before she made contact.

The Fae pinned her arm behind her back and yanked her to his chest. "Little one," he said in a cool, serious tone, "I like your spirit, but do not attempt to best me. There is no comparison."

He cradled her head with his other hand and drew his face down as if to kiss her. Only instead of kissing her, he stopped above her lips and dipped his face into the crook of her neck.

Reese's body trembled, her breaths growing shallow.

Derek didn't know what the hell he was witnessing, but he didn't think it was disgust—more like lust.

Keen released her arm and skimmed his hand down her ribcage and waist.

Derek should leave, give them privacy, but there were some serious sparks flying, and not all of them romantic. He waited another second just to be sure Reese was okay.

A scowl came over her face and she shoved Keen away.

The Fae stepped back and turned from her, his hands low on his hips, head bent as he seemed to collect himself. He appeared stunned, as if he couldn't believe what he'd done.

Neither could Derek. He knew Keen liked Reese, but this was intense.

Reese stormed past Keen and grabbed her keys and

purse from the counter. She walked out the front door—in her slippers.

Shit. Elena was right. This was a bad idea. No more leaving Keen and Reese alone together. These two were volatile.

Keen's head rose and he stared over his shoulder at the door, then glanced at the hallway, as though trying to decide if he should run after Reese or stay and protect Elena.

Keen couldn't leave Elena to run after Reese. Elena was too important to his people.

He must have determined that as well, because he strode to the window and slammed a fist against the frame. The impact sent a tremor through the walls, rattling the glasses in the cupboards.

The Fae had serious strength. Nothing like causing a minor earthquake to impress people.

Keen turned and strode toward Derek, stopping a couple of feet from Derek's invisible form. His mouth tensed. "Begone, Halven."

Damn. Could all Fae see him?

That was a nuisance. How was he going to spy on them if they all knew where he was? Even Elena could see him.

Derek heeded Keen's warning and returned to Reese's bedroom, where he'd left Elena and Mateo. Only Mateo was gone and Elena had fallen asleep.

Mateo must have given up his big-brother vigilance and gone into Elena's room to crash for the night.

Elena's head was propped against the headboard and slightly tilted to the side, a magazine lying loosely in her hands. Derek considered giving her privacy, but where would he go? Keen would kill him if he returned to the living room, and Derek wasn't leaving the house. He'd already decided to stay by Elena's side until this was all over.

Derek took off her shoes and removed the magazines from her lap, somehow managing to get her under the covers without waking her. She had to be exhausted. They'd left Emain early tonight, but she was still depleted from all the training.

He peered around the room, thinking about what he'd witnessed. He was worried about Reese. She'd probably gone to a friend's house, but he didn't know that for sure. He felt like an ass for disregarding Elena's worries about leaving Reese with the Fae.

How could Keen screw things up so badly? Hard to imagine Keen didn't have game, with his passable looks. The sparks had flown between them before Reese fled the house. Maybe the Fae wasn't the only one fighting an attraction?

Derek shook his head. It was obvious they'd get no information from Keen. Whatever secrets the Fae hid, neither Keen nor Leo seemed inclined to share. It had been a long shot to think Reese could befriend Keen. Attempting it had only made the tension around Elena greater.

Their best move was to focus on building Elena's powers, only Derek hadn't wanted to think about what that meant. If Elena was right about the Tertullian Codex and she needed to travel to the Fae realm, what kind of danger would that put her in?

Worried for Elena and unable to sleep, Derek checked his phone for messages.

His father had called. Twice.

"Derek." His father's cultured voice rang out in the voice message. "Good news. I bumped into Philip Rand at a humanitarian luncheon last week. I may have boasted of your accomplishments at Dawson, and, well, in short, Rand believes he could get you admitted into the program this late in the semester. He says they're always open to exceptional students. I wanted to let you know right away in case you've changed your mind about finishing off your education at Dawson.

"Your mother and I understand you wanted to go in a different direction from cardiovascular health, but please consider this opportunity. Not only is it an Ivy League school, but Rand says he could find you a private lab to continue your work if you wanted. You'd also be near your mother and me, which would make your mom happy. Call us when you get this message, son. I'm eager to talk to you."

Derek rubbed his eyes. He loved his parents, and part of him longed to share his secret with them. But if his admission about who he really was went badly, he could lose his family forever.

Portia hadn't lied. His adoptive parents weren't forward-thinking. They were conservative politically and socially. Derek had already lost his biological parents. He didn't want to lose his adoptive family too. And there was no reason for that to happen. As long as he did what the Fae asked, he could keep his secret.

Limbs and mind suddenly heavy, Derek walked over and pulled the covers up to Elena's chin. He lay down beside her and studied her profile. The elegant line of her cheekbone, her smooth, baby-soft skin. A strand of wavy hair had fallen across her lips, fluttering with each exhalation.

Derek had put up walls when he realized what he was, but Elena had caught his attention even after that. He'd told her the truth when he said he didn't peep on her and her roommate. But his intentions were never totally platonic. The more he'd watched her from afar, the more beautiful she became to him. And now, it felt like she had a piece of him.

It was terrifying as hell.

Derek let out an exhausted breath and sank deeper into the mattress. His hand slipped across the bed like a magnet toward her body until his index finger brushed her bent knee. He closed his eyes and sleep took over.

TWENTY-ONE

Elena walked along the bank of a clear river, its water rushing by. The sound of leaves rustling on the wind floated across the cool, earth-scented air as the sun descended on the horizon in flames of burnt orange.

She wrapped her arms around her torso to keep warm and glanced at the forest a short distance away, expecting to see the trees moving in the breeze. But that wasn't what she saw.

The forest was made up of trees bearing leaves in impossible colors—traditional red, orange, and yellow, but also pink and deep violet. And the leaves didn't sway in the wind, they *shifted,* relocating to different branches and causing the rustling sound she'd heard.

She stared in disbelief. A moment later, the leaves did it again.

Like iron filaments attracted to a magnet, each leaf fluttered to a new branch.

"Beautiful, isn't it?"

Elena's shoulders jerked, and she turned. "Deirdre?"

She released the breath that had caught in her throat. "I thought I was alone."

Deirdre smiled warmly. "Never alone. We are here." She gestured to the forest and the area around them.

"Where is here?" Elena had never seen this place before, but it seemed familiar somehow. "And what's with those trees?"

Deirdre peered at the forest. "The *allon.* Some call it the tree of life. It is said to be a gift from the heavens. The allon only grows in Tirnan."

"The library in Emain is named after it," Elena said absently, watching the leaves repeat their mysterious migration.

Deirdre walked along the river and Elena did too. "You will find a great many representations of the allon within Emain and Tirnan."

"Is that where we are, in Tirnan?" She looked around them.

"We are in your dream, but yes, every Fae dreams of Tirnan."

"But I'm a Halven."

Deirdre paused, as if considering. "That is true... Your powers are also unusual. Perhaps that is why you dream of Tirnan when other Halven do not."

After a moment, Deirdre pointed to the water. "This river is called the Fates. It separates two of our kingdoms, the Old and the New."

Elena studied the stream, which seemed to widen up ahead. "Which kingdom are you from?"

"Old Kingdom, but I live in Sunland now."

"What is Sunland?"

Deirdre smiled. "Sunland is a land beyond the two king-doms, unclaimed in the traditional sense. Sunlanders believe in your human democracy. We wish to live simply off the land, care for each other, and stop the war."

"There's a war?"

The corners of her mouth turned down. "There will be. Old Kingdom and New Kingdom have fought to control Tirnan for over a millennium. More bloodshed will come. Soon."

"But Fae are dying from disease. Why would they fight in a war right now? Can't they put their differences aside long enough to get through this?"

Deirdre glanced out at the trees, her eyes sad. "When you have battled as long as we have, it becomes a part of your essence. Oldlanders and Newlanders despise each other. Disease or not, that remains a constant."

"That sounds morbid. And miserable. Aren't you supposed to be descended from angels?"

"Ah, but even angels have waged wars. With hell most commonly, but also amongst themselves, according to the legends."

Elena stepped onto a pretty, curved bridge that crossed the river.

"Stop." Deirdre held up her hand. "Don't go beyond this point, Elena. It's dangerous. Old Kingdom lies beyond. *Never* trust Oldlanders."

"You just said you're from Old Kingdom."

"And now I am a part of Sunland, a neutral zone. Those loyal to Old Kingdom, intent on fighting the Great War, will destroy you."

Elena woke with a start, Deirdre's words ringing in her ears.

Just a dream—not real.

No one was going to destroy her. No battle was being waged, other than the Fae's battle to survive the disease.

Elena reached for a glass of water on her nightstand, and stared at the unfamiliar neon clock.

Reese's neon clock.

She was in Reese's room, but she didn't remember falling asleep last night.

It was still early, though not early enough to go back to sleep. She'd have to return to Emain soon.

Where was Reese, anyway?

Elena tried to push down the covers to get up, but they were stuck. And that was when she heard him.

Derek's breathing—deep, familiar—filled her senses, and she shifted around. He was asleep on his stomach beside her, his body on top of the blankets. His head was turned away, one arm curled beneath a pillow—one bared, muscular arm. The rest of his torso was naked too.

Elena automatically glanced down.

He still wore his jeans, but his bare feet dangled off the bed.

And wow. Those Fae clothes she thought fit him so well didn't do him justice. His skin was smooth and lightly tanned, and the muscles the snug Fae clothing hinted at were on full display, making her chest and other parts of her body overly warm.

Instinctively, she reached out and lightly trailed her fingers over his shoulder and down the firm waves of his back muscles. Those corded muscles jumped beneath her fingertips, and Derek's breathing changed.

She froze, but it was too late. He lifted his head and glanced around as if trying to figure out where he was. His gaze landed on her, and he shook his head as if to clear it.

"Sorry. I tried to move the blankets down, but you were on top." She sounded like an idiot. She'd groped him while he slept, and that was the best she could come up with?

Derek sat up and leaned on his elbow. He stared at the blankets, then yanked them below her waist in one swift movement.

Seeing their bodies side-by-side made her think about last night—before she'd fallen asleep. Their kiss, the taste of him... Had she dreamed about being with Derek the way she'd dreamed of Tirnan?

Derek's gaze trailed up her body, over her T-shirt and up her neck, where she felt the blood rise and warm her face. The look in his eyes—as if he could devour her—had her heart hammering.

Okay, maybe she hadn't imagined the kisses.

Taking the same liberty to touch that she had, Derek reached out and smoothed his fingers over her cheek and down her neck, pausing at the bottom of her throat above her pounding pulse.

After the dream she'd woken from, his hand was like a salve. The dream hadn't terrified her in the traditional sense, but it had burdened her just the same. It was like an omen. And having Derek here soothed her.

He flattened his hand over her sternum, the edges of his large fingers grazing her breasts as he slid it down her middle. He slipped his palm around her waist and tucked her against the hard line of his body.

"You're beautiful." He leaned down and ran his lips over her hairline, tickling her skin. His body pressed lightly over hers, causing her eyes to flutter closed. Her breath became audible, but Derek didn't seem to notice, or maybe he didn't care that he had her panting. Maybe that was the point.

He kissed her cheekbone, her nose. She lifted her knee to get closer, and his large hand caught her hip, pinning her leg to him. He paused above her mouth, then kissed her bottom lip.

Elena wrapped her arms around his broad shoulders, squeezing him to her chest. She fully comprehended the restless energy between them now—the tension that sometimes built and had caused them to bicker in his lab that first night, or in Emain while she worked toward a cure. Attraction was like that. When two forces were close enough, tension built until the two attracted pieces united.

Derek's mouth came down on hers, and she responded by curling her fingers in his hair and trapping his head. His tongue caressed and tangled, sending those spasms of pleasure shooting through her again. He broke away and dropped feverish kisses down her neck. Her head fell back and he nudged her T-shirt lower with his chin, showering attention on the top of her breasts. Inarticulate little sounds erupted from her throat. God, his mouth felt good.

After a moment, Derek raised his head. Elena looked down to find him staring at the place he'd kissed.

Shit. Men liked breasts, but hers were so obvious she chose clothes that toned them down.

Derek cupped the bottom of one breast as if he were holding something precious, then gently squeezed, trailing his palm over the nipple thinly covered by her lace bra. And *wow.* She'd had this before, this type of touching, but it had never felt this good. His hands, the way he smelled, the warmth in his eyes—they melded into this perfect force she couldn't fight, nor did she want to. Derek brooded and stomped around, but in the end he protected her, watched over her. Was there for her.

And suddenly there wasn't a barrier that seemed too great to cross in order to be closer.

Elena ran her hands down his chest and along the sides of his ribcage, mapping out his upper body. Derek's breathing grew shallow as he caressed and kissed along her exposed skin, pushing her T-shirt up more and tugging the lace of her bra to the side. His mouth and tongue moved where the material had been, and Elena gasped. She arched to get closer. He slid one palm over her hip to the inside of her thigh, where he stroked between her legs over her jeans.

The sensation he stirred was so raw and urgent, her breaths came fast and she thought she might pass out. Need burned a swath through her belly and limbs, consuming her. She tried to calm down, to think rationally like she always did—she'd never gone this far with a guy before—but her mind wasn't sending the normal signals. She kept thinking about how amazing it would feel if his hand was *under* her clothes.

Would it be so bad to make love to Derek? Because right now that seemed like the most natural thing in the world.

Somehow a piece of logic crept its way into her hormone-drunk thoughts. "Derek, wait."

He stilled, then eased his hand to a safe zone at her hip, trailing his fingers across her bare stomach. He nuzzled her cheek and ear. "Yes?" His voice was a notch lower than normal, craggy, and doing nothing to cool the heat of her blood.

There were more important things she should say, like *We need to leave for Emain.* Or *This is the wrong time.* But what came out was, "How come you never asked if I have a boyfriend?"

His lips paused above her ear. "I know you don't," he finally said.

She thought about that for a moment as his kisses resumed down her neck. *"Peeping Tom."* He smiled into her skin, and she gripped his shoulders. "The thing is... I've never had a boyfriend before. Never done—you know."

Derek froze. He lifted his head to look into her eyes, as if searching for something there.

The truth to the universe?

Nope, probably just checking to see if she was serious about being a virgin. And now her mortification was complete.

She grimaced and shut her eyes. Why had she brought it up?

He dropped a soft kiss on her mouth. "Good. Don't like thinking of you with other guys."

She drew a hand through his silky, rumpled hair. "Aren't you worried I'm too much of a nerd for guys to want me?"

He snorted. "Believe me, guys want you. They're just intimidated by smart girls. Especially beautiful smart girls. It's a good thing I'm smarter than you. I'm not intimidated."

She swatted his shoulder. "Hey!"

He smiled and pinned her hands above her head, clutching them both in one of his own. It was a move Mateo had made a million times to gain control of the remote—or to piss her off.

Derek's version did not feel the least bit brotherly. His fingers and arms warmed her chest where her skin lay exposed from her lacy bra skewed every which way.

"It's not like I've never kissed anyone—"

He put a finger to her lips. "I don't need to hear it.

Thinking about you with someone else makes me —irritable."

"Fine. What about you?"

"I've had sex, if that's what you're asking."

Just like that, he went and said it. "Do you have to be so blunt?" She wasn't thrilled with the idea of him and someone else either. But she understood most people weren't virgins at their age.

He loosened his grip on her hands, and she tugged her top down and sat up.

He shrugged. "It's what you're asking, isn't it?"

"I guess." She frowned.

He pulled her onto his lap and wrapped his arms around her. He kissed her frown, but she couldn't get her face to soften. "I never felt for them what I feel for you. Not even close."

Them? There was a them?

He kissed her neck and mumbled, "Matter of fact, my mind draws a blank when I think about it. All I can think of is you."

Typical line. But it worked. Her body loosened and she fought a smile.

Lying close and touching Elena, Derek's body wanted to explode, but what he'd said was true. Elena was the only girl he thought about. He didn't care what they did as long as he was with her.

"We should get up. We need to be in Emain soon." She sounded as disappointed by it as he was, but she was right.

Derek wanted this Fae business over with, and the only

way to accomplish that was to give them what they wanted.

"I'd like to return to Marlon's lab today," he said as she untangled herself from his arms. "I found things there. I should have gone back already to search for more, but I didn't want to leave you last night."

"You think Marlon had something to do with the virus?" Her hand rested on his bare shoulder, and just that warm touch alone gave him a sense of peace he hadn't known since he'd discovered what he was.

"Yeah. Marlon's definitely involved."

Derek quietly told Elena about the virus and the F-18 ingredient from Marlon's notes, conscious of keeping his voice low, with Keen in the living room. He'd prefer to tell her without Keen around, but that didn't seem likely, and they were running out of time. He explained how he wanted to take samples from the antique bottles in the back of Marlon's lab to search for F-18.

"It should be safe for you to come with me today if you think you can get away," he said. "The place hasn't been touched. And Keen will be with us as backup. I don't trust the jackass to not tell people where we went, but he won't know what we're doing there."

"Beginning to rely on my bodyguard, are you?"

In a flash, he pinned her beneath him and tickled her sides. "I'm the bodyguard. Keen is the lookout."

She giggled and fought the fingers he dug into her ribs. "Okay, okay. You win. You're the bodyguard."

He eased up, and she wrapped her arms around his shoulders. "I like having a personal bodyguard."

He kissed her on the mouth, enjoying how good it felt to hold her. "So you'll go with me?"

"Of course. But it might be best if we leave now and go

early. I didn't make progress yesterday. I need all the training with Leo I can get."

Derek sat up. "You're not due in Emain for another hour. If we hurry, we can swing by Marlon's lab on the way."

TWENTY-TWO

When Elena entered Marlon's lab behind Derek, something was different. She glanced up and caught a wary expression on Derek's face, as if he noticed it too.

He nudged her forward. "Let's get this over with."

Derek headed for the wall of old bottles, but about halfway there he came to an abrupt stop.

The room was silent except for a dripping sound, probably from a faucet that hadn't been turned off properly. The droplets created a steady drum inside the stainless steel basin. *Drip, drip, drip...*

Elena placed her hand on his arm. "Everything okay?" The muscles beneath his clothes had bunched with tension.

He raised his nose and breathed in, then stepped back, looking around. He grabbed her arm and shoved her toward the door. "Go, go, go!"

They rushed toward the door, but Elena's foot caught the leg of a stool and she stumbled. She righted herself before falling, but it wasn't quickly enough.

A roar like thunder clapped right by her head, a

second before a burst of energy tossed her in the air. Elena landed hard on the ground, a large weight pressing on top of her. Disoriented, her head pounding and her ears ringing, she couldn't breathe, her chest compressed beneath the heavy weight. Pain lanced through every limb of her body, pulsing in tune to her racing heartbeat.

Dark boots appeared in front of her nose and the weight above her lifted.

And then she was lifted.

By Keen.

He held her up like a rag doll, his arm wrapped around her waist. Her ears were still ringing as they made their way into the hallway, but she detected the faint sound of a fire alarm.

Elena looked back. "Where's Derek? We can't leave him!"

Keen turned her chin to face him. "He's right behind you," he seemed to shout, though she could barely hear him. "Do not breathe the air."

He covered her mouth with his sleeve and hauled her toward the exit.

She looked back when they reached the stairwell, and experienced a moment of relief. Derek stood outside the lab door. He was bent over and struggling for air, his hands braced against his knees, but he was in one piece.

Derek straightened and jogged toward them. "I smelled bleach and ammonia."

The two chemicals combined were highly volatile, which would explain the explosion. And then she realized something else; she'd heard him clearly, and the sirens were louder too.

They raced down the stairs and into the open, the

ringing in her ears dimming, while the fire alarm grew louder with each step.

Outside, a crowd milled. Not a large one this early, but big enough that she worried about being discovered.

Derek and Keen must have had the same thought. They headed for a copse of trees off in the distance. When they were out of earshot, Derek said, "Someone must have planted it to trigger after we entered the room. I'm the only one with access besides Marlon. Had to have been meant for me."

"Or me," Elena said. "Marlon could have discovered my involvement with the Fae."

"It could have been meant for either of you," Keen said. "We must go to Emain immediately." He continued to drag her across the quad toward a cluster of buildings where the Physics Hall stood.

"Derek," she said, as they made their way across campus, "how did you know the ammonia and bleach weren't from the janitors? The smell could have been from cleaning chemicals."

"Some of the antique bottles on the back wall were missing." Derek coughed several times, his breathing labored. "The scent of chemicals was too strong for cleaning products." He reached behind his back and winced.

"Are you hurt?" She pulled out of Keen's hold and grabbed Derek's arm, urging him to turn around. Her chest tightened as she peered at his blood-soaked T-shirt. Holes dotted the material as if it had been torn by shrapnel. "Oh my God."

Derek put his hand on the small of her back. "Keep moving."

"What about your back?"

"I'll be fine."

"Are you insane? You're gushing blood." Elena tried to see his face, but he pushed her relentlessly forward. At this point, she could walk just fine, but apparently not fast enough for Derek or Keen.

There was no reason to rush to Emain if where they really needed to go was a hospital. Fae didn't get sick or hurt the way humans did. They wouldn't have the supplies needed to help Derek. When they were far enough away from the explosion, Elena pulled Derek behind a large spruce and planted her feet.

"What are you doing?" he said. "We need to hurry, Elena."

"Turn around."

He stared at her. "We don't have time for this," he said, but he rotated his broad shoulders.

She lifted part of his shirt, her hands vibrating from adrenaline.

The holes in his T-shirt were there and so was the blood, but his skin was clean and smooth. From the side, she caught him glancing at Keen, a silent message passing between them.

"Elena," Keen said in his calm Fae cadence, "your friend has healed. He or I will explain later. Right now, we must reach Emain. You are in danger."

TWENTY-THREE

Elena and Derek were ushered into one of Emain's dorm-like rooms—small, but way cleaner than the dorms at Dawson, and the furniture was all antique. Elena crossed and sat on the bed.

She'd never had the privilege of seeing this part of Emain before, because the Fae had kept them in the laboratory or the gymnasium. Few Fae had entered those parts while Elena and Derek trained. But here, in the dorm section, many tall, beautiful Fae in dark clothing milled about.

And stared. As though she and Derek were freaks. Or enemies of the state.

They were Halven. To Fae, who were being attacked by a virus created by Halven, Elena and Derek *were* the enemy.

"What happened out there, Keen? You heal quickly and Derek does too?" She glanced at Derek and did a double take. He'd stripped off his bloodied T-shirt and his muscled chest was on full display.

Images of him above her, his mouth and hands

touching her, flashed in her mind. Her heart thumped erratically.

Derek wet the T-shirt at a small sink in the corner and wiped his back clean. It had been shredded and bloodied less than two hours ago and was now smooth and healthy. They'd had to hide out for a while before entering the Physics Hall. Derek's blood wasn't very discreet, and emergency crews were everywhere. The university had even quarantined part of the quad. Keen didn't want to take a chance on being seen by whoever was behind the explosion.

Derek pulled out a long-sleeved shirt from his backpack and tugged it over his head.

"Fae and Halven heal quickly," Keen said. "Fae from birth, Halven once they reach their majority. Derek has been healing since he reached his majority two years ago."

"But I just reached my majority and I don't heal like that."

"You have already healed," Keen said. "You had sustained a large bruise across your forehead when I pulled Derek off your back."

Derek shielded me?

He sat beside her on the bed and stared down, hands clasped between his legs.

"And you could not hear me talking to you," Keen continued. "How do you feel now?"

"Fine. No pain. Even the ringing in my ears is gone." She glanced away, thinking. "What does that mean? Are Halven immortal like you?"

Leo burst inside the room before Keen could answer. His uniform was impeccable, but dark shadows weighed down his eyes.

Emain had beds. Fae could heal, but they clearly needed sleep. More than Leo was getting, based on his appearance.

"The university is investigating the explosion," Leo said. "Humans recognized you and Derek running from Marlon St. Just's laboratory. They are searching for you as we speak."

Great. So hiding out until they could slip into the Physics Hall undetected had been only half productive. The bomb's creator hadn't gotten to them, but the university had connected them to the bomb.

"You will remain in Emain until we find a cure," Leo continued. "Reparations for the explosion will be made through our campus representatives."

He turned to Derek, a firm look in his eye. "Why did you foolishly return to your lab when your business is here while we seek the cure?"

"There is no rule saying I can't go to my lab," Derek shot back.

Leo sighed like an exasperated parent.

Derek looked at Elena, and she nodded. The Fae needed to know about Marlon. It might help them with the cure. And maybe if they worked together, the benefits would outweigh the risk of the Fae knowing that Derek had helped create the disease spreading throughout their land.

Derek stood and paced the room. "I believe Marlon masterminded the virus."

"What are you talking about?" Leo said.

"I went to the lab a couple of days ago and found evidence that the fast-acting flu virus we'd been working on had been tested on Fae tissue." He stopped and turned to Leo. "Elena and I returned today to see if we could recover the ingredient that Marlon indicated in his documentation blocked Fae healing."

Leo's face reddened. "How dare you keep this from me?"

Elena sat straighter. "He wasn't hiding it to prevent you from finding a cure. Derek had every intention of taking what he'd learned and helping the Fae, but you've threatened us since we arrived. He feared you'd use the information against him. Can you blame him?"

Derek put his hand on her shoulder and squeezed. "I only recently discovered the truth about Marlon. These last couple of years, I never knew, Leo. I went to Marlon's lab a couple of days ago, because I suspected he might have been involved once I learned about the Fae virus. This morning, I returned with Elena to find F-18, an ingredient that was key to making the virus lethal. I'd hoped that if I found it, Elena could manipulate the molecules into an antidote rather than try to pull a healing solution from thin air. We share the same goal. Elena and I are not working against you."

"That's all very well, this scheme of yours to create a cure behind our backs."

Derek sighed. Leo was willfully misinterpreting his words, and Elena was frustrated too.

"But in your incompetent efforts to investigate Marlon St. Just, you now have campus authorities looking into the explosion with your names pinned to it, and they are not so understanding."

Elena sank her head into her hands. Dawson was within their rights to expel her if they believed her responsible for the lab's destruction.

"You said you'd take care of it. You can't let us take the fall for this," Derek said angrily.

Leo inspected the back of his hand casually. "There may be something we can arrange." He looked at her, his expression determined. "We'll discuss it after Elena produces the antidote."

More leverage to force her to help? Wasn't she already helping? Or was there something else they wanted from her? Would she be at the Fae's beck and call forever?

Leo strode to the door.

"What about the guy Marlon was working with?" Derek called out.

Leo stopped and turned. "What *guy*?"

Derek rubbed his forehead. "There were emails between Marlon and a guy named Beorhtric, both of them using Dawson email addresses. Most of the emails were an exchange of information on general scientific findings and instruments they were using, but Marlon saved the emails with his virus files.

"The emails were friendly at first, then Marlon and the guy had a falling out. Marlon wanted access to more ingredients—wanted to visit Beorhtric—but Beorhtric refused him and didn't answer Marlon's last email."

"Beorhtric?" Leo said, as if surprised. "Many scientists have traveled between Tirnan and Emain, but only one with that name is notable in this instance. If the man you speak of was who I think, he wouldn't have had anything to do with the virus. He is dead. A transmutation wielder who succumbed to the disease." Leo turned to Elena. "Your uncle."

Her uncle?

Elena let out a shaky breath. She had never known her mother's brother, but she couldn't help hating Marlon just a little bit more for the loss of so many.

Derek looked over, concerned, and she smiled weakly. She would have liked to know her mother's family, but right now she couldn't fixate on it. She had to focus on saving everyone else.

"Beorhtric provided Marlon with F-18," Derek continued. "That was the only connection I could detect, but Beorhtric didn't seem to know Marlon's true purpose, and he appeared to get cold feet when Marlon asked for other things from him. Marlon wanted ingredients only Beorhtric could provide."

Leo looked down. "Likely ingredients only found in Tirnan. It seems St. Just used a rare connection to our people and turned it against us." He shook his head. "Beorhtric was a scientist and a brilliant magic user. It is possible he put the differences between Halven and Fae aside and trusted Marlon with an ingredient he thought might further science. He was more patient with humans for his sister's sake than the rest of us, and he paid a heavy price with his life." He stared accusingly at Elena.

She straightened, frustrated by the accusation. Beorhtric had been kind to Marlon because his sister, Elena's mother, had married a human. But not all humans or Halven were like Marlon. Beorhtric had chosen the wrong person to trust.

"There is much to think about," Leo said. "It can't be a coincidence Beorhtric was one of the first to fall to the virus. If Marlon and Beorhtric were in communication, it's possible Marlon passed the virus through a contaminated instrument or some other means before the lockdown with Emain. We may never know how Marlon managed to spread the disease to Tirnan, but now we know he had the means. There is nothing that can be done now except to fight this virus."

Leo spun and grabbed the doorknob, but before he

opened the door he said, "Elena, I will give you time to compose yourself after your ordeal this morning. I expect you at the lab in one hour. Keen will escort you."

His heavy gaze landed on Derek. "Your room is down the hall, where you will remain while Elena works. Keen has been instructed to intervene if you do not comply. You and Elena have spent too much time alone. I see the danger in it now."

Leo stepped outside, and Derek followed. "What's that supposed to mean?" Derek said. "Is this because of the lab, or... *Is this a dad warning?* If we want to be together, it's none of your damn business!" he shouted at Leo.

Heat crept into Elena's cheeks. She sprang up and grabbed Derek's arm, pulling him inside, but it was like moving an angry bear.

Leo faced them and calmly said, "I will not risk complications. With your lineage, if you and Elena were to... You were never meant to form a connection. No matter what, the lines must remain as pure as possible. Too much dilution has been introduced as it is." His gaze cut to Elena then back to Derek. "You will assist Elena with her work, but that is all you will give her. Otherwise, you will find yourself dismissed and you'll never see her again."

His words confirmed the thought niggling the back of her mind—that her freedom had vanished the moment she'd agreed to help the Fae.

Could Leo really keep them apart?

She wrapped her arm around Derek's waist. "Let it go. There's nothing we can do about it right now."

This time he came willingly when she pulled him inside.

Keen moved to the door. "Say your goodbyes. You have one hour." He lifted his eyebrow as he stared at Derek.

Elena had the impression Leo didn't want her and Derek alone at all. Was Keen disobeying him? Leo hadn't specified that Derek leave immediately, but it was implied. She supposed that was a technical error on Leo's part. Which meant Keen was taking advantage.

Those angsty moments with Reese last night must have softened him up.

Derek locked the door behind Keen, strode across the room, and slumped on the bed. His mouth compressed into a thin line. "Why does he care if we're together?"

Are we together? She hadn't tried to define what they were, but after last night she couldn't imagine being torn away from Derek. Not when she'd only just realized how much she cared about him.

She walked over and stood in front of Derek, resting her hands lightly on his head. She smoothed the thick, unruly locks of his hair. "I don't want to think about Leo. I want to be with you while I can."

Derek leaned forward until his forehead touched her stomach. He wrapped his arms around her waist.

She couldn't lose him. He meant something to her. Meant more than even she was willing to admit. He saw her in a way no one else did. Yes, he understood her Halven side, but he also saw her nerdiness and magical flaws, and he still thought her beautiful. Still wanted to protect her.

She tipped his chin up and kissed him, releasing all the emotion welling inside her. Fear, love, anger, lust...

When they parted for air, Derek's gaze searched hers. Whatever he saw on her face, he read it accurately. He stood and scooped her up, kissing her like he'd never see her again. If he hadn't recognized the danger and acted quickly this morning, maybe he wouldn't have.

They could heal, but heal from a point-blank chemical

explosion? Keen had told them Halven were susceptible to guns. Why not bombs? The only reason Elena and Derek had come away in one piece was because they'd made it nearly to the door before the bomb had gone off, thanks to Derek's sharp senses.

"I could have lost you," he said between kisses, putting words to her thoughts.

He eased her onto the bed, his knee parting her legs so he could reposition himself between her thighs in a full embrace. His arms bracketed either side of her head. "I don't want to lose you." He leaned down, his lips and breath mingling with hers.

"You won't. I—I want you."

"You have me."

"No. I mean, I *want* you."

He looked up and there was a question in his eyes.

She leaned in and kissed him, her fingers trailing over his shoulders and slipping down his sides. She rucked his shirt up his back, wanting to see him without the audience of Keen in the room. And yes, feel him too.

"You'll tell me if I go too far?" he whispered.

"You won't. You couldn't."

Derek reached back, yanked his shirt over his head, and tossed it aside, the muscles in his arms and chest flexing with the motion.

Her mouth went dry, her brain a bit frenzied. She leaned up and kissed his torso and he sighed. His large hands dropped to her waist and he slowly pulled up her top.

It was as though no time had passed since this morning when they'd kissed and touched, and at the same time, it was as if this moment was all they had left. She didn't know that with certainty, but she wasn't taking chances. If she had nothing else, she wanted this.

Elena ran her hands down his stomach, faintly registering Derek unhooking her bra. The muscles on his stomach tensed the lower her fingers got, and a shiver racked his body. He leaned forward, edging her back so they were skin to skin, with nothing and no one between them.

"God, Elena—" His mouth landed on hers, and the heat, the rawness, took her breath away.

She ran her palms around his trim waist to his back, then slipped them beneath his jeans and squeezed the muscles beneath his boxer briefs. Derek rocked his hips forward.

The feel of him between her legs had that urgency she'd discovered when they'd kissed this morning building again.

He covered her moans in a frantic, deep kiss, moving his hands over her breasts, down her stomach to her waist. "I'll stop whenever you want."

"Do *not* stop."

The "last night on Earth" scenario might be the perfect pickup line—and Reese would give her such shit for this— but Elena trusted her instincts.

The intensity she and Derek shared was real. She wanted this moment with him because she was falling in love with him.

His hand dipped to her inner thigh over her jeans, his fingers swirling over the sensitive place between her legs. She moaned into his mouth and gripped his back, her breaths a gaspy mess.

Derek leaned to the side, slowly unzipped her pants, and slid his hands to her lower back. He eased her jeans down her legs. Just that, the barest touch of his naked stomach and hips against her side, created a lightning storm of sensation.

His hand skated down her leg and pulled up her knees

so he could remove one shoe, then the other. He rose and pulled her pants all the way off until the only thing she wore was her panties.

She was pretty shy about her body, but the way he looked at her with reverence and desire—it didn't matter. She felt beautiful.

His heat-filled gaze took in every inch of her, and he slowly inhaled. "Why do you hide all this?" He shook his head. "You know what? Don't answer that. More for me."

He bent and kissed her breast. His soft lips trailed their way down to the top of her panties, then the inside of her thigh. "You are so beautiful, Elena."

When she couldn't take those soft, tempting touches of his mouth anymore, she wrapped her hands under his thick arms and urged him up. He covered her with his body and she reached between them, fumbling with the snap at the top of his jeans.

If she was in her underwear, it was only fair he should be.

He eased to his side to give her access and cupped the back of her neck, kissing her deeply as she tried to undo his pants. His tongue distracted her enough that she fumbled with the zipper before she managed to push his jeans down with his help. He kicked them off in a heap beside the bed and rolled her on top of him, her thighs straddling his waist.

Aside from the thin layer of underwear they both wore, she felt the long, hard ridge and sharp angles of his body beneath her.

Elena shivered, her fingers gliding over his chest and arms.

"Cold?" he asked.

She shook her head, but he pulled the covers up and

rolled until he was leaning over her, the heat of his body warming her. His hand skimmed up and down her leg, her stomach. Everywhere he touched, her skin ignited. Very effective warming technique.

Derek ran his palm up her chest and cupped her breast, his thumb rubbing the sensitive peak. Her body arched, and he replaced his hand with his mouth, the backs of his knuckles skimming down her belly and beneath her panties.

He touched her the way she'd imagined him doing this morning. The intimacy of it was awkward at first, but then his fingers slid over a place that made her limbs melt and she really didn't care anymore.

He moved in a steady rhythm over the spot that had her writhing, her hips lifting toward his hand, breaths coming quick as he kissed and touched her.

But she wanted more. She wanted to touch him too.

Tentatively, she trailed her hand down his chest and palmed the part of him that was so foreign, yet infinitely fascinating.

His fingers stopped their deft seduction on her body, and the muscles in his shoulders bunched. "Elena, I don't think I can last if you do that."

"I don't want to stop what we're doing. I want this. With you."

He let out a slow breath. "We can wait. I would wait however long you want. We don't have to do this now. Jesus," he said, as if coming to another conclusion. "Keen's somewhere outside the door." He lifted up slightly, as though he was about to rise. "We shouldn't do this here."

She held on to him. "He's not with us. It's just you and me, and I don't know when they'll let us be together again."

It was the oddest thing, but given everything that had

happened today, the notion of being separated from him was what brought burning tears to her eyes. She blinked them away.

His face went taut. "Those bastards. Don't worry about them, Elena. I won't be far. I'll find some way to stay with you."

She reached behind his neck and brought his mouth down. "You *are* with me. Now." She kissed him and pulled his body closer. "I want this."

Derek pressed his forehead to hers and took a steadying breath. He kissed her tenderly and ran his mouth down her neck, his hand finding her breast again. "I can't think clearly when you look at me like that... I promise to find a way to be with you, Elena. But I'm also not leaving you now. I don't have the strength."

They kissed and his hands skimmed over every inch of her body. When her breaths grew embarrassingly erratic, he reached over the side of the bed and grabbed something from the pocket of his jeans.

He set a condom packet beside them and kissed her again. She tugged at his boxers, and he slid her panties off.

Derek tore the condom wrapper and fit it on. He settled over her, and she felt him circling and pushing gently where his hand had rubbed earlier.

She wanted this moment, but she was nervous. She wrapped her arms around his shoulders and kissed him softly.

"You okay?" he asked.

She nodded, and his eyes held hers as his body rocked slowly into her. His head dropped and he kissed her mouth, her neck.

Derek breathed slowly through his nose as if trying to

maintain control, and all the while his body entered her and retreated, until there was no space between them.

He stilled. The tips of his fingers settled at her temples as his large hands cradled her face, a look of longing and love filling his features. "Elena."

Just that one word—her name with so much emotion behind it. He moved again, and she stopped thinking entirely.

She ran her hands over the contours of his upper chest and arms, breathing in his scent, and that fluttery feeling he'd built earlier began again, only deeper this time.

Derek was everywhere, surrounding her body, her head, her heart. Nothing else mattered.

And when that fluttery sensation caused the muscles in her stomach to convulse, she felt no fear, no loss, just love and pleasure and Derek.

DEREK LAY ON HIS SIDE, his arms locked around Elena, their legs tangled. He waited for his breathing to calm, but somehow he didn't think it ever would. He squeezed Elena tighter, brushing his mouth along her hairline. She smelled so good. And what he felt for her... She was his. Simple as that. He didn't want to let her go, ever, let alone leave her room.

Damn, Leo. What an asshole. If Leo thought he could keep the two of them apart, he was wrong. Derek's ability to Blend meant they couldn't keep him trapped in one place for long.

"I wish you could stay," she said, her breath tickling his chest.

He pulled her closer. "I'll stay if you want me to. Screw Leo. He needs us, not the other way around. And if I have to tell my family what I am, so be it."

She sat up. "No, Derek. Not if you think they'll abandon you. I can't imagine why anyone would want to, because you're amazing and brilliant, but I've lost my parents. I wouldn't wish that on anyone, especially the person I care about."

Derek snaked his arm around her soft curves and pulled her close, kissing her tenderly. This girl was everything to him.

He had known Elena from afar since the start of school, lingering around her without putting reasons to his actions. He made stupid justifications to himself for why he'd visit his neighbor's apartment building when he was on scouting missions, though she was no threat. Not to his body. His heart was another matter.

Now that he knew her… She was it for him. He loved her, and he'd give his life for her.

Elena was good, and stronger than she gave herself credit for. And she was important.

Leo and Keen and the rest of them wouldn't admit how special she was, but Derek knew they weren't telling her everything. She was more valuable than they let on, and Derek wouldn't allow anything to happen to her. Not just because he loved her, but because of the good she could do. The world needed Elena, and he wasn't so selfish a bastard that he'd deprive others of her abilities just to save himself the heartache of losing his family.

"Let me worry about my parents. You worry about staying safe and doing what the Fae ask for now. I promise to stay close."

Her mouth twisted. "I want to be near you, but maybe we should listen to Leo. We need their help as much as they need ours. It's not safe for either of us anymore."

He let out a sigh through his nose. "Though it pains me to admit this, I trust Keen to keep you protected while I'm in whatever room they throw me in for the afternoon. He'll look out for you in the lab, I'll make sure of it. And I won't be far. Call if you need anything and I'll come running, because *I'm* the bodyguard." He grinned cockily.

She smiled at their inside joke, then her eyes dropped to his mouth and her lips parted.

His blood fired. When she looked at him like that, he wanted to—"Elena, you better stop looking at me that way, or I'm going to do something about it and you'll be late."

She gave a light pout he didn't think she was aware of.

"Fine. Have it your way," she said, but a spark lit her eyes, and she leaned over and kissed him. Adrenaline shot through his body at the press of her naked skin against his, and for a moment, he kissed her back, forgetting where they were.

He pulled away. "When this is all over, there's going to be a ban on clothing when we're alone. Only skin on skin, and lots of kissing." She smiled and just about stopped his heart.

One way or the other, this girl might be the death of him.

They dressed, and Derek dipped his head out the door long enough to threaten Keen with bodily harm should anything happen to Elena.

He stepped back in and closed the door, dragging Elena to his chest and holding her close to his heart. "Don't leave Keen's side, okay?"

Derek glanced around as if he could see through the walls to what the Fae were really doing behind closed doors. But again, he wasn't a superhero and he didn't have that special ability. Maybe if he did, he could protect Elena better.

"Be careful," he said. "I don't trust this place."

TWENTY-FOUR

Keen escorted Elena to the lab where Leo waited, but all Elena could think about was Derek. Every touch, sound, or word uttered in the Emain dorm room would forever be branded in her mind. She'd felt cherished and protected in his arms. Her body was a little sore, but she'd never imagined sex could be so amazing, and it probably wouldn't have been if it hadn't been with Derek.

She'd never regret the moments they'd stolen together.

Elena stifled the perma-grin that wanted to etch itself on her face, and focused on the training Leo had for her today, but it was no use. For the second day in a row, she made no progress with transmutation.

"This isn't working." Leo's face was more strained and tired than it had been earlier. "Go to your room. I need to focus on an approach to the cure that doesn't involve your abilities."

An ominous statement coming from Leo, who'd thought all along she'd be their salvation.

Elena walked back to her room with Keen, but she

worried the rest of the afternoon about what to do. Innocent people would die because of the disease and the battle between Fae and Halven. It wasn't right. Her own mother would die if she didn't find a cure. She had to stop it.

Over and over she considered the words in the Tertullian Codex. If only she could safely travel to Tirnan—

It wasn't until the second vibration that Elena realized she'd missed a text message.

She reached for her phone and looked at the time. Well after dark. Keen had dropped off dinner, but she'd been so preoccupied, she'd barely touched the food.

There were two text messages on her phone, both from Reese.

Reese: *Where are you? I'm so excited you messaged me about the party! But I'm here and I can't find you :(*

Reese: *You said Alpha Chi, right? I checked everywhere but I don't see you. It's a total sausagefest tonight. The male vultures are starting to swoop in. Hurry up and get here, I need some girl backup.*

Elena sat up, her heart racing. She hadn't sent Reese any messages.

Elena: *Reese, that wasn't me! I don't know anything about a party. Get out of there!*

Oh God, who had messaged her? And how had they made it look like it was from Elena? Whoever it was must have hacked into her iCloud.

Elena: *Please go home! Not safe!!! Text me as soon as you get this so I know you're okay.*

Elena waited for Reese to respond. Reese always returned texts quickly, but this time she didn't.

When ten minutes passed, then fifteen without a word or call from Reese, panic tightened Elena's chest. "Keen!"

Keen burst through the door, his white-blond hair

whipping against his face as he searched every corner. "What is the matter?"

"I can't get hold of Reese. I texted her and she hasn't responded."

His mouth twitched in what she thought might be annoyance. "This is not an emergency. Your roommate is flighty and unpredictable."

"No, Keen. Someone pretending to be me sent her to a party." Elena scooted to the edge of the bed and held up her phone as if he could see from across the room. "Could they—is it possible Marlon would have done that? After today..." She pinched the bridge of her nose and shook her head. "Would they go after my roommate?"

Keen let out a sigh—a long one. Did Fae have greater lung capacity?

He stepped into the room and slammed the door closed. Elena jumped.

He stalked over and read the messages on her phone, his face growing angrier. "What do you propose?"

"It's been twenty minutes and she hasn't gotten back to me. Reese never answers her phone, but she's a consistent texter. I'm worried something's happened."

Mateo had left a voice message earlier saying that he'd met a woman while grocery shopping to replace the food he, Derek, and Keen had inhaled over the last few days. He was out with her tonight and Mateo went MIA when he was on dates, or Elena would ask him to go after Reese. It made perfect sense that Mateo wouldn't be around the one time she actually needed him.

"What if you or I go to the party and find her?"

Reese had gotten sucked into this thing because of her proximity to Elena. Elena couldn't leave her friend out there to fend for herself if the Halven were after her. And Elena was pretty sure Leo wouldn't authorize guards to be sent in search of a human they cared nothing about.

"Out of the question," Keen said. "How can you even think of leaving after you were nearly killed this morning?"

"I wouldn't think about it, except it's *Reese*, Keen." Elena couldn't let anything happen to her best friend.

Keen scrubbed a hand down his face, which was another shockingly emotional gesture for him. He rarely showed emotion—unless Reese was involved.

"You are not to leave Emain and I cannot leave *you*, which means we both must remain here. Emain is on lockdown while we devise the cure, and there is little time left."

She rubbed her temples. "You're right. And we can't send Derek. He's in danger too."

"No, and you are not to see Derek. Leo's orders, if you recall."

Her fingers froze and she looked up. "What's the deal with that?"

Keen shrugged. "He feels you are getting too close."

If only they knew. "Leo thrusts us together and he doesn't expect us to become friends?" Keen raised his eyebrow, and she blushed. Either Emain had cameras in its rooms, or her and Derek's relationship was more transparent than she thought. "Fine, what if you and I go together to the party and get Reese out."

"No."

"Keen! I'm not letting anything happen to Reese."

His jaw shifted as if he were reconsidering it, or just flaming pissed.

She jumped at the hesitation. "I'll stick to you like glue the entire time. We'll be fast—in and out. If we leave through one of your portal thingies, no one will see us and we can get there faster."

She looked around and nodded to the opposite wall. "You could open one here."

Keen frowned. "That is not how it works. Some Fae possess the ability to create temporary portals, but they are rare individuals. And I am not one of them."

"Well, whatever. I don't care how we get there." She paced a few steps. "Believe me, I don't want to leave—that bomb scared the hell out of me—but I can't stay back while Reese is in danger."

Keen's gaze fixed on her. For a moment, she thought he'd refuse her again. "Grab what you need. I will give you one hour, *beginning now*, to find your friend. Not one minute longer."

Holy shit. He'd do it?

Elena didn't waste time overanalyzing Keen's motives. He left the room and she stripped out of the Fae top she'd changed into for the lab this morning. She slipped on the blue tank top she'd worn beneath her pullover when she entered Emain, so she wouldn't stand out, but her black Fae pants and boots would have to do for the rest of her outfit. She didn't have time to change them.

Elena emerged from her room seconds later, and Keen ushered her down the hall.

"You had better hope we find the girl over the next hour. This is the only chance I will give you, and somehow I think I will regret it."

They turned into a corridor she'd never been to before, and then Keen pushed her through a door that looked like every other door inside Emain, only it wasn't.

It's a rainbow. Lights flashed before her eyes.

A second later, she landed on her shoulder and the side of her face with a thud. A building she recognized from the north end of campus—half a mile from the

Physics Hall where Emain was situated—stood in front of her.

Portals weren't a bad way to travel, if not for the sense of tumbling through a washing machine and being expelled like refuse from a garbage chute.

Keen landed smoothly on his feet beside her. He pulled out a key fob and aimed it at a nearby parking lot. Car lights flickered a row over.

Elena rubbed her shoulder and scurried toward the car.

Keen slowed his sedan as they neared the massive Alpha Chi fraternity house, which looked more like a 1970s medical building.

Dawson didn't boast palatial antebellum Greek houses. That would be too classy. Dated fraternity houses went with the town's primarily seventies façade and the manure-scented air that swept through campus from nearby agricultural fields on hot or windy days.

Elena hadn't chosen Dawson for its architecture, but for the small-town feel, the proximity to her family, and because it boasted a top pre-med program. The dated seventies buildings were a tacky bonus.

She stepped out of the car, the evening dark and shadowed by a new moon. Most of the party was off to the side behind a fence, but a few stragglers trolled the lawn in front of the fraternity house. In a darkened corner, one group stood out because they were huddled with their heads bent together.

One of the guys glanced up directly at Elena before dipping his head back to the group, and a chill zipped down her spine. She couldn't make out the guy's features from this distance, but it didn't matter. She needed to grab Reese and get the heck out.

Elena and Keen headed across the lawn to the entrance. While they walked, Elena caught sight of a girl peeling off from the group huddled in the corner, her pale ponytail swinging behind her.

Elena stopped and stared. For a moment she thought it was Beatrice. The clothes were all wrong, but the set of the girl's shoulders, her height and hair, seemed uncanny.

Keen pushed her toward the gate. "Be quick."

Right, *Reese*. Elena had less than an hour now to find her roommate. As long as she stuck close to Keen she'd be safe.

She inched closer to her Fae bodyguard as they made their way past the gate and through the crowd, hip-hop music blaring in her ears. She would have felt better if Derek were here, but at the same time, she was glad at least one of them was safe. Worrying about Reese was enough. She didn't want to have to worry about Derek too.

Bales of hay were pushed up along the sides of the Alpha Chi backyard, evidence of some kind of western-themed party. They saw no sign of Reese on the patio, and her long golden hair tended to stand out.

Elena peered at a set of stairs to the fraternity house, covered with students holding plastic red cups. "She must be inside," she told Keen loudly so he could hear.

He nodded and led her up the steps, the stench of beer, sweat, and urine assaulting her senses as they entered the house. Despite the volume inside, which was marginally quieter than outside, her normally super-silent boots made tearing sounds on the sticky hardwood floor as they crossed into the main room.

How do guys live like this?

Elena edged toward the back wall to avoid the stickiest parts of the floor in the center of the room, and looked from one face to the next, while Keen peered over heads. He was so tall he could take everyone in at a glance, and she wasn't the only person who noticed. Keen received several appreciative gazes from the girls in the room, but he didn't seem to care. He appeared wholly focused on finding Reese.

Elena had turned her attention to a room off to the side, when an elbow nailed her in the stomach, knocking the wind out of her. The stocky guy she'd collided with appeared to have dodged a playful punch from his friend.

Keen darted over and grabbed the guy's shoulder, shoving him back.

"Sorry," the guy mumbled, holding up his hands. He disappeared into the crowd.

Her heart sprinting, Elena took a deep breath and tried to clear her head. The guy was just drunk, not a threat, but she couldn't shake the edgy feeling she'd had since Reese's text. "Let's keep searching," she said.

Keen stayed with her near the wall, his hand on her shoulder, but they didn't see Reese anywhere.

"What about the bathrooms?" she suggested. "It's the only place we haven't looked."

They walked to the hallway where two doors were labeled in black Sharpie, *The Little Girls' Room* and *The Men's Room*, set a ways apart.

Elena didn't think Reese would be in the guys' bathroom, but you never knew at these things. Girls got desperate when they had to pee and there was a line.

A girl with brown hair walked out of the women's bathroom, her head bent down. Elena gestured to the other door. "You check the men's, I'll check the women's."

Keen nodded and paced down the hallway.

Elena entered the room the girl had exited. Filthy urinals stood on one side, a few stalls with crooked doors on the other.

She peered under the stalls and walked to the back of the bathroom where two sinks hung beside a window, but no one was there. *Where could Reese be?*

Glancing in the mirror, she caught the image of herself, paler than normal, her hair tangled at the ends, but otherwise unharmed from the laboratory explosion, just as Keen had said. She turned on the faucet and splashed water over her face.

When she straightened, a scream caught in her throat. A man stood behind her, his angry face reflected in the mirror.

She parted her lips to call for help, but the man's large hand was already clamping down over her mouth, cutting off her air supply.

Elena yanked at his fingers to clear her nose, but his grip tightened and he wrapped his other arm firmly around her waist. He lifted her from behind and carried her kicking toward the window.

The window where another man was waiting—reaching for her.

TWENTY-FIVE

Derek's eyes opened with a start, his heart racing. Dammit, he must have fallen asleep.

He sat up quickly and rubbed his face, his head woozy from moving too quickly.

When Keen had taken him to his room after dropping Elena off at the lab, Derek had lain down for only a second, but it was one second too long. He felt like he'd slept for hours.

He'd been dreaming of Elena, and not one of the good dreams that left him wanting. Elena was lost, calling for help, and he couldn't get to her. The harder he searched, the farther away her voice grew.

He turned to the clock on the side table. *"Son of a bitch."* Hours *had* passed since he'd left her.

Over the last few days, Derek had grown sleep-deprived too, but it was no excuse. As soon as Keen had left with Elena, Derek had meant to Blend and keep an eye on her.

He shook the sleep from his head and stood, searching for his phone. He hadn't been away from her for long, but the idea of losing her, like in his dream, made his mind want to curl in on itself in the fetal position.

He had agreed to separate rooms because Leo was being an ass and because he figured he'd Blend and follow Elena anyway. The dream brought back doubts.

He shouldn't have left her. Not even for a second.

Derek spotted his phone on the side of the bed and grabbed it. His ability to Blend might not help Elena find a cure for the Fae virus, but it enabled him to maneuver around Emain undetected. Fae could see him if they were paying attention, which was a bitch, but he'd use caution.

He transformed quickly and stepped carefully out of his room, watchful of anyone passing the hallway.

He'd half expected Leo to post a guard outside, but there was no one there. Either Leo wasn't concerned about Derek leaving his room, or the Fae had bigger issues to worry about. It was the bigger issues that had Derek worried as well, because they involved Elena.

He jogged down the hall, making several twists and turns inside the complicated Fae building on his way to the lab Elena used in Emain. He stopped a couple of times to dodge Fae guards, but otherwise, the hallways were empty.

And so was the lab.

Derek raced back to her room, his heart pounding. Where the hell was she?

"Traitorous bitch," the guy holding Elena growled. "You're working for the wrong side."

A loud bang sounded against the bathroom door.

The man holding her slammed her shoulder against the metal frame of the window as he raced to hoist her through. She wasn't making it easy. She braced her foot against the wall, fighting him and the other man leaning through the window from the outside who was pulling her up at the same time.

The bathroom door burst open on a loud splinter. The man behind her let go, and the other man jerked her toward the wall, nearly dislodging her arm from its socket.

Scuffling and smacking sounds, like fists hitting a dummy bag, or in this case, flesh and bone, sounded from behind. Elena had only one person to contend with now, but he was making decent progress in pulling her through the window.

She did the only thing she could. She bit his arm.

He yelped and boxed her ear, loosening his hold enough that she fell back.

Her vision blanked as she landed on the floor. Then Keen was suddenly in front of her, pushing her against the opposite wall. "Stay here."

The man outside was no longer at the window, and the one who'd grabbed her from behind was limping for the door.

Keen crossed in two long strides and yanked him by his preppy pink polo shirt, dragging him to the ground. Keen twisted the man's hands behind his back and pinned him to the floor with one knee. "Who sent you?"

"No one. Can't a guy have a little fun?"

"How many of you work for St. Just?"

"I-I don't know what you're talking about."

Keen nodded and released him, allowing the guy to half crawl, half run out the door.

Elena's head cleared, the pain from the blow ebbing. "Why did you let him go?"

"He doesn't know the answer to my questions, but he could lead us to St. Just."

Keen lifted her under her arms and helped her to the door. "We suspected a group of Halven were behind the virus, but it seems St. Just has built an army. Your attacker is more use if he leads us to the others."

Elena was dazed, but not entirely out of it. He wasn't making sense. "Then why aren't you following him?"

He glanced at her out of the corner of his eye. "Did you never wonder about *my* ability?"

Keen had an ability? Other than being a giant, ruthless bodyguard? "Leo said Fae have mental or elemental powers. I figured yours was weak and that's why they put you on guard duty. I assumed brute force was your main talent."

He smiled arrogantly. "That too, but like all Fae, I possess a power. Put in the hands of a bodyguard, it becomes extremely useful."

"Don't leave me hanging." She glanced down at his arm holding her up. "Okay, bad pun. Just tell me what it is. Otherwise, I really think we should go after this guy. We haven't found Reese and they might have her."

"There is no need to go after him," he said as they made their way out of the fraternity house. No one seemed to pay them a second glance as Keen held her up. Probably because she looked like any other drunk girl getting help from a guy. "Now that I've touched Marlon's thrall, I can listen in on his thoughts."

Elena leaned back to stare at his face. "Hold up. You're following him... *in your head*. Have you always been able to read minds? Is that how you knew I was in danger?"

"Yes."

She glanced around, trying to make sense of it all. "If

you can read minds, then where the hell is Reese? You must know what she's thinking."

Keen urged her on. "I do not believe your friend is here. We must leave and return to Emain."

"What do you mean, you don't *believe* she's here? Don't you know? Why did we come all this way if you can read her mind?"

Keen went silent.

"You *can* hear her, can't you?"

Keen's gaze flicked to her, then peered straight ahead as they crossed the backyard toward the exit. "No. Your roommate's mind is a blank to me."

TWENTY-SIX

Derek rounded the corner, heading for the room they'd given Elena. And staggered to a stop. Something wasn't right. Keen wasn't guarding the door.

Had that bastard screwed up again?

The sinking feeling in the pit of Derek's stomach spread to his chest. His heart raced as he leapt through the wall.

The room was empty.

Several hours had passed since he'd last seen her. Between his sleep of the dead and the time it had taken him to go to the lab and now back to her room, she could be anywhere. And he had no idea how to reach her.

Just like in his dream.

Where had they taken her? If they hurt her, he'd... What would he do? Let them rot and die from the disease Elena risked her life to cure? The thought was tempting.

Derek had nothing riding on finding the antidote, except exposure of who he really was. And that had become minor in the scheme of things. Right now, the only thing he cared about was finding Elena and keeping her safe.

He stepped back into the hallway, and started searching each door he passed, sticking his head through the wooden surface. He'd search the whole damn place if that was what it took to find her.

All the rooms in this corridor were empty, though. He turned and searched down another passageway, and another. Finally, he spied a hallway of occupied beds. All the people sleeping inside were men. Fae, from the size of them. Most hadn't bothered to remove their clothes. They had simply fallen face-first onto their mattresses, booted feet and arms dangling off the sides.

Half the rooms in the hall were empty and half were occupied. Were they working on a cure for the virus in shifts?

Derek left the men's section and a few minutes later encountered two Fae women approaching him down a different hallway, a tall Fae girl—about his height—and Beatrice.

The tall girl yawned. "Where were you this evening? I thought we were on the same schedule?"

"I had to take care of something," Beatrice said. "I'm going to the lab now. Go to bed." Beatrice opened a door for her. "You look like you're about to fall over."

The tall girl nodded. "I feel like it. You shouldn't work through your rest periods, though. Without sleep, you'll be no help. Talk to Leo. Someone should take your place in the lab when you're on official business."

"I'll be fine." Beatrice urged the girl through the door. "Good night."

The girl walked inside in a daze and Beatrice closed the door behind her. Beatrice stared at the surface for a long moment, then she spun and turned in the direction the two women had come from, disappearing around a corner.

Derek checked each of the rooms in the hallway, finding a similar scenario to the men's quarters. Half the rooms were empty, the other half housed sleeping women.

Unlike the men, the women took the time to cover their clothed bodies with a blanket before passing out. And none of their limbs dangled off the sides of the beds.

That was one good thing about Fae dorms: extra-long beds. He was short compared to most Fae men. He actually fit on his bed with room to spare, which was probably why he'd slept so long, dammit.

At the rate his body grew, there was no telling how tall he'd end up. Already, the baggy clothes he'd purchased a few weeks ago fit him better. He'd have to ask Keen about the growth spurt—just as soon as he got his hands on the bastard.

Where had he taken Elena?

Derek decided to skip the rest of this corridor. It appeared to be only Fae women catching a couple hours of sleep. He needed more active areas—the labs the tall girl had spoken of. If they had taken Elena anywhere inside Emain, it would be the labs.

Derek jogged around the corner Beatrice had turned down—and nearly ran into her.

"Derek," she said as he skidded to a stop inches away. She stood with her shoulder against the wall, as if waiting for him. "Show yourself, so we can—talk." She gave him a small smile.

The way she'd snuck up on him was disturbing. He needed to be more careful. Humans couldn't see him, but Fae were getting surprisingly good at it.

Derek solidified and glared at Beatrice. "Where's Elena?"

Her eyebrows shot up. "Don't you know?"

His hands clenched at his sides. "If I knew, would I ask?"

"I'm happy to tell you where your little friend is"—she glanced conspiratorially from one side to the other—"but not here. Let's talk in your room."

Derek stretched his neck and let out a deep breath. "Don't screw with me, Beatrice. I don't have time for it. Tell me where she is."

"I will tell you where I last saw her, but we must go someplace private to discuss it. I'm certain you would not want the others knowing what I know."

DEREK SHUT the door to his room. "We're alone, Beatrice, now tell me."

She walked to his bed and sat on the edge. She put a finger to her lips. "Come closer, so I can whisper it in your ear."

Derek's jaw clenched. She was jerking him around.

There weren't any cameras in the rooms as far as he could tell, but Fae had powers. Who was to say they couldn't listen in without him detecting it? Whispering seemed stupid, but right now Beatrice was his best bet at finding Elena.

He did as she requested and sat on the bed next to her. With his elbows braced on his thighs, hands dangling between his knees, he kept his head forward so she could talk close to his ear.

She leaned in and her voice took on an odd, lilting tone. "Elena is not here. She is with Keen at a party off campus."

Beatrice ran her finger down his cheek. He wanted to pull away, but he couldn't move.

Panic coursed through his veins. She was doing something to him. The most he could manage was one word. "Where?"

She leaned closer. "Kiss me and I'll tell you."

His mind jerked in repulsion, but he couldn't get so much as a foot to slide away. In fact—against his will—his body leaned closer.

"You fight it," she whispered. "How interesting. Most don't know I am doing it, but I sense you know. It must be difficult to have lost control." Her voice held mock remorse.

She placed her slender hand along his jaw and turned his head toward her. She kissed him, and he couldn't do anything to stop it. Beatrice moved his hands to her sides, running them up and down her body. "Touch me. Caress me like you caress Elena."

"No," he managed to get out, but he couldn't get his hands to stop touching her. He felt like a puppet, while his mind lashed out.

His hands sought her chest and traveled down to her stomach, and around the small of her back.

Beatrice leaned closer and moaned in his ear. "Feels so good. Kiss me like you kiss Elena."

His mouth responded before his mind could fight it. He growled against her lips in anger.

She giggled and wrapped her arms around him, pressing her body to his. He ran his hands up her sides to her shoulders and pushed her down, pinning her to the bed, one of his legs wedged between both of hers.

"Yes," Beatrice hissed, while Derek's mind bellowed, thrashing against the chains that held him prisoner.

CHAPTER

TWENTY-SEVEN

Elena's head no longer throbbed from the hit to her temple, and she was fairly certain her faculties were in operating order. What Keen had just said made no sense. "But if you can read minds, why can't you read Reese's?"

Keen opened the passenger door to his car for her. "Humans are more difficult to pick up. Halven come in clearer. Fae are perfectly clear. Reese's mind I cannot hear."

"Because she's a human?"

He didn't respond.

"Is that why you're so pissed off with her? Because you can't hear her thoughts?"

He looked confused. "I am not angry with Reese."

"The two of you fought the other night."

His mouth compressed. "We do not understand each other."

"That's obvious," she muttered. "At least let me stop by my apartment. Maybe Reese went home early. She should have gotten back to me by now if she had, but it's worth a try."

Keen agreed to stop by Elena's house, but when he pulled up to the walkway of her apartment, he peered around warily. "If Reese is not here, we return to Emain immediately. This day has been filled with danger. I do not like the feeling I have."

Normally, she preferred her own bed, but after today, the relative safety of Emain sounded better. And Derek was in Emain. She wanted to be near him, even if he slept in a different room.

When Elena walked into her apartment, Reese wasn't there, and she hadn't been there by the look of things. The place hadn't been disturbed.

There was always the possibility that Reese had found a friend, or met a guy, and had gone home with someone else. Elena hadn't lied when she'd told Derek her roommate didn't sleep around, but that didn't mean Reese was a nun.

Mateo wasn't home either, but he'd texted earlier to say he was crashing at his date's house for the night. Big surprise.

Elena grabbed a duffel bag and stuffed a few overnight items inside. She didn't know when she'd be returning. Leo had been adamant about her remaining in Emain for the time being.

She texted Mateo to tell him not to wait around, that she had a huge project at school and would be on campus or crashing with study pals for the next couple of days. He probably wouldn't buy it, but she'd deal with the aftermath later.

After leaving one final note on the counter for Reese to call as soon as possible, Elena and Keen drove to the parking lot near the brick building's portal.

Elena stepped out of the car and peered at Keen across

the roof. "What if they have her, Keen? What if those men who tried to take me took Reese?"

Keen glanced around the parking lot. "Right now, we must get you safe. We will address other possibilities later."

Elena stared at the wall that somehow housed the portal. "Is it safe for me to bring my bag through?"

"Yes, but I should carry it until your landing skills improve." His lips twitched.

"Are you going to give me pointers, or allow me to land on my face every time? Why isn't this portal like the one inside the physics auditorium? This one is so disorienting, and the one in the Physics Hall just feels like I'm walking through a door."

"The physics auditorium portal has been augmented for ease of entry, and it is at the heart of the energy source that supplements our magic. The other portals are permanent, but...rough. For these rougher portals, transporting through them is like jumping off a cliff into a pool of water. Imagine how you might keep your body upright. Would you flail your limbs, or attempt to maintain form and body alignment? There is a moment toward the end of the portal when pressure builds before the final landing. Search for the pressure, and when you feel it, bend your knees to soften the impact."

"You make it sound easy, but this portal spins me around like a washing machine. And the rainbow lights are blinding."

"Ignore the lights. They are disorienting."

She thrust the duffel at him. "You could have told me all of this before you pushed me through the first time."

Keen shrugged lazily and stepped within inches of the brick wall. "I will go first to make sure everything is clear on the other end. We cannot risk someone from Emain seeing you. I must tell Leo about tonight, but as for the others… It would be best to limit our confidences. Enter the portal immediately after me. I will count to five. If you do not emerge in that time, I will return for you. Do you understand?"

She looked nervously over her shoulder. "Believe me, I don't want to be out here by myself. After today, I plan on sticking to you like a seat cushion on a hot day, so you better move it if you don't want me landing on your ass."

Keen nodded in approval and passed through the portal. Elena waited exactly one second and dove through.

The same disorienting flux engulfed her, but she followed Keen's instructions and, shockingly, landed on her feet. Mostly. She might have tripped a bit, but she caught herself before falling on her face. Her catlike reflexes from hours of soccer practice with Mateo were finally paying off.

Keen looked at her with his brow raised.

"What? That was graceful compared to the last time."

He shook his head and proceeded down the hall. It was empty, as usual.

"Where is everyone?" she asked, trying to keep up with his long stride. "How come I never see the students in Emain? This place is some sort of Fae University, isn't it?"

"Among other things." He glanced at her.

Right. The monitoring station for Halven.

"The students are in the labs working," he said, "as you should be. Under the circumstances, however, you should gain some rest. Tomorrow will be a big day. Possibly the last."

That did not sound good. But he was right. Portia said they only had a week to find a cure. How many days had it been so far? Four? Five? "Just a couple of hours and then I'll get back to work. You guys do sleep, don't you?"

"Yes."

Wow, a straight answer. She peered around in case she'd missed something. "Then where is everyone? This is the dorm area. Why aren't people coming and going from their rooms?"

"They reside in another section of Emain."

She laughed. "What, am I contaminated goods?" His face turned stoic, and he didn't respond. "That's it?" She hurried to keep up. "Your people don't want to be near me?"

"The leaders believe it best to maintain a degree of separation."

She rolled her eyes. "You mean *segregation*. Good God, Keen, did Fae learn nothing from American history? You ever think you might not be in this situation if your people would accept Halven as equals? You know, work together to create a better world instead of treating Halven as specimens to be tagged and monitored? And as far as the monitoring goes, you're not doing such a good job, considering you let Marlon slip through the cracks."

"He had no powers. We weren't focused on him," he said.

They reached the door to her room and she searched his face. "I know what racism looks like. I might be a minority among Fae, but I'm considered a minority in the Earth realm also. We're all people. We need each other. I'm half Fae, with my own powers. I'm like you."

"No. You're not."

The words, spoken kindly, burned. She'd thought Keen respected her. He teased her, though stoically, and he was willing to help even when it wasn't in his best interest. She believed they were friends, but they couldn't be if he never saw past their differences.

She walked into her room, and Keen turned his back to the door, standing guard outside.

She threw her bag on the floor and walked right back out.

Keen looked over. "Where are you going? You are not to leave. Leo made that very clear. I made one allowance because your friend was in danger, but do not think I will do it again."

She spun around. "Yeah? Well, she's still in danger, remember? You can't hear her, Keen, and you don't know where or who she's with. I'm going to tell Derek about Reese. No one else cares what happens to her."

"I never said I don't care." He wouldn't meet her eyes.

Trying to figure out his allegiances gave her whiplash. "Prove it. Let me speak to Derek."

Keen hesitated. "You will not like what you find, Elena. But perhaps this is for the best. You will no doubt heed Leo's warning afterward."

"What are you talking about?"

He stepped aside, allowing her to pass, and she stopped on a frustrated sigh. "I don't know where Leo put him."

Keen strode past her and motioned for her to follow. He took her down several more empty hallways—*friggin' Fae labyrinth!*—and stopped in front of a door. An odd expression crossed his face. "Are you sure you wish to do this?"

He was worrying her. What had they done to Derek? Elena turned the knob and burst into the room.

Derek lay on his bed—on top of a woman. Kissing her. His hand beneath her top. Touching her.

Elena's stomach clenched. *"Derek?"* Her voice came out light and shaky. A burning pressure built behind her eyes. She shut them and swallowed the ball lodged in her throat.

Derek swiveled his head toward the sound of Elena's voice. He sprang off Beatrice, relief rushing through him. He could move again.

How had Beatrice done it? Trapped him in his own body?

Beatrice sat up and locked his face in her hands like a clamp. She leaned forward and mumbled against his lips. "Forget everything, except that you touched me and what we did in your room."

Derek twisted away, stunned and confused. A wave of nausea roiled through him. He bent forward, tamping down the urge to puke. His chest heaved. What had he done?

He'd never kiss Beatrice…but he had. Why had she been in his room?

Beatrice sauntered past Elena, pretending to wipe a smudge of lipstick from her lips. She wasn't wearing any.

He shook his head. This couldn't be real. He'd never do this. He hadn't thought of another girl since the day he'd discovered his pretty neighbor next door. If he was honest, he hadn't thought much of girls since he'd turned. Elena had been the only one he coveted, even when he didn't want to.

He looked over desperately. Elena's body was stiff, shaking, and some of the fog cleared from his mind.

God, he'd missed her, and they had only been apart a few hours. She… What was she wearing? Her tank top clung to every curve. Had she gone out?

A flash of jealousy ran through him. "You were supposed to stay in your room. Where did you go tonight?" He stared at her chest, a mixture of appreciation and frustration burning through him. "What were you doing with Keen?"

"*You're* chastising *me*? I found you making out with Beatrice. *Beatrice*, Derek!"

His brow furrowed. For a moment, he'd forgotten what had happened in his room, and his memory was nearly photographic. It was as though the whole sordid thing had happened to someone else.

"I—I don't know what that was. I don't remember…" He shook his head. "Elena, I am not interested in Beatrice. I can't stand her. You know that."

"Yeah, well, it seemed like you stood her just fine." She turned and took off running.

Derek scrubbed his face, attempting to clear the rest of the fog from his mind. He leapt unsteadily to his feet and flew out the door. "Elena!"

She disappeared down a different wing and he raced after her, Keen silently at his side. They arrived at Elena's door, but she had bolted it shut.

He turned to Keen. "What the hell, Keen? What's going on?"

Keen raised his eyebrows.

"Not with me. I know I screwed up—I didn't want to. I don't know how it happened." He shook his head again, attempting to clear the memories he didn't understand.

There was no way he'd want to be with Beatrice, or anyone, after he'd made love to Elena. "It wasn't me. I don't know who that was, but it wasn't me."

Derek squeezed his eyes closed, then opened them again. "Where did Elena go tonight? I searched and couldn't find her. Is she okay?"

Keen glanced away. "She is fine."

Derek pressed his forehead to the door. "What

happened to me tonight, Keen?" He rolled his head to the Fae and pierced him with a glare. "And don't tell me you don't know. It was like someone took over my body."

Keen broke eye contact and sighed. "We had better speak to Leo."

Elena thrust the door open, her eyes red and watery. Derek caught himself by the frame before he fell on her. "I'm going with you," she said.

TWENTY-EIGHT

Elena followed Keen as he led them through Emain, the memory of Derek with Beatrice tearing at her insides. She'd given herself to him, and hours later he was with another girl? The logical part of her brain said there was more to the situation, but her insecure side said he'd used her. Which wasn't like the Derek she knew. It was all so confusing.

Elena's throat clenched, and her stomach balled in a tight knot. She clamped her arms around her middle.

Keen glanced over and quickly looked away.

He directed Elena and Derek down several staircases until they emerged in a section with checked vinyl flooring and concrete walls that looked like some sort of underground basement. He stopped at a double door where guards were posted.

Keen addressed the head guard, an especially tall Fae—at least seven and a half feet—with dark chestnut hair and pale green eyes. "Marcus, we are here to see Leo. It is important."

The guard, armed with half a dozen knives and other

menacing weapons, moved gracefully with all that armor and swept the double doors open.

A laboratory the size of an airplane hangar lay beyond. There had to be four hundred Fae working inside the room. More technicians sat at computer stations on a mezzanine overlooking the main floor.

What was this place? And why hadn't she been working in here the whole time? With so many people focused on the same project, they might have had a chance at finding a cure. It was as if they'd never wanted her to succeed.

In spite of the mass of equipment and numerous bodies, Leo stood out. He was older than the rest, but that wasn't what drew Elena's attention. Leo exuded authority.

He looked up as they walked over. A line appeared between his brows as he took in Elena's modified uniform. "Why are you not resting?" he said, though his own face wore the telltale signs of great fatigue. The shadows beneath his eyes had darkened and his pale skin appeared sallow.

"My roommate is missing. I went to search for her." Leo's gaze darted to Keen, but Elena spoke before Leo could. "I was only gone an hour and Keen protected me."

"A lab explosion nearly killed you today. Was that not enough incentive to remain where you are safe?"

She waved her hand at the room. "Why have you kept me locked away? Why haven't I been working with everyone in here to find a cure?"

"This lab is different," he said. "They work on numerous projects—yes, searching for a cure. But honing your magic was more valuable." Leo sighed. "What will it take for you to understand the severity of the situation?" He gestured to the room the way she had. "This is what matters. Your friend does not. No single life is more important—except perhaps your own."

"I understand what's at stake," she snapped. "But as much as you might prefer it, I can't forget the people I love."

Admitting the rest of what had happened tonight would merely prove Leo's point, but he needed to know. "Someone tried to kidnap me while I was away."

Leo's chest rose, a look of indignation crossing his face.

"What?" Derek said.

"It wasn't Keen's fault," she said hurriedly. "If not for him, I wouldn't be here."

Derek thrust his fingers through his hair. "Christ, Elena. What were you thinking?"

She shot him an angry glare. "I was thinking of my best friend. Not that it's any of your business."

Leo and Keen exchanged an awkward look.

Elena took a deep breath and tried to calm down. "We have to find Reese."

"It's true, the girl is missing," Keen said. "We haven't heard from her in hours. I am following Elena's kidnapper, but so far he's made no move. He failed his mission and fears the one in charge. While questioning him, I confirmed Marlon St. Just commands the group of Halven. He has over ninety disciples and the list grows each day. They wish to take over Tirnan and rule as Halven."

Leo pressed his thumb and forefinger to his brows and bowed his head, letting out a deep sigh.

"There is more," Keen said, and glanced at Derek, whose face reddened, hands balling at his sides. "We have reason to believe Beatrice enthralled Derek."

Leo's head rose. He studied Keen for a moment, then peered past him to the door. "Marcus, bring Beatrice. Immediately."

Marcus turned and exited the aircraft hangar laboratory.

"It is odd," Keen went on, "after the other incident."

"Yes," Leo said. "We will withhold judgment until we speak to her. I did not wish to believe the daughter of a dear friend capable of treachery, but I cannot ignore the evidence."

Within minutes, Marcus returned. "Beatrice is not in Emain. She left the premises seventeen minutes ago."

"Her movements reflect this," Keen said. "She blocks me from her thoughts, but her physical movements do not mimic the makeup of Emain. The fact that she blocks me is incriminating."

"I saw her tonight," Elena said, her comment catching everyone's attention. "In front of the fraternity house. At least, I think it was her. The woman had the same hair as Beatrice, the same build and walk. I wasn't sure at the time, but after the men attacked me... If that was her, she was talking to three men on the lawn of the fraternity house before I was attacked."

"Marcus," Leo said, "have security search for Beatrice. Guard all entrances into Emain. When you find her, take her to the holding cell."

Holding cell? Emain has a prison?

"Let us convene in my office, where it is"—Leo glanced around—"private."

They followed Leo several flights up in an elevator and entered a room that looked like a Victorian gentleman's smoking room. Two settees faced one another in front of a huge desk. Ornate built-in bookshelves covered the walls. Tall windows with diamond-paned glass peered onto a copse of trees.

Leo gestured to one of the settees. "Please, have a seat."

A servant brought in a tray that held tea and small cookies, and Elena stared at it. What was with Fae using British customs?

Leo observed her expression. "It is not true, what the myths say about Fae and food. You may eat without becoming ill or beholden to us, just as you've eaten from our kitchen without injury."

Wow, she wasn't even thinking about that—didn't even know she should fear receiving food from Fae. If she had appeared uncomfortable, it was because the atmosphere inside Leo's office was like stepping into another century.

Derek grabbed a handful of cookies and ate them two at a time.

Elena poured a cup of tea and tried not to look at Derek at her side. As upset as she was about seeing him with Beatrice, she couldn't shake the instinctual comfort of having him near. Which only meant she couldn't trust her instincts. Not until she figured out what really happened between him and the girl. *Enthralled,* Keen had called it.

"St. Just's laboratory was destroyed in the explosion," Leo began. "We searched for the ingredient you mentioned, Derek. Nothing of consequence remained of the room. You are fortunate you left when you did. Had you stood within ten feet of the walls, there would be little left of you as well. Are you certain this F-18 ingredient is needed for Elena to create the cure?"

Derek nodded. "According to Marlon's notes, it's the key."

"Then we must find it."

Elena caught Leo's eye. "That's not our only problem. I need knowledge of what I'm creating in order to make something. I could develop the virus using F-18, but I'd still need an antidote for it in order to save Fae, something the notes Derek retrieved don't contain. But I've thought about the Tertullian Codex—"

"No, Elena," Derek said.

Elena had thought that by controlling her environment she would never lose anyone she loved again. But sometimes life had a way of pushing you in a new direction despite your best efforts, just as Leo had said days ago.

What if, in order to make something of herself—to make her family proud and to protect them—she needed to be what she was born to be? To embrace her Halven side with all the powers and complications that entailed?

She turned to Derek. "You have no right to tell me what to do. If I'm the only one who can help, then I will. It's *my* decision." She let out a sigh and turned to Leo. "I think—I think I need to go to Tirnan."

The Emain Fae could be stuffy, unpredictable, and some of them—Beatrice—seemed to be working against their own, but they'd also kept her safe and had fought for her. She said her next words not simply to ensure her family's safety, but because it was the brave thing to do—the right thing.

"According to the book, I need contact with the land, and possibly Fae of noble origins. I believe if I go to Tirnan, I'll figure out how to transmute and create a cure."

Leo shook his head. "Fae from Emain cannot escort you to Tirnan to ensure your safety. The risk to our soldiers of exposure would be too great. We will not chance losing more Fae lives. And if our soldiers cannot go with you, you will be unprotected."

She didn't like it, but what other option did they have? "I understand."

"Do you?" Leo said gravely. "Portia left for Tirnan against my wishes yesterday to retrieve healing potions for testing. We've lost contact with her and fear the worst. Under normal circumstances my people would not tolerate you, but with the threat of mass death... I cannot express how extraordinary our agreement is with you as a Halven here in Emain. Even so, your presence is barely tolerated among those said to be liberal. It will not be tolerated at all in Tirnan."

Leo let out a deep sigh. "Unfortunately, our brethren have made little progress on an antivirus. I convinced the others to take a chance with you in the beginning, believing that with your lineage lay potential. You have proven adept, you learn fast, and you are exceedingly powerful for a Halven, yet we still do not have a cure. The fact that I am willing to let you go to Tirnan, knowing you may not survive long enough to develop a solution, shows how dire our circumstances have become."

Elena's hands turned cold, as if all the blood had drained from her extremities. "If I go there, will I be susceptible?" Bad enough she'd have Fae after her. If she caught the disease too... "I'm a Halven with Fae blood. Can I contract the virus?"

"Humans and Halven are immune."

She shook her head. "You can't know that for sure unless you've exposed people and tested the theory."

He stared at her.

"You tested it... on Halven? Like guinea pigs?"

"We had no choice. We've assessed every possible strategy to save our people."

Elena rose from her seat, her knees wobbly. "I need rest. I'm going to my room... going to try and call Reese again."

"Rest," Leo said. "We will plan how to get you in and out of Tirnan unharmed if at all possible. I will notify you if we discover your friend's whereabouts. Understand, however, that she is not our first priority."

"Oh, I'm crystal clear on that point." She reached for the back of the settee for balance. Exhaustion, Derek's betrayal, shock at the Fae's use of human lives to test the virus—all of it made her stomach lurch and her head spin.

Derek grabbed Elena's elbow, but she jerked her arm away. She couldn't stand him touching her. Not after…

She made her way unsteadily out of Leo's office toward her room while Keen and Derek walked a few paces behind.

"Give us a minute," Derek said to Keen when they reached her door. He followed her inside and closed it behind him.

She rubbed her eyes and sat in the chair next to the desk. Derek sat on the edge of the bed.

Seeing him on the mattress brought back images of them together. It seemed like days or weeks ago—but only hours had passed. And then he'd been with Beatrice.

"I don't want you here, Derek." She swallowed the lump in the back of her throat. "Please go."

He leaned forward. "Elena, I don't know what happened earlier, but it wasn't within my power to control it. I have never wanted Beatrice. I'm sorry if what you saw hurt you. You're the only person I think about. I want *you*."

They were the words she yearned to hear. Beatrice might have done something to influence Derek—*enthralled* him. Leo and Keen seemed to think so. It didn't erase the images of Derek with another woman.

The knot in her stomach tightened and she bent forward. "I need to be alone."

Derek stayed a moment longer. He shifted his feet. When she didn't move or say another word, he stood and walked out, slamming the door behind him.

Elena spent the next hour calling and texting Reese, without success.

Unable to push aside her exhaustion any longer, she pulled her father's leather jacket over her shoulders like a blanket and crawled across the bed. With dried tears on her cheeks, she fell into a fitful sleep.

TWENTY-NINE

Red stars sparkled in a black sky like pale rubies. Elena walked along the river's edge, staring up, her feet and the rest of her body clad in the comfortable Fae clothes. The sound of leaves rustling and water trickling were the only signs of life.

She looked down and stars and moons reflected in the river beside her.

Moons? She peered up again, and tracked not one, but three white moons in different lunar phases.

A gentle breeze swept a lock of hair against her face and she wrapped her arms around her torso, but this time the breeze didn't penetrate her clothes. She remained warm, the Fae material, like a thin, stretchy wetsuit, molding to her, as if the clothes were protecting her from the cooler Tirnan climate.

Just ahead, she made out the arch of the bridge from her last dream. As she neared, a familiar female shape appeared.

"Remember what I told you," Deirdre said as Elena reached the bridge. "You must never cross the Fates.

Danger resides on the other side. More danger than simply entering this realm."

How did Deirdre know Elena planned to go to Tirnan?

"I remember. But why do you only visit me in my dreams now?"

Deirdre looked down at the water, flowing steadily south. "It is safer this way. No one observes you here."

"But you do."

Deirdre smiled. "Yes. That is my special gift. Not many have the ability to enter dreams. A dreamwalker may only enter the dreams of someone they know."

Deirdre had entered her dreams twice now, bestowing knowledge about Tirnan. Maybe she'd have advice about traveling there. "After reading the Tertullian Codex, I think I need to travel here to build my powers." Elena glanced around. "It seems Fae of noble blood can enrich their powers through the land."

"It is possible." A forlorn look crossed Deirdre's face. "The only other Fae with your ability was a nobleman. Connecting with his descendants may help in your search as well. They are a part of New Kingdom." She paused a moment and sighed. "I feared you would end up in Tirnan. You must speak to Leo and learn all you can before traveling here. Great danger awaits you."

"Leo mentioned that, but if I'm the Fae's only hope, why wouldn't they help me?"

"Long-held beliefs are difficult to extinguish. Fae believe Halven are an abnormality. Like the mother of a deformed pup smothers it to spare suffering, our people will sense your energy level and end your life before they listen to reason."

"Can't Keen telepath a message and let people in Tirnan know that I'm coming to help?"

"Keen's telepathy works in one direction. He may listen to others, but they cannot hear inside his mind. And his ability does not work across realms.

"Even if he could communicate with our brethren, they would not listen. It would take time we do not have to convince them to put aside prejudices about the Halven. Most know Halven are responsible for the deaths of their loved ones, and they are not in a charitable mood toward your kind."

"If that's the case, how will I survive long enough to create a cure?"

Deirdre gently squeezed Elena's arm. "Protect yourself through your ability. Use it to defend as much as to create. For now, Derek is on your side. If traveling to Tirnan is the correct course, Derek's power will help you enter unsuspected. There is always the risk that…" She trailed off, concern crossing her face.

"What?"

"Trust your instincts. They will guide you well." Deirdre's figure flickered.

"Wait! I don't trust my instincts. That's the problem."

Deirdre was gone.

CHAPTER

THIRTY

Derek went to Elena's room a few hours later, but Keen wasn't out front and Elena didn't answer the door. A brief moment of panic washed over him, before he remembered that Leo had wanted Elena to put in one last defense training session before traveling to Tirnan. Derek jogged to the Emain gym, and found Elena crouched and facing Keen.

Keen lunged for her, and Derek's entire body tensed. But in the next instant, Elena hit Keen in the throat with the side of her wrist and elbowed him in the solar plexus. Keen faltered and Elena mimicked kneeing him in the groin.

Keen stepped back and nodded, still recovering from the throat blow.

Derek clapped. "Not bad. Thanks for waiting for me this morning."

Elena grabbed her water bottle, her tanned skin pale, eyes rimmed with red. She walked to the side of the room and proceeded to stare at the wall.

He hated to see her like this. Felt helpless to fix things, since he was the cause. Wisps of what had occurred the night before rendered a hazy, disjointed image in his mind, but one thing was clear. He hadn't wanted to be with Beatrice.

The thought of being with the Fae female made bile rise in his throat. He had scrubbed his skin raw last night trying to erase lingering memories of her touch. He was a guy; of course he'd hooked up with girls he didn't have strong feelings for, but never against his will. Call him crazy, but he liked to choose his partners.

After spending time with Elena, he had no interest in anyone else. The knowledge that he'd hurt her after what they'd shared tore at his insides, and Elena's cold shoulder made him itch to punch something. Preferably a Fae something.

Derek strode to where she stood and addressed Keen. "What's the plan?"

"Weapons training for you, more hand-to-hand combat for Elena before she meets with Leo for final preparations."

"Why aren't you teaching me how to use weapons?" Elena glared at Derek as though she wanted to shiv him— for last night, for being the one who received the weapons training, for everything.

And maybe he deserved it. He'd been an ass to her in the beginning when she'd caused an explosion in Marlon's lab, redeemed himself somewhat by helping her with the Fae, and then he'd kissed another girl right in front of her. It didn't look good.

"We need to teach you more defense skills," Keen said. "You put up no fight against the Halven at the party."

Elena threw up her hands. "It was two against one, and the one guy clocked me in the head. How am I supposed to respond under those conditions?"

Keen pinned her with a glare. "Do you think you will

find yourself in a padded, air-conditioned room the next time someone attacks you? You will be given no warning, likely under impossible circumstances. You must be able to defend yourself in the worst of conditions, and I don't have time to properly train you. Derek has proven his combat skills are sufficient for him to advance to weaponry."

"His skills haven't been tested in a real-life situation. How do you know how he'll fight when the chips are stacked against him?"

"Enough." Keen waved his hand and walked to the edge of the mat. "I will not argue with you, Elena. Do as I say and you may survive the next time someone tries to kill you."

"Don't sound so smug," she grumbled, and turned her back. "If I don't survive, you won't either." Elena chopped the dummy bag with the move she'd practiced on Keen's throat moments before.

Keen moved to the weapons wall and pulled knives and guns down. He checked the chamber of a handgun and raised it to Derek. "Have you used one before?"

Derek shook his head, most of his attention on Elena chopping the hell out of the dummy bag. "Only a Benelli shotgun and a Magnum .22."

Elena landed one last punch on the bag. "Great. He kills Bambis."

Derek dropped his hands low on his hips and turned to her. "We have a large property back home. I've shot birds, but most of my experience is limited to tin cans." He nodded at Keen. "I have good aim, though."

Keen handed him a Magnum .22 and ammunition, then pulled several small knives from the wall. He sheathed them, and pointed to where they fit along Derek's belt. Once Derek had the items secured, Keen reached inside a drawer and handed him two more belts, both of them small and made of the same rubberlike material as the belt at his waist.

"For your ankle and forearm," he said, handing him two more knives. "Attach the smaller knives to these straps and cover them with your clothing."

The guard from the basement lab walked in and stood at attention beside the door.

Keen glanced up. "Marcus will take you to firing practice and show you knife maneuvers while I finish training Elena."

Marcus peered at Elena. "Nothing on your roommate yet, miss. I have my men searching all possible leads. Leo asks that you meet him in the small laboratory."

Elena squeezed her eyes closed and nodded.

She'd been through a lot, and there was more to come. Derek wanted to comfort her, but she wouldn't like that right now. Maybe she never would.

Probably best he left with Marcus. Elena hated him for what'd he'd done, and there was no easy way to explain his actions.

He strode through the door, leaving his heart back in the room.

KEEN HAD TAUGHT Elena a few more defense maneuvers she hoped she'd remember if she ever needed them. He even relented and gave her a few pointers on how to handle a small knife and gun. He said if she needed them she was probably dead, but he gave her tips on proper handling just in case she got lucky.

How optimistic of him.

Elena left to meet Leo in the lab and made one last-ditch effort to transmute.

She looked up from her latest failed attempt, a granite rock that had ended up a pile of granite sand. "Do you really think I'll be able to improve my powers in Tirnan? What if I misinterpreted the Codex? *Land. Ancient. Noble.* Those are the words that stick out in my mind as keys, but that's not exactly a road map."

Leo set aside a petri dish. "Fae magic is most powerful among the royal lineages, one of which you come from. Royals, if they've survived the disease, live in Tirnan. And the land itself is magical, gifted by our original fathers."

"The angels."

He nodded.

"But what makes the royals so magically powerful?"

"Persistence. We've managed to keep those lines pure, intermarrying to preserve the lines and their connection to the angels."

"As in *incest?*"

"In most cases no, but cousins marry. After years of trying to conceive, they may partner with another. The goal is conception, which can take decades, possibly centuries for most women. Fertility is much stronger between Fae and humans, thus the Halven problem."

Elena chuckled humorlessly. "And that doesn't tell you something? Did God ask you to keep your bloodlines pure, or is that a Fae interpretation?"

Leo's mouth became a thin white line. "Of course not, but Fae were gifted by God with abilities. Those abilities weaken the farther down the line our brethren are from the original angels who sired them. It is only logical to keep the bloodlines strong through purity."

She shook her head. Maybe that was true, but in nature

the ability to reproduce was critical to the survival of a species. If Fae could be wiped out by a manufactured disease, they weren't impervious to death. And if successful reproduction meant mating with humans, maybe Fae should listen to biology.

Tired of trying to convince Fae that their prejudices were stupid and harmful not only to Halven, but to themselves, she focused on what mattered. "I'm wasting time here, Leo. I should leave for Tirnan. It makes sense to seek help from the nobles I'm descended from."

Of course, how to get those nobles to talk to her before immediately killing her was something no one had the answer to.

"Yes." His face was weary and drawn at the edges. He actually appeared sad. "I had hoped we could protect you, Elena. You are more special than I presumed, with Fae-like abilities. You could have been one of the few Halven with a legitimate claim to a place in Tirnan. I have always respected your family... I am sorry I cannot protect you."

Leo's compassion stunned her for a moment. "I'm not dead yet, Leo. My mother and the rest of you will be, if I don't do something." She remembered Deirdre's words about asking Leo for information on the Fae realm. "What can you tell me about Tirnan? How can I best survive while I'm there?"

Leo nodded and spun on his heel. "Come with me."

He led Elena to the classroom where it had all started—the place where she'd first encountered Keen and the other Fae.

An image of an allon tree, carved into a wood panel on the back wall, presided over the room, gold filament covering the leaves. It was subtle, but magnificent. How had she missed it before? The allon was everywhere in Emain, now that she knew what to look for.

Leo stopped in front of the unusual framed map she *had* noticed the first day. The one Portia had identified as Tirnan. The massive land formation in the center differed from anything she'd ever seen, yet the map itself appeared aged, worn at the edges, as if it had been around forever.

Leo pointed to the singular landmass. "At the center of Tirnan lies a large crater, a frozen, uninhabitable wasteland." He placed his hand on the surrounding area colored in faded blue. "Ocean covers the rest of the realm. The kingdoms lie along the rim of the landmass, near the ocean. Volcanism does not affect Tirnan, so the land is fairly flat and easy to traverse. Tirnan is densely vegetated and rippled with interconnected streams, rivers, and lakes, all of which may be used as drinking water."

He pointed to a place at the top left of the landmass. "The land here is a part of Old Kingdom. The sovereign of that land holds with ancient customs and ways of living. The buildings in this region resemble human fourteenth-century architecture. Though the lifestyle is outdated, the king is very powerful magically, and uses his ability and that of the others in his land to stay current with battle weapons. Do not underestimate these people by their lifestyle. The king is a formidable opponent."

He dropped his hand to the lower middle of the landmass. "New Kingdom embraces most modern conveniences, with buildings constructed in the human realm's eighteenth-century style." Leo glanced at her. "It is from here, Elena, that your ancestors descend. You may find less opposition should you enter the realm in New Kingdom. Their use of magic as a weapon is not as advanced as in Old Kingdom, but they too are lethal."

"Old Kingdom and New Kingdom are deadly, but what about the third kingdom? Is that the land on the right?"

"Sunland. Yes." Leo took a moment to answer. "Sunlanders are an open-minded people. Passive. They do not fight for power. They live with the land rather than use it."

She chuckled. "Sunlanders are environmentalists."

He nodded. "Among other things. They desire peace for Tirnan, which is unrealistic."

She wanted to ask him why, but figured she didn't have enough hours in the day to argue peace not war with Leo.

"If you venture to Sunland, you will find the dwellings odd, many built into craters or low to the ground. Sunlanders are less combative, which would be safer for you, but noble Fae do not reside in Sunland. And if your interpretation of the Codex links your development of transmutation with the nobles, you will need to enter one of the other two kingdoms."

Leo stepped away from the map. "It would be best to portal you to New Kingdom, close to the castle. I've already mentioned that the streams and lakes may be used as drinking water in Tirnan. You need not travel more than a kilometer in any direction to encounter a fresh source. Animals may be caught for sustenance as well, but you are not acquainted with these particular species. We will supply you with food for your journey. And, of course, the leaves from the allon may be eaten if all else fails."

At her questioning look, Leo scanned a bookcase beneath the map that held what looked like encyclopedias. The titles on the spines were in an unusual language.

He selected a book and quickly flipped through the pages. "Here is the allon leaf." He pointed to a broad, round leaf in varying colors, the edges frayed like worn fabric— exactly like the colorful branch-jumping leaves she'd spied in her dreams. "The leaves alone will not sustain you, but you could survive on them for a few days if needed."

Leo returned the book and seemed to be considering something else. "I would tell you of the weapons used in Tirnan, but most you've seen or heard of before: bows, knives, some guns. The best advice I can give you is to remain hidden and try never to encounter a Fae soldier."

Why did she think that was going to be a nearly impossible task?

Leo ushered her back the way they'd come. "The sleep deprivation you've sustained will hinder your ability to manifest the power you need for transmutation, despite your body's rapid healing. You are still half human, after all. I feel it best that you take a short nap while we prepare the food packets and inform those among us of the journey you are about to embark on."

Another restless nap in Emain? If this was it, a sort of last rites, she had one final request.

"Leo, before I leave for Tirnan, I'd like to go home. I'll take a short nap there and return immediately. I'll be gone an hour at most, just enough time to say goodbye."

If she needed sleep to have any hope of success, a twenty-minute nap in her own bed would be best. Also, she wanted to see if Reese had been home.

Marcus's men didn't know what to look for, but Elena knew her roommate's routines and could tell if anything had been disturbed. Reese should have called or texted by now, but Elena couldn't help wanting one last chance to see for herself—and one last moment in her own space.

Leo sighed. "You cannot tell anyone of your journey."

"I won't actually say goodbye. It'll be more of a visual farewell."

He studied her face, then gave a short nod. "Very well. I

will send extra guards with you." As if reading her mind, he added, "And I will see what Marcus has discovered of your roommate. We will speak to the authorities if she still has not been found."

"Thank you."

Either Leo was softening his stance on Halven, or her chances of survival were astonishingly low. He never wanted her to leave Emain. His agreeability didn't bode well.

Within minutes, Elena was led to the exit of the physics building with no fewer than five additional Keen-sized bodyguards, one of whom was the weapons master, Marcus. Several more guards followed, hidden in the surrounding area. It was a good thing it was dark out, and few people were about. Keen with his atypical height was unusual, but a group of Keens walking the campus would not have gone over well. They didn't exactly blend.

"Elena, wait up," Derek called from behind as they left the building, and her heart constricted.

He caught up and walked home with them without a word, then veered off to his house, taking the porch steps two at a time.

At least he didn't have delusions of coming over to her place. She was still confused and hurt after seeing Derek with Beatrice. She wouldn't be able to relax, let alone rest up for the biggest challenge of her life, with him nearby.

And that made her sad. Derek had been the one person throughout all this whom she could depend on.

Elena entered her apartment and breathed in the scent of home. A moment of peace swept over her, until she realized Reese hadn't returned.

No dishes lay in the sink. Reese never washed hers, so if she'd been home and had eaten something, the dishes would be there. And Elena's note to her roommate rested where she'd left it the night before.

Elena went to Reese's bedroom and discovered her bed hadn't been slept in. She braced her hand on the doorframe, taking a deep breath.

If she'd gotten Reese hurt, she'd never forgive herself. She had to make it back from Tirnan—she needed to find her roommate.

Returning to the living room, her heart heavy, she realized she'd missed a second note beside the one she had left for Reese.

You better not be avoiding me, ER. I got my eyes on you! I'll be back in a few days. By then your "project" should be finished. Besides, I've got another date lined up with Isabelle.

Mateo had drawn an image of two large breasts next to the girl's name.

Life might crumble around her, but some things never changed.

The note that would normally have made her laugh brought tears to her eyes. She tried not to think about her cousin, or the rest of her family. She could do nothing for them now, except what she was already doing.

She glanced longingly at the stove. What was one last meal at home, all things considered? It would relax her more than any nap could right now, and good food would help her energy.

Elena peered at the five guards and Keen. They'd squeezed their massive bodies onto her couch and living room chair, and were watching a reality dating show. Keen held the remote, which explained their choice in television.

"Are you guys hungry?" No one said anything, but each of the Fae stared over eagerly, like a band of puppies eyeing a pork chop in their mother's mouth.

She walked to the kitchen and opened the refrigerator. Mateo had gone berserk. Packages of chicken weighed down the racks, and the bins and other shelves were filled to capacity. The kitchen cabinets were equally stuffed with dry goods.

A burning sensation filled her chest. Her cousin was the biggest jackass she knew, and she loved him with all her heart.

Elena spent the next forty-five minutes making quick recipes of chicken mole and Spanish rice. She didn't have time to cut up a salad, but she'd made a ton of the mole, so it would have to do. When it was ready, she called the Fae to the table.

Keen and the five guards joined her with disconcerting speed for their size. Funny how inferior she was, unless she was cooking for them. Then she was their best friend.

Men. Speaking of...

Everyone had sat, the table overcrowded with large Fae tucked up against each other, when the front door creaked open.

For a moment, Elena's heart stopped. She half stood, thinking it was Reese, only to sink back in her seat.

Derek stepped inside and closed the front door behind him. "Smells good." He walked to the kitchen and grabbed a plate from the cabinet.

Elena turned to Keen. "Did you text him?" she said under her breath.

He shrugged.

She glared at Derek. "You come to eat my food, knowing how I feel about you right now? Why are you hurting me this way?"

He froze, his throat bobbing in a gulp. "I never meant to

hurt you. If it had been within my power to stop it, I would have."

The guards around the table darted their eyes at the drama unfolding.

"It is true what Derek says." Keen held a serious expression.

After a moment, Derek scooted a chair over and ladled a helping of rice, but his hand shook. He was upset. Maybe as much as she was.

The guards shuffled their plates to make room for Derek at the table.

Both Derek and Keen said Beatrice had done something to Derek. Elena hadn't believed he could lose all control that way, but Beatrice had somehow manipulated Keen into leaving his post when she'd trapped Elena in the library. It was possible Derek told the truth.

"I'll never know what really happened," she said.

Derek looked up, and her breath caught. Pain and an emotion she couldn't define pooled behind his eyes. "It wasn't my choice. I'd take it back if I could."

Derek's hand on Beatrice's breast had been damning, but the look in his eyes now... he meant it.

Elena had been so hurt by what she'd seen that she barely listened to Derek when he said he never wanted to be with the beautiful Fae. Elena couldn't believe it possible. But he'd said all along he'd been powerless to stop it. Now, with that look in his eyes of utter hopelessness and pain... He was telling her the truth.

Whatever had happened between Derek and Beatrice, it wasn't Derek's fault. He was innocent.

THIRTY-ONE

Keen had texted Derek that food was on at Elena's house, and Derek deliberated for all of two seconds before heading over. He couldn't turn down her cooking, and he wanted any excuse to be near her. The distance between them was killing him.

Without a chance to talk to Elena in private—there was no such thing as privacy with Fae guards surrounding her—he didn't know where they stood. He'd told her the truth in front of Keen and the other guards. He hadn't wanted Beatrice; he'd been forced to touch her. That was all he could say. Unless Elena experienced the utter loss of control Derek had, she'd never understand.

Derek left shortly after dinner, not wanting to overstay what little welcome he had, convinced Elena would never trust him again. His chest ached, his head pounding despite the vast amount of excellent food he'd eaten. He opened the front door to his place—his home foreign and cold from the moment he'd returned—and his cell phone rang.

He glanced at the number, and took the call.

"Hi, son. I'm glad I caught you. We need to talk."

Derek wasn't interested in the opportunities his father had talked up. He wanted to be here with the others like him—if he ever got a chance to meet other Halven. And he wanted to be near Elena, though in some ways it might be better if he left. She wasn't happy he'd showed up tonight. Being near her, yet not able to be with her would be brutal.

"Sorry I haven't called. I've been busy with school."

"Of course. That's to be expected. I'm happy you're making the most of your college experience, though I hear you've run into some bad luck this year. I just got off the phone with Professor St. Just."

What?

Derek kept his voice steady. "When did you talk to Marlon?"

"About two hours ago, right before my meeting with the hospital administrators. Is something wrong?"

"No—it's just—did Marlon say where he was?"

"On campus, I assumed. He told me about the lab explosion. Thank God you weren't around at the time. It's unfortunate what happened, but it does provide the perfect incentive to reconsider other opportunities. You still have two more years of college. Plenty of time to assimilate on a new campus."

Would his father never let up?

"There's nothing keeping you at Dawson anymore," his father continued. "Marlon explained how he's taking on a new project and won't be able to mentor you anymore. He agrees that without him and the private facility, your talents are best utilized elsewhere. He suggested you transfer as soon as possible while it's still early in the semester. With your capacity to absorb information, he believes you'll have no problem getting up to speed."

His father said more, but Derek's ears rang with what

he'd already said. Marlon, the man responsible for murdering thousands of Fae, had contacted his father.

Putting aside the danger Marlon posed to his family, he couldn't help wondering why Marlon would want Derek to leave Dawson. If Marlon was worried about what Derek knew, why not just kill him like he had Fae?

Oh yeah, Marlon *had* tried. Or his people had. The bomb in Marlon's lab could have been targeted for Derek and not simply a random attempt to protect Marlon's secrets... And when that hadn't worked, there was Beatrice to put a rift between him and Elena, ensuring they no longer worked well together.

"I'll consider it, Dad."

"Derek, your future is nothing to play with. The right education opens doors. There's no limit to what you can accomplish. It's critical you make the right choices."

Critical for the future his father had planned for him, not for what Derek wanted. "I understand. Give me a couple of days to think about it."

His father would have said more, but Derek cut him off, telling him he had an important test to prepare for.

In some ways, his father's insistence he change schools was a way out. He could leave Dawson, the Fae, and Elena. Start a new life. Meet a different girl. One who didn't hate him.

But he didn't want a different girl. He wanted Elena.

After a warm shower, Elena lay on her bed, alone for the first time in what felt like forever. She glanced at the corner of her room where Derek had slept not long ago, the ache in her chest returning. She missed him, and in just a short while she'd return to Emain, where she didn't know when or if she'd ever see him again.

She hadn't gotten a chance to tell Derek before he left tonight that she believed him about Beatrice. Too many Fae were around, preventing any semblance of privacy.

There was no way Derek would go to Tirnan with her now. The Fae hadn't ordered him to go—they didn't even think Elena could do much good there, let alone survive. They supported her traveling to their homeland as a backup plan. Derek might have gone with her before this afternoon, but now…he'd be a fool to risk his life for her.

Derek had left her house this evening with the same closed-off expression he'd used to shield himself with when they'd first met. She hadn't realized until now that he looked at her differently. His gaze was warm, deep blue turning black when he kissed her, expressing his feelings more than his words.

She didn't want his life in danger. If she mended things now, he might try to leave with her, and she couldn't let him make that sacrifice.

The only thing more frightening than putting her life in danger was putting Derek's life in danger too. He'd lost enough because of her—his lab, a peaceful existence before he'd found her with the Fae—and she'd never forget it. But she couldn't let him pay the ultimate price, should anything happen to him inside Tirnan.

Elena returned to her bed and curled into a fetal position. Sleep wasn't happening; she had to return to Emain in a few minutes. And she couldn't call and say goodbye to her family, because they'd flip out if they even suspected something was wrong. There was still no word from Reese…

Maybe she should leave her roommate another note? Or send an email explaining what had happened?

Email. Elena hadn't checked her email. Reese could have left a message.

She jumped up, grabbed her laptop, and returned to her bed. Reese preferred texting, but what if she'd lost her phone? What if she was trapped and the only way she could get hold of anyone was by sneaking onto a computer and sending an email? Elena was grasping, but she was desperate.

Of the hundred new messages in her inbox—nearly all junk mail—she found nothing from Reese.

And then an instant message popped up on her screen.

She was about to hit delete, like she did all IMs she didn't recognize, when she took a closer look at the profile.

HalflnzRule.

Heavy footsteps stormed down the hallway. Keen burst through the door and took in her expression. He crossed the room and glanced over her shoulder at the screen.

"Were you listening to my thoughts?" she asked.

"No, his—Marlon's vassal. Yours give me a headache. I gave up listening to them a long time ago. Same for Derek. His revolve too much around you."

Okay, as insulting as that statement was, it explained why Keen hadn't said anything to Leo about Elena and Derek's early suspicions about Marlon.

"Click on the message," he said. "The vassal has information for you."

"If you know that, why do I need to click on it?"

Keen's mouth tensed as he glared at the screen. "He's blocking me. I'm only picking up general impressions."

"What is the point of your ability if everyone blocks you?"

His eyes cut to her in annoyance. "Most do not know how to block me. St. Just trained your abductor, or perhaps he gave him drugs. Some drugs interfere with the brain waves I read. St. Just had the boy send the message, knowing his soldier wouldn't have enough information in his mind to be a danger to the army, and that we would read his message. Which is what you should do if we are to learn anything new within the next century."

"Sarcasm is a human trait, you know." She clicked on the IM.

HalfInzRule: *A trade? You for the girl?*

Elena's stomach dropped. Her hands started shaking. She looked down, realizing for the first time that they had stopped jittering sometime between now and when she'd first acquired her powers.

"They have her, Keen. Marlon has her."

"Confirm he speaks of Reese."

"Who else would he be talking about?"

"Do it," he growled.

Elena: *Which girl are you referring to? There are about fifteen thousand on campus.*

HalfInzRule: *Who do you think, bitch? The blonde. Your roommate. Meet me tomorrow at 10p.m. White farmhouse off Hwy 89. Turn left at Exit 12. No physical address. The sign on the drive reads The Millers. Be there or the girl dies. It'll be my pleasure to play with her before I kill her.*

Keen grabbed the laptop and yanked the screen back. He stared at the words, his eyes turning into emerald fire. "I will kill him."

THIRTY-TWO

At Keen's urgent text, Derek rushed over to Elena's apartment.

Keen pointed to the chair in the living room, indicating he should sit. "Elena must leave for Tirnan immediately."

He knew Elena planned to travel to Tirnan, but it seemed like something had happened. Keen had the look of a desperate man. And Keen never looked unnerved.

"Someone want to fill me in?"

Keen's gaze locked with Elena's. She looked so small between him and one of the other Fae guards.

"Marlon has Reese," she said, her elbows on her knees, fingers digging into the waves of hair at her temples. "He'll release her in exchange for me. The meeting takes place tomorrow night."

Derek wagged his head. "Not gonna happen."

Elena looked up and her brows drew together in confusion, or surprise.

What did she think? That he'd stopped caring just because she didn't trust him?

Keen let out an exasperated sigh. "We will not sacrifice Elena for the girl, but we will not allow harm to come to Reese. That is why Elena must leave for Tirnan now. St. Just and his band of Halven threatened Elena through Reese, but they will not stop there. More attempts on Elena's life will follow. At this point, Elena is better off in Tirnan, where she has a chance of developing a cure and besting Marlon. Our people have been weakened. We can protect Elena better once the disease is contained."

Interesting how they needed Elena to regain their strength. And it was not something they readily admitted to either.

"Even if she left this minute, how could she possibly find what she needs, make a cure, and return in time?" Derek asked.

"Tirnan runs on a different timeline than the human realm. The timeline varies from season to season, but as of now, it runs slower by about three days. That allows enough time—if she hurries."

No matter what Derek told himself about changing colleges, there was no way he'd let Elena go to Tirnan alone. He tapped his finger on the chair, thinking through their options.

They had none. Reese would die if they did nothing.

"Since when do your people care about one human life?" he asked.

A strange look crossed Keen's face, one he quickly checked. "We do not risk lives unnecessarily. We can save the girl if we act now. You both would have left for Tirnan in an hour, regardless."

Elena's head popped up. "What? Derek isn't going. Leave him out of this."

"I'll go, but when Elena and I return, I'm leaving

Dawson." He stared hard at Keen. "I'm transferring to a different school, and I don't want interference from your people."

"Accepted," Keen said.

Elena searched Derek's face. "Why? Is it because of what happened? I know it wasn't your fault, Derek. I don't blame you. You don't have to leave."

She said that now, but what if something like this happened again? Would she hate him in six months? What if some other Fae or powerful Halven tried to warp his mind and pit him against her?

Elena had something the Fae wanted. The best thing for her would be if he left. One less person the Fae could manipulate to get to her.

"My reasons have nothing to do with you." A lie, but he didn't want her to feel responsible for why he was leaving. "I've been offered a better opportunity at a different school, and I'm taking it."

He'd help her in Tirnan because as a Halven he was the only person who could protect her there. He figured Beatrice's purpose in enthralling him had been to cause a rift between them, thereby making Elena vulnerable. Why Beatrice, a Fae, would want to do that, he didn't know. It looked like she had become a traitor to her own people. Either way, he wouldn't give Beatrice the satisfaction. Elena needed him, and he'd be there for her.

Elena sucked in a breath, her face pained.

"Very good," Keen said. "I'll portal you to the outer wall of the New Kingdom castle as planned. Get Elena inside and find her a hiding place. When it's safe, search for her mother."

"My mother?" Elena blurted.

Keen's face softened. "Yes, Elena. She's your only ally in Tirnan. Trust no other."

"Deirdre told me the same thing about not trusting anyone, except she never mentioned my mother."

Keen raised an eyebrow. "Deirdre?"

Elena's mouth parted, a look of chagrin crossing her face. "Deirdre sort of comes to me in my dreams."

"She is from Old Kingdom," Keen said. "She married your mother's brother. Her allegiance is to Sunland now. You may be able to trust her. Only you can know for certain."

"Deirdre is my aunt?" Elena said, her tone surprised.

"Beorhtric Rainer's wife, yes."

A small smile played on her mouth. "That explains a lot. She's always been kind to me. I'm not sure why she didn't tell me who she was, though."

It was good to see Elena smile, if even a small one. And it was good to know Deirdre had Elena's back.

"We've been instructed to give you as little information as possible. Deirdre went against orders telling you as much as she did."

"And now it's okay to inform me of things? Now that I'm risking my life?"

Keen shrugged.

Typical, thought Derek. They kept all this from Elena until now, when it was too late.

"How do you know so much, Keen? Shouldn't Leo be giving me this information?"

"He would if he were here." Keen waved at one of the guards outside, circling his finger.

Signaling for the guard to patrol the area?

"Fae do not lead like your military, particularly inside Emain," Keen continued. "Most of us have been around a long while. We work together, and generally follow one command, but there are times in battle when a single warrior must make a decision for the good of us all. Leo understands that you might be our last hope. He will support my judgment under the circumstances. I'll notify him directly of what has transpired once we return to Emain." His gaze fell on Derek. "One more thing. There will be times when you must transform Elena along with you. Getting past the guards at the portal will be the first test."

Derek shook his head. "Impossible. I've tried to Blend larger objects like my backpack. It can't be done."

"Elena is not an inanimate object. Your backpack is wider than she is. It will work, but you must hold her close."

Derek closed his eyes, trying to remain calm. He didn't want to hold her close. As it was, he battled every instinct to reach out and comfort her, when the best thing was for him to keep his distance.

Instead he said, "What would be the point of Blending with her if all you Fae can see me anyway?" Portia, Keen, and even Elena had sensed him while transformed.

"We cannot see you in the way I see you now. A shimmer in the air notifies us of the disguise, but it is nearly impossible to observe in low light. Even in full daylight, one must be looking for it."

Elena's face looked hopeful. "Let's try it, Derek. If it works, it could save us. We'd have a chance of escaping."

She was right. If they had any hope of surviving, they needed his ability.

Derek mentally braced his senses against the onslaught he was about to subject them to. Elena stepped past Keen and the guards, and stood in front of him.

Keen scanned their stances. "You'll need to hold her as

close as possible. Tuck her head beneath your chin and center her between your legs. Wrap your arms around her."

Derek glared at Keen.

The corner of Keen's mouth twitched. Keen knew Derek had feelings for Elena, just like Derek knew Keen wanted Reese.

Derek grabbed Elena's arms and wrapped them behind his back, breathing out of his mouth so he couldn't smell her. Bad enough her soft flesh molded to his chest. Her hands tentatively flattened on his shoulder blades and his heart began to race. She wedged her feet between his, and tucked her head close, her hair tickling his nose.

The itch to his nose distracted him and he breathed in, instantly regretting it.

Elena's fruity scent, mixed with the smell of her skin, made his hands sweat and adrenaline surge. He wanted to mash his lips to her mouth and consume her. Instead, he tucked his head to draw closer, grazing her ear with his lips. She stiffened, but she didn't move away. Derek Blended before he started thinking of other things he wanted to graze his mouth on.

The transition from solid state to air occurred the same as usual, evidenced by a slight tingling sensation, only faster. The adrenaline caused by Elena's nearness helped quicken the process.

"Good," Keen said. "We cannot see either of you. Try moving."

How the hell was he supposed to move with her wrapped around him like cellophane?

Derek tried moving anyway, but Elena ripped from him like a piece of Velcro, his body jerking and shuddering from the separation.

"Elena has come into view, Derek."

Derek made himself solid. "I told you it wouldn't work."

"You'll need to figure out a way to move without breaking the transformation."

They tried for several agonizing minutes, and every time Derek took a step, Elena returned to solid state.

"I have an idea," Elena said hesitantly. "Derek somehow modifies the atoms in our bodies while we're stationary. When I'm close enough to him, his body perceives me as part of him, like his clothes. What if when we move, the shifting takes me out of range?"

Where is she going with this?

"I think—I think some part of him must meld with me when we transform. That way there's no question we are one."

Marcus cleared his throat. Keen smirked. The other guards simply stared, as if preparing for the entertainment.

Derek was too stunned to reply.

Elena let out an exasperated breath. "I'm not suggesting what you perverts are obviously thinking. I was considering something more along the lines of...a kiss."

Derek was speechless. He wanted to do a lot more than kiss Elena. He wasn't sure he'd ever recover from making love to her. She'd taken a piece of him. But he'd made up his mind to stay away. Even if her kissing idea made sense— and unfortunately, it did—distance, separation, that was what they needed. Kissing went in the opposite direction.

He turned to Keen. "You have any other ideas?"

Elena crossed her arms over her chest. "Oh my God, I'm not going to molest you. I know this isn't ideal, but it's logical. If we're connected..." She shrugged.

He glanced at each of the Fae, hoping one of them might come up with something better. Instead, they stared mutely back at him.

Great help, guys. Derek shook his head in frustration.

Elena dropped her arms and put her hands on her hips. He'd seen that stance many a time on his mom and scores of Southern female cousins. Elena was pissed. "Look, if you have a better idea, by all means inform us."

Maybe he liked the fire, because at the moment, the only thing he wanted to do was grab hold of her and kiss her feisty lips the way she'd suggested. Derek's gaze dipped down her body. She wanted a kiss, she'd get a damn kiss.

He grabbed her hand and yanked her to his chest. Elena's eyes widened, but she didn't pull away. With one hand braced on the back of her head, he lowered his mouth and took her full, rosy lips.

Small problem. She responded in kind.

And he was gone.

The kiss took on a life of its own. Tongues clashing, lips meshing, filling a desperate void, as if he'd been starved of oxygen and could finally breathe again.

After a moment, Derek sensed Elena hesitating. She pulled away a fraction. "Transform," she mumbled against his mouth.

Oh yeah. *Shit.*

Ignoring their audience, who had at this point received an eyeful, he stopped kissing her. "Wrap your legs around my waist."

Her eyebrows climbed up her pretty forehead, but she clamped her hands on his shoulders and jumped into his arms, her legs locking around his middle.

She weighed about as much as his weapons belt. He could run for miles with her like this, which might come in handy in Tirnan. Derek repressed the urge to fantasize about her in this position and let out a slow, calming breath. He made his body transform, and transformed hers along with it.

"We cannot see either of you," Keen said.

Time to test the theory. Derek pressed his mouth to Elena's, and her lips parted. He ran his tongue over hers, tasting her... After a long moment, she nudged him in the butt with her heel.

Dammit! How was he supposed to focus like this? He'd like to see the Fae warriors keep their heads under these conditions.

He adjusted the angle of the kiss so he could see where he was going, and carried Elena to her bedroom. Once inside, Elena pulled away and they stared at each other.

She loosened her grip and slid to the ground, taking a tentative step back. Their connection ripped apart and Elena went solid.

Derek focused all of his attention on not feeling anything. He would not allow his mind to go where it wanted to go. To her, to them, and being together. The kiss had meant nothing.

Her gaze cut away, as if she too was affected and didn't want to acknowledge it.

Derek returned to solid state and exited the room. The Fae soldiers faced the opposite wall where he and Elena had stood moments ago. She joined him at his side.

"Mission accomplished," he said.

The men spun around at the sound of Derek's voice.

"What's next on the pre-Tirnan training regimen?"

"Nothing," Keen answered. "You are as ready as you can be. As long as you don't get distracted"—he gave Derek a knowing look—"you might survive."

THIRTY-THREE

Since Keen was in such a sharing mood about her family, Elena grilled him on the way to the brick building portal. It was nighttime, so no one should see them, and this portal was closer to her apartment than the Physics Hall entrance to Emain.

"According to Deirdre, my mother is a New Kingdom princess. Is that true?"

"Yes."

The fact that Keen was freely sharing information disconcerted her about as much as it had when Leo had opened up to her earlier. It was like getting more of those last rites. They really didn't think she'd come out alive, so in a sense, the Fae had nothing to lose by giving her all the information she asked for. And that was scary.

"While my mother and father were together, she went by the name Theda Rosales, taking my father's last name after marriage. My family said they knew little about her. She didn't share much about where she came from. No one knows her maiden name, and my father refused to speak of her after she left. How do I find her?"

"Your mother was born Theodora Joelle Rainer, daughter of Sihtric Rainer, king of New Kingdom."

A shiver ran down Elena's spine and she gripped her elbows. Her mother and grandfather's names sounded old-school, and totally foreign.

"When your mother returned to Tirnan, they imprisoned her. She resides isolated within the New Kingdom castle."

Imprisoned? Leo said her mother had been punished, but he hadn't mentioned how.

"Rainer valued his only daughter, but he lost all trust when she ran away and married your father. She has no freedom within her land. The king keeps her near, though no one knows exactly where. The castle is vast. Finding her will be difficult. The advantage you have is that few people in New Kingdom possess Derek's ability. Newlanders are not likely to recognize the signs of his transformation. His mental powers dominate in Old Kingdom, while elemental powers are prominent in New Kingdom."

"Are you sure they won't see the shimmer? It seems pretty obvious to me."

Keen eyed her. "It is unusual for a Halven to see a Fae once they've gone into the elements. Only a Fae of pure blood who knows what to look for may identify the disguise."

"Do you think it has something to do with my family and where I came from?"

"Yes," he said, his eyes distracted. "They do not speak of Halven with royal blood. The gentry strictly regulate blood-lines, mating for the sake of the kingdom. Rainer is one of the oldest Fae—and one of the closest to the original angels. Perhaps his line passes our magic more purely than others. It would explain your powers as well as your late uncle's."

"Speaking of angels, where are they? Why aren't they saving you from the disease? You're like their children."

He smiled wryly. "All life originates from the heavens, even human life, and the angels do not save *you*."

"I agree we all come from the same place," she said with emphasis. "But some of us—*cough, cough*—believe themselves above others. I figured if you were as superior as you claim, the angels would save you."

"It is not what I believe, it is truth. Some of us are more pure." He held up his hand at the look on her face. "Let us not argue the point; we haven't the time. In response to your earlier question, several millennia ago, the angels returned to the holy realm. No one has seen or heard from them since. Not even Fae may enter the holy realm."

Keen stopped in front of the brick wall. "Marcus and the other guards will go first. Elena, you and Derek follow. I will enter last."

Elena figured that was about as much as she was going to get out of Keen before she left for Tirnan. It was more than she'd hoped for.

She watched the guards enter the portal one by one, then she stepped through behind them.

Elena felt the spinning, the suction, and tried to remember Keen's instructions for a smooth landing. Shockingly, she came out the other end on her feet with only a mild stumble, and considered the effort a success. She waited for Derek, who popped through next as if stepping down a stair, damn him. Keen swept through last, like a ginormous, graceful dancer.

They made it look so easy. She rolled her eyes and turned around.

And was greeted by a wall of seven-foot muscle with semiautomatic weapons pointed at her heart.

Even the Fae guards who'd traveled home with her waited off to the side for instructions.

Keen approached the Fae at the center of the living blockade, a guard with spiked white hair and a protruding brow. Keen seemed to know him, and relayed a message in a language that sounded like a variant of Greek.

The guard nodded, and, without taking his gaze from Elena or Derek, spoke one word: "Leo."

One of the soldiers in the blockade peeled off and disappeared down the hall. The other semiautomatic-bearers broke formation and allowed them to pass.

Keen took Elena and Derek down a convoluted but quick path through the hallways and one grand Victorian ballroom—*where the heck had they been hiding this place?*—to the corridor where they'd trained. He stopped at the restrooms with the lockers. "Change into your Fae clothes. The guards will notify Leo of what has transpired. Leo will meet us at the portal to Tirnan."

Elena and Derek changed, and this time Keen loaded their belts with weapons—mostly on Derek. Apparently, Keen still didn't trust Elena with the weaponry. Trusted her to save his life, but not her own. Fae were a contradiction.

Elena's hands shook from the adrenaline surging through her. She was about to enter a deadly realm from which she might never return. The need to leaven the situation before she collapsed in a heap of hysterics had her sticking out her leg with her hands on her hips.

"I'm feeling rather Fae with my uniform and weapons."

Considering Fae in Emain were extremely pale and almost all light-haired, there was no way she fit in, but she couldn't pass up the opportunity to tweak Keen's cool façade one last time.

He looked down her, his gaze returning to her face, eyes reflecting an emotion that could only be described as fear. "Do not get killed." He turned on his heel and stormed down the hall.

Elena couldn't get past the expression on Keen's face. If he was scared, they were truly screwed.

Keen stopped at the top of a long flight of stairs. A massive bronze door stood at the bottom, engraved with the allon tree and inlaid with leaves of what looked like polished turquoise, lapis lazuli, and other natural stones.

"A last word of advice," he said, looking from her to Derek. "Fae from Old Kingdom and New Kingdom, as well as Sunland, come together in Emain to educate themselves for the advancement of our people. It is the only place where we treat each other with immunity. In Tirnan, borders cannot be crossed without dire consequences. Should you pass into Old Kingdom, Elena, they will not only see you as a Halven abomination, as will those from New Kingdom, they will see you as an enemy of the state. Your chance of survival in New Kingdom is precarious. In Old Kingdom..." He let the unspoken words hang there.

A few more words of advice from Keen and all hope of survival would be lost. Elena swallowed and clamped her jaw to keep her teeth from chattering. "I think I've got it."

He pulled out small, thin packets from a black satchel. "Food. Bland, but they provide the necessary nutrients."

Derek stared at the packets Keen handed him. "You got any more of these—like, say, twenty?"

Keen arched a brow.

"I'm *growing*," he said.

Keen nodded and pulled out two dozen more packets.

Enormous food consumption must be a male Fae thing. Come to think of it, it was kind of a young guy thing, because Mateo fit the rule as well.

Keen showed them where to attach the food beneath their uniforms. "You have three days' worth of packets. That is all the time you can spare in Tirnan before Marlon expects Elena for the exchange. Use the time and your powers wisely."

After a short pause, Keen's gaze slid to Marcus. "Leo should have arrived by now."

A silent message passed between the two guards, and then Keen's nostrils flared. Marcus pulled out a crossbow and Keen unlatched a gun from his belt. He edged Elena down the stairs toward the door. "We cannot wait for—"

A group of unfamiliar Fae descended the steps, crossbows raised.

Arrows sang before Elena could figure out what was happening, one of them stinging the top of her shoulder.

Keen shoved Elena behind him and Marcus fired arrows at Fae at the top of the stairs.

"I thought this was neutral territory!" she shouted, pressing a hand to the light wound and small slice in her shirt.

"Given Beatrice's betrayal"—Keen fired two shots from his gun—"there was a breach. You must leave. Now!" He reached behind and pried the bronze door open while Derek blocked her with his body.

"Wait! Keen, if I don't come back, promise me... Promise me you'll save Reese."

He gave one swift nod and shoved her through the door. Disoriented by the lights and color, Elena spiraled through the portal. She tripped, and landed on her rear on top of gravel in the dark of night, a mix of pine and peppermint filling her senses.

Elena looked up, and red stars stared down at her.

Tirnan. The place she'd known only in her dreams. She was actually here.

She breathed in the crisp, clean scent, blinking in wonder. And then Derek crashed down on top of her. Their limbs tangled, and one of Derek's hands shot out and caught her head before it slammed into the ground.

"Are you okay?" he asked breathlessly, his dark blue eyes inches from her face.

She tried to move. "I think so. You're a little heavy."

"Sorry." He eased onto his knees, scanning the area, his expression as mystified as hers had been a moment ago. Then he looked over her head and his eyes widened. He sucked in a deep breath. "We gotta go."

Shouts rang out in the distance.

Elena started to turn, but Derek fell on top of her and kissed her, his teeth biting into her lip. The tingling sensation of Blending passed through her limbs. Her heartbeat slowed, and then they were rolling.

Derek shifted her on his lap, and she caught sight of what had frightened him. A terrified squeak erupted from the back of her throat.

Dozens of Tirnan soldiers in dark uniforms ran toward them with their crossbows raised.

Arrows arched into the night air and Elena's heart raced as she vividly recalled her brush with an arrow minutes ago inside Emain. But she and Derek were no longer solid. The arrows whizzed right through them.

Still kissing her, Derek braced her legs around his waist

and secured one arm to her back. He deftly lifted her and ran.

Elena tucked in close, holding her breath as he rounded the soldiers. She'd had only a few seconds to take in the place she'd dreamed of before they were being attacked. It couldn't be a coincidence that the soldiers found them so quickly.

After a moment, she brushed a swath of hair from her face and glanced to the side, lips still connected to Derek's.

A towering rectangular building, about a city block in length, stretched before them. The structure stood sharp and imposing, with ornamental pillars, the entire thing protected by a tapered cement wall. The wall modified what might have been a leisure palace into a fortified castle.

And Derek was running straight for it.

Elena slammed her eyes shut a second before her skin zapped. When she opened her eyes, they were on the other side of the wall in some type of courtyard.

Soldiers poured out of the main gate behind them, presumably after her and Derek, whom they couldn't see, while other Fae swept the courtyard, weapons raised. It was dark out, and what Keen had said about Derek's Blending not being visible in low light was holding true.

Derek sprinted to the side of the building a football field away. As he rounded the corner, he skidded to a halt. He turned to the side as if to go back the way they'd come, and that was when Elena saw what had stopped him.

Soldiers approached at a fast clip from the opposite end, swords in front of them.

One Fae raised his hand and threw what looked to be a small fireball, only once released, the sphere expanded and grew to the size of a bowling ball before slamming home a few feet to their right. The ground vibrated, heat from the fireball slamming into them.

What if the fireball had hit its target?

Derek must have had the same thought, because he squeezed her waist, darted for the castle wall, and leapt through it. Elena experienced the sensation of being airborne, before he crashed to the ground and she lost her hold on him. They were ripped apart, her body skidding in a bruising heap across smooth, pale stone.

Shouts echoed off the cavernous walls inside the castle, and the end of the hallway filled with soldiers.

They could see Elena and Derek. Because the crash landing had torn them apart, their bodies no longer Blended.

Derek jerked Elena toward him by the arm and grabbed the back of her head, slamming his mouth to hers. He picked her up and transformed, running in the opposite direction of the soldiers rapidly approaching. At least these Fae didn't appear to see them while Blended. No one had thrown fireballs yet. Either they didn't know what to look for, or they didn't want to incinerate their palace.

At a speed that made her eyes water, Derek tore through the hallways, heading to what appeared to be the back of the building. They came to a narrow flight of stairs and he climbed the steps three at a time.

On what must have been the fifth floor, a Fae in dark livery carrying a tray entered the stairwell.

Derek shoved Elena into a corner. His tongue dipped into her mouth as he kissed her deeply. Her body shook, and it wasn't from the Blending or the fear of being caught. There was real emotion behind this kiss, and it stole her breath.

She opened her eyes, which she hadn't realized she'd

closed, to find Derek staring at her, his pupils dilated, his irises rimmed in navy. He held her like that for a moment, waiting for the servant, or whoever, to leave, but his gaze and firm grip on her waist said he'd felt what had passed between them too.

The servant's footsteps faded, and Derek tipped his forehead to hers, but only for a moment. In the next instant, he was climbing again, taking them up two more flights of stairs to the top of the building, which appeared deserted.

Poking their heads inside each door they passed, Derek scouted out the rooms on this level. Several of them seemed to have been recently occupied, but eventually they came to a few with unmade mattresses and dusty antique furniture. All of the rooms were simply furnished: a bed, dresser, maybe a nightstand—what might be found in a servant's wing.

Derek walked through the wall of one of the empty rooms and transformed to solid state before breaking their kiss. He set Elena on the mattress and sank next her, his breathing only mildly elevated despite the running and climbing he'd done. "Are you okay?"

"Yeah, you?"

He nodded and gave her a weary smile. "That was close." He glanced around. "This room's abandoned. If I go alone, I can scout quickly before they search the entire castle. I don't want to leave you, but..."

"No, it's best. You can Blend easier without me. I'll wait here."

He studied her for a moment before nodding. "I'll only be gone a few minutes." He smoothed his hand down her hair where it lay on her back in a mass of waves.

Such a simple gesture, but it made her insides melt.

Standing, he unhooked one of the guns from his belt and handed it to her. "Take this, just in case."

She stared at it with a sense of unease. "Guns won't kill them. If I use it, they'll only come at me more pissed."

"Yeah, but it'll slow them down." He wrapped her hand around the handle, his large palm engulfing her fingers. "I'll feel better if you have it. Use your knives if you need to. Do whatever it takes to remain safe. And don't leave unless you hear someone approach."

"Okay, *Keen*," she teased, but his eyes held too much worry to smile back.

"I'll search for your mother and return in ten minutes. You should be okay until then." He rubbed his forehead, as if reconsidering.

"I will be," she quickly reassured him. "But you need to go. They'll find us if we stand still too long."

He glanced at his phone. "No cell reception, but our phones work. We can keep time. If we get separated—"

"I'll send a signal."

"Elena." His voice had dropped a notch, a warning that had the opposite effect, sending a sultry shiver down her spine.

She smiled. "A teensy-weensy signal to let you know I need you. What's the point of my ability if I don't use it?"

Derek breathed in through his nose and stared at the ceiling. "Because everyone will know where you are." He peered down again. "They're already onto us. Don't use your powers unless you have to. Fae sense your magic, remember? That's how they found you at Dawson to begin with."

Good point. "But my powers have grown. How will they know if it's me, or someone else here? We're in my ancestral castle. Their powers are similar to mine."

He seemed to consider her words for a moment. "Maybe, but don't use your ability unless you absolutely have to. And be careful."

"Aren't I always?" she said sweetly.

"No." He dipped his head and planted a kiss on her brow.

THIRTY-FOUR

Derek scoped out the floor plan of the enormous castle at a dead run, memorizing everything he passed—the most lifesaving use of his photographic memory yet. He'd always had the ability, a gift he'd been born with, not something he'd acquired once he turned eighteen and his Halven powers emerged.

He ran through walls, hopped down flights of stairs, and gathered the layout within the first five minutes. His Fae abilities allowed him to pass through solid surfaces, but he had to focus on doing so, which was why he could stand on solid ground instead dropping through it.

The interior of the New Kingdom castle looked like Emain, with intricate plasterwork and square wooden floors in the formal areas.

Oh, and it was crawling with Fae.

Derek kept to the shadows or leapt through walls when anyone approached. It was bright enough inside the palace that he didn't want to risk being seen in his Blended state. Besides, that one guard outside had seen him, and it had been dark. Not all Newlanders were oblivious to his power.

There were seven floors total. Small bedrooms he assumed were for servants made up the top level where he'd left Elena. The other floors were either for housing various rankings of royalty, congregating, or for supporting various palace jobs. Most of the populace inside the walls appeared to be on the first two levels, half of them organizing a hunt for him and Elena, based on the formations. The rest of the people were in some sort of top-level meeting in a large assembly hall.

Derek followed the flow to the assembly hall and crossed a well-guarded thick metal double door on the heels of a tall Fae. Hundreds of soldiers, legs braced in a stance of relaxed readiness, filled the room—with one woman at the center. She was tall, like the rest of the Fae women, around six feet, with long blond hair pulled into a low ponytail, and she wore a flat gold band on her head.

The soldiers, all men, regarded the woman with an *I will die for you* devoted stare.

She could only be a part of Fae nobility, unless everyone walked around wearing gold crowns. But neither Keen nor Leo had mentioned a queen in charge.

Derek had less than three minutes before he needed to return to Elena. He wouldn't risk leaving her alone a minute longer with Fae actively searching the premises. The search party hadn't reached the upper levels yet, but they would.

If he didn't figure out where Elena's mother was being held now, he'd have to return with Elena later, and that would make staying hidden more challenging. Keeping his head on straight while kissing Elena was no easy feat, and he couldn't maneuver as easily with her in his arms.

He paced to a corner of the room, out of sight of the soldiers but with a clear view of the woman in charge.

"We've isolated brethren presenting with symptoms, as

well as everyone they've been in contact with over the past week," one of the guards said.

"You used the suits and masks I specified?" the woman asked.

"Yes, everything as you ordered, my queen." So she *was* the queen. "Will it contain the virus?"

"I don't know." The woman's mouth pursed as if she were considering. "But it has worked before."

"Before, my lady?"

Her narrow shoulders straightened. "With humans. I lived among them for a time, if you recall, Samuel. The humans deal with disease every day. They have learned to contain infection. The practices we have employed come from my observations during my time in the Earth realm. Most of you believe humans inferior, but there is much to be learned from them."

The soldiers visibly stiffened, glancing at one another.

"Relax. All of you," she said. "I am not suggesting you mingle with humans, merely learn from them." Her gaze slowly touched on several of the soldiers. "Humans have dealt with disease for millennia. The practices they have employed over the last couple of hundred years to slow the spread of disease have saved lives. We must look past our pride, as we have with many of their modern technologies, and utilize whatever means are necessary to save our people."

"My queen," Samuel said, "I speak for the rest of us when I say we understand the unusual circumstances and agree with your logic. The king's passing was a great loss, and proof that we are all vulnerable to this most horrendous attack on our people. It is to our advantage that our new queen holds special knowledge in these matters." He scanned the faces of the soldiers. "As you said, we've adopted technologies humans have created, improving on them, of course. This is no different."

"Thank you, Samuel. I share everyone's desire to destroy those who seek to harm us. The Halven trespassers must be found and interrogated. For now, the best way to fight the enemy is to contain the disease. It is our only chance at survival."

Not their *only* chance. But how would he and Elena get the queen to listen to them? She'd see them as one more threat in an already charged environment. They needed to find and rescue Elena's mother. She was the only Fae who might listen to them.

"You will be our salvation, my queen," Samuel said. "My sincere apologies for the years of mistreatment you suffered."

Whoa, what?

The queen gave a wry smile. "Ironic, is it not? My father confined and punished me for marrying a human, and in the end, my compassion for humans may save us." A murmur of discomfort swept the room, but the queen didn't seem to notice. Or maybe she didn't care.

She couldn't be...

"I imagine the isolation saved me. Had I been allowed to mingle with my family and the others of our court, I would have perished along with them."

The queen was Elena's *mother*? Theodora?

Elena and the woman before him looked so different. The queen had jewel-green eyes with skin as fair as Keen's... but something about her delicate bone structure and the way she carried herself reminded Derek of Elena.

It was possible.

A second woman Derek hadn't noticed among the throng of men stepped forward, her back to him. "Theda, we are most pleased you did not perish with the rest of our leaders and that you stand today as our rightful ruler."

That voice. Familiar, but not familiar.

The woman bowed to the queen, her silver-white hair pulled in a formal knot at the back of her head. She turned and faced the room, and Derek's stomach dropped.

Portia. Here. Referring to the queen as Theda in an informal way, as if they were friends.

Leo said Portia had left Emain for Tirnan and hadn't returned. He thought she'd died from the disease.

Even though there was no communication between the realms, something didn't sit right.

Portia grabbed the queen's hand, smiling with warmth, something Derek had never seen on her face before. And maybe that was why her voice was familiar but different. She spoke in a kinder, softer tone.

And Derek would swear it was fake.

"Thank you, Portia," Theda said. "Your loyalty and friendship goes far in overcoming the past and creating a future for our people. I rely on your strength and integrity." She addressed the rest of the soldiers. "I rely on all your strength, in magic and spirit."

Everyone in the room bowed, and Derek slipped out.

Daylight streamed through the allon trees, and the leaves shuffled to new branches. Elena spun in a slow circle at the edge of the forest and spotted the river Deirdre had called the Fates trickling beyond.

She must be dreaming again.

"Deirdre, are you here?" she whispered, for no logical

reason. This was her dream. She could shout at the sky and no one would hear.

Deirdre floated from behind a particularly large allon, a serene smile on her face. "I am pleased you've made it this far. You must be extremely careful inside the palace walls. Your mother is heavily guarded. Get her alone before you attempt communication."

"How do I get her alone?"

"You underestimate yourself, child. You have an extremely powerful ability." She smiled. "Get creative. You have everything you need to succeed in your mission."

"A few hints wouldn't hurt!" she called as Deirdre's figure wavered, then broke apart into tiny dust motes.

Elena hated it when she did that.

"WAKE UP, BEAUTY. WE GOT TROUBLES." Derek's voice jolted Elena awake.

She had closed her eyes for only a second to try and summon Deirdre, but she didn't actually think she'd succeed and fall asleep. *Crap.* What if the soldiers had found her?

She sat up and pressed her fingers to her eyes, shaking her head to clear it. "What did you find out?"

Derek sucked in a breath. "Well, there's no easy way to put this, but...I think your mom is the new queen."

"*What?*" Elena sat up straighter, her mind instantly alert. "What are you talking about? Keen said she was imprisoned. That we'd have to search the dungeons."

Derek dragged his hand through his hair, squatting to make himself level with her. "I'm sorry, Elena. Her entire family died from the virus. She's the last in the succession.

They made her queen, and from the sound of things, it's a recent turn of events."

"My mother's entire family—is dead?" she said in shock.

He nodded and placed his hand on her leg.

That meant all of Elena's Fae relations were gone. Forever. She'd never know them, and they were the last nobility in New Kingdom—the people she'd hoped would help her gain her powers.

But there *was* one noble left. Her mother. And if Elena didn't do something soon, she'd lose her mom as well. "We'll have to change our plans. At least we don't have to worry about rescuing my mom too."

"Right, we don't have to break her out of prison, but she's also got a million loyal followers protecting her. Followers with Fae standards that include extreme prejudice toward humans. It's a twisted conundrum if you consider she married one." Derek sat beside Elena on the bed. "She's saving New Kingdom by isolating the sick, a practice she learned from her life on Earth. I get the feeling they don't completely trust her because of her past, but they're going along with her commands for now to save their people. Your mom's walking on thin ice. One wrong move and they may revolt."

"My mom... It sounds strange to hear you say that, like she's a living, breathing thing."

Her father had destroyed all pictures and videos of her mother. Given what she now knew, she wondered if he'd done it to protect Elena.

Derek smiled. "She's alive, though..." He sighed and leaned forward, resting his arms on his knees. "They think we're vermin, Elena. This won't be easy. Makes me wish we were back in Emain. Emain Fae are prejudiced bastards, but at least they want to keep you safe. Never thought I'd wish we had Keen with us, but he'd be a good ally right about now."

"No." She shook her head and stood, pulling him up with her. "Keen has to save Reese if I screw things up here."

Derek tucked a lock of hair behind her ear. "You won't screw up. However, when we approach your mother, we have to be careful. She'll be divided, forced with the choice between loyalty to her people, or helping us. Daughter or not, you're a Halven. Your mother's followers won't trust you, they won't trust me, and if she sides with us, they won't trust her either."

"You're right." She paced the room, trying to think quickly. "When Keen told me where to find her, I figured she'd be in bad shape. That we'd be saving her from a terrible life and I'd get my mother back." She stopped and stared at him, her arms hugging her chest. "Now, I don't know what will happen." Elena felt her nose grow warm as she forced back tears. "She doesn't know me. So much time has passed. What if she won't help us?"

Despite her efforts to hold it in, an escapee tear spilled down her cheek. Derek stepped forward and wiped it away with the pad of his thumb, his fingers trailing gently over her chin. "She loves you. Mothers don't stop loving children because they're separated. She'll help us."

He leaned in and kissed her, a delicate sweep of his lips, but it caused heat to spiral through her chest. It was the first genuinely given kiss since the Beatrice incident that hadn't been initiated in order to Blend.

Derek's eyes were warm. Loving. He was here, risking his life for her. Always with that burning heat when he looked at her.

She'd never mistake his loyalty again.

He glanced away and tapped his finger on his leg, which she realized he did when he was thinking. "We need to confront your mother when she's alone, but I'm going to take a random guess and say she's never alone."

Elena swallowed. "No, she won't be. While I slept, Deirdre came to me. She said my mom's heavily guarded. Deirdre told me to use my magic." Elena smiled at the memory. "Get creative."

Derek groaned and shook his head. "That's not a solid plan. That's like telling a toddler to man the barbecue, or giving an arsonist a torch. Anything can go wrong."

Elena crossed her arms. "Hey, I've learned a lot since that day in your lab. Besides, I have an idea. It's not a good idea, mind you, but I think it will work as long as it doesn't piss Theodora off too much. Let's pray you're right about her loving me. Because we'll need all the motherly sentiment we can get."

THIRTY-FIVE

"You're sure you want to do this?" Derek asked for the tenth time.

Elena sighed. "I told you, I'm open to suggestions, but you haven't given me any."

Why was he being so skittish? This was a pretty good plan, all things considered.

"I'm too busy trying to keep my body upright, what with my knees knocking from the four hundred seven-foot-plus Fae guards in residence and the additional two hundred along the perimeter. We're entirely outnumbered."

"But they haven't found us yet, so we're good." She smiled, proud of her sound logic.

"For now. I wouldn't rely on it lasting." Derek stretched his neck, making it crack. "There's something I forgot to mention. I saw Portia. She was the only other woman attending the meeting, and she seemed very chummy with your mom."

"*Portia?* She's alive?"

"Exactly. I've never trusted her, and seeing her all sweet

and supportive of your mother makes me wonder if she's up to something."

An uneasy feeling settled in Elena's bones. Portia had defended Beatrice over the locked library incident, and Beatrice had disappeared under incriminating circumstances…

"What if Portia's working for the other side?"

"It's possible. All the more reason to get to your mom. Come on." He nudged her toward the door. "Let's not worry about that right now. We need to reach Theda."

Elena stopped in front of the door and reached up, wrapping her arms around Derek's shoulders, the warmth of his body easing her distress.

Nothing had gone right since they'd arrived in Tirnan, but they'd made it this far. As long as they were together, everything would be okay. "You're going to get sick of kissing me," she teased, trying to lighten the mood.

Heat filled his eyes and he clenched her waist. "No. I won't." He dipped his head, his mouth scorching her in a deep, languid kiss that sent heat down her chest.

Point taken.

Elena's body tingled and her heart slowed as Derek transformed them.

He skimmed his hands over her hips, beneath her thighs, and picked her up. She clutched the sides of his face, lost in the kiss.

"Elena," he murmured against her lips. "You ready?"

God, right. She opened her eyes and tightened her legs around his torso. Derek walked through the door into the abandoned hallway. From there, he carried her to the third floor of the castle, the level where he'd said the royals slept.

They crept down the hallway, making slow progress as they darted out of the path of sporadic passing Fae. The rooms were farther apart on this level, but one by one, they poked their heads through walls and doors, checking out the space.

Two of the three elaborate apartments were covered in sheets, but the third one, closest to the courtyard, had polished, elegant furniture and at least two guards inside.

Derek clutched the back of her head and pulled them out as one of the soldiers walked toward them and into the bedroom they were staring in. The guard seemed to be coming from a living area.

Derek looked in her eyes and she nodded lightly. These must be the queen's rooms.

He walked down the hall and carefully peered around the corner to the entrance of the suite. Four large Fae stood in front of the door, each sporting swords strapped to their backs. These guards even carried guns on their belts.

Definitely the queen's rooms.

Derek's lips and tongue kept a constant connection with hers while he eyed the guards at the entrance. After a few seconds, he walked back to the bedroom they'd spotted, and stuck their heads through the wall again. The guard who'd been on his way in there must have gone back to the main living area, because the room was empty now.

Derek stepped through, the surface making Elena's skin zing. A canopy bed big enough to accommodate a giant loomed in front of them. But no Fae.

They were safe for now.

Derek strode across the bedroom and peered into the main living area. There were two guards in the suite. One of them stood beside a gold brocade chair, pushing a ruby floor-to-ceiling drape aside while he scanned the area beyond the window.

Emain's interiors were nice, but the New Kingdom's palace stepped it up a dozen or two notches.

The guard at the window moved away and made what appeared to be an orchestrated sweep of the living area along with the other soldier. They took in every detail as they crisscrossed the space, but primarily the two Fae orbited a large chaise... where a beautiful woman sat.

The woman had pale, flawless skin, and wore a thin gold crown on her head, her feet tucked beneath her bottom as she stared at a laptop resting above a pillow on her lap.

She appeared to be no more than a few years older than the students at Dawson—definitely within the realm of college-aged—and she was so beautiful she took Elena's breath away.

Could this really be her mother?

Elena only managed to see the woman's profile from her angle, but something about the lady's face, a slanting of the cheekbone, the angle of her eye, reminded Elena of what she saw when she looked in the mirror.

Elena's lighter shading and hazel eyes came from somewhere, and it wasn't from her father's side of the family. Every Rosales, except for her, had jet-black hair and eyes to match.

Derek used his tongue to caress along the inside of Elena's cheek and mumbled, "Theda," without breaking contact.

Talented boy.

So this was the queen. Her *mother.*

Elena clung to Derek a little too tightly. She was nervous and scared, but it would all work out—it just had to.

Theda's head lowered to the screen in front of her, and

her brow furrowed. "Samuel, why does the west-end portal have only one guard? We're on lockdown because of the breach. Where are the men?"

Elena's fingers dug into Derek's shoulders. *Theda's voice.*

Elena should have been too young to remember the sound of her mother's voice, but she recognized the tone, the cadence when Theda spoke.

Derek's eyes scanned her face. He made a questioning sound in the back of his throat.

There was no time to explain how strange this moment was for her. They needed to forge on. She closed her eyes and gave a quick shake of her head that wouldn't dislodge their connection.

"I do not know, my queen," Samuel said. "There should be at least a dozen. I will speak to the lead guard on the ground and find out what has happened." He exited the room.

This was it. They'd anticipated dealing with interior guards, and now only one remained.

Elena needed just enough time to convince Theda they meant no harm. She hoped a minute was all it would take, because that was probably all they had.

Mouth connected to Derek's, Elena tried to pool her energy while focused on the ceiling.

Nothing happened.

She tried again, but felt none of the power that normally surged beneath her skin when she called her abilities to the surface. Something was wrong.

Crap. She'd wondered if this would happen. There hadn't been time to test every scenario.

Holding Derek's kiss, she squeezed his shoulders and yanked him, jerking their bodies to the side. He followed her lead and carried her away from the door to the back of the room.

Elena broke the kiss, tearing apart their connection.

Derek reemerged instantly. "I hate it when you do that. Feels like I'm being disemboweled. Pinch me next time, before you rip us apart."

"Keep your voice down," she whispered.

He glanced over her head at the door. "What happened? Why didn't you do the waterfall act?"

"I couldn't. Apparently, I can't manipulate the elements if you've got me transformed."

He rubbed his brow. "We can still do this. I'm the only one that needs to be Blended for the sneak attack," he whispered. "We thought there'd be more guards and that we'd need to hide, but there's only one. This could work."

She nodded, and Derek Blended. Elena inched to the open doorway and took a steadying breath. She concentrated on the sensations running through her.

Power billowed beneath her skin, and within seconds, a small cascade of water burst from the ceiling in front of Theda.

Theda yelped and hopped on top of the chaise. She crouched, staring at the flow. "What is going on today?"

The solitary guard standing by the window had spun around and now stood with his sword drawn.

He carefully returned the sword to its sheath. "Plumbing, my lady. I'll get it taken care of immediately." He peered around once more, as if to ensure everything was okay, then strode out of the room.

Before he came back, or another Fae could replace him, Derek quietly appeared behind Theda.

He placed his hand over her mouth and picked her up.

This was the worst part of the plan, but neither of them could think of a way around it.

They didn't want to risk talking to her mother out in the open when neither of them knew who could be trusted. And honestly, they hadn't even been sure they could get Theda alone. There was no guarantee the guards would leave her even for a second. But they had.

Derek acted fast. He couldn't Blend Theda without the extra... ah—*kissing*—connection. But he had her tucked away in the bedroom within seconds.

The moment Derek removed his hand, Theda spun around to glare at him. "Do you know who I—"

"I'm your daughter."

Theda turned slowly, eyeing Elena. "What did you say?"

Derek silently shut the bedroom door.

"Please," Elena said. "We're here to help." She tucked a lock of wavy hair behind her ear, suddenly nervous, and not at all sure how to go about this. "Were you once married to a man named Alex Rosales?"

Confusion and anger warred on Theda's face. "How do you know my husband?"

Elena took a deep breath and squared her shoulders. "I'm his daughter. And that makes you my mother." Elena pulled out her mother's necklace from beneath her clothes. The amethyst in the center winked in the dim light.

Theda's eyes widened. Her gaze rose to Elena's face. "It can't be..."

"Mom"—the name felt foreign on Elena's tongue— "please don't call the guards. They'll kill us if they know we're here. We only want to help."

Her mother gave her a look she couldn't quite read.

If Theda cried out, the game was over. Everything rested on her mother's support. Derek didn't believe Theda would turn on her own daughter, but Elena wasn't so sure. She couldn't predict from one moment to the next what the Fae would do.

"Are you responsible for the pipe bursting?" her mother asked.

"Yes," Elena said meekly. "But it wasn't a pipe bursting. It was a stream of water that only seemed like it came through the ceiling."

"Where is your father, Elena?"

"Dead."

Her mother's head snapped back as if she'd been slapped. Color rose to her cheeks. Her eyes turned suspiciously glossy before she closed them completely. When she reopened them, Elena started.

A world of pain and longing glistened within the green pools of Theda's gaze.

Most Fae hid their emotions to the point that Elena wondered if they had any besides anger and frustration. Theda appeared to control hers equally well, but when Elena had mentioned her father's name—and then his death—Theda's mask had come down.

Elena couldn't breathe, couldn't speak. This woman had cared for her father. *Really cared.* Elena had wondered, regardless of the reasons Leo and Deidre had given for her mother's desertion, but now she knew.

"I am sorry for your loss," Theda finally said, her expression troubled. "How...?"

Elena's chest tightened. "Farm accident. It was a long time ago." Her mother swallowed and looked away. "What matters now is saving you and your people from the virus. I made a promise to Fae in Emain."

Theda looked back at that. "Why? You have nothing to do with the virus."

Elena glanced at the puddle in the main room, and Theda did too. "You have the ability to manipulate the elements," her mother said. "It runs in our family. Several Fae possess this power. Your ability cannot save us from the virus."

"I share your opinion, but apparently the people in charge disagree."

"*I* am in charge." Power surged with her mother's words.

Elena peered at the walls to see if they'd shaken.

She looked cautiously back, not wanting to anger Theda further with her next comment. "I'm not sure you are, and I say that with all due respect. Plan your next moves carefully. We have reason to believe some of your people may work against you."

Elena thought of Portia. She didn't know for a fact that Portia was up to something, but too many things had happened in Emain with Beatrice and the guards who'd attacked them before they left for Tirnan for Elena to believe all Fae were loyal to finding a cure.

Theda chuckled humorlessly. "Of course they do. An entire kingdom wants my demise more than their next breath, but they won't have it."

"I'm aware of the dispute between Old Kingdom and New Kingdom—"

"*Dispute.*" Bitterness seeped from Theda's voice and she shook her head. "It is not merely a dispute, but a history-long loathing between one kingdom and another. There will be no peace. Not in this lifetime, or the next."

"I'm not simply referring to Old Kingdom. I mean here, within these walls. There may be others who are untrustworthy."

How much did Theda know about Portia? Elena had to tread carefully.

She explained to Theda what had happened with Beatrice, and how Fae guards had attacked them before they entered the portal to Tirnan. She also explained her dealings with Portia, and how the Portia they knew in Emain behaved much differently than the one Derek had witnessed here.

Theda's flawless features set in a frown. "Thank you for that information. I will remain guarded. But you must leave, Elena. You cannot stay here." Her mother raised her arm as if to reach out, but quickly lowered it to her side. "You are not safe in Tirnan. That is the reason I left you with your father. You were never safe with me. They would have destroyed you."

"I'm not safe in the Earth realm either. More important, I have an ability the Fae are willing to risk my life for."

Her mother's jaw set. "You will not risk your life. As I said, many Fae possess the power of manipulating the elements, particularly in New Kingdom—"

"Yes, but can they transmute something that has never existed? Leo—I don't know what his last name is—he's one of the Fae who recruited me to Emain. He believes I can create a cure for the virus through transmutation."

"No." Theda shook her head. "It is not possible. My brother was the last to possess the power of transmutation, and he was full Fae. Magic is rare among Halven. Only those with noble blood possess it. That particular ability is unheard of in one such as you. And if it is true"—her face paled—"you are in more danger than I could have imagined."

Her mother reached out, and this time, she grazed a finger on the center stone of the pendant Elena wore. "I thought of you. I always think of you, but particularly on your birthday. I prayed you would be normal. I feared something like this would happen. That they would seek you out."

Theda dropped her hand and balled her fist. "We must hide you." Her voice sounded unsteady, not at all rational.

Elena touched Theda's arm, hoping to get her to listen. "I don't want to hide. The Tertullian Codex indicated that if I came here, I could gain my full powers. I can help you and your people."

Theda put her hand over Elena's. "What you ask will get you killed. Leo—if it's Leo of the Phelans—he knows the risk. He is a good scientist. A moral man. I do not believe he would have sent you on this mission unless the alternative were dire, but"—Theda's voice shook—"I cannot risk your life."

Her mother cared for her as strongly as she'd cared for her father. The notion filled Elena with hope, and it also worried her. Because Elena had to do this.

"You're not risking my life, I am. It's my decision. I'm not a child anymore."

Her mother rolled her lips as if she were holding back emotion. "I understand I missed—everything. But that does not mean I will throw you into a world where you will not survive."

"I'm stronger than I look."

Theda's eyes softened. "I have no doubt, but—"

Elena squared her shoulders. "You won't change my mind. I am here. This is what I'm doing."

To prevent further argument, Elena changed the subject and brought up something her mother had mentioned. "I'm glad to know more of Leo's character. There were times I wasn't sure I could trust him. His determination put me off."

Theda peered at her as if she knew what Elena was doing by changing the subject, but she didn't push it. "Desperation will do that to a person. You understand what we face as a people?"

"Yes. Most will die. Considering the attack we witnessed before we left, I'm not sure even Emain will survive."

Her mother looked away, her gaze disturbed. "That is most unfortunate. Emain was to be the one safe place. Your presence here, and what you suspect of Portia—we are up against a much larger battle than I thought. And my predictions for how this would affect our people were not good to begin with. I've implemented measures that will save some of us, but the majority of the population will perish." Her mother's voice grew clipped. "They do not listen to me. We are an ancient population of millions, and we've lost nearly half, if the numbers are to be believed."

"That's why I'm doing this," Elena said, returning to the subject she'd tried to avoid. "Whatever the risks, I'll take them. Coming here is my fate."

"I did not wish this for you," Theda bit out. "I spent years locked away to save you from this—" She waved her hands around angrily. "I wanted a safe world for my daughter. It is not safe for you here, Elena." Her attention moved to Derek. "Not for your friend, either..." Theda paused and tilted her head. "Who are you, boy?"

"Derek O'Brien."

"No—who *are* you? Your Fae parentage? You look like—"

Pounding came from the locked bedroom door. "My queen, are you safe? I hear voices?"

"I am fine," Theda called out. "This computer is making sounds."

Which it was, Elena realized. Derek had grabbed Theda along with her laptop still in her hands, and the machine was making beeping noises on the ground.

"You have connectivity?" Derek whispered.

"No," Theda said. "Not in the sense you mean. We have electricity and electronics we've mobilized from your world, but not the Internet you speak of. New Kingdom is more modern than other parts of the realm, but there are some technologies even we do not embrace. Our forms of communication are more primitive and, when needed, magical."

Elena glanced at the door. "They can't find us here. Not everyone is loyal to you, and even if they were, they wouldn't support your decision to help us."

"You must leave," Theda said, but Elena got the impression she said it to save Elena and not because her mother feared recrimination from her people. She ushered them to the back of the room, as if hiding them in a corner would help.

Elena halted. "Before we leave the palace, do you have any clue as to how I can gain the rest of my powers? Three things were mentioned in the Tertullian Codex: nobility, ancient, and land—which I took to mean Tirnan. I had a strong feeling I needed to be here, but other than that, I'm lost."

Theda closed her eyes briefly and let out a deep sigh. "I know the answer you seek. But it is pointless for me to tell you. The place you would need to go is dangerous. You would not survive long enough to use the powers, even if you managed to gain them."

Her mother knew?

Elena had hoped her family in New Kingdom could point her in the right direction, but she'd never expected her mother to know exactly how. "Tell me anyway, for the heck of it."

Her mother's mouth softened into the semblance of a smile. "Your uncle often used that expression, *for the heck of it.*"

"My uncle is dead. I don't remember him. Mateo, his son, says it all the time, though."

Theda's expression fell, and her gaze flickered to the wall, where an image of a smiling baby hung. "I left you alone, didn't I?"

"Not entirely, but"—she waited for her mother's head to turn back—"now you understand why I have to save you? Why I must save all of you? We are family. We are connected."

There was a pause, then, "I will tell you what you need to know, on one condition. My guards and I will travel with you and assist you."

That would make her mother an enemy of the people she was supposed to rule.

Elena didn't want Theda in danger, but this was her only hope for saving Tirnan in time. There was no other option.

"Agreed."

"In that case, we will venture to Old Kingdom, where the Ancient Allon grows."

Of course they would, because that was the one place Deirdre had warned Elena never to go.

THIRTY-SIX

Derek grabbed Elena's arm and dragged her to his side while her mother changed in another room. "This is insane. We can't do this. You heard what your mom said about the danger."

"I knew what I agreed to when I came to Tirnan."

His eyes grew worried. "That was when we thought we had a chance at surviving by using my powers. Your mother seems certain you won't make it."

Considering all the warnings Elena had received to not venture into Old Kingdom, there was a distinct possibility she wouldn't come out alive, but... "There has to be a way for us to get what we need and return safely. We can do this, Derek. Look how far we've come. We have my mother's support now. There may be others she trusts who can help us too. We aren't defenseless."

He studied her face. His jaw hardened, but his eyes remained warm and caressing. "I don't like this, but if we go through with it, you have to promise me you'll stay with me at all times. No daredevil maneuvers, or I'll kill you myself." Harsh words, but the hand he placed at her waist rubbed softly up and down her side.

She curled in closer. "I'll stay with you. We'll come up with a good plan, and it will work."

He pulled her to him in a tight hug and kissed her forehead, burying his nose in her hair.

Theda walked out of the changing room, and her eyes flashed distress at the two of them holding each other.

Because Elena was with a guy? Her mother barely knew her, but she seemed to have the mom instincts intact. Or maybe her mother was some sort of Fae Puritan who didn't believe in sex before marriage?

Averting her gaze, Theda addressed the room as she opened a cabinet on the wall filled with knives. "To gain the power you seek, we must access the Ancient Allon inside Old Kingdom, as I mentioned. All allon leaves are life-giving, but the Ancient Allon connects mystically with the realm's life force. Its leaves, in particular, enhance magic.

"I've called to Samuel. He and his team will escort us to the border."

Elena eased away from Derek, who had a vise grip on her waist. "You called to him? Is he a telepath?"

"No." She turned and faced Elena. "We only have a handful of mentalists in our kingdom, and no one with that ability. I used allon leaves and my magic to reach out to him. My magic transcends language barriers. I can send messages to anyone through the leaves, including animals." Her mother paused and her brow furrowed. "How do you know about telepaths?"

"My bodyguard in Emain is a telepath."

"He must be from the Old Kingdom." She shook her head slowly. "You know more about our kind than most Halven."

This seemed as good a time as any to ask something she had wondered about. "Did my father know what you are?"

Theda froze in the act of attaching a sharp little knife to her belt. "No. I believed I could keep you both safe by not telling him." She resumed attaching the knife, and grabbed two others, affixing them stealthily beneath her clothes. "It became apparent that if I stayed any longer, there would be terrible consequences. Your father knew something of my past. He may have suspected more than I told him. Enough to know the importance of keeping you protected."

Elena peered at the black and white sketch her mother had glanced at earlier. The rough drawing, framed in velvet and gold, looked uncannily like Elena's baby pictures.

A rush of confused emotions flooded her: happiness, sadness, and, finally, frustration.

"What happened? How did you meet my dad? Why did you leave us?"

Theda's eyes glossed over as she gazed at Elena with something close to desperation. "I never wanted to leave you and your father. I would have done anything to stay with you." She thrust another knife into her belt. "I had no choice but to leave before you were discovered." She paused and gave a delicate sniffle, shifting a sleeve that cloaked a small gun attached to her forearm. "It seems you were found regardless of my sacrifices. And now you are here," she said flippantly, but with an underlying edge.

Theda swiped at her eyes and stared at Elena. "I met your father after the king, my father, promised me to a man I detested. I ran and escaped to the Earth realm through Emain. I traveled down the California valley." She looked away, a small smile on her lips. "I hid inside unlocked storage sheds at night. It was nothing like what I was used to. I don't know where I thought I was going. I suppose anywhere seemed preferable to returning home." She looked back at Elena. "Your father, Alex, found me in one of those sheds. He worked for the man who owned the land. Alex was very handsome, and—ah, charming."

She turned back to the weapons case and pulled another knife from the cabinet. "We were married shortly after."

Elena's brow furrowed. "That seems kind of quick for someone escaping another marriage. What was the rush?"

The side of her mother's face turned pink, and a niggling suspicion entered Elena's mind.

"You weren't—you couldn't have been—" Elena started, then stopped, unsure how to proceed without insulting Theda.

Her mother's shoulders squared and she lifted her chin, still not looking Elena in the eye.

"He knocked you up?" Elena blurted, forgetting all manners.

Theda frowned. "I never liked that human expression. But yes, technically, we were expecting. We were in love and overjoyed at the prospect of having a child. Marriage was a natural transition."

Sex before marriage. *Not a Puritan, then.*

Samuel walked silently into the bedroom, quickly scanning the area, then gazing at Theda in a guardian sort of way—and, if Elena wasn't mistaken, a not-so-guardian way.

Samuel was attractive, with dark blond hair and a strong, bulky build. His nose was a little large for his face, but his lips were full and sensual. He looked to be about her mother's age, maybe a little older, and he had an air of stability and quiet strength.

Theda had been gone seventeen years, but the idea of

her mother with someone other than Elena's father was too weird to contemplate right now.

"What's our plan?" Derek asked.

"There is a portal from the castle to the Bridge of Fates that divides our two kingdoms, but we won't use it," Theda answered. "The portals are heavily guarded, or at least, they should be…" A worried expression crossed her face before she regained her composure. "We'll travel on foot. After night falls, you'll cross the bridge of the Fates River that divides our lands and enter Old Kingdom. Oldlanders will know immediately of your arrival because of the Presence Charm, which reacts to intrusions magical or corporeal, but at night, Derek's ability will help keep you hidden."

"That doesn't sound like much of a sneak attack," Derek said.

She turned to him. "There is no way to *sneak* into Old Kingdom. Just as there is no way to sneak into New Kingdom."

"What about Sunland?" Elena asked. "Would it be easier to enter Old Kingdom from there because they're more peaceable?"

"Anyone may enter Sunland, but no one can enter Old Kingdom or New Kingdom without our knowledge, followed by the full force of our armies, such as they are after the disease."

"This is ridiculous," Elena huffed. "We're trying to save everyone. Why won't they let us do our jobs? Why do the kingdoms hate each other so much?"

Her mother peered wearily at Samuel as his mouth formed a straight line. "There is the prejudice toward Halven—" Elena opened her mouth to say something, and Theda raised her hand. "I understand the hypocrisy of it.

Fae created Halven, but it doesn't change their beliefs. Our people strive to keep the bloodlines as close to pure as possible."

"As close to their angelic ancestors, you mean?"

"Yes. And that plays into the differences between the kingdoms. The wars waged in heaven among the angels were brought to Tirnan. Descendants of the different angelic factions created their own kingdoms, and fight to this day. That is why there is very little mixing, and why our powers can be traced by kingdom. Suffice it to say, deep hatred has existed for thousands of years. If our people survive the disease, there will be a reckoning between the kingdoms the likes of which no human can fathom. It will make your world wars look like a skirmish in comparison. Everyone within the realm will be affected, even the docile Sunlanders. No one will be safe."

"What a waste of time, trying to save a group of people determined to kill each other anyway."

"There is always hope, Elena. It was the one thing I clung to all the years of my confinement, and here I am, reunited with my daughter." Her mother gave a sad yet determined smile. "Never give up."

Her mother was right. Theda had suffered in ways Elena couldn't imagine, and had not only survived, but had also prevailed and become queen.

There was a chance Fae could overcome their differences, including their prejudice toward Halven. Elena saw it in the way Keen and even Leo had softened toward her. They hadn't reached the level of believing Halven equals, but there was hope there.

Theda looked at Samuel. He nodded as though reading her silent thought.

"We'll send two of our men with you into Old Kingdom

to create a distraction." She turned to Derek. "The guards said you transformed my daughter after you exited the portal. Transform her with you once you cross the bridge. They won't see you and Elena if you keep to the shadows along the forest line. Old Kingdom guards will catch sight of our soldiers and take them for the intruders. As long as you remain transformed, there is a chance they will not search for you. The Presence Charm is not so specific as to identify numbers or locations of trespassers, and once you reach the castle boundary, you will become a part of the kingdom's inhabitants. The charm will no longer react to your presence."

The plan sounded dangerous for her mother's people. "When they see your soldiers, what will happen to your kingdom? Will it cause a battle?"

"That is a possibility, but I do not believe it likely. Only two of our men will enter, and they will be wearing commoner clothing and quickly depart the land. It will appear more of an accident than an attack. War is unavoidable, but neither kingdom wishes to be the one to initiate it. Nor are we prepared, with our men and women dying."

Theda grabbed one last knife, a fancy-looking ice-pick thing, and sheathed it beneath her sleeve. She closed the cabinet, apparently sufficiently armed.

The clothing her mother had changed into was different from the clothing Elena wore in Emain and what she'd seen of the New Kingdom inhabitants. Baggy and earth-toned, the two-piece set Theda wore appeared a cross between a Chinese peasant outfit and a *Star Wars* Jedi uniform, with a belt in the middle and the secret pockets her mother had tucked weapons into.

Theda removed her thin gold circlet and handed it to Samuel. Samuel, wearing the male version of the commoner clothing, carried the crown out of the master suite, presumably to somewhere safe. Theda placed a brown hat on her head that would have resembled an old-fashioned pillbox, if it hadn't been for the flaps hanging over her ears and the leather cords that tied beneath her chin.

"Derek's ability to keep you hidden is your best asset for staying alive," she said. "Follow the Fates River. It leads directly to the castle. Breach the castle, but do not approach the Ancient Allon unless it is dark outside. If the sun grows high on the horizon, hide yourselves in the castle. Old Kingdom castle is not as large as the New Kingdom palace, but it is large enough that one could become lost, or, in your case, hidden."

This was a lot of information to remember, and they needed to leave before they were discovered. Derek probably had it all down with his amazing memory, but Elena didn't. "Should you be telling us all of this now? Why not wait until we get to the river?"

"We'll go over it again at the river, but there is no margin for error. And I don't know what troubles we may run into along the way. Should anything happen to me, I want you to have the information. It is my gift to you."

Elena pushed back the tears that had suddenly welled behind her eyes. Her mother didn't know her, but she was going to risk her life for Elena.

"The Ancient Allon," Theda continued, "is the oldest allon in Tirnan. It grows directly through the center of the castle and out the roof. An invisible barrier allows nature's elements to filter to the tree while protecting the castle against cold and rain. The tree is visible from every floor, but can only be accessed from the trunk located on the first level. Guards protect the tree at all hours. Were it not for

Derek's gift, there would be no way to reach the leaves without discovery." Theda smiled at Derek. "A fortuitous ability you possess. Even so, you must climb at night, when the likelihood of discovery is at its lowest. Our people in New Kingdom have a more difficult time identifying your disguise, because few possess the same magic. Many have mental abilities similar to yours in Old Kingdom, and they'll be able to see you."

Samuel returned and Theda nodded to him, though he hadn't said a word. She walked over to stand beside him.

"The rooms inside the Old Kingdom castle are lit by fire and are dimmer than what we have here. Old Kingdom has access to electricity, of course, but they choose the old ways." Theda sighed in exasperation. "Under any other circumstance, the fact would baffle me, but in this case I am glad they cling to old customs. It will help you maintain your disguise. When you approach the tree, remember the changing of the leaves. The shifting is a part of the allon's magic. The leaves change every forty-five seconds. Climb the tree and gather five leaves immediately after a shift, then run from the premises as quickly as possible. Samuel and I will wait for you on the other side of the bridge, where I will show Elena what to do from there."

Theda held Elena's gaze, her eyes intent. "Do not get caught. Should anything go wrong, *run*. Leave with Derek and do not return. I will find you."

Elena smiled, trying to reassure her mother, though she didn't know why. She barely knew her mom. Maybe every child had an innate desire to shield a parent from worry. "The plan sounds simple enough, as long as we remain disguised."

"The plan may sound simple, but it is not." Theda

peered at Derek. "Do not leave her alone. Your parentage may save both of your lives if you should run into trouble."

Derek grew visibly skeptical. "My dad's a cardiologist. I'm not sure how that's gonna save us."

"Your human father may be a cardiologist, but your Fae father... If my guess is correct, he is nothing short of my sworn enemy."

Derek's face turned to stone, taking on a grayish hue. He stared at Theda as if she'd told him his house was on fire.

Portia had made a comment in Emain when they'd first agreed to help the Fae, about the person Derek had gotten his temper from. Elena hadn't thought much of it at the time, because she hadn't understood it. But now she wondered. Had Portia been referring to Derek's biological father?

Theda smiled. "I do not hold it against you. You are here to protect my daughter, and for that I am forever grateful."

Derek held up a hand. "Wait—maybe you should tell me who you think my father is."

Theda took Derek in from head to toe. "Your stature is not as grand, though you are young and still growing, but your face is nearly identical to that of Osulf Niall."

Derek shrugged. "And he is...?"

The name meant nothing to Elena either.

"The Old Kingdom's ruler."

Elena clenched Derek's hand when he didn't seem able to move or take a breath.

Theda looked at him with sad eyes. "It is unfortunate the two of you have become... friends, but fate makes fools of us all sometimes. Let us hope your differences continue to complement one another and do not put you at greater risk."

Derek's grip tightened on Elena. "How can you be so certain I'm the king's son?"

"I am not certain, but the pieces of the puzzle fit. There was a time when Old Kingdom and New Kingdom had reached a truce. I was a child then, but I remember it clearly, for it was the only time we lived amicably. The kingdoms allowed egress between the lands during the truce. Nobility from each side came to know one another. Your father was older than me—closer to middling years—but very handsome. I remember his face well from those encounters."

Theda looked down, as if thinking back. "Later on, rumors spread that a human bore Niall his only child. He is said to have searched for his child for years." She looked straight at Derek. "By the look of you, my guess is that the child has found the father instead."

CHAPTER

THIRTY-SEVEN

Derek sank into a squat and locked his hands behind his neck, taking in deep breaths. A part of him had always wondered who his true parents were. Never had he imagined this.

Elena rested her hand on his back and rubbed his spine up and down, her touch warm and comforting. "Are you okay?" she whispered.

He shook his head.

"Do you really think the king would help us if he thought Derek was his son?" she asked her mother.

"There is a chance I am wrong and Derek is not who I think he is. Either way, it is safer that you do not alert the king to the possibility of Derek's identity. Unless all hope is lost."

Theda paced a few steps. "The Oldlander king is self-absorbed and greedy. He's been known to show little or no mercy toward others. He has searched for his son at great length." Her face filled with compassion. "I'm sorry, Derek. If he discovers you are his child, he will not easily release you."

Derek slowly raised his head and unfolded his body. The muscles in his jaw tightened as fury built in his chest. Elena needed him. The Oldlander king was mistaken if he thought he would ever leave her.

Which meant Derek needed to keep his identity a secret, even if they were caught. "It's getting light out. I'm assuming we have a long way to travel. We should go if we want to rest before it's dark."

Minutes later, Derek Blended with Elena in his arms and followed Theda and Samuel through a secret passageway. The four of them slipped out of the palace and beyond the cement wall that protected New Kingdom castle.

They traveled at a brisk pace while the sky slowly lightened, the strange red stars disappearing against the blue.

Theda explained before they left how few people traveled at night, but that they rose early with the sun. The roads in Tirnan didn't have modern highway lighting, so commoners kept to country hours, rising early and returning home before twilight.

It would be bright out soon, and in a little while they would have to stop and hide for a few hours, which would give Elena time to sleep. Derek couldn't remember the last time she'd slept for long. A lot had happened since then. She needed her strength.

Hidden in the forest, Samuel's team of twenty of the queen's trusted soldiers guarded Derek, Elena, and her mother from afar as they traveled. They joined the men in the forest to rest when the sun rose too high in the sky to go any father without being seen.

Derek sat against a tree and Elena leaned into him, her head against his shoulder. She was asleep in seconds, but his mind spun. He couldn't stop thinking about his true father and what it all meant.

He must have dozed, because the next thing he knew the soldiers were departing and Theda was speaking silently to Samuel. She drank from a leather pouch and appeared to point out a path through the woods.

Elena rubbed the sleep from her eyes. She brushed off the needles clinging to her clothing and approached her mother.

"We must go," Theda said. "It is still light out, but the sun grows low. We will remain along the forest edge and tread carefully. The bridge is only a few miles away."

The sky darkened as they made their way through the woods close to the road. Their pace was slower, but eventually, they saw the bridge off in the distance.

Derek could tell something was different about the Bridge of Fates. It may have looked like a crusty old brick arch, like something from an Irish pasture, but a powerful force drifted from it. The force brushed in sizzling waves against Derek's skin, sending the distinct message that this crusty old bridge was not to be messed with.

Theda made a sharp left, heading deeper into the woods, and they soon arrived at a whitewashed two-story cottage.

"The Gatekeeper's Hovel," she announced.

The hovel looked as ancient as anything Derek had seen while traveling through the Irish countryside with his parents years ago.

"This dwelling resides on our land," Theda explained, "but during the peace accord, a gatekeeper lived here and collected a toll to cross the bridge. As you would expect, the hovel is abandoned now. We are safe here to go over the plan again and eat before you venture across the bridge."

They followed Theda toward the hovel, but about ten

yards from the old building, the hairs on the back of Derek's neck stood at attention.

He stopped and looked around. "Are you sure no one's here?"

Theda gave him a reassuring smile. "Few remember the existence of the Gatekeeper's Hovel, and those who do are too busy fighting the disease to worry about an abandoned house."

Despite Theda's words, something about the place seemed off. He made certain to enter the building before Elena, and stood in front of her while he took in the space.

Samuel closed the door behind them. The air in the center of the room shimmered. That was when Derek knew his instincts had been right.

A liquid wall dropped from the ceiling like a heavy velvet drape, a dozen soldiers standing armed and ready for battle on the other side. Along with Portia.

Elena tried to step around Derek, but he put his arm out, forcing her to stay behind.

"It's about time you arrived," Portia said.

Derek glanced out the windows. More armed Fae surrounded the house.

Portia smirked. "I'm surprised you didn't sense the glamour that hid my team, Theda. Then again, glamours are *my* specialty. And my daughter's." She stared at Derek. "You remember Beatrice, don't you, Derek?"

His body tensed. *Her daughter?* How long had Portia been planning to betray them? From the beginning?

"I planted men in area farmhouses as well, but I figured this would be the most likely place for you to bring the Halven. You always were predictable, Theda. Until you ran off with that human." Disgust oozed from Portia's words.

"When they told me Halven had come through one of

the portals, I'd hoped it was one of Marlon's disciples, and that they'd do my job for me and have you killed." She gazed at Elena. "It seems it was only your daughter." Portia shrugged, her mouth twisting in a happy little grin. "Ah well, I wanted to get rid of her too. Kill two birds with one stone, as the human saying goes." She tapped her chin. "You know, I've come to appreciate the human metaphor. Very clever."

Theda slowly shook her head. "Why? We took you in and treated you as one of our own after your grandfather escaped Old Kingdom. We built centuries of trust between our families. Was it all a lie?"

Portia's smile faded, replaced with cold malice. "Had my grandfather remained in Old Kingdom, I could have been a princess—a queen! Yet it was you who were given every privilege imaginable, only to waste yourself on a human." Her mouth puckered. "There is no accounting for taste."

Samuel shifted. It was subtle, but Derek caught it. And so did Portia, apparently.

"Ah, ah, ahhh." She wagged her finger and waved a guard forward.

The guard stripped them of their weapons.

Portia fingered the hilt of a knife strapped to one of the Fae guards beside her. "I walked among you, Theodora, but I was not one of the *great New Kingdom nobles*. When I heard of your disgrace and what you gave up to be with *that man*, I knew my time had come."

"You were given the same privileges I was. Why betray your leader? The palace cared for you and your family."

Portia's nostrils flared. "My ancestors are only once removed from our ancient forefathers, and I was treated as second best to you. What makes you better than me? Nothing, I tell you! I am more clever, more powerful than your silly ability to speak with the animals." She turned her back to them, seemed to compose herself, then spun back around. "It's more about what should have been mine. New Kingdom royals needed a change of blood. A cleansing, if you will, and my line is the one to replace the line you've tainted. You are not fit to rule."

"That is not your decision to make," Theda said. "Not even I can make that decision. The angels did when they bestowed the kingdoms and land upon us."

Portia raised her chin. "Our forefathers are gone and have left us to rule our land. And rule we shall." She looked at Derek. "It was simple to convince your insane but brilliant Halven mentor to create the virus for us. He, like so many, would do anything to gain access to Tirnan. Of course, he may have been misled as to the power he'd wield here, but he'll discover that soon enough."

She sighed dramatically and stared directly at Theda. "For now, no one but me and a few select Fae know how this will play out. Of course, I would never have sanctioned the creation of such a virus unless I could immunize those I wanted to keep around. But you're not one of them."

Derek's mind raced. Portia had the antivirus. Her own blood must contain the antibodies. But weaponless and surrounded, they were in no position to do anything about it.

"You are alive, Theodora, because of the irony of life. The isolation imposed on you for your misdeeds spared you from the virus. Until now." The guards behind Portia raised their weapons. "You will die today, and I and the leaders I've chosen will control New Kingdom, as is my destiny."

Derek caught a movement in his peripheral vision.

Theda had lifted her hands. She held them cupped around her mouth, as if to call to someone at a great distance.

Portia chuckled humorlessly. "Don't bother trying to beckon the others with your silly communication ability. The soldiers hiding in the woods have already been disposed of."

Theda's eyes narrowed on Portia, and then her chest fell as she let out a burst of breath into her palms, a faint puff of powder escaping the gaps between her fingers. Only then did she lower her hands to her sides.

Portia glanced up as if exasperated. "You know, before I smite you, I must say, your daughter and her Romeo were an interesting twist."

She turned to Derek. "I hadn't planned on your involvement. I considered it best to keep you out of it with the knowledge you possessed of Marlon's work. But then you insisted on following Elena the day we sent for her." She shook her head.

Elena was still partially hidden behind his back, though she kept trying to change that and inch around him. Stubborn girl. He was trying to protect her, and she chose now to get feisty? No matter how hard she pinched him to get him to move aside, he didn't budge.

Portia swept her gaze across them. "The three of you have given me no small measure of amusement, but I'm afraid the fun must end." Portia signaled, and the guard in front of Derek raised his crossbow.

Portia's guard aimed his weapon at Derek's chest, and the faint sound of angry dogs barking snapped Elena from her fear-induced paralysis.

She didn't think. She acted.

Elena jumped on Derek's back, ripped his shirt down, and said, "Run," a split second before she bit into his muscled shoulder.

Derek jerked at the impact, but quickly wrapped his arm behind her, at the same time the sensation of Blending took over.

Elena tasted the copper flavor of his blood running over her tongue, and felt the whiz of arrows and swords through her Blended body as Derek ran for the opposite wall. They passed through weapons, Portia, the guards, and anything else that stood in their way. Her flesh zapped like static electricity as they swept through live bodies, but finally they made it to the outer wall and beyond.

The sound of dogs barking grew louder outside, but Derek didn't stop. Not even when a flash of fur swept past her.

Teeth embedded in his flesh, Elena rolled her eyes to the side. Dozens of—not dogs, something else—passed them. Their bodies resembled stout, hairless pigs, held up by powerful, heavily muscled legs. The muzzles were shaped like those of a pit bull—all jaw—with long, sharp teeth like a lion. The beasts sniffed the air, seemingly sensing her and Derek's presence, but they didn't stop to attack. They continued on toward the Gatekeeper's Hovel.

Seconds later, high-pitched squeals rang out, the kind an injured animal makes.

Theda had said she could speak to animals. Had she summoned the beasts? Would they protect her?

Her mother could survive injuries, but there were so many soldiers and they'd taken her weapons.

Theda and Samuel were trained to fight. She had to

remember that and not think about worst-case scenarios, or fear would freeze her like it had inside the hovel.

She peeked over Derek's shoulder, careful not to loosen the tenuous connection she had to him. They were almost to the Bridge of Fates, and suddenly all the warnings to not cross the bridge pummeled Elena's mind. She sucked air in through her nose, holding on to Derek as tightly as she could, her eyes closed. She felt him sprint up the cobbled slope, oblivious to her fears, and jump off the other end.

When she opened her eyes, they were on the other side of the bridge. In Old Kingdom.

Derek raced toward the forest Theda's soldiers were supposed to have used to divert the guards. Her mother's men would have looped around south and crossed the bridge back into New Kingdom, but Derek ran at a northern angle toward the castle, delving deep into the forest until the dense canopy of trees choked off the sunlight.

Elena didn't dare look back. She kept her teeth lodged in Derek's shoulder, blood running down her chin. It was a crude way to create a physical connection, but it was the best she could come up with while a crossbow was aimed at Derek's chest.

She couldn't see or hear anyone, her view narrowed to the small slit above and slightly to the side of Derek's shoulder, but Theda had said the castle would dispatch soldiers as soon as they entered the land. She and Derek wouldn't be alone for long.

After what seemed like ten miles of thick forest passing them by, Derek slowed and stopped in front of a tree with a large hole at the base. The tree resembled a huge pine, with a trunk like an upside-down mushroom.

He turned them solid and Elena unlocked her teeth

from his shoulder and slid down his back. Her jaw had cramped and a spasm of pain shot down her neck.

Concerned about his shoulder, she held his T-shirt away and watched as the wound stopped bleeding, the edges slowly knitting together.

Her body would heal this quickly too. The pain in her jaw was already ebbing.

Derek turned to face her, his breathing slightly elevated.

"Sorry about the bite." She wiped blood from her chin. "It looks like it's heal—"

Before she could finish, Derek grabbed her waist and pulled her close. He buried his face in her neck, running his mouth along her jaw, kissing her skin in desperate brushes of his lips until he reached her mouth, coming down hard. His tongue dipped inside, and his hand cradled the back of her head.

Elena's heart raced and she tangled her tongue with his, desperate for the connection and comfort he offered.

If she had acted one second later inside the hovel...

Derek raised his head, his breathing elevated. "I appreciate the improvisation, but I think I prefer your kisses."

Elena sank into his arms and he tightened his hold on her, tucking her head in the crook of his neck.

He dipped his face into her hair and breathed in through his nose. His body trembled. "Elena—"

For a moment, she just stood there, allowing his unspoken words to seep through her skin along with his warmth. They had almost been separated in the most permanent way imaginable—and the idea had desperation bubbling up inside her.

She wanted to tell him how she felt, that she loved him, even though he could be bossy and overprotective. But telling him now while their lives were in extreme danger might not come across as genuine. And her feelings for him were the one sure thing inside the mercurial world of Fae and magic that had become a part of her life.

"Are we safe?" she whispered.

"I think so. For now." He raised his head and looked around.

She wanted to yank his face back, to feel his breath in her hair, on her skin—active reminders he was alive and well.

"We'll wait here until dark." He peered up through the trees at the dimming light. "Another hour or so."

He guided her to the hole at the base of the tree, tearing away branches and exposing more of the opening.

Half the trees in the forest were allon, the rest this weird variant of pine.

Derek peeked inside, then turned and gave her a lopsided grin. "Welcome to my Tirnan lair." He waved his hand across the opening. "Care to join me for some refreshments?"

She smiled weakly and got on her hands and knees near the opening. The smell of dirt, pine, and mildew assaulted her nose. "I hope you have a couch in here."

"I'll add that to the list next time."

He followed her in and covered the hole behind them with the branches he'd removed.

Derek leaned against the wall of the trunk, pulled out two food packs, and handed her one, along with a flat metal water bottle from a strap beneath his clothes.

Elena reached over and pushed up his shirt. "What else do you have under there?"

He cut her a flirty grin she caught now that her eyes had adjusted to the darkness inside the tree. "Come closer and I'll show you."

He slid her to his side, and she curled into him. They sat like that for a while, neither of them moving.

"Derek—do you think they made it?"

She looked up, and he was frowning at the freeze-dried packet in his hand.

He let out a long breath. "I don't know. Your mom's resourceful and strong, and she had Samuel with her. She didn't expect things to go perfectly, which was why she gave us instructions back at the palace before we even got here. She must have had a contingency plan. The best we can do is continue on to Old Kingdom castle and collect the leaves. We have to create that antidote. Until that's done, no one is safe."

He was right. She sat back and opened her food packet. As nervous as her stomach was feeling, the last thing she wanted to do was eat, but she needed the energy. Elena ate-drank the mushy contents of the packet in small increments. The stuff was disgusting.

Derek polished off one of the packets and grabbed another. "The kingdom may know we're here, but there's still a chance we can get in and out without them finding us."

They were at a disadvantage with their presence officially recognized, but that would have been the case no matter what. The only difference now was that Old Kingdom was looking for Derek and Elena instead of her mother's soldiers, like they'd planned.

"What do you think about what my mother said— regarding your real father?"

Derek's face hardened. "My father's in Ohio. *If* what your mother says is true, the person who donated sperm means nothing to me."

"So you won't tell the king who you are?"

"No way. It would only make things more difficult. You heard what your mom said about him searching for his son. If he thinks it's me..." He shook his head. "I don't want any part of that."

He finished the other food packet and started on his third. Derek didn't seem to mind that it was barely edible.

Men.

He turned to her, their faces only inches apart. "We can do this, Elena. Your mom told us how to sneak past Old Kingdom guards to get to the tree. We grab the leaves and we get out."

"Blending via kissing instead of biting, preferably." She smiled.

His lips quirked and he tossed his empty food packages over his shoulder. He leaned in and pecked her lips. "Kissing's good." He dipped his head, his nose tickling her neck. "Nibbling's not bad either."

Elena leaned back to give him better access, because whatever he was doing sent shivers down her chest and limbs, her skin oversensitized after their brush with death.

It felt good to be in Derek's arms again. Because he wanted to be there and not because they needed to Blend. She'd not trusted Derek about Beatrice. She wouldn't make that mistake again.

His fingers trailed down the base of her throat, pushing aside the pliant Fae material, along with her bra. He swept kisses and tongue along the delicate skin of her breast.

Elena gripped his biceps and dragged him closer until he was half lying on her. She needed this—needed to remember they were alive and that not all hope was lost. They'd never survive if she allowed herself to doubt even for a second.

Elena's breaths quickened when Derek rolled them to

the side and grabbed her bottom, bringing their bodies together. She ran her hands up his broad shoulders, over his neck and into his hair that smelled faintly of soap. As much as she wanted him, they couldn't afford to be distracted like this. They should stop before things went too far.

"Derek," she said, resigned.

He stilled, then groaned. He gave her one last kiss and eased onto his back, throwing an arm over his eyes. "I know," he said hoarsely. "Bad timing. I'll be good." His arm dropped back and he slid her a look. "We're okay, though?"

He was talking about them as a couple, not the team taking down a deadly virus.

"Yeah. We're good." She smiled and pressed in close, resting her head on his chest. He wrapped his arms around her, and soon Derek's low, even breathing began to lull her. She couldn't keep her eyes open any longer.

She wondered briefly if that would be a bad thing, but before she could decide, sleep took her.

CHAPTER

THIRTY-EIGHT

Derek shook Elena awake, adrenaline pounding through his veins. How long had they slept?

He didn't remember falling asleep—damn sleep deprivation. They could have been out for hours. He'd awakened to the sound of a twig snapping outside their tree. Peeking through the hidey-hole to check it out, he hadn't seen anything. But that didn't mean much.

The forest was dark. Anyone could be out there and he wouldn't know it. More importantly, they had to race to the castle now that it was full night.

Despite the time difference in Tirnan, they only had so long before harm would come to Reese on Earth. And every day it took them to find a cure, more Fae died. The next could be Elena's mother. If she'd survived the attack.

Derek hadn't wanted to worry Elena, but he didn't think it likely that Theda and Samuel had made it out of the Gatekeeper's Hovel. But that wasn't something he wanted to bring up when she'd only just reunited with her mother.

"What's wrong?" Elena sounded groggy, but she sat up quickly. "What time is it?"

Derek considered the amount of fatigue left in his system and estimated they had a few more hours before sunrise. There was no way of knowing for sure, since his cell phone had stopped working.

He put a finger to his lips. "Time to go," he whispered. "Check your cell phone. Mine died."

She attempted to turn her phone on, but the screen wouldn't light up. They should have turned them off to conserve batteries. *Hindsight.*

"A sound outside woke me. I don't know if anyone's out there. It's tight in here, but I'd feel better if we Blended inside the tree. Hop on my lap."

Elena's eyes narrowed and she gave him a questioning smile.

As if he could think of *that* right now.

Okay, he could, but he was capable of pushing it to the back of his mind in an emergency. He dropped his chin and leveled a frown at her. "I don't mean it that way."

Later on he would mean it that way, but not right now.

Elena maneuvered onto his lap, facing him. She wrapped her legs around his waist. Under less dangerous circumstances, the position would have wreaked erotic havoc inside his mind. Right now his heart thrummed from adrenaline, not lust.

Okay, some lust, but mostly fighting adrenaline.

Derek cradled her face with his hands and kissed her.

Elena pulled back. "Wait—the biting thing worked. We could try something else besides kissing, if that makes it easier. I could... put my finger in your mouth? Or your ear? I don't know, something so you can see better."

Let's see... kiss Elena or have her finger in my ear. "I'll stick with kissing. I've gotten used to maneuvering around with it. I can manage."

She smiled as though she could see through to his motivation. And yeah, he was probably transparent, but what sane guy wouldn't be?

He pressed his mouth to hers, and Elena's lips moved rhythmically with his to keep the connection. He ignored the automatic heat her mouth sent through his body, and kept fear of capture at the forefront of his mind.

Derek couldn't risk anything happening to Elena, and not just because she was the key to saving them. She was a part of his life now. How could he ever have considered leaving her to attend a different school? He'd been bitter after she refused to believe him about Beatrice. At the time, moving to a different school seemed like a solution to his problems. Now, he regretted ever saying it. He wouldn't leave her as long as she wanted him near.

Derek Blended and passed through the tree with Elena in his arms. He bolted across miles of forest until he came to the clearing.

The Fates River swept southeast in a steady stream. Keeping to the tree line, Derek saw several dark figures patrolling the area, and down farther toward the bridge. Supposedly, more soldiers would be scouting the woods, but he hadn't encountered any on his way out. The forests in this realm were massive, which helped.

Derek headed north toward the Old Kingdom castle. He remained in the shadows of the trees, careful to steer clear of the guards and the moonlight.

Soon, he and Elena closed in on a massive gray structure up ahead. The castle loomed before them, reminding Derek of Hunyad in Romania, only bigger.

Derek had visited Hunyad Castle with his parents—the place where Vlad the Impaler had been imprisoned for seven years. Hunyad had creeped him out then, just as Old Kingdom castle did now.

A dark, stagnant moat surrounded the castle, giving off the scent of sulfur and rotting vegetation. Night hindered visibility, but the structure appeared to have several turrets or towers along the perimeter—and a large billowy center jutting into the sky.

The billowy center must be the Ancient Allon. Theda had said it grew right through the middle of the castle.

From what Derek could tell, the castle had about six levels and stood roughly twelve stories high, taller if you factored in the turrets. The tree must be at least two hundred feet in height.

Derek scrambled down the moat and up the other side, passing seamlessly through the water as if he was water too. He came to a large stone wall, similar to the one that surrounded the New Kingdom palace.

Shifting Elena in his arms, he noticed two guards approaching him from either end. They walked at a leisurely pace, taking in the foreground, probably making rounds. Soon they would crisscross right in front of him. Standing exposed out in the moonlight, Blended or not, wasn't a good idea.

Derek quickly stepped through the wall to avoid the guards—and landed in a beehive of Fae soldiers.

Just like at the New Kingdom palace, a couple hundred heavily armed Fae milled about on the Old Kingdom berm. Heart hammering, Derek flattened his shoulders against the stone wall and tightened his hold on Elena. He looked for patterns, a way to cross the yard without attracting attention.

Some soldiers stood in pairs, scanning the grounds, while others paced in what seemed to be a patterned sweep of the area. And then Derek realized something. These guys didn't look so good. Several of the Fae were coughing, and more than a few showed signs of deep fatigue with hollowed cheeks.

Fae didn't get sick, which meant Old Kingdom hadn't taken the precautions Theda insisted on for New Kingdom. They hadn't separated the sick from the healthy. And that worked in Derek's favor. They wouldn't be in top form if things came down to a fight.

Elena grabbed his chin and swiveled their faces to the side. A soldier headed straight for them a few feet away.

Forget patterns. Derek sprinted to the center of the berm, swerved around several soldiers, and ran through the castle's gray exterior.

They ended up inside an interior hallway that appeared to be deserted. Derek dragged in deep breaths through his nose, his heart hammering. It was a miracle no one had shouted out as they had passed through the yard.

The castle was nearly as dark as the night, illuminated by candles, just as Theda had described. Wood shutters covered the windows instead of glass, causing a draft. And the place reeked like a stink hole.

Forced to breathe through his nose and inhale the stench while his mouth was occupied on Elena's, Derek eased down the corridor, slipping inside alcoves whenever someone approached. Several twists and turns later, he found the castle's main hall.

In the center of the room, like a great Parthenon pillar, rose the Ancient Allon.

Though the trunk took up a large portion of the space, the room was big enough to accommodate another few hundred Fae. At present, fifty or so patrolled the area, a quarter of whom protected the tree.

Derek scanned for gaps between the guards, taking a few minutes to consider his options.

Elena kicked him in the butt like she was urging on a horse.

Growling quietly, he pierced her with his gaze. Her eyes laughed back, looking pointedly from him to the tree, as if to say, *Hurry the hell up*.

The girl had no sense of self-preservation. Their lives were at stake. He was being careful. Though he took her point.

Unless they waited for the guards to drop off one by one from the disease, they wouldn't find a better opportunity to gather the leaves. The sun would soon be rising. The cavernous room was as dim as it was going to get. Even better, no one knew they were here.

Derek sucked in a deep breath through his nose and walked to the base of the tree, sidestepping Old Kingdom clansmen and slipping past Fae guards stationed at the base.

So far so good.

He stepped over the thick ornamental twine roping off the trunk, and gazed up at the tree's crown, blocked from this angle. There was no way he'd be able to climb the tree with Elena in front of him. He'd scrape up her back, and getting a good hold would be a bitch.

He'd have to resort to a finger in the mouth after all.

Derek grabbed her hand and carefully inserted her finger from the side. She nodded and pulled her head away slowly, as though cognizant of how dangerous it would be if their connection tore apart and they were suddenly exposed.

No ripping sensation. The connection was intact.

Derek swirled his tongue around her finger and she narrowed her eyes. *What?* He needed a good connection.

Elena slipped around to his back, and Derek started to climb the tree.

"Intruders!" A shout sounded from behind.

Goddammit. They were still Blended, so someone must have seen through the disguise.

Without looking back at the person who'd shouted—wouldn't make a difference anyway—Derek did the only thing he could. He raced up the base of the tree with Elena clinging to him.

More shouts erupted, then a loud blast went off that ended on a strange pinging sound.

Derek and Elena ripped apart like Velcro and fell to the ground. They landed with a thud on the soil at the base of the tree, Derek's shoulder and head pounding from taking the brunt of the impact.

Ignoring the pain shooting through his shoulder and head, Derek swiped at the slippery, bubblelike film that covered him and reached for Elena. Guards swarmed in, but Derek quickly pressed his body to hers and kissed her to Blend.

Nothing happened.

He kissed her frantically, trying to make the connection, and still there was no sensation of Blending.

"It was only a matter of time before we caught you, Halven," said one of the Fae guards, his hair fire-engine red. "The energy you triggered baffled us at first, stronger than typical for a Halven, but not strong enough to be one of us."

The Fae smiled, revealing a dimple in his cheek that should have been cherubic, but instead looked lecherous as he watched Derek repeatedly attempt to kiss and transform

Elena. "Don't worry. It will be our pleasure to take care of your female's needs."

Derek pushed Elena behind him and jumped to his feet. He kicked the redheaded Fae in the gut and pulled out a small knife Portia's guards had missed. One of the hidden knives Derek had strapped to his ankle.

Before he had a chance to use it, Elena shrieked.

Derek spun around. A different guard had his arm wrapped around her waist from behind, the other across her breasts. He was speaking in her ear, his words making her face contort with anger.

Derek surged forward to slice the bastard to ribbons, but a large hand clamped over his head, halting him in his tracks. He sank to his knees and fell flat on the floor, facing Elena.

He couldn't move—could only lie there and watch the other Fae assault her with his words, the Fae's hand roaming her body.

Derek's head felt like it would explode as panic and anger coursed through him, while his body remained frozen on the ground.

Elena angled away from the Fae who was pressing his hand to her stomach and talking in her ear, and peered down at Derek. Her mouth tightened.

She elbowed the Fae in the gut. He grunted but didn't let go—until she slammed her foot along his instep. The Fae hunched forward and she tucked her chin and threw back her head, cracking him in the jaw with the back of her skull.

The guy released her and dabbed at his bleeding chin, limping. Several guards stepped forward, but the one Elena had attacked stayed them with a raised hand. He wiggled his jaw, eyes blazing, and grabbed her just as she was about to reach Derek. He jerked her back by the hair, and Elena screamed.

The rigor mortis in Derek's limbs—or whatever it was —slowly released, but he was still basically frozen. All he could do was watch the scene unfold.

He couldn't protect Elena, and he was about to lose his mind.

Bracketing the front of her within the folds of his large body, the Fae guard held her so tightly Derek didn't think she could breathe.

Perspiration broke out along Derek's forehead as he focused on moving the joints in his legs. His knees popped free, and he concentrated on moving his elbows. Slowly the rest of his body began to respond. He moved his leg a couple of inches. The guards around him were so focused on Elena and the Fae that they didn't notice his subtle movements.

The guard holding Elena suddenly howled and released her, blood streaming down the side of his shirt. Feet apart and braced for an attack, Elena gripped a small, bloodied knife in her hand. She must have had one still stashed as well.

The rest of the men watched raptly, weapons at the ready, but seemingly not concerned for their comrade's safety. Which wasn't a good sign. It meant that the Fae didn't fear Elena.

Derek had lost his Halven ability from the blast that hit them in the tree; Elena must have lost hers too. Without her powers, she was no match for the Fae.

But Derek couldn't consider that right now. He had to get them out, no matter the odds.

The injured Fae reached for Elena, but she jabbed the

knife at him. When he dodged it, she twisted and elbowed him in the stomach.

The Fae stepped back, catching his breath. In one quick movement, he knocked the knife from her hand and grabbed her arms, wrenching them behind her. Anchoring his leg along the bend in her knee, he shoved her until she fell on the ground and then he followed on top. He pulled her arms over her head, holding them in place with one hand.

"Derek!" she screamed, her pitch too high. Panic-filled.

Derek slowly lumbered to his knees...and then his feet. Not everything was working perfectly, but good enough. He grabbed the knife he'd dropped earlier and barreled through the guards, landing on top of the Fae attacking Elena. He managed to stab the guy in the back before two shots rang out.

A searing pain blazed through Derek's shoulder and hamstring, but he didn't let go. He wrenched the Fae off Elena and stabbed him in the shoulder, his movements jerky and weaker than normal, but effective.

Another shot rang out, and this time the pain pierced Derek's lower back.

He slumped to the side, rolling off Elena's attacker. The edges of his vision went hazy.

The redheaded cherub in charge glanced around at his comrades. "This has been fun. How shall we dispose of them? Quickly, or let him heal a bit and torture them?" He smiled at Derek. "Maybe we'll keep him conscious while we entertain ourselves with the girl." He leered at Elena, who was squirming beneath the Fae Derek had attacked, while blood poured from the wounds in the man's back. The guard had her trapped again, but he hadn't made a move, apparently awaiting orders. "Her form has interesting attributes Fae women don't possess to the same degree."

Derek gasped for air, choking on the blood pooling in his mouth. His vision began to wink. He could be dying or passing out. Either way, he wouldn't be able to save her. Not like this.

"My father...Osulf Niall," he croaked. "I demand to speak to him."

THIRTY-NINE

A low chuckle rumbled from the lead guard. "You jest, filthy Halven." He held his mouth in a tight smile, but uncertainty crossed his eyes.

"I'm not lying," Derek managed to get out. "The king—he's my father."

One by one the Fae's subordinates inched closer and studied Derek. Silence filled the room.

"I'll notify his majesty," one of the soldiers said, and separated from the rest.

The leader grunted. His gaze slid to Elena and his mouth quirked at the corner. "This one is mine."

Derek ground his teeth. "Lay a hand on her"—his breaths came in quick, jerky bursts; the itch of his flesh healing offered hope he might actually survive the bullet wounds—"and I'll snap it off."

Elena caught his eye and frantically shook her head.

Before any of the guards could react to Derek's threat, the men parted and a tall, commanding Fae about the same physical age as his adoptive father came forward. The man must have been following the commotion from someplace nearby to arrive so quickly.

Derek sucked in a breath. The Fae leader's hair was long, hitting the top of his shoulders in thick blond waves with streaks of gray. His eyes glowed a striking bottle green. The eyes and hair weren't like Derek's at all, but the face... Derek never thought he'd meet anyone he resembled, but this man looked like him. Or rather, Derek looked like Niall.

Osulf Niall sent a cursory glance toward Elena, then studied Derek for several minutes. "If I didn't know it by your appearance, the power my guards say you yield confirms it."

Niall flicked his fingers and two guards stepped forward.

"My son, how unusual that after all my years of searching, you have come to me. We will discuss your future in my chambers." He strode away without glancing back.

The two guards grabbed Derek under his arms and dragged him behind their leader.

"No!" Derek shouted. "I won't leave without Elena."

Niall halted on the massive planked staircase, casting back a calculating look. "As you wish. I will allow you this boon." He scanned his men. "No harm comes to the girl within the walls of my castle." His gaze returned to Derek. "And you will give me something in return."

DEREK KEPT a watchful eye on Elena as they entered the king's apartment, similar in size to the one Theda occupied in her castle. There the similarities ended.

Niall's rooms were not rich and opulently decorated.

Instead, woven rugs covered the floors and large tapestries decorated the walls. Nothing in the rooms spoke of luxury.

"How did your guards take away our powers?" Derek asked.

They hadn't much time. The more information they gathered, the better their chances. And right now, Derek had Niall's attention.

Niall approached a carved wooden chair set on a dais and sank down, one leg outstretched. "A null gun. Clever device. We do not eschew all modern technologies. Of course, this one is composed primarily of magic, which makes it as ancient as time."

"How long do the effects last?"

His father smiled mockingly. "You may be my son, but I will not disclose all our secrets."

Derek's face burned with rage. Niall's men had disarmed him and Elena in minutes. He couldn't let it happen again. He *wouldn't*.

Niall laughed. "Such passion—I see it on your face. You're just like your mother. She had beautiful blue eyes and golden skin. Her beauty and passion drew me to her, but that was a mistake. I underestimated her determination to protect you. It was unfortunate she took her own life to prevent me from finding her and *encouraging* her to tell me where she had hidden you." Niall shook his head. "Such a waste. You lost your mother and I was denied my son. I learned to select biddable females after that."

His real mother was *dead*?

And this man had driven her to take her own life.

Derek's head pounded from the force of the blood pumping through his system. His mother had *saved* him, not abandoned him. Just as Elena's mother had saved her. Or tried to.

Niall glanced at Elena. "You would do well to learn from my mistakes, son. This female—the Newlander, whose elemental magic I sense—will only cause you grief and frustration. She has too much spirit and bad blood. No good can come from such a union. You have strong mental powers. We must keep the bloodline pure and cleanse it of your mother's dilution."

"I don't need relationship advice, *Father*. And Elena's bad blood is the only thing standing between you and certain death."

Niall's jaw twitched in agitation. "Oh? And why is that?"

"Because without her abilities, you'll die from the disease. Or have the Fae collapsing around you escaped your notice?"

Niall lurched forward in his chair, anger—maybe hatred—contorting his features. "Watch your mouth," he growled. "I will not hesitate to smite it from your face."

"So much for unconditional love," Derek muttered sardonically.

"Stop, Derek," Elena pleaded. She peered up at Niall. "What he says is true. We are risking our lives to save your people. We want to help."

Niall eased back. He rubbed his thumb along the armrest. "And why would you do this?"

"I have an ability Fae in Emain believe can save your people from the virus—and my mother along with them."

She left out the part about Leo and Portia threatening Elena's human family, but Derek wasn't so certain Leo meant to follow through on that. It could have been all Portia's idea, and she'd left Emain to spread her hatred in Tirnan.

Now that Derek knew Portia's true purpose, he doubted

she ever believed Elena would find a cure. Had probably banked on her not finding one and had only used Elena as a convenient distraction for her real goal—to take over Tirnan with the virus as her weapon.

Niall studied Elena. "Interesting arrangement. I'll need to confirm your story."

"It's the truth," Derek interrupted. "And there's no time to confirm it. Even if Emain Fae allowed you through the portal—which they would not—most of your kingdom is exposed to the virus, or will be by the end of the week. If I were you, I wouldn't risk my life to confirm something Elena can prove in a matter of minutes."

"You are not me," Niall boomed. A warning. "However, I am willing to see this proof."

"Then I ask again, how long do the effects of the null gun last? Elena will need her powers."

"They've returned by now." He paused and nodded to one of the guards. "If she attempts to harm me in any way, shoot her through the temple."

Derek's heart raced as the guard aimed his crossbow. Elena wouldn't harm Niall, so there was no risk of the guard shooting her for that, but the Fae's finger could slip. Anything could happen.

Niall gestured to Elena. "You may begin."

She had her chin set in that stubborn way that usually meant all hell was about to break loose. Derek stretched his neck, the popping sound filling the silence. She had better not do something risky. He wasn't certain they had any more luck left.

Elena breathed deeply and closed her eyes, her shoulders dropping as if relaxed. A faint wind whirled around the room, picking up speed.

She opened her eyes and the wind stopped, but the air

in the room condensed. Droplets of water sprinkled on their heads from a charcoal cloud that had coalesced along the ceiling. The wind picked up again, and the pressure in the room shifted. A deafening crack boomed across the room, followed by a bright light that zipped past Derek's shoulder.

The guard at Elena's side shrieked like a little girl, his hand smoking where the bow had been.

Elena's mouth twitched. "You are unharmed, your majesty."

Derek shook his head, his ears ringing from the thunder. She was going to get them killed.

Niall's face remained stoic. "Interesting. But manipulation of the elements will not cure the virus."

"Which is why we're here," Derek said. "Elena only recently acquired her abilities. She hasn't had time to fully develop them, and she won't before the disease completes its spread. Unless you help us. Elena is descended from nobility, as you may have surmised, otherwise she wouldn't have abilities. According to the Tertullian Codex, she can gain her full powers in Tirnan."

Niall's gaze narrowed. "I see. And what do Fae in Emain believe is her ultimate ability?"

"Transmutation. She'll develop an antivirus to the disease."

Niall was silent for several seconds. Derek's palms were sweating, but he refused to look away. He had nothing to hide and he wouldn't back down.

The king slowly tapped his finger on the armrest of his chair. "The secret for manifesting a Fae's innate magic has been passed from one generation of nobility to the next." He sat forward, his body going eerily still. "I will provide Elena with what she needs and tell her how to fully possess her powers—on two conditions. First, I want sole control of the antivirus. Second, you agree to remain in Tirnan. With me."

Elena spun to him. "No."

She had agreed to help the Emain Fae create a cure to the virus. In turn, they wouldn't harm her family. There was no rule as to who controlled the cure.

Derek rubbed his jaw. Niall's second condition was more complicated. He wasn't sure why the Fae wanted him. Maybe for posterity; maybe to murder. It was a toss-up at this point. Derek wasn't getting warm, fuzzy feelings from Daddy.

He looked at Elena, who seemed to be pleading with her eyes.

He didn't know when it had happened—maybe subconsciously from the first moment he'd set eyes on her —but he'd do anything to keep her safe.

Elena turned abruptly to the king. "I won't leave Derek behind," she said, and Derek groaned.

She still had no sense of self-preservation. They'd have to work on that.

"Elena—" Derek began.

"You have no choice, my dear," Niall answered. "Consider it the boon Derek promised in exchange for your protection within my castle. The first condition... Well, we both desire that, do we not? Develop a cure and fulfill your agreement with our people. I will make sure this Fae mother of yours survives the virus."

FORTY

What an evil bastard Derek's father turned out to be! How was Elena going to get Derek out of here?

She racked her brain for an alternate solution while they stood in front of the king, but her mind kept drawing a blank. Not even a whisper of a clever scheme flickered through her gray matter.

Fear of losing Derek must have forced her better judgment to the forefront, leaving one option. "I will give Old Kingdom the antidote," she said.

This ruler was just arrogant enough to think of himself and Old Kingdom as one and the same. By the pleased look in his eye, she could tell she'd been right.

The next condition was trickier. She had to be careful. "What do you want with Derek?"

The corner of Niall's mouth curved up. His face twisted with forced sincerity. "What any father wants. He is blood of my blood, and my only son. I wish his fealty."

A tremor of unease swept through her. She didn't understand the meaning behind Niall's saccharine words or what exactly he meant by fealty, but figuring that out would take time. A luxury she didn't have.

"My mother said I need five leaves from the Ancient Allon in order to manifest my full magic. I want Derek to retrieve the leaves." She didn't trust Niall, or his men.

Niall studied her for a heartbeat then nodded to Derek. "Go."

Derek looked from Elena to the guards, as if mentally calculating her safety in his absence.

Niall had promised her no harm within his castle. Derek must have surmised the same, because he swept out of the room followed by two guards with null guns pointed at his back.

Her mother was supposed to show her what to do with the leaves, but Elena didn't want her mom brought here—assuming she was still alive.

Elena's stomach twisted and she pressed her wrist beneath her ribs. She'd only known her mom a few hours; it was ridiculous to mourn someone you barely knew. But she did. There was still a chance her mother had survived. She had to hold on to that possibility and hope for the best.

"What do I do with the leaves once I have them?" she asked.

Niall's head tilted and he studied her for a moment. "You mentioned your mother. Who is she, dear?"

The fine hairs on Elena's neck stood at attention and her fingers twitched. She'd hate to give Niall information that put her mother in danger. "Does it matter?"

Niall smirked. "I think it does."

Every gaze in the room focused on her.

"Theodora," she murmured.

Niall leaned forward on his wooden dais. "Theodora who?"

"Rainer."

"Speak louder," he commanded.

Elena pushed her shoulders back and raised her chin. "My mother is Theodora Joelle Rainer."

A hush swept the chamber.

The king's expression blanked, and then he leaned back and laughed loudly, his surprisingly lyrical chortle cutting through the silence like a sharpened blade. "My son and the daughter of..." He pressed a fist to his grin, shaking his head in disbelief.

Elena crossed her arms. "Will you tell me what I need to know, or not?"

Niall's smile faded and his expression turned serious. "Grind the leaves into a thin powder. Pour warm water over the granules and drink it down. Be forewarned: royal blood withstands the power of the Ancient Allon leaves. Lesser Fae become ill. A Halven..."

Might not make it, she thought.

She might not survive no matter what. With the leaves, she had a fighting chance, and so would her mother and the rest of the Fae.

"That's it?" she asked. "There's no other ingredient, no voodoo waving of the hands to make the formula more magical?"

"I assure you, the Ancient Allon is plenty magical."

Derek returned, and one of Niall's men brought in a *molcajete*—an herb grinder like the one her aunt had passed down to Elena on her sixteenth birthday.

Derek handed her the leaves, and she ground them into a thin powder with the *molcajete*. The leaves were surprisingly brittle for being fresh from the tree, but then, these leaves never dropped. They shifted from branch to branch, but never fell.

She carefully scooped the granules into a cup and filled it with the warm water procured by a servant.

Derek stared at the concoction, his gaze leery.

Without hesitating, Elena brought the blend to her mouth and gulped it down.

The leaves tasted like bark with a hint of peppermint. Not horrible, but not exactly a coffeehouse tea.

"My guards will escort you to your chamber," Niall said. "Rest for a few hours and allow the leaves to take effect. When the sun reaches midmorning, we will see how you've fared and if the scientists of Emain were correct."

ONE OF THE guards kicked Derek in the back, launching him inside a small, dusty chamber.

He stumbled and whirled around.

"Do not attempt to use your powers," the guard said. "Castle alchemists will monitor you and your female's power levels. Present a spark of magic and you won't enjoy the consequences."

He slammed the door in Derek's face, the sound of a large wooden object sliding home coming from the opposite side.

Good. Derek wanted privacy.

He walked across the room, past the thin cot hugging the wall, to a narrow window with metal bars.

He surveyed the soldiers pacing the castle periphery. One of the guards glanced up from the yard, and Derek withdrew, pressing his back to the stone.

The nice thing about a crusty old castle with no modern conveniences? No possibility of surveillance cameras.

Derek gently pulled out the five additional leaves he'd

extracted from the Ancient Allon when no one was looking. Well, they may have been looking, but with his powers returned, he'd made part of his arm invisible and snatched the extra leaves, stuffing them inside his pocket with no one the wiser.

Silently, Derek carried a small table that held a ceramic bowl and cup away from the window. He picked up the cup in one hand and used his other to grind the leaves over it. Small grains and a few larger pieces flittered to the bottom.

He poured tepid water from the bowl over the leaf particles and allowed them to steep for a moment, hoping the extra time would provide the same effect as warm water.

Derek drank down the mixture, chewing and swallowing the larger chunks of leaf.

He came from royal Fae too, and if it was possible to help Elena by enhancing his own abilities, he wanted in.

Because he didn't trust anyone inside Tirnan, least of all Niall.

FORTY-ONE

Soldiers entered Elena's room a couple of hours after she awakened. The last of the nausea the leaves had caused finally relented, leaving her throat sore from dry heaving and her body weary from a night of poor sleep.

Surrounded by guards, she was guided to Niall's chamber, her toes pinched inside her boots.

"How are you feeling this morning?" Niall asked, eyeing her as she entered.

"A little woozy, and—" She held out her arms, revealing sleeves a good two inches too short.

"You've grown. That is to be expected. Had you been male, the growth after drinking Ancient Allon leaves would be dramatic." Something flashed in Niall's eyes. Anger?

"I must admit, I am surprised, Elena." A boyish smile crossed his face, as if he'd been caught with his hand in the cookie jar. "I did not believe a Halven could survive the leaf of the Ancient Allon." His expression turned thoughtful. "This morning has been full of surprises."

Niall's ominous tone brought a fresh wave of nausea to her belly. This man made her extremely nervous, particularly since he was hellbent on keeping Derek. Something she had no intention of allowing.

Niall's eyes narrowed and he tapped his finger on his thigh atop the dais.

That mannerism... How many times had she seen Derek doing that same finger tapping when he was thinking? The uncanny physical resemblance was weird enough, but the finger-tapping thing had her freaking out. What other similarities did Derek share with his biological father?

No. She mentally shook her head. *Derek is nothing like Niall.*

"Come." Niall rose suddenly and strode across the room. The guards in his chamber flanked him and surrounded Elena. "We will see what other changes the leaves have wrought. You will use the castle laboratory. The alchemists have abandoned it in favor of a more isolated domain."

A few minutes later they entered a large room Elena wouldn't go so far as to call a lab. Some of the instruments looked like they belonged in a museum, not capable of withstanding heat and chemicals. More important, something else was missing, or rather, *someone.*

She spun in a circle. "Where's Derek?"

Niall peered at an ancient glass vessel in his hand. A flask? A bong? It was so old, she wasn't sure what it was.

"Indisposed. You work alone today."

No way.

"Look, sir, your majesty, king—whatever—I need Derek. You may not know this about him, but he's a brilliant immunologist. That was one reason the Emain Fae coerced him into helping me. It's essential he be here."

Really, she just needed to know he was okay. She didn't like being separated from Derek, and no matter what he had agreed to, Elena wouldn't leave him behind with his zealot father.

The corner of Niall's mouth twitched. "It seems my son was very busy last night. He is being disciplined for his defiance. However, under the circumstances, I will withhold the remainder of his punishment until later."

That didn't sound good. Not good at all.

What had Derek done?

NIALL STATIONED a handful of guards outside the door to the lab while Elena waited for Derek. She distracted herself by inspecting the first microscope ever created. She wasn't certain it was the first one ever created, but it was mostly made of wood, which made it way too old to be of any use to her.

Twenty long minutes had passed, when she heard a buzzing sound.

Elena swatted the air near her ear and what she thought was an insect, only to realize the buzzing was coming from inside her head.

The noise faded and softened into an echo of her mother's commanding voice.

Elena, I pray this message finds you safe. Samuel and I are in hiding. Whatever you do, do not return to New Kingdom. Return to the human realm as soon as possible. A revolution stirs in Tirnan...

Elena experienced a moment of deep, shuddering relief. Her mother was alive.

But what was this about a *revolution*? They hadn't cured the virus. Why were Fae preparing for war?

Too much to worry about right now. Thank God her

mother was okay. Elena would return to the human realm as her mother said, just as soon as she survived Old Kingdom and Niall.

Seconds later, a brigade of guards entered the lab. They parted like a flower opening for the sun, and Derek stepped out. *Stepped* being figurative.

Derek lumbered forward, one leg dragging behind him, blood oozing down his shirt from a split lip. He cradled his wrist in one hand, the joint contorted at an odd angle.

Elena's body shook, her breathing unsteady as rage overwhelmed her. How could Niall do this to his own son?

She glared at the guards. "Leave us. Now!"

One of the guards, a short one, which meant he was probably slightly less than seven feet, stepped forward. "We are to remain while you work."

Elena counted to ten and took a deep breath. "Fine. Watch from the other side of the door. I can't concentrate with you people around. You make me sick!"

The guard's nostrils flared, but he walked out. The others followed, leaving the door ajar.

The moment they left, Elena raced to Derek, stopping just shy of touching him, afraid she might hurt him. "What can I do?" Her voice quivered and she swallowed back a bitter flavor in her mouth.

"Help me sit." Blood gushed down his chin with each word.

She gingerly lifted his good arm around her neck and guided him to a chair. "What happened? Why did they do this to you?" Her voice caught. If she wasn't careful, she'd start crying.

"I drank the mixture. They could tell as soon as they entered my room this morning." His swollen, battered mouth twisted in a mock smile.

"What do you mean, you drank the mixture?" She stared, taking him in from his arms and broad torso to his long, muscular legs and—did a double take.

He was hunched over, the bloody gore a massive distraction, but even so, she didn't know how she could have missed it.

"You grew," she choked out.

"I stole extra leaves. Made more of the tea in my room and drank it. Wanted to be as strong as possible."

The leaves could have killed him. But then, he'd been out of the room stealing leaves when Niall had explained *that* potential outcome.

She waved her hand down his body. "I grew a couple of inches, but you—how tall are you now?"

"I don't know. Best guess, the drink added an extra seven inches to my height and more bulk. My old clothes were literally choking me when I woke. Before they beat me, they were kind enough to offer new ones." He flicked a finger at a ripped sleeve.

"Seven inches?" The clothes fit his new height and build, but they were now bloodied and torn in several places.

He flexed the fingers of his bad hand, gently working the wrist back and forth as it healed. "I wanted to improve my powers and help you. I had no idea I'd turn into a giant."

She shook her head. "Not a giant." She glanced past him to the door. "You—*we've*—become like them," she whispered.

What exactly had the Ancient Allon done to them? They'd both changed physically, and if all went correctly, magically.

How else might they be like Fae?

Derek scowled. "Don't say that. That's what Niall

wants. He was pissed that I disobeyed him, but not that I'd grown and become more powerful. He expects me to rule with him. To lead one of the other kingdoms he plans to take over. He thinks that with the Ancient Allon in my blood, I'll live longer."

That was Niall's plan and why he wanted Derek? "Well, he can't have you," she said, determined.

A shadow passed over Derek's face. "He's powerful, Elena. Before the beating, he had one of the alchemists put his hand to my head. I felt the magic, but I don't know what it did. No matter what, you have to make the cure. Promise me."

"Yeah, of course."

He let out a breath. "Good."

But she wasn't leaving Derek with his father, if that's what he was thinking. She didn't care what Niall wanted.

Derek continued on, oblivious to her silent promise. "I'm not like them and neither are you. We're still part human. I'm tall, but not as tall as those guys—" He jerked his thumb at the door. "We're still Halven."

Derek was taller than the shorter Fae men, but she didn't think he'd appreciate the observation. "How are you feeling?" she asked instead. "Can you walk?"

He eased out of the chair and stretched his back to full height.

Elena's breath caught. Derek had always appealed to her in some innate way, but he really was the most beautiful man she'd ever seen. His cuts were healing and he stood evenly on both legs now.

He peered down at her with a sweet smile and pulled her into his arms. She pressed her nose to his upper midriff and breathed in his scent.

He smelled the same. At least that hadn't changed.

The sense of being connected and safe settled over her. Not everything was different. They were still *them*.

She looked up, but he was gazing over her head with a frown. "What is this stuff? Because it sure as hell isn't laboratory equipment."

"Tell me about it. But it's okay." She beamed. "I have an idea."

Derek gazed at her warily.

Where was the trust?

She held out her hands like a surgeon before an operating table, fingers waggling. "Let's put the tea to the test and make our own equipment."

FORTY-TWO

"Christ, Elena. What do you expect me to do with these?"

Elena glanced at the cotton swabs in Derek's hand that she'd created and named E-tips.

"Swab their noses?"

"They're Fae, not gorillas. Can you come up with something smaller?"

She glared at him. "My apologies, master. So sorry the size doesn't work for you. Would you like a different color? Perhaps the cotton in a polka-dotted pattern?"

Derek let out a slow breath and tapped his finger along the side of his leg. "This is serious," he growled.

She smacked him on his newly sculpted pecs. "I know that. Give me those."

Elena grabbed the E-tips the size of pencils and threw them on the counter. She closed her eyes, drew from the atoms in the air, and opened her hands, producing four smaller versions to accommodate a Fae nose.

With her heightened powers, Elena didn't need the exact element to manipulate matter. She could take an air or water molecule and create metal if she wanted, as long as she understood the properties of what she was changing the molecules into.

Two hours later, after a few more fumbles she considered practice rounds, she managed to pull together the tools they needed to create a cure. *Maybe.*

Elena wasn't a pharmaceutical company with the capacity to produce complicated antiviral compounds. Not yet, anyway. Instead, she would try to cure Fae by mixing a bit of nature with magic.

After talking it over with Derek, they decided their best bet was to create a type of virucide.

Virucides come from the environment, like peppermint oil, which attacks certain viruses. As long as Elena could study infected Fae tissue and figure out how the Fae virus surpassed their rapid healing, she could design a virucide for it. Derek had taught her enough back home about flu viruses that she knew her way around the biological aspects, but it helped to have him near.

They needed infected epithelial tissue to study diseased cells, but that shouldn't be difficult to acquire. Several of the guards outside the lab were coughing, and Fae weren't susceptible to other infections. Those symptomatic had the virus. Convincing Fae to let her take a nose swab was another issue.

Elena did the smart thing. She sent the newly ginormous Derek to collect samples with the E-tips.

Derek returned a few minutes later with a disgruntled look on his face.

She gestured to his cheek. "Is that a new bruise?"

"Fae are crappy patients."

"What do you expect? They've never been sick before. It's like a bunch of men with man colds, only times ten."

"What are man colds?"

Definition of man cold: an affliction only caught by men, exhibiting cold-like symptoms, but no one has ever been as sick or as tired as the man who catches the man cold.

Mateo got man colds all the time. They were the worst.

Which was another reason Elena had sent Derek to collect the samples. Fae were legitimately sick and had to be grumpy as hell, between the deadly symptoms and never having been ill before.

"Um, never mind. It's just, you know, a bad cold," she said.

Derek grumbled some derogatory response about Fae, and prepared slides for the archaic microscope she'd modified to increase magnification.

He placed a slide beneath the lens and stepped aside, waving her forward for the first look.

Elena bent over and peered through the eyepiece. Several minutes later, she raised her head. "Slight problem."

"What? Sample no good?"

"No—well, I don't know. It might be, but I can barely make out the individual cells, let alone see what's going on inside of them."

Derek leaned over and took a look.

He pushed the microscope away. "This thing sucks. Why don't you create a better one?"

Elena pulled her fingers through the hair at her temples and paced the room. "I can't just make a better microscope. I tried, but I'm not an engineer. I need schematics, some sort of blueprint. Something—*anything*—to show me how to do it."

"Calm down," he whispered, and pulled her to the far corner.

"Look, we have one thing working in our favor right now." His voice was low and secretive. "They want us to use our magic. They *expect* it."

She studied his eyes. "What are you saying?"

"They won't attack us if we use our powers—which means we can use them to get out of here. We have what we came to this castle for. Let's create the cure somewhere else, away from Niall. We'll supply Tirnan with the virucide and return to Emain."

Elena's gaze flickered to the doorway. It could work. It was daylight, which put them at a disadvantage, but if they stayed they'd accomplish nothing with the tools at hand.

If the castle's own laboratory didn't contain a modern microscope, it was unlikely anywhere else in the kingdom would. And Elena wanted nothing more than to leave this place.

Niall wanted his son and control of the cure. He knew that if he allowed Elena to leave, the first thing she'd do would be to create more virucide for the rest of Tirnan. They were both stuck. Unless they did something about it.

They could do this—leave while no one was suspicious of them using their powers. But instead of creating a cure in the antiquated lab, they'd use their magic to escape to someplace safe. And modern. "Let's head for Sunland. They're less likely to harm us there."

Pissing Niall off could result in disaster, but they were in danger no matter what choice they made. At least this way they had a chance at escape.

"What about trying to find your mother?"

Elena shook her head. "My mom sent me a message with her magic. She told me *not* to return to New Kingdom. She said to leave the realm as soon as possible."

Derek peered at the stone walls, then back at her.

"Nothing is stopping us. Let's do it. I have the Tirnan map memorized. We'll head straight for the woods separating Old Kingdom from Sunland. The forests are dark. That'll make it difficult for anyone to see us while we're Blended. We can also hide inside a tree like we did the last time, if needed."

When they'd entered Old Kingdom, the guards had confiscated their food packets and the last weapons they'd managed to hold on to after Portia's men disarmed them. They had nothing but the clothes on their backs, and a plate of cheese and bread the servants had brought to the lab while they worked. Elena pocketed the bread and cheese. "What else should we take?"

He looked around the room. "A null gun would be nice."

"We won't find any of those lying around. If we manage to make it back to Emain, I'm demanding schematics so I can make one."

He leaned down and kissed her, cradling her jaw with his large hand. "We will return." Tipping his head toward the counter, he added, "Grab the E-tips. Took you too long to get those right the first time." Humor filled his voice and she frowned, but she grabbed the E-tips.

Derek peered at the four walls. "We should go. Hop up."

She craned her neck. "Do you expect me to climb you like a tree?"

He smiled. "Not my fault you're such a shorty now." He bent and lifted her, and she wrapped her legs around his waist. She clung to his broad shoulders, their faces at eye level. "No finger business this time. I want full lips." He grinned, and Elena's stomach fluttered. Her attention went straight to his mouth.

They might be running for their lives, but it didn't stop

the scattering effect he had on her. She glanced about to distract herself. "Nice view you got up here."

"Elena—"

She looked back. "Hmm?"

"Kiss me."

She leaned forward, her breaths coming in unsteady puffs as she gently brushed his mouth with her lips.

Derek's hand spread along her back, sliding up to the nape of her neck. He urged her mouth open and slid his tongue along hers.

Her body heated—and they transformed.

CHAPTER
FORTY-THREE

Derek avoided the doorway and went straight to the back of the lab, easing through cabinet and stone as if it were air. He ran full force with Elena in his arms to what he hoped was the exterior wall, but to tell the truth, he wasn't certain.

Normally his mind was like a steel trap, but he hadn't been completely lucid when they'd dragged him from the torture chamber.

Having the living shit beaten out of him wasn't an experience he wished to repeat anytime soon. It also had illuminated the kind of father Niall would have made. Ruthless, unforgiving, not the kind of person you wanted raising you. Derek appreciated his adoptive parents more than he ever had in his life.

Derek had believed his biological parents had given him away because he was unwanted. In fact, his mother had made the ultimate sacrifice with her life in order to set him free of Niall. One day he'd mourn the mother who'd done so much for him. Right now he needed to get Elena to safety.

Taking a risk, Derek leapt through the stone surface he hoped led to the berm. And instantly regretted it.

He skidded to a stop. Inside the great hall, where dozens of soldiers stood in front of Niall as he gestured and commanded his men.

Very slowly, Derek stepped back, silently retreating the way he'd come.

A shout rang out. "Over there!"

The room whirled into motion. The scuffle of footfalls sounded, along with the pitch of metal sliding through sheaths, and strings tightened as Fae drew weapons.

Derek ditched his plan to go back, and on instinct, sprinted straight for the entrance of the castle and the light he saw through the panes of a small window high above the door. Later, he'd consider whether that had been a smart move—running through a swarm of guards instead of retreating to an uncertain maze within the castle—but right now, he went for it.

He swerved around null blasts, breezed through bodies and arrows, and burst through the castle's exterior into the open air.

Derek darted across the berm; the Fae outside were a second behind the action going on in the castle. All too quickly, though, the guards trained their crossbows on Derek, likely zeroing in on the telltale signs of his transformation, thanks to the bright sunlight.

Unless he slipped up or was torn from Elena and went solid, crossbows weren't a deterrent in his transformed state.

Null guns were.

Derek adjusted Elena in his arms. Turning solid from a null gun while running through an eighteen-inch stone defense wall would not be good. He held the back of her head to keep their mouths together, and glanced back.

What he saw jarred his senses.

Not a null, or at least that wasn't what caught his attention.

Niall appeared from inside the castle. Along with his army—through the walls, not the door. Each of his guards held a crossbow in one hand while the other touched the shoulder of a fellow soldier. They connected to a single point in the middle. Niall.

The king had Blended an army of Fae with one touch.

Holy shit.

Derek darted to the left, bypassed two null blasts, and hurtled through the defense wall.

He stumbled on the other side, caught his footing, and leapt over the moat, one arm windmilling, the other latched on to Elena.

As they crashed to the ground, Derek bit into Elena's lip and she squeaked. His leg disappeared into the soil as he stumbled upright, his mind so muddled he wasn't focused on his transformation. If he didn't give it the smallest amount of concentration, he'd walk right through something instead of on it.

Derek jerked his foot free of the earth amid a rain of arrows, and ran for the northern forest.

Somehow, they managed to make it there without getting shot by a null, thanks to some zigzagging on Derek's part and the sporadic cover of trees. Old Kingdom Fae might be able to see Derek while Blended, but he wasn't a clear target. Not at the speed he was going.

He entered the forest and dodged thick foliage and ancient trees for miles as he ran without slowing his pace.

Eventually, they lost sight and sound of the guards behind them, and still Derek ran.

Hours passed. Finally, he slowed and abruptly broke the transformation, sliding Elena down his body to the ground. His breaths sawed in and out, and he hunched over, grasping his knees. His lungs burned, and for a moment his vision blurred.

"Are you okay?" she asked, worry in her voice. He couldn't see her. Could barely make out the ground in front of his face.

After a moment, he straightened. "Fine," he said, his breathing returning to normal. "We have to keep running, though. I think we lost them, but I want to move deeper, just in case. We'll make better time if I'm not carrying you."

A cry like a wailing baby, followed by the clap of wings flapping, came from above. Derek flinched.

Birds didn't cry. Then again, the animals here weren't normal.

Elena peered at the trees and rubbed her upper arms. "Yeah, let's keep going." She studied him some more. "You sure you're okay, though?"

He breathed in deeply. His lungs no longer burned and he felt better. "Good as new."

Aside from the growth, the Ancient Allon leaves seemed to have increased the speed he could run and heal.

They took off through the forest, running faster than any human should, and something occurred to him. He grabbed Elena's hand and slowed. "Stop for a second."

"You need a break?" She didn't seem winded, and he definitely wasn't. That wasn't why he wanted her to stop.

"No, I want to try something." He peered at their entwined fingers and concentrated, allowing the transformation to sweep through him.

The difference between pre-leaf transformations and post was like comparing a dying battery to one fully charged. He'd seen what Niall had done with his soldiers. He wondered...

Derek mentally projected his powers to encompass Elena.

There was no one to tell them what they looked like, so he pulled Elena toward a tree.

She held back. "Wait. What are you doing?"

"Trust me," he said, and walked through the base, staring as Elena's hand touched the bark, then dipped into the tree. He pulled her through and out the other side with him.

She glanced back. "I felt it, the transformation, but... how did you do that?"

With her mouth pressed to his during their escape, she couldn't have seen the king. Wouldn't have known it was possible, just like he hadn't.

"While we were running from the castle, Niall Blended an entire regiment through the walls with one touch. As long as his men had one hand on each other with Niall at the center, they Blended."

A mix of worry and wonder crossed her eyes, then her chin firmed. "Good. I'm glad your powers have grown. That will make travel easier."

Was she glad? Her expressive eyes appeared frightened.

If he had the same powers as his biological father—plus the speed, strength, size, and build of a Fae—*was* he still human?

Derek squeezed her hand. "Come on. We're only about half a mile from the border. The Oldlander guards may cross too, but I'd feel better knowing we're off Niall's land. If we're lucky, we'll find allies in Sunland."

They jogged the last stretch, hands clasped, bodies Blended using Derek's new heightened power, and reached a wide creek.

"This is it," he said. "The border runs along the creek bed. Staying Blended will keep us dry as we cross."

Derek stepped into the water a stride ahead of Elena, his hand stretched back and holding hers to maintain the connection. They glided through the water as if it were air.

Midway across the creek, a piercing pain jarred his head, vibrating down his spine and freezing him in place. His muscles spasmed and a groan burst from deep inside his chest. Derek dropped Elena's hand, tearing apart the Blending and leaving them submerged in the cold creek.

"Derek!" Elena splashed to his side.

He tried to move forward, but the pain intensified and his legs buckled, water lapping his torso. He couldn't think, couldn't get his lungs to inhale. Paralysis oozed up his chest like drying cement, closing off his airways.

Small, spindly arms wrapped around his waist from behind.

Elena was dragging him through the water back to the shore they'd come from. Most of his weight floated along the surface, but once they reached solid ground, her breathing increased and she grunted as she heaved him to dry land.

He was twice her size. She shouldn't have been able to maneuver him at all.

"Derek, your chest isn't moving. Can you breathe?" She frantically waved her hand over his face and lowered her cheek to within a millimeter of his nose.

Sensation slowly seeped into his limbs and he breathed in deeply. "Yeah," he said, panting. "I can now."

She leaned back and exhaled, her eyes wild. "What happened back there? I thought you were dying."

A memory flashed of Niall leaning over him while a guard beat him senseless. "You cannot leave, Derek," he had said while another guard pressed electrode-like fingers to Derek's forehead. "You are mine."

He'd felt the magic at the time, but hadn't known what it meant.

What had Niall done to him?

"I don't think I can leave Old Kingdom. They did something to me. You—you have to go ahead." The words ripped from Derek's tongue like tearing flesh from his body.

He rolled his head against the gravel shore, his chest aching. He would rather lose a limb than leave her alone in Tirnan. "You have to go now," he said. "While you still can."

"You idiot! I'm not leaving without you." Her voice shook and tears glistened in her eyes.

He sat up on his forearms then pushed to a sitting position. "Listen to me, Elena. We betrayed Niall. He'll kill you if you stay here."

She shook her head, and he moaned. So stubborn.

He liked her stubborn, feisty side. Liked everything about her. But right now her obstinacy would get her killed.

Derek grabbed her slender shoulders, his voice softening. "I don't know how the magic he used works, but Niall made it impossible for me to exit the kingdom. You have to go. You have to create the cure." *And then get the hell out while you can.* Derek swallowed. "You can do this, Elena." His fingers dug into her skin and he shook her gently, trying to relay the urgency bucking inside him.

Elena's liquid hazel eyes softened—*so beautiful.* She was the most beautiful girl he'd ever seen. Would ever see.

Her lips quivered. A tear ran down her cheek and she swiped it away. "I can't—"

He kissed her. Hard. Consuming. She was so soft and warm, and *his*. Or maybe he was hers; it didn't matter. He'd do anything for her.

Derek lifted Elena onto his lap and dragged her against his chest. He broke from her mouth to sweep kisses across her cheek, her chin. He pressed his face to her neck and inhaled her scent, memorizing it. He couldn't let her go...

"You have to leave. Please," he whispered, his voice hoarse.

The wailing birds roared above.

A small sob escaped her, but he felt her nod.

Derek pulled back to stare one last time at her beautiful face.

She raised her chin ever so slightly. "I'll find you."

FORTY-FOUR

Elena watched as Derek's mouth tensed, then frowned. "Damn it, Elena! What you have to do is more important than my life. Don't you dare risk yours for mine."

"Of course I won't risk my life." *Of course* she would. "I'll get help and we'll get you out." She'd do whatever it took to get him back, she silently vowed.

He continued to frown, as if he could read her thoughts. "Go. Before they get here," he said. "I'll find a hiding place in the woods. Head straight." He pointed across the river to a copse of allons surrounded by tall pines, all bowed in as if guarding the magical trees.

Derek stood and pulled her up with him. His lips pressed together and he stared off into the distance, his throat bobbing.

Elena glanced across the creek, then back at him. "Derek—"

"Leave. Before they get here." His voice came out grave and commanding, just the way it had the first day they'd met. This moment reminded her so much of that day, with him pushing her away.

But the Derek she knew now held her, guarded her. He would never leave her, unless there was no other way.

She clenched one hand on his shirt and pulled him down, kissing him softly on the mouth. She lingered a moment to savor the feel of him, before she turned and ran through the water to the opposite side of the creek.

When Elena looked back, Derek was gone, with not even a shimmer in the air to trace him.

A hollow feeling settled over her. Her clothes were wet, clinging to her calves and thighs like leafy seaweed pulling her under. But she wouldn't go down. She had to fight for all of them now.

Elena turned and headed for the Sunland forest, determined to create a cure and return for Derek.

HOURS later and deep inside the forest, Elena's clothes hadn't dried and she was shivering from cold. With the canopy of leaves blocking most of the sunlight, the moisture and cool air had seeped past her protective Fae clothing and into her bones.

The shadows had turned from gray to nearly black, making it difficult to see. She wrapped her arms around her waist and searched for a place to sleep for a few hours. No matter how good her vision, she couldn't see without any light.

After walking another mile, she found a place she felt would be safe enough to rest in for a while—a tree like the one Derek had discovered when they'd hidden from the Oldlander guards. The upside-down mushroomed trunk was smaller than the one he'd found, but big enough for a single person.

Elena looked around one last time to make sure no one had followed her then crept into the hole. She copied Derek's technique and used a bush to smooth out her footprints near the base, then blocked the hole with the shrub.

Inching as far from the opening as she could get, she found it more confined inside than it looked like from the outside. She couldn't lie flat no matter which way she moved. Instead, she rested her head against the bark and covered her feet and legs with dried needles.

A shiver racked her body—from the cold, from fear. What would happen to Derek if Niall's men found him?

Elena's eyes burned. She cleared her throat and shifted her shoulder, searching for comfort.

"Deirdre, please come to me..." she whispered into the dark.

It was daylight and Elena stood inside a small village. If she gazed broadly, the village looked fogged and blurry, but if she focused on details—yellow flowers planted inside a red flowerbed, a cart full of grain—the image sharpened.

A dream?

"Deirdre?" she called out.

Elena walked across the street of the abandoned town to what she thought was the front of a store. When she clasped the doorknob, the metal rippled like water.

Her pulse raced with panic, and she ran to the building next door. But as soon as she approached, the image broke apart like soggy bread in water.

The lines of the town ran together in a messy watercolor. Her legs cramped, and something pinned her arms. "Deirdre! Help!"

"Wake up," a woman's gentle voice said.

Elena blinked awake, her heart pounding.

"Poor child. It is only I." Deirdre was kneeling on the ground with her head inside the hole. "Come. We must get you to the village."

Elena crawled from her tree cave to find it fully light outside. She had slept too long. Anything could have happened to Derek by now.

"How did you find me?"

Deirdre appeared thinner as she stepped over a log. "Not long after we spoke in Emain, I worried you'd end up in Tirnan. I prepared by coming here." A vicious cough racked her body. She hunched over, her shoulders and chest convulsing as she gasped for air.

Elena bent to help her aunt, but Deirdre waved her away. "I'm fine, but we must hurry. Sunland has been hit hard by the virus. I was in Emain performing diplomatic work when it first surfaced. I wasn't there when your uncle..."

Her Uncle Beorhtric had been murdered with the virus, and now Deirdre would succumb too if Elena didn't do something. "Where do we go?"

"To your uncle's laboratory, where you will find the tools you need."

"How did you know—"

"The dream. I read your thoughts. I gathered your location and tried to show you the way to my village, but my powers are weak. I came to you instead. I've not been gone from Emain long, but time passes differently here. I've been infected almost a week now. We haven't much time." She paused, her gaze settling on Elena. "I am sorry about your friend..."

Derek. Elena wrapped her arms around her waist. *Please let him be okay.*

Deirdre was silent as they made their way out of the woods, but her aunt managed a slow jog once they were out in the open. Soon they came to an agricultural field.

Elena stopped, stunned for a moment. The landscape looked so much like the California Central Valley, minus the highways. "*This* is Sunland?"

"Yes." Deirdre pointed to a cluster of low buildings in the distance. "And there lies your uncle's laboratory."

FORTY-FIVE

Elena took in the sophisticated laboratory her uncle had built beside the single-story home he and Deirdre shared. "This place is amazing."

Deirdre's thin face widened in a proud smile. "Most Fae rely on magic for their abilities. Your uncle embraced magic and science. He would have found a cure had they not..." Her voice trailed off and a blank look crossed her eyes, as though she still couldn't believe he was gone.

"I'm sorry, Deirdre—for your loss."

She blinked and looked over. "He would have liked to have met you, Elena. I'm sorry he didn't get the chance."

"Me too." Elena stared down, wondering if she'd have any family left when this was all over, and praying Deirdre and her mother would survive.

Her aunt drew back her shoulders. "Let us not lose more lives. We must get to work."

Deirdre paced to the opposite side of the room and pulled down beakers and petri dishes lined in perfect rows in a glass cabinet. "What else do you need?"

Elena took in the six microscopes against the back wall.

All modern, all capable of in-depth cellular magnification. "This is more than enough. Oh—well, there is one thing. Can I take a sample from your nose?"

In the end, it took longer for Elena to figure out how to operate her uncle's fancy microscope than it did to solve the riddle of the virus.

Once Derek had discovered information linking Marlon's flu research to Fae, he'd given Elena a quick tutorial on flu strains. Not enough to be an expert—but enough so that she had an understanding of how they worked. Flu viruses contain keys, or knobs, along the surface that connect with locks on healthy cells, and that's how the virus spreads.

According to the data Derek had pulled from the thumb drive Marlon kept stashed away in the locked cabinet of his lab, Fae cells sealed their locks at the sight of a virus, and that was how Fae avoided communicable disease. But with the Fae virus Marlon created, the cells didn't seal their locks. They allowed the virus to enter, killing the cells at a rapid pace.

Derek's theory was that Marlon's virus put some sort of glamour over the diseased cells, so that the healthy cells didn't recognize them as a threat. And F-18, the ingredient Marlon had obtained from her uncle Beorhtric, had been used to achieve it.

Elena looked up. "Deirdre, have you ever heard of something called F-18?"

By the time Elena and Derek returned to Marlon's lab on campus, the blast had nearly killed them and had taken out all of Marlon's ingredients. But maybe in her uncle's laboratory, where F-18 had originated, she'd find it among his possessions.

Deirdre was lying on a chaise her husband kept in a corner of the lab, her face to the wall. She turned and peered over.

Elena gasped. In the two hours since she'd arrived, her aunt's eyes had sunk more and her checks had hollowed. The skin of her face was thin and gray, and her body trembled lightly beneath several woolen blankets.

"I've never heard of that name, but then, I am not a scientist. Beor's supplies are stored along the back wall." She lifted a bony finger and pointed to a wall partially hidden by stacks of neatly organized wooden crates.

Beor must have been Deirdre's pet name for her husband.

Elena rushed over and inched the crates aside. Her aunt wouldn't make it much longer. She had to do something now.

She scanned the shelves full of glass bottles and jars. Several containers were labeled in a strange language, but everything seemed ordered according to the English alphabet. Some contents she recognized: elements from the periodic table, and common herbs and flowers.

F-18 sat next to eucalyptus.

Elena grabbed the glass container and carried it to Deirdre. Her aunt's eyes were closed, so Elena placed a hand on Deirdre's shoulder, and flinched. Intense heat radiated off her aunt's body, bleeding through clothes and blanket.

Deirdre's eyes fluttered open.

"I'm sorry. I know you're weak, but do you recognize this? Some background on what it is might help me formulate a cure." Elena held up the jar, which contained large broken leaf bits like those in the eucalyptus bottle.

Deirdre nodded. "It is—" Long, wet-sounding coughs seized her aunt.

Elena reached for a glass of water from a side table and placed it to Deirdre's lips once the coughing had subsided. "Drink first."

Her aunt sipped the liquid and shut her eyes. "Allon," she breathed. "The leaves...come from the allon."

Elena studied the leaves, dryer than the brittle fresh leaves Derek had picked from the Ancient Allon, but close in appearance. "Are you sure?"

Deirdre gave her a weak smile. "Yes. I would know them, even if I couldn't see them." She laid a thin fist above her heart. "I feel them here. They are a part of us."

And that was probably why the tree's leaves could be manipulated to destroy Fae.

The solution Elena couldn't quite reach back home came down to this one tree found only in Tirnan. The tree capable of giving life—and taking it, if used in the wrong context.

All allon contained magical properties, not simply the Ancient Allon growing through the center of the Old Kingdom castle. Marlon had taken the precious leaf given in good faith by Beorhtric for scientific purposes, and used it to destroy Fae.

After examining the foliage under a microscope, Elena came to a conclusion about its makeup and poured the leaf bits into a bowl. She used her power to manipulate the molecules and reform the dried leaves into fresh ones. Then she extracted the watery sap they produced.

She mixed the sap with her aunt's diseased cells.

Pinpricks erupted beneath her skin, a rush of power and

heat forming in her hands, but this time when she released her magic there was no painful kickback like there was in Emain. Her amplified powers simply crossed space and did what she asked, transmuting the molecules into a new pattern—one that would produce a virucide that blocked the virus from entering healthy Fae cells.

Elena rested her hands on the counter and stared at the sap that looked the same, but now possessed a different molecular structure. After drinking and surviving the infusion of Ancient Allon leaves, her abilities had in fact stepped up to the level she needed to transmute and create a cure.

Whether she'd transmuted the sap correctly was another question. The sap would need to be tested, and she knew just how.

Before she gave the virucide to her aunt, Elena mixed it with more of her aunt's cells. The sap worked in a healing wave, blocking the virus and allowing Fae tissue to heal. So quickly, in fact, Elena missed it the first time she viewed it through the microscope. She had to place her eye at the eyepiece before applying the virucide the second time in order to catch the reaction.

Elena let out a deep, shuddering breath. She'd done it. And there was no time to celebrate. Pretty soon, it wouldn't matter what she'd accomplished if she didn't distribute the cure quickly enough.

Using a dropper, Elena placed a single drop of the allon virucide into her aunt's water glass. With her hand behind her aunt's neck, she brought the water to Deirdre's mouth.

"Drink. It will heal you."

Deirdre sipped the elixir and within minutes sat up straight. Her color changed from pale gray to just pale.

"How do you feel?"

Her aunt's brow puckered. "Hungry." She stared at Elena warmly, a healthy glow suffusing her face. "And much improved. Thank you, dear niece."

She cupped Elena's cheek with her hand. "You've risked much for those who've shown you so little kindness." Deirdre stood carefully, walked away from the chaise, and began rifling through drawers. "Now we must help the others."

Elena gazed at her aunt warily. "Maybe you should take it easy."

Deirdre smiled over her shoulder. "I am fine now, thanks to you. But we must move quickly if we are to disperse the cure in time."

Elena stared off. "I've been thinking about that. Leo said the streams and rivers of Tirnan connect. The virucide is natural—derived from the allon—it won't hurt people." She looked up. "Is it possible to put it in a main water source?"

Deirdre nodded slowly. "The lakes. Every kingdom, including Sunland, owns a large lake connected to numerous rivers. We could pour the cure into the three lakes and tell people to drink the water."

Elena bit the inside of her lip, a skittish sensation filling her stomach. "The Sunland lake should be easy to access with you by my side, but what about the others? Derek and I weren't exactly welcome when we entered the other two Kingdoms. In fact..." Elena looked away, worried about how her actions in Old Kingdom might hinder her ability to help the Fae and get to Derek. "I betrayed Osulf Niall. He's going to want my head if he sees me. Is it possible to enter his land undetected?"

She would enter his land no matter what, but it would make life easier if Niall didn't find out about it. At least, not until she'd poured the cure in the water and escaped with his son.

"If Niall doesn't know I'm there, it will make getting Derek out easier," she added.

Her aunt paused in her packing and looked over. Worry etched her eyes. "Are you certain Derek will come with you?"

Elena's lips parted. "Of course he'll come. He wants to go home as much as I do. Niall is forcing him to stay."

Deirdre walked over and squeezed Elena's arm. "Yes, very well. We will go and find your boy. It is unusual, the connection you share, but who am I to judge? I was originally an Oldlander, I married a Newlander, and now I live in Sunland. We are a family of mixed heritage."

"That goes without saying. I'm Halven."

"Excellent point." Deirdre smiled then laid out clean clothes while she worked out a plan. "I will tell my neighbors to spread the word about the water. We have someone in town with your mother's abilities who can notify the other kingdoms about the cure once we've had a chance to release it. I fear you are right about Niall. He must not discover our plans until we've implemented them and escaped. For this to work, we will need quick transport to the other kingdoms. A portal is our only option. Unfortunately, the kingdoms will notice once we enter their land. We will have little time before they find us and attack. Escape will be a problem."

"Derek can help us with that."

Deirdre shook her head. "His mental ability will keep him hidden, but you and I will be exposed."

"Derek's abilities have grown."

Her aunt's brow rose. "Oh?"

"Derek drank from the tea of the Ancient Allon leaves as

well. Believe me, this could work. His abilities have become very powerful."

"Good. We will need them. Between the portals, the antidote you created, and Derek's powers, we just might save the rest of the realm and make it out alive."

FORTY-SIX

Elena rushed through her shower, attempting to chisel two and a half days' worth of grime off her body in under a minute, while Deirdre spoke to her neighbors about the cure they would release into the water. Thankfully, Sunlanders were peaceable. Elena didn't have to worry about being attacked, whether she was here to help or not.

"We will see if a friend of mine can assist us," Deirdre said, after she'd given Elena clean clothes and new boots that fit a heck of a lot better than her old ones, which were too small on her now.

They jogged a couple of blocks from Deirdre's home to a door built into a hill of green grass. Large boulders littered the hilltop, along with what looked like solar panels secured aboveground. Two steps down an incline, an awning covered a carved turquoise door.

"Your friend lives *here*?" The exterior smelled like grass and dirt, which, she supposed, it was.

"Camille." Deirdre twisted her lips lightly. "No one

knows where Camille originated. Some say the Dark Kingdom."

"The Dark Kingdom?"

Deidre waved it off. "A myth. There is no evidence the Dark Kingdom in the center of the realm exists. No one could survive in the land of ice and snow. Regardless of her origin, Camille has been a Sunlander for as long as I've known her, and she is very powerful. She senses magic. Given the right amount of energy, she can create portals."

Elena nodded. "Definitely helpful."

"Yes, but there are limits to the number of portals Camille may construct in a short span of time. We will need Derek's ability if he has grown as powerful as you say."

Elena didn't doubt Derek's ability. She worried about whether or not she could help *him* escape Old Kingdom with Niall's spell in place.

"Let us hope Camille has survived the virus. She is a recluse. Perhaps she avoided exposure."

Deirdre knocked on the turquoise door. After a moment, it swung soundlessly open.

The room inside appeared empty, lit by a single candle. Which didn't provide much light, because the home was a windowless cave. Most of the light poured in from the open door.

Deirdre stepped inside and slipped a hand beneath her tunic to her arms belt, the only sign she was on her guard. "Camille? It is Deirdre. Are you here?"

A smallish Fae with long raven hair stepped out from the shadows, her body clothed in a flowing red dress. Her pale porcelain skin and bright blue eyes glowed even in the dim candlelight.

Elena had never seen a black-haired Fae—didn't even know they existed.

After a moment's hesitation, Camille stepped forward and grasped her friend's hand. "Deirdre," she said in a relieved tone, her voice light and feminine. "I apologize for the rude greeting. Many of the sick have come, insisting I take them or a beloved one somewhere safe. If I knew of such a place and had the power to move everyone, I would gladly do it. Unfortunately.... " She shrugged sadly. "Instead, I have maintained a distance."

Camille looked at Elena with curiosity. "Whom have you brought?"

Deirdre placed her hand on Elena's shoulder. "This is Theodora's daughter. My niece, Elena."

Camille's gaze was about as penetrating as Derek's, and seemed equally capable of reading Elena. More so, because a warm heat swept past Elena's exposed skin, as if Camille *was* actually reading her.

"She is not Halven—nor fully Fae."

"No," Deirdre said. "Elena drank from the Ancient Allon. Her powers have increased. She has the ability to rid us of the disease."

"Yes," Camille said. "I see that she can. Come inside and tell me what has happened."

They quickly informed Camille of what had transpired inside Emain and Tirnan over the past several days, and why they required her assistance to enter the kingdoms.

"I'd also like your help finding my friend," Elena added.

If Camille could sniff out power sources like a hound, she could find another Halven with Elena's unusual strength—not quite Fae, not quite Halven, as Camille had pointed out.

Right now, Derek could be anywhere. He might have managed to hide from Niall and his guards in the woods, but considering the king's determination to have Derek, she feared the worst.

"I believe I could detect him, but we must move closer. We'll travel to the border and see if he remains where you left him. The Fates River that separates the two kingdoms runs downstream from Old Kingdom into New Kingdom. If we travel to Old Kingdom first, we can pour the cure into the fast-moving river. It will not take long to reach the Newlanders. First, though, let's go to the Sunland lake; it isn't too far from here."

Camille changed her clothes into standard Fae garb and led them to a lake so vast Elena couldn't see to the other side.

Elena had made a batch of highly concentrated virucide to have on hand, but it wouldn't be enough for all of the lakes. For now, they collected a large batch of allon leaves from the forest nearby and threw them in the lake. Elena transmuted the leaves into a virucide with the same properties as the sap in the jar she carried, and created a heavy breeze along the surface to mix the cure with the rest of the water.

Afterward, they ran to the Sunland-Old Kingdom border, making quick time now that Deirdre was healthy.

Camille paced the edge of the creek. "Your friend Derek is not here. I sense a large magical flame near a power source similar to Elena's in the location of the castle. It seems Derek is with his father, the king. No one else possesses that much strength. It will be very difficult to reach Derek if he is already with the king."

Anger replaced fear. No way was Elena leaving Derek with Niall after what the Fae had done to him.

Her limbs tingled and a rush of power bloomed at her fingertips. "I won't leave without Derek."

Camille and Deirdre exchanged a look. "We can try to get to him," Camille said and paced some more. "It is risky, but I could create a portal to the castle. Do you remember a quiet section—someplace shielded from view?"

Elena considered it for a moment. "The laboratory. They don't use it, but it's right in the middle of the castle."

"Perfect," Camille said. "They'll sense intruders, thanks to the Presence Charm, but the charm will wear off quickly with us in the heart of the castle and surrounded by other Fae. My portal will throw them off further. They'll search the borders and static portals before they search the castle. By then, the charm will have ceased working, and they will assume the intruders became lost in the woods or are off the land. They may consider the possibility that we entered the castle without being discovered, but the chance of success in doing that is very low. Most would never try, and they know this." Camille smiled. "Few in our land possess my ability. They will not be expecting it."

She peered across to the Old Kingdom's trees. "I sense the position of the castle by the king's energy and the number of Fae in the area. There is a pattern in my mind that gives me an idea of perimeters, but I will need more information if I am to take us to the abandoned laboratory."

In the dirt, Elena sketched a rough diagram of where she thought the lab was located within the castle.

Camille nodded. "Very good. I'll use this to get us inside the walls of the room."

"This map probably isn't very accurate. What if your portal is off and we wind up in the wrong place?"

She gave a light shrug. "We run."

Nice. A solid plan. It sounded like something Elena would throw together, and this was no time to improvise.

"Any way we attempt to access the castle, we risk failure," Deirdre said gently. "Camille has two, perhaps three portals within her. After that, she'll need significant recovery time before formulating another. The portals she creates are not like the ones you are used to, Elena. They are transient—good for a minute, at most. Once she forms one, we will need to move quickly."

So, only two or three one-minute portals that needed to be in the exact right place, or they were all screwed.

No problem.

FORTY-SEVEN

The brilliant rainbow of flashing lights stung Elena's eyes. Her back bowed, arching through atomic matter until the pull of gravity signaled the end of the portal. She tucked and bent her knees, bracing for impact the way Keen had taught her, only instead of a smooth landing she came to a sudden, jarring crash.

Elena tumbled forward until she smashed into a solid surface, buckling up against it like a fly on a windshield, the air whooshing from her lungs.

Deirdre had entered the portal before her. She lay on the ground, collecting herself a few feet away. A second later, Camille swept through. She stumbled mildly, but caught her balance without crashing into furniture.

Deirdre stood and dusted off her clothes. "Camille's portals are a bit bumpy."

Slight understatement. But they'd made it into the lab, thank God.

Elena peeled herself from the laboratory's blackened

cabinets and wobbled to her feet. "Do you think they heard us?"

Deirdre walked to the door and carefully peered out. "No one approaches. They are most likely forming search parties at the borders." She scrunched her nose. "I see Osulf still refuses to update the castle plumbing."

"It does smell awful in this place," Elena said. "No wonder people migrated to New Kingdom."

"Elena," Camille said patiently. "The politics of Tirnan are more complicated than that." She shook her head at Deirdre. "Now that the king's sanitation system has been dismissed, may we proceed with the plan?"

Deirdre pulled out a machete she'd strapped to her back beneath her tunic. "I suggest we confiscate arms from the next guard that passes."

Elena eyed the frightening blade. "Confiscate?"

"Render him unconscious and grab his weapons," Deirdre said, as if the meaning wasn't clear.

Camille pursed her lips thoughtfully. "Excellent idea. Oldlanders may be outdated in lifestyle, but they possess advanced weaponry, perhaps the best."

Memories of Elena's last physical encounter with Old Kingdom guards made her heart race. She had no issue with attacking an Oldlander, she was simply less optimistic about the outcome. And if they used null guns... Her stomach did a nauseating twist. Hit by a null and without her magic, she'd be defenseless.

"I wouldn't mind getting my hands on a null gun or two," she said, "but are you sure we can take one of these guys down?"

Camille pulled out a club and smacked it in her palm a couple of times. Where the hell had she been hiding that? "Of course we can."

Deirdre—with her machete between her teeth—flexed her arms and cracked her knuckles. She peered out the door again and held up one finger behind her back.

"Guard coming," Camille mouthed.

Elena gasped. Were they really doing this?

A moment later, Deirdre tightened her hold on the handle of her blade. Faster than Elena thought possible, she swung the door open and plucked the guard from the hallway, slamming the butt of her machete into his temple. While he stumbled inside the room, she silently closed the door, then turned and kneed him in the groin. The guard collapsed, hands gripping his man parts.

These women are ruthless.

Camille touched Elena's shoulder, and Elena jumped. "Rope, cloth," she whispered.

Elena transmuted cloth and rope, but had to redo the rope twice because she'd made it too thick to tie the first two times. Even with the delay, they had the Fae bound to a chair and gagged before he could recover.

Deirdre set down her weapon, and she and Camille divested the guard of his knives, strapping them on their belts and inside the hidden pockets of their clothes. Deirdre handed a couple of knives to Elena, and she attached them to her belt as well.

With the guard tied up and incapacitated, Elena stepped forward gingerly and searched him for a null gun.

An idea was working its way into her mind about how to get Derek out of Old Kingdom, and she needed that damn gun.

Without warning, the guard yanked at the ropes and growled at her. She scuttled back and fell on her ass.

Deirdre stepped forward. She studied the guard for a

second, then stabbed him in the chest with one of his own knives.

He swayed forward, gasping for breath—she must have punctured his lung.

Deirdre reversed the knife and knocked him out with the butt. "That should hold him for a while."

Elena had no idea her sweet aunt was so bloodthirsty. She seemed so delicate...but Leo had said all Fae could fight. Elena had newfound respect for her aunt's skills. She'd look into more defense training if she ever survived this.

She crawled to the unconscious Fae and continued feeling around for the null, fingers trembling. She found a holster at the back of his belt and unlatched it, pulling the gun inside it forward.

Thank God. The gun looked just like the null guns she and Derek had been shot with—squat, yet wide at the muzzle. All of the guards must be equipped with them.

Which wasn't a reassuring thought.

Camille gazed at the ceiling. "Your friend is on the second floor. He paces the room above us." She raised her hands and closed her eyes, pointing to the far corner of the laboratory. "There."

Derek. They were so close.

They could do this—save Fae with the virucide and escape the realm together.

She followed Deirdre and Camille out of the laboratory, pulling the door shut behind her. They jogged to the back of the castle, using Camille's ability to detect if any Fae neared. After winding their way up a narrow flight of stairs to the second floor, they slowly edged down a long hallway. They traveled to the end and stopped in front of the last door.

Camille looked over at Elena and nodded.

Elena eagerly twisted the knob and stepped inside. Deep relief filled her.

Derek was standing with his back to her, gazing out a window. He looked poised and powerful, and incredibly handsome in the clothes the king had given him—embroidered at the wrists like Niall's, and tapered at the waist, highlighting the new breadth of his shoulders. He didn't appear to have been mistreated, but she couldn't be sure until she saw his face.

His head shifted slightly in her direction. She muffled a cry and ran to him, throwing her arms around his wide back.

Derek stiffened and slowly turned to gaze down at her, an odd, blank look on his face. "They told me you would come. I said you were smarter than that. I misjudged you."

She understood why he'd made her leave at the creek. They never would have found a cure if she hadn't left Old Kingdom. But now, he had no reason to push her away.

Elena swatted his chest. "Derek, we're getting you out—"

His hand snapped to her neck, squeezing and blocking off air.

She clawed at his fingers. *"Wha—why?"* she mouthed.

He glanced at Deirdre and Camille, who had drawn their weapons and were rapidly crossing the room. "Move another inch and I kill her."

Derek gazed down at Elena. A muscle twitched above his eye, his face momentarily softening. He shook his head, and the fierce, impenetrable mask returned. "You shouldn't have come. I am my father's man now. You will be too. You will work for Old Kingdom as an alchemist slave to his majesty's will."

What had they done to him? This wasn't Derek. His body, yes, but not his mind.

Elena kicked him in the shin and clawed at his fingers, but his clasp tightened.

"Don't fight this, Elena. You will not win."

She slid her hand to her belt, searching for something to defend herself with, her head growing woozy from the lack of oxygen.

A shot rang out and a glossy bubble encompassed Derek and the front of her.

Derek blinked several times. He glanced at his hand around her throat and dropped it as if her skin had scorched him. He stumbled back, looking startled. "Elena?"

She dropped the null gun she'd pulled from her belt, and bent over, coughing and gasping for air.

When she could breathe again, she straightened to find Derek's eyes wide, his body shaking. He was gripping the wrist that had choked her, his face contorted with anguish.

"It's okay," she said, her voice broken and scratchy. "It's not your fault."

Elena would never doubt Derek's loyalty again. She'd done that once after the Beatrice incident, when the evidence had been stacked against him. She'd forgotten for a split second what her heart knew: Derek would never harm her willingly. Was always, in fact, protecting her.

Elena had planned all along to zap Derek with the null, which was why she'd taken it from the captured Fae to begin with. She'd hoped to remove whatever charm Niall had placed on him to keep him from leaving Old Kingdom. But when she realized Niall had turned Derek against her, she didn't wait.

Derek stepped forward and collapsed to his knees,

sliding to her. He wrapped his arms around her waist. "I'm so sorry," he breathed into her belly.

She stroked his hair. "I'm okay. Everything's okay."

After several deep breaths, his body tensed and he stood, still holding her close.

"Goddamn Fae," he growled. "I'm not a pawn!"

He stepped away and paced the room.

Elena picked up the null gun and reattached it to her belt, then touched his arm. "We have to go."

"Yes," Camille said, gazing off as if listening to something the rest of them couldn't hear. "They are coming. The gunshot was very loud. As was Derek's outburst."

Elena turned to Camille. "Can you make a portal to the river? We can't escape these walls by Blending right now. Derek's abilities won't work for a while because of the null gun." She reached for the jar at her waist and set it on a nearby table. "If you can get us to the river, we can pour the virucide in the water, but we'll need a portal out."

Camille grabbed the virucide and tucked it in her pocket. "We could portal farther down the river, away from the bulk of the guards, but my powers will diminish. Fae abound at the castle, and their energy strengthens me. If we remain close, I may have enough power to portal to the river, then get you home."

"Virucide?" Derek said. "You made the cure?" She nodded, and he pulled her close. "Of course you did. I never doubted it."

Elena tipped her head back and peered up. "We'll pour it in the river outside the castle for people to drink from, then escape from there. Camille makes portals, but they aren't like the others. They only last a minute, and she has two left before she has to rest."

The sound of several people running came from down

the hall. Elena's heart raced in her chest as she looked to Deirdre.

Camille lifted her head as if sniffing the air. "Seven to ten soldiers approach." She spun around and ran her hands over the stone beside the door, tracing out the shape of a large rectangle. "I'll have the portal take us to the north end of the castle beside the Fates River."

Her palms rose from the surface, and the area within the rectangle she'd invisibly outlined wavered. Camille glanced back, nodded, then walked through the wall and disappeared.

Deirdre looked over. "We must hurry." She rushed to the stone Camille had disappeared through, and entered behind her.

Before Elena and Derek could follow, the door to the room burst open.

And before Elena knew what was happening, Derek shoved her into the portal.

She went tumbling through space and lights, landing near the river on her right knee and elbow, pain shooting through her joints.

Camille and Deirdre stood in front of her, staring at something over her head with equal looks of horror on their faces.

Elena glanced back, and wished she hadn't.

A steady stream of seventy—maybe a hundred—guards sprinted for them, weapons drawn. The pounding of their feet explained the low rumble and vibration coming from the ground.

Camille ran to the edge of the river and hastily poured the virucide into the water.

If they didn't survive, at least they'd have accomplished what they came for. They'd gotten the cure to the people of

Tirnan. But Elena wasn't giving up hope yet. She wasn't defenseless, not since her powers had been increased.

Derek burst through the portal and rolled on one shoulder, popping up into a crouch. He looked past Elena and his eyes widened. "Shit."

"Make the portal," he shouted to Camille, then disappeared.

Which meant his powers had returned. But where had he gone?

Elena frantically scanned the area and found no trace of him, until a fist came out of nowhere and struck one of the guards leading the herd of soldiers.

The guard stumbled and fell, taking two other Fae down with him.

Derek couldn't fight everyone on his own. If she didn't do something, the soldiers would be on them in seconds.

She held up her hands—

Deirdre grunted a few feet away.

"Deirdre!" Elena shouted.

"I'm fine." Deirdre pressed her hand to a patch of blood blooming on her arm where an arrow had anchored.

Elena peeled her gaze from the bright red pouring from her aunt's wound and focused on creating fine water droplets. She engulfed the Fae guards in a thick fog.

Judging by the sounds, they were stumbling into one another blindly. Their hands popped out wildly from the dense blanket surrounding them, as if searching for a stronghold—or a captive.

Deirdre ran forward and stabbed anyone who came close. The guards had stopped firing their bows. Even they weren't stupid enough to shoot indiscriminately. They were as likely to shoot one another as they were to shoot Elena and the others.

Elena backed from the blinded Fae over to Camille, who was kneeling at the river. A wavy illusion appeared above the water.

Perspiration dotted Camille's forehead as she peered over her shoulder, a panicked look on her face. "Where is Derek?"

"I don't know." Elena hadn't seen him since he'd punched the Fae, and soon their mode of transportation would be gone.

"Elena, I cannot make another. This is the last of my powers until I have time to rest. If we wait, we will be captured or killed. You must come with me now."

Camille stood and placed her hand on Elena's shoulder. "Niall does not wish to kill the boy. Leave with us, and we will return for him later."

She gave one last sad smile, then moved to the edge of the bank and into the portal.

"Camille is right," Deirdre said from her side. "We must go. We will find him later."

Elena nodded and approached the edge of the bank with Deirdre, which apparently gave her aunt the reassurance she needed.

Deirdre glanced to make sure Elena was right next to her, then stepped into the portal.

But Elena didn't follow. She looked back, searching for Derek.

She glanced every few seconds at the wavy portal to make sure it still existed, her heart fluttering with each moment that passed. Turning in a circle, she peered around frantically. Looking beyond the thick fog that held the disoriented soldiers, toward the castle and other guards approaching, she saw no sign of him. Where was he?

"Derek—" she began to shout, her voice cut off on a whimper.

A large hand had pinched her collarbone, somehow making it impossible for her to move.

"You think you can escape me?" Niall's frigid voice doused the hot adrenaline coursing through her body. A mirage-like shimmering floated from the side and moved in front of her, Niall's body coming fully into view.

Her muscles weakened in cold fear—would have rooted her to the spot even without the magical hold.

Niall's soldier released the power that kept her motionless, and stepped in line with the others.

The guards fanned off Niall on either side of him like the wings of a dark angel.

Elena lifted her hand to the horde of new Fae approaching from the castle and encased them in fog, hoping that would help Derek return before the portal closed. She quickly went to immerse Niall and his men as well—but not fast enough.

A shot rang out and the clear, bubblelike liquid of a null dripped off her body in a cool, slippery glaze.

She had no more powers. No more hope of using the elements for escape.

Elena scrubbed the slime from her eyes with her sleeve. She had hesitated, but there was no way she could have left without Derek. Her heart wouldn't allow it.

"I honored my promise to keep you safe within my castle, but we are no longer there." Niall raised his hands as if to prove the change in venue.

Elena took the opportunity to glance around one last time, still searching for signs of Derek. She bit the inside of her cheek to keep her features in control, though her insides rioted in terror on all levels. For Derek. For herself.

As if reading her mind, Niall said, "You are nothing. Not worth the ground my son walks on."

"Derek is Halven, like me." She tried to sound strong, but her words came out weak and trembling.

He smiled. "Derek is more than Halven, and soon he will be *much* more, while you will cease to exist. He is my only son and heir. He will rule Tirnan with me." Niall reached back and slid a sword from a sheath at his back. He touched the edge of the blade with his thumb and a bead of blood oozed down the silver metal.

Elena's throat tightened, choking her. Her shoulders trembled and sweat dripped down her palms as Niall slowly raised the sword above her head. His guards spread out more, giving their leader a wide berth. She tried to say something—anything to stop what was about to happen—but the only sounds coming from her were strangled, gasping noises, as if she were drowning. That was what fear did to you—it locked you in place until you couldn't think straight.

Elena had meant to protect the people she cared about when she stepped out of her sheltered world and into this one, but she never really believed it would result in her death. Even if she had believed it, it wouldn't have changed her decision. She would rather die than allow harm to come to the people she loved. And if she saved innocent Fae too, her choice had been worth it.

Niall smiled, his teeth like pearls in the sun peeking through the dissipating fog. The muscles in his shoulders bunched as he arched his arms for the killing blow.

Elena closed her eyes.

A second passed. And another...

When nothing happened, she blinked her eyes open. Niall's sword was still raised, but it had dropped a fraction and his smile had faded. He grunted and looked dazedly down at his chest, blood bubbling from the corner of his mouth.

The air rippled, sending the dissipating fog into a frenzied whirl. And then Derek appeared over Niall's shoulder.

Niall's body jerked back. Once. Twice.

His eyes glazed over and he slowly turned. *"No,"* he gurgled, and fell at Derek's feet, a gaping hole in his back where his heart used to be.

Derek clenched the organ with a shaking hand, his eyes wide, jaw tensed.

Every one of Niall's guards stared in what could only be disbelief. Slowly, one by one, they knelt and bowed at Derek's feet.

"Fealty to King Derek," one said.

The others chanted the words in return.

Holy crap.

Could Derek actually be…

Didn't matter. *Leave—they had to leave.* Elena glanced back.

The portal flickered, as though it were about to close.

There was no time to shoot Derek with another null to ensure he could leave the land. And anyway, the magic the king had imposed to keep him here might have died with Niall. "Hurry, Derek!"

He jerked forward, grimacing as he stepped over Niall's prone form, the former king's heart still clenched in one hand. As if momentarily coming out of whatever shock he was in, he looked over his shoulder. "Spread the word to every corner of the kingdom to drink the water," he commanded. "It holds the cure to the virus."

Then Derek grabbed Elena around the waist, and dove into the portal.

FORTY-EIGHT

Three days ago, the portal out of Tirnan had dumped Elena and Derek, along with Deirdre and Camille, onto a pile of burned-out stone and rubble where the lofty halls of Emain had once stood.

While Elena and Derek had been fighting for their lives in Tirnan, Leo, Keen, and the rest of the Emain Fae had waged their own war against the Halven Army, which, ironically, included several full-blooded Fae. They won the battle, but the surviving Halven Army managed to escape through a portal to Tirnan, where it was assumed they'd joined Portia, who'd taken over New Kingdom. No one had confirmed it, but Marlon St. Just was said to be in New Kingdom as well.

Through his telepathy, Keen had sensed Elena after she entered the Emain realm, and escorted her and the others to safety. Ever since then, Elena had been trying to put back the pieces of her life.

"I came to discuss your promise," she said as she dogged Leo's steps off Dawson campus to the New Emain, which she had yet to see. "I created the cure for you, but my mother's life is still in danger. She's missing, and the Halven Army and Portia have taken over her kingdom."

After putting together the connection between Marlon and her uncle, and with the disease now contained, they'd had Fae in Sunland search her uncle's laboratory for more information. Communication between the two realms was spotty, but they'd managed to find more email documentation between Beorhtric and Marlon when both men had worked together in Emain. Leo deduced that Marlon's longstanding frustration with not being allowed into Tirnan, coupled with Beorhtric's refusal to provide additional Tirnan ingredients, had been the driving forces behind Marlon's collaboration with Portia and his final retaliation against Fae.

It seemed Marlon wanted to carve a place for Halven in Tirnan, and he had been willing to wipe out a race in order to achieve it.

How Derek played into Marlon's plans was less clear. All they knew was that Marlon and Portia—two people with the same goal to take over Tirnan, but with different motivations—had banded together. It was possible Portia had ordered the bomb inside Marlon's lab without Marlon's knowledge, intending to remove all remaining links to their plans and take out Derek in the process. That was the only reason they could determine for why Marlon had warned Derek away by appealing to his father. He may not have wanted his protégé in danger. Or perhaps it had been a warning for Derek to stop looking into the virus. Either way, they might never know. They'd found little to no physical trace of the mad genius behind the deadly Fae disease.

Leo glanced around as if to ensure no one overheard their conversation, and turned down the street to her apartment. "Ah, yes, our agreement. We did not say we would save your mother from her enemies. Merely that we would make sure she wasn't intentionally exposed to the disease."

They passed Elena's apartment complex. Where exactly *was* New Emain?

"She's the rightful queen of New Kingdom now. Why aren't you putting all of your energy toward finding her and ridding New Kingdom of Marlon and Portia? And if we're getting technical, you said you'd do your best to keep my mother safe if I agreed to help cure the disease. You didn't specify from what."

Take that, Fae, and your twisted truths.

Leo stopped abruptly and peered at her. His mouth quirked into a small smile. "You are learning. And yes, you are correct. Your mother's safety and her return to her rightful place in the palace are our top priorities."

He resumed walking, and Elena scurried to keep up. "We told you that if you came up with a cure for the virus, we would have the means to help your mother."

He'd better not be telling me what I think he's telling me.

"In short, you will use your powers to help us save your mother from those who seek to take over Tirnan."

Yup, that's what he was telling her.

"Are you saying that I risked my life, Derek's life, my roommate's life—who's still missing, and I want her back! —to find myself in the exact same place, with the burden to save your people resting on my shoulders?"

Thanks to the differences in the passage of time between the Earth and Fae realms, Elena and Derek had returned in time to make it to the farmhouse where the Halven Army had told her to meet them in exchange for her roommate. Of course, the Halven Army had wanted to take

Elena instead, but Derek and Keen weren't going to let that happen.

Even though they were still recovering from the brief but savage war in Emain, Keen had dozens of Fae surrounding the perimeter to ensure Elena got out safely. Elena worried that the Halven Army would figure out their plan and do something terrible, but in the end it didn't matter. Reese hadn't been there. No one was at the farmhouse, and it seemed the place had been abandoned for some time.

The only thing they could imagine was that Marlon had somehow heard about what was going on inside Tirnan and run. With her roommate as collateral.

"The burden was not entirely resting on your shoulders. If you recall, Fae in Emain worked tirelessly to find a cure. And do not forget, in the beginning you did not have the capacity to heal a fly. It took a great amount of dedication on both our parts to develop your powers to full capacity."

"By throwing myself on the mercy of that madman Niall to help your people. Yes, I remember, thank you."

He continued as if he hadn't heard her. "The enhanced ability you acquired in Tirnan afforded you the power to heal our people and do what no other Fae was capable of. You are the last of our transmutation wielders until more are bred. With the strength of your powers behind us, we will work together to save your mother. Our soldiers are looking at all angles for how to wrest back control of New Kingdom for your mother. We will keep you informed and involved every step of the way."

Something about the breeding statement didn't sit well, considering she was the last in the line of transmutation wielders, but she chose to ignore it for the moment. At least they were working on helping her mother.

Leo turned up the walkway to a massive, dilapidated Tudor-style house at the end of her street. She'd heard it lodged a gaggle of sorority girls some years back. "Keep in mind, however, you may use your powers for Fae activities, but you must never use them to heal or otherwise help humans."

"*What?* Why not?"

"Your abilities would be exploited—"

"Like you're exploiting them?"

"—and your life as you know it would dissolve." He stopped at the threshold and turned to her. "Our people would be exposed, as would you. We cannot take the risk, Elena. For now, you've proven yourself trustworthy and have performed a great service to Fae. Because of that, we have allowed you to resume your previous human activities on the condition that you not reveal your powers."

How magnanimous of him. And what the hell? *Previous human activities?* Why would they ever think they had a say in whether or not she returned to classes?

Leo had made sure she and Derek hadn't been charged in Marlon's lab explosion, but he'd owed her that.

"Leo, you have no control here. You said so yourself, there are no transmutation wielders left. If that's true, you need me, I don't need you." Her mouth twisted as she considered. "However, you make a good point, and I'll not reveal my powers to humans. I'd like to continue to blend in and not be a freak."

That didn't mean she couldn't help people without anyone knowing.

Leo nodded. "Very good. And please"—a charming smile spread across his face—"consider this your second home." He waved a hand at the ramshackle interior. "Our new station will be up and running by the end of the week."

Elena scanned the room inside the doorway. Drop cloths littered the scuffed wooden floor, beside half-painted walls. The place was a mess. Not to mention her apartment was just down the street.

"Seriously, Leo? This is where your new headquarters are located?" New Emain was so close she could throw a rock and nail her front door from where she stood. Their old compound had been a hundred times larger than this house.

"It is temporary." He guided her through the tall arched entry and they walked past half a dozen carpenters working on the repairs.

At the back of the house, Leo entered a room decorated exactly like his office in Emain.

"How did you manage to salvage the settees and desk?"

His original office had been destroyed. The only things that remained of Emain after the twenty-four hours of battle while Derek and Elena were in Tirnan were exterior walls and part of the massive basement laboratory. Elena was almost happy she'd been gone. Fae could throw a serious war when they wanted to—one more reason to be concerned about the brewing revolution in Tirnan that her mother had spoken of.

Leo's brow pinched. "I did not salvage them. These are what the designer brought to replace the old."

Elena shook her head in disbelief. Fae were serious creatures of habit.

Leo strode across the room and sat behind his desk, plastering on a smile that seemed too cheerful for his typical disposition. "I hope you will visit us often."

Was that why they'd chosen a place near her apartment? "I thought your kind despised me and sought my help out of desperation. Why do you want me around all of a sudden?"

Leo shrugged. "You have proven more valuable than we presumed. Whether we wish it or not, you carry our blood. It is why our people have monitored the Halven. However..."

When he didn't finish the sentence, she prodded him. "Yes?"

"Perhaps we were wrong—to keep such a distance between our two species."

Wow. Elena never thought she'd hear Leo say those words.

She'd argued with Keen about acceptance and he hadn't budged one inch, despite their sort-of friendship. He still believed Fae were superior to humans. Though the way he was behaving over Reese, maybe there was hope for Keen too.

"Fae have a long memory," Leo added. "We will not forget what you have done for us. Others of your kind are another matter. They cannot be trusted."

Here we go. "Just like some of *your kind* can't be trusted." She thought of Beatrice and Portia, in particular, who had orchestrated the ultimate betrayal of their people and nobility.

Leo harrumphed.

"I'll visit," she said, "but don't try and twist the truth anymore." Elena leaned forward. "And, Leo, if we're to work together, I expect your help in finding Reese as well, not just my mother."

Reese could be dead, but Elena just didn't believe it. Or maybe she didn't want to.

Leo sighed. "We will continue to search for your friend. Marlon's disciples took her, and we suspect there was a reason beyond baiting you, since she is still missing. We'd like to find out what that reason was. Every attempt will be made to rescue her."

Elena sat back, satisfied. Fae-Halven relations weren't perfect, but her having saved the Fae might be the catalyst for the first step in the history of the realms toward acceptance.

Her mother had held out hope for a better future while imprisoned for all those years. Elena would hold out hope for a better future with Fae too.

FORTY-NINE

Elena returned to her apartment after her meeting with Leo. She had just set her books on the desk in the bedroom and pulled off her leather jacket when the sound of a key grinding in the front door made her freeze.

Reese.

Elena ran into the living room with her heart pounding in her throat. But it was just Keen sweeping inside like he owned the place.

Somehow Keen had pilfered a key to her apartment and proceeded to use it at his leisure.

"Dammit, Keen! You can't just walk in and out whenever you like."

He pocketed the key, ignoring her as he headed into the kitchen and opened the refrigerator.

Her shoulders sank. Elena didn't really mind Keen showing up. She was only disappointed it wasn't Reese.

"Any news?" she asked. No need to be specific. She asked the same question of Keen about ten times a day.

His cool face strained in a grimace. Since their failed

farmhouse rescue, Keen hadn't faltered in his search for Reese. Dark patches camped out below his eyes, and his hair had even taken on the Derek O'Brien no-comb appearance.

"Sources loyal to your mother confirm Reese is in Tirnan. She is being held captive. For what purpose, no one knows. They have nothing to gain by keeping her there." Keen's large hand squeezed the refrigerator door and he slammed it shut, the bottles rattling inside.

Elena let out a loud breath. "Thank God she's alive. I mean, it's not ideal that she's in Tirnan, but it's better than the alternative."

Marlon's vassal had initially threatened to kill Reese if Elena didn't show up at the farmhouse. This meant there was hope. "We can get her back, Keen."

He spun around. "Not *we*. You're finished traveling to Tirnan."

"No way." She shook her head vehemently. "I have to find Reese. It's my fault she's there to begin with."

"Do not mistake your run of luck in Tirnan for anything other than what it was. You will leave the rescuing of Reese to my men and me. I will find her, and I will return her to you." Keen straightened, his chin all proud, sharp edges. He was serious.

"Why? Why do you care what happens to Reese?"

He broke eye contact. "I told you I would find her. Fae do not lie."

Yeah, sure. She'd bet that wasn't the only reason. Keen cared about Reese. He just wouldn't admit it to himself, or to anyone else.

Well, she cared about Reese too. Elena had been irritated when Leo suggested she rescue her mother, because she felt Fae needed to step up and help, but she'd planned on doing it anyway, just like she planned on saving her best friend.

Keen's help was welcome—because he cared about Reese, even if he didn't acknowledge it—but she would search for Reese no matter what. "Keep me informed every step of the way. And come to me if you need help."

"If I need you, I will find you." He said this only for her benefit, she could tell. The chances of Keen believing he needed her help were one in a million, so he wasn't actually lying.

Keen grabbed an apple from the counter and a few granola bars from the cupboard before ducking out the front door—just as Derek stepped in.

After seeing where New Emain was located, she understood why her place had become the community living room. As she was located between campus and the Fae's new headquarters, the convenience of food and smutty reality TV were apparently too much to pass up. Plus, Keen was still technically her guard, though he'd simmered down a bit and had stopped watching her every move.

Keen and Derek exchanged the proverbial guy nod before Derek closed the door and scrubbed a hand down his face. He looked up and their eyes met. His shoulders relaxed, and he strode over and grabbed her in a hug. "I missed you."

She wrapped her arms around his waist and squeezed him back. "You were only gone for a couple of hours."

"Yup. Still missed you." He smiled and leaned in for a kiss.

Derek, especially, had taken what had happened in Tirnan hard. Camille had to pry Niall's heart from his hand once they'd made it through the portal. Elena didn't even think Derek knew he still held it. He seemed to be walking around in a state of shock.

They'd held each other all night that first night, Derek sleeping fitfully. He'd called his parents the next morning to "check in," but Elena could tell he'd needed to hear their voices, though he couldn't explain to them why.

Derek didn't disclose the Fae to his parents. This time, though, it appeared his reasons for not telling them that he was a Halven stemmed from the need to protect his family, rather than from fear of abandonment. He'd gained perspective after his time with Niall. But no matter how horribly the Fae king had treated Derek, Derek hadn't wanted to hurt the leader.

Had Derek simply maimed Niall, neither she nor Derek would be here right now; Fae healed too easily. Derek would have been imprisoned in Old Kingdom and Elena would be dead. Derek had done what he had to do.

"I'd do it ten times over if it meant protecting you," Derek told her when she'd asked him if he regretted it. And she believed him. Traveling to Tirnan hadn't only brought them closer, it had made their relationship rock solid. After all they'd been through, she trusted Derek more than anyone.

Their fates might have been divided, but not their souls. They were meant to be together.

"Where's Keen headed?" Derek asked as he set his backpack down and sank onto the couch.

"To see about rescuing Reese," she said, and joined him.

Derek studied her face. "Really? They found her?"

Elena told Derek about Reese being trapped in Tirnan.

He looked down and shook his head. "I'm sorry, Elena. But if they've got her imprisoned, they must need her or they would have... Anyway, it just means they're not likely to hurt her."

Elena pressed a knuckle to her mouth. "I know. You're right," she said, but she was still worried.

Derek wrapped his arm around her shoulders. "Keen's a badass. He'll find her and heads will roll."

She smiled and turned to him. "You two forming a bromance?"

He sat back, stretching his legs out wide. "His golden good looks are appealing"—he pulled her onto his lap—"but I like my lovers saucy." He kissed her cheek and lingered, rubbing his lips across her skin.

She squirmed, but kept her expression blank. "Keen's saucy too," she countered.

He growled and she giggled. "So insolent. If you must know, I also like my lovers soft." He ran his mouth behind her ear, a puff of breath teasing a surprisingly sensitive location below the lobe that had her squirming again. "And round in the right places..." He glanced down at her chest and quirked a brow.

She looked to the ceiling and shook her head. *Men.*

Derek grinned and leaned over her until she fell to the side on the couch, his weight lightly pressing her into the cushions. His face grew serious. "And you—I only want you, Elena." He lowered his head and kissed her, butterflies, or whatever you wanted to call them, fluttering around in her belly and bouncing off one another like heated molecules.

Her sensitive, magical fingertips ran over his shoulders and down his sides to the gap between his T-shirt and jeans. She rubbed a slow circle against his bare skin, and the press of his mouth intensified.

She pulled gently away. "Stay with me tonight?" This

time, it had nothing to do with protection or comfort. She was safe for now. She just wanted him.

"'Course," he mumbled, and returned to kissing her, his lips moving down her throat to the top of her breasts—

A cell phone rang.

Derek stilled at the base of her throat as if considering whether or not to answer it, then sighed.

He sat up and pulled out his phone, glancing over with a look of apology. "My dad. I'd better get this." He put the phone to his ear, but before answering the call he pointed a finger at her. "Do not move. We will continue our *conversation* in a moment."

She grinned at the hidden meaning, and used the break to grab a glass of water from the kitchen.

While Elena stood behind the peninsula drinking her water, she thought about how Tirnan had changed her too. Becoming a doctor had been her goal, until she realized it was her family's dream, not hers. Having the power to help people the way she did in Tirnan settled something deep inside her. For the first time in her life, something else interested her besides science—the mixing of science and magic. Alchemy.

The tone of the call on the other side of the room changed and Elena glanced up.

"I'm not going anywhere, Dad," Derek said.

He'd mentioned that his dad hadn't relented on trying to convince him to attend a better school. Because Derek didn't want to tell his parents about Fae, his reasons for remaining at Dawson escaped them.

"I like it here and I'm plenty challenged with the coursework. My girlfriend's here, and I have no intention of leaving her."

Elena's fingers gripped the glass, her heart thumping

rapidly. No one had ever referred to her as their girlfriend. In some ways, she and Derek were so much more than boyfriend and girlfriend, but the reference made her giddy just the same.

"Yeah, sure. I'll call in a week and let you know the name of my replacement advisor. Tell Mom hi."

Elena waited until they were secluded in her bedroom before she asked him about the phone call. Lying on their sides atop the comforter and facing each other, she said, "Did you mean it? What you told your dad?"

"Nah." The side of his mouth kicked up as he tucked back an escapee curl that had fallen across her eye.

"Oh." She tried to not look disappointed.

"Dawson's classes aren't all that challenging, but what I learn from Fae will be. Besides, it looks like I'll be needed in Old Kingdom."

Her forehead puckered. She didn't like the idea of Derek returning to Old Kingdom. "That doesn't sound like a good—"

He leaned over and silenced her with a peck on the lips. "Either that, or we risk another dictator ruling. Fae live a long time, Elena. I can't do that to Oldlanders. And who knows. Maybe having a Halven as their king will endear us to them?" When she continued to frown, he added. "Okay, probably not. But think of it this way: I'll be able to update the plumbing."

That *would* be an improvement, but she couldn't smile when gripped by fear for his safety. She lived with enough anxiety over her mother and Reese. "Are you sure you have to be their leader?"

"For now, yeah. Being a king in Faeland wasn't my dream, but maybe I can do good there. I'm not subject to their long history of war against each other. A Halven as leader could help smooth things over. I'd be able to rule with wisdom, instead of emotion and power in mind."

She ran her fingers through his hair. Not happy, but also understanding his point. "You would make a great king. I just don't want to lose you."

Replacing Niall with an even more barbaric ruler wasn't the solution. Until they found someone else, Derek *was* their best option. And who knew, maybe this was his calling the way alchemy was hers.

Elena thought about the rest of Derek's conversation with his father and ducked her head into his shoulder, hiding her face. "But when I said, 'Did you mean it,' I meant what you said about your girlfriend."

He leaned back and rolled her on top of him. "I love you, Elena." His heart pounded beneath the hand she had pressed to his chest. "When I'm not near you, I'm thinking about you and wondering how long until I see you again. When I'm with you, I'm thinking of ways to get close and touch you, even if it's only to hold you. And when you smile...I wonder if there is anything more beautiful in the world. Make that *worlds*." He grinned.

His words stole her breath. He loved her.

She stroked his brow with her fingertip, and bent to kiss his lips with every spine-tingling, happy emotion he stirred in her.

And then the full magnitude of what he'd said kicked in, and she smiled so widely her cheeks ached. She squirmed and bobbed giddily on top of him. "I have a boyfriend," she said in a singsong voice.

Derek grunted as a stray elbow landed on his ribs. He flipped her so she lay beneath him again. "How should we celebrate your first official relationship?" he asked in a deep, sexy voice, his hand snaking down her collarbone to the top of her breast.

She smiled slyly. "By holding hands?"

His palm stilled and he frowned, shaking his head.

"Hmm... With a kiss?"

He put his mouth on her neck and kissed and licked his way down. "Getting warmer," he murmured.

She tapped a finger on her mouth, trying not to move while his lips and hands made her face heat and her breath catch. "No hand-holding, but kissing is okay, yet not enough. What to do, what to do... I've got it. How about a heavy make-out session?"

"Warmer still," came his response from the general area of her belly button, where he'd lifted her top a few inches and exposed her skin. His hands continued their wonderfully tormenting path down her torso to her hips.

She closed her eyes, breaths shaky and uneven as her stomach and thigh muscles clenched beneath his fingers. "Fine—you win." She reached down and yanked his T-shirt over his head.

He sat up as though affronted, his eyes sparkling. "Hey, I'm not that kind of guy."

She smiled. "You're a terrible liar. Is that drool on the side of your mouth?"

He raised his hand to his lip and grinned. She took that opportunity to shove his chest until he fell with little effort onto his back. Then she straddled him.

Her fingers glided along the muscled landscape of his chest and stomach. "I like the new and improved Derek." Was that *her* husky voice?

Derek tried to frown, but she could see the smile creeping through. "Is that all I am to you? A hot body?"

She looked up and scratched the side of her head.

"Pretty much." She leaned down to place a soft kiss on his mouth. "Are you okay with that?"

"Fine by me." He beamed.

The next several seconds saw a frenzied loss of clothing.

Derek's large, hard, beautiful body loomed above her, the expression on his face thoughtful. He placed a gentle kiss on the corner of her mouth. "I was only joking about celebrating with sex. I just want to be near you. I don't care what we do. Though this is amazing."

"I know that, and if I haven't said so yet, I know you would never willingly betray me. I'm sorry I doubted you for even a moment. I love you, and I love that you're my first boyfriend."

His arms tightened around her. He grinned widely. "And if I have my way—your last."

The next book in the Halven Rising series, *Fates Entwined*, tells the story of Keen and Reese and the future of the Fae realm...

Grab ***Fates Entwined*** Now!

Sign up for J. Barnard's newsletter, and **receive a FREE bonus scene that takes place after *FATES DIVIDED*,** along with writing updates. By signing up here, you'll also be the first to know when new books go live:

FATES ENTWINED

He must make a choice. Betray his people, or lose her forever...

Humans are inferior.

A scourge on the Fae and on the magic passed down to them by angels millennia ago.

Keen won't add to the half-breed problem that threatens his people's existence by giving in to his attraction to Reese.

Reese can't stand Keen. He criticizes her clothing, won't answer a straight question, and is too handsome for her peace of mind. Her entire life, Reese has been pegged as a shallow, ditzy blond. She won't take the stereotype from the arrogant Fae too.

But when her life is threatened, Reese sees a side of Keen that is protective and dangerously seductive. And she wonders what else lies beneath the soldier's hard exterior.

The Fae realm's battle for power forces Keen to make a choice: betray his people, or lose Reese forever.

Grab* <u>Fates Entwined</u> *today!

Also by J. Barnard

HALVEN RISING SERIES

Fates Altered (Prequel)

Fates Divided (Book 1)

Fates Entwined (Book 2)

Fates Fulfilled (Book 3)

About the Author

J.Barnard is the fantasy pen name for USA Today Bestselling Author Jules Barnard. Library Journal calls her Halven Rising series "...an exciting new fantasy adventure." To find out more, visit jbarnardauthor.com or follow @jbarnardauthor on Instagram.

Sign up for J. Barnard's newsletter, and **receive a FREE bonus scene that takes place after *FATES DIVIDED*,** along with writing updates. By signing up here, you'll also be the first to know when new books go live:

Please spread the love for the Halven Rising series and *FATES DIVIDED* by leaving a review or rating it, and sharing the series on all things social. Don't forget to tag me!

www.ingramcontent.com/pod-product-compliance
Lightning Source LLC
Chambersburg PA
CBHW061902310726
48972CB00004B/1133